BY ALLEGRA GOODMAN

This Is Not About Us

Isola

Sam

The Chalk Artist

Intuition

The Cookbook Collector

Paradise Park

Kaaterskill Falls

The Family Markowitz

Total Immersion

The Other Side of the Island

THIS IS NOT ABOUT US

THIS IS NOT ABOUT US

| *Fiction* |

Allegra Goodman

THE DIAL PRESS
NEW YORK

The Dial Press
An imprint of Random House
A division of Penguin Random House LLC
1745 Broadway, New York, NY 10019
randomhousebooks.com
penguinrandomhouse.com

The following stories have been previously published, sometimes in a different form: "Ambrose," *The New Yorker,* September 30, 2024; "$," *Freeman's,* Fall 2023; "The Last Grownup," *The New Yorker,* February 27, 2023; "A Challenge You Have Overcome," *The New Yorker,* January 25, 2021; "F.A.Q.s," *The New Yorker,* September 11, 2017; "Apple Cake," *The New Yorker,* July 7–July 14, 2014; "Sheba," *Subtropics,* Winter, 2011

Library of Congress Cataloging-in-Publication Data
Names: Goodman, Allegra author
Title: This is not about us / Allegra Goodman.
Description: First edition. | New York, NY: The Dial Press, 2026.
Identifiers: LCCN 2025029763 (print) | LCCN 2025029764 (ebook) |
ISBN 9780593447840 hardcover | ISBN 9780593447857 ebook
Subjects: LCGFT: Fiction | Domestic fiction | Linked stories
Classification: LCC PS3557.O5829 T48 2026 (print) | LCC PS3557.O5829 (ebook)
LC record available at https://lccn.loc.gov/2025029763
LC ebook record available at https://lccn.loc.gov/2025029764

Printed in the United States of America

2nd Printing

Book Team: Production editor: Kelly Chian • Managing editor: Rebecca Berlant • Production manager: Sandra Sjursen • Copy editor: Julie Ehlers • Proofreaders: Kathryn Jones, Evan Stone, Barbara Jatkola, Megha Jain

Book design by Susan Turner

The authorized representative in the EU for product safety and compliance is Penguin Random House Ireland, Morrison Chambers, 32 Nassau Street, Dublin D02 YH68, Ireland. https://eu-contact.penguin.ie

To my sister Paula

Contents

THE FAMILY

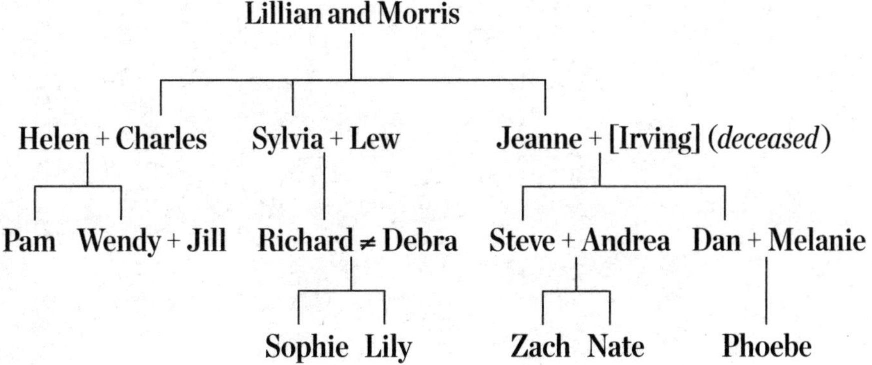

Lillian and Morris
Helen + Charles
Sylvia + Lew
Jeanne + [Irving] (*deceased*)
Pam
Wendy + Jill
Richard ≠ Debra
Steve + Andrea
Dan + Melanie
Sophie
Lily
Zach
Nate
Phoebe

THIS IS NOT ABOUT US

1

Apple Cake

Her sisters flinched because she was the youngest, but she looked so old. Jeanne was just seventy-four, and no one ever thought . . . They didn't speak of it. They would not allow themselves, but Helen was eighty, Sylvia seventy-eight. They'd married first, been mothers first. They were older. They should have been frailer. How could Jeanne be first to go?

In the Brooklyn house, their baby lay propped up on pillows. Jeanne, who had celebrated her first birthday in eyelet lace, a slice of cake on the tray of her high chair, and her sisters on either side. Their living doll with her blond curls and round blue eyes. In the mountains, in Kaaterskill, they'd pulled her in their wagon over grass bumpy with apples from the apple tree. Later, when the family moved to Boston and the Brookline house, Helen and Sylvia had walked their little sister to school. Now it was dreadful to approach her—hair just wisps, voice nearly gone, her cough breaking every sentence. Horror, pity, shame. Jeanne's older sisters felt all that at once, to see her now and to remember her as she had been. They were sorry and they were glad to feel so alive, steps firm in their low-heeled shoes. Their own bodies sound, rejoicing with each breath. What a terrible thing to say! They would never admit it. Their own strength, their good fortune, and their guilt—they could never put it into words. No one should!

"How are you, darling?" Helen asked.

Jeanne didn't answer.

"Did you see the orchid Richard sent?" Sylvia turned a tall white orchid toward Jeanne's chair.

Jeanne looked briefly at her nephew's gift. There were so many flowers. Blossoms filled the first-floor music studio where Jeanne had to live because she couldn't take the stairs. The orchid from Richard, the sunflowers from her daughter-in-law, Melanie, the roses from the Auerbachs next door. Wherever she looked, she saw arrangements. The piano tuner had sent a basket of mums, which were losing petals, shedding everywhere. The cards said, "All our love," and "Thinking of you," and even "Healing light." This from her niece Wendy, the music therapist.

"Look how beautiful they are." Sylvia meant, Do you see how much everybody cares for you?

Jeanne made a face. The flowers depressed her, especially those already wilting. When she looked at the mums, she felt she wasn't dying fast enough.

Her sisters sat chattering about the heat, the traffic, and the rain. They were afraid to leave her alone—although she had lived by herself for years, a widow. She lived alone because she liked it. Her late husband had been difficult, to say the least.

According to her sons, Jeanne's Tudor home was much too big. According to Phoebe, her twenty-year-old granddaughter, Jeanne's house wasted energy. For years, everybody had been telling Jeanne to move. Now nobody mentioned it.

These were the privileges of hospice. You didn't have to blow insulation into your walls. No one suggested assisted living, or criticized your carbon footprint, which would disappear entirely in weeks, or even days. On the other hand, everyone came to see you and confide in you. Jeanne didn't believe in God or any kind of afterlife, but lung cancer made believers of her family, so that she, who despised superstition, became touchstone and talisman for the rest of them. Her sisters were always pressing her cold hands.

Helen told Jeanne, "Pam and Wendy are coming up this weekend."

Jeanne nodded.

"Richard's coming too," said Sylvia. Her only child was having a terrible time, switching jobs, divorcing, and she felt he deserved credit for dropping everything to see his aunt. Pam was coming up from Providence, and Wendy lived in Brooklyn, but Richard was driving all the way from Philly.

Jeanne closed her eyes and listened to her sisters say she's tired. She's exhausted. She heard them echoing each other. She has to rest. Yes, she has to rest. She was looking at the sun, red through her closed eyelids.

That autumn red felt good, but dark was better, because everybody left except for Shawn, the night nurse. Then Jeanne lay awake in her rented hospital bed and listened to symphonies and choral rhapsodies, quartets, concertos on WCRB, Boston's Classical Radio. When she heard a solo violin, her fingers curled reflexively; her left hand knew.

Her sons had pushed away her music stands and moved the piano to make room for Shawn, now dozing in his straight-backed chair. Jeanne imagined he had another job during the day, and she saw that he was trying to study as well. He was always reading a textbook, but he never got far. Just before dawn, the book slipped off his lap onto the floor.

Shawn started up and saw Jeanne staring at him from her bed. "I'm sorry. I'm sorry, ma'am." He bent down for the book.

She said, "You rest."

"No, I'm here if you need something."

"Sleep."

His eyes widened. There was no way he was going back to sleep. He'd lose his job.

"I'll let you know if anything happens," Jeanne said.

Her sons and their wives came to see her every afternoon. First Steve and Andrea would sit by her side. Andrea showed videos on her phone of their huge boys, born just eighteen months apart, lion cubs who played high school soccer. They were coming to see Jeanne right after practice. Andrea was going to drive them straight from the field, cleats and all.

Next came Dan and Melanie. They had just the one daughter, Phoebe. Melanie had gained fifty pounds when she was pregnant. She never had another child, and she never lost the weight. "Phoebe sends her love," said Melanie.

Dan explained, "She wants to be here, but she won't fly."

Jeanne tried to picture her ecological granddaughter biking from Ann Arbor. She couldn't help laughing as she imagined Phoebe's long blond hair streaming out from under her helmet. Jeanne's breath came short and quick. For a few moments she couldn't breathe at all, and then she couldn't see. With help from her nurse, Lorraine, Jeanne sat up, and wiped tears from her eyes.

"What's so funny?" asked Dan.

Melanie said, "She wants to study eco-poetry."

"Stop!" said Jeanne because she was laughing again, and her lungs couldn't take it.

Dan and Melanie looked crushed, and Jeanne felt sorry for them—but why did everyone expect her to be so concerned?

Illness did not bring out the angel in her. At first she had appreciated visitors, but as she lingered on, they didn't leave. Her sisters kept bringing in their middle-aged children—for what? Goodbyes? Advice? Some final blessing? Sylvia begged, "Tell Richard to stop smoking!"

Oh really, Jeanne thought. That's what I am. Exhibit A. She studied her ruddy nephew. His wife had just won custody of the children and the dog. "I enjoyed smoking," said Jeanne. "Your mother did too."

Sylvia shrank back as though Jeanne had struck her, but she said nothing. It was too late, apparently, to retaliate.

Jeanne's sons returned, and they looked terrible, both of them. Dan wore wire-rimmed glasses. He was thick in the middle, and he had hardly any hair. It amused and saddened Jeanne to see him look so much like his late father. As for Steve, he had a bad back, so he had to walk around the room. He made Jeanne dizzy, pacing up and down.

Her daughters-in-law got emotional—especially Melanie, herself a doctor. Please, thought Jeanne. I lost both my parents by the time I was your age.

She pretended to sleep, and then she really did drop off. When she woke, her sisters hovered over her. Some of us have overstayed our welcome, Jeanne thought—and then, with sudden shock—no—I'm the one. That would be me.

Sardonic as she was, husk that she'd become, she shuddered to disappear, to lose consciousness and irony, her music, her unrenovated house, her sun. Cancer had consumed her body; drugs clouded her mind. Even so, Jeanne held on. Barely eating, scarcely speaking, Jeanne endured. Her nieces and her nephew sat with her. Wendy came to sing and strum her battered guitar. Jeanne's soccer-playing grandsons arrived. Zach cracked his knuckles. Nate jiggled his right leg. The boys were all ears and feet.

The hospice nurses said that Jeanne would drift away in just a day or two, but four days passed, and then a fifth. It was awkward, because her sons had to take off work, and her grandchildren could only miss so many days of school. Should they stay, or should they go? Did it make sense to return home and then come right back for the funeral?

Helen said, "We need a plan." Oldest and bossiest, she told Jeanne, "We need to know your wishes."

"To get well," Jeanne said immediately.

Later in the hall, Sylvia turned on Helen. "How could you speak to her like that?"

Helen drew herself up. "Well, we can't ask her what she wants when she is gone!"

Sylvia began to cry.

"Don't get hysterical," snapped Helen.

"I'm not hysterical. I have feelings. Be considerate."

"I am considerate," Helen said. "I'm doing for Jeanne what I hope someone would do for me. If I didn't have a living will."

Weeping, Sylvia retreated to the dining room to criticize her husband, Lew.

That afternoon, at Jeanne's bedside, Helen appealed to her daughter Pam, a tax attorney. "She left no instructions."

At the word instructions, Jeanne opened her eyes. It was disconcerting the way she did that. Just as you slipped into the past tense, Jeanne would rouse herself to glare straight at you. Then everyone would hurry to her side again.

Jeanne stared at her sons and daughters-in-law gathered at the foot of the bed.

"Melanie," Jeanne whispered.

"What is it?" Melanie asked. Already the tears. Always the tears.

"Half a bagel," Jeanne said.

That sent them off again, scrambling to Rosenfeld's. The two couples took Dan's Volvo to Newton Centre, even as they told each other there was no way. Melanie, the doctor, said, "She'll never eat a whole half a bagel."

"Does that matter?" Dan demanded, as he drove.

"No," Melanie said, "of course not."

"If my mother wants a half a bagel. She's getting half a bagel."

Melanie said, "No poppy. She could aspirate the seeds."

"Get her an egg bagel," Steve suggested from the back seat.

Andrea corrected him. "She doesn't like egg. She likes plain."

By the time they returned with a dozen bagels, two large containers of whipped cream cheese, a side of lox, and a chocolate babka, Jeanne was sleeping again.

The nurses stopped predicting when Jeanne would drift away. Now they said that only Jeanne would know when it was time. Lorraine suggested that everybody share a moment. Was there unfinished business in the family? Sometimes people had to forgive each other before they could let go.

Tremulous, angelic, Sylvia told Helen, "I forgive you."

"Oh, for God's sake," Helen said. There was nothing to forgive. Simply the great divide between them. Helen told the truth, while Sylvia tried to paper over everything.

"Helen never listens to me," Sylvia declared in front of the entire family assembled at Jeanne's bedside. "I'm invisible to her."

Amazed at this mixed metaphor, Helen said, "Obviously I see you."

At this point Dan spoke up. "I think we need to focus on the time we have together."

"Amen," said Lorraine, and everyone was jealous, because she liked Dan best.

Look at you, thought Jeanne. All vying for attention! Even so, she forgave everybody. Good night, she told her family silently. Farewell. She wished she could send a blanket dispensation. After which she could stay, and they would leave.

In fact, she looked a little better. She drank some juice and tried a bite of toast. She asked for her violin. She couldn't play it. She couldn't even open the case, but she kept it on the table next to her bed.

Like a cat, Jeanne slept most of the day, but waking, she seemed a heightened, sharper version of herself. When Pam drove up the second time from Providence, Jeanne asked why she'd never married. When Melanie sniffled, Jeanne snapped, "Stop feeling sorry for yourself."

Obviously, Melanie was sad because she was afraid of her own death. Jeanne could see it in her eyes. Jeanne's sisters were just as bad. They looked at her and thought only of their own mortality.

But this was cruel! Not only unkind, untrue. Jeanne's sisters thought nothing of themselves. Sylvia berated Lew all the way home to Weston. Helen stayed up late in Brookline, baking. Lemon squares, brownies, sticky pecan bars, apple cake, sandy almond cookies. Alone in her kitchen, she wrapped these offerings in wax paper and froze them in tight-lipped containers.

Her husband, Charles, told her, "You should get some rest."

What a thing to say! How could anybody rest? Helen had not pursued a career like Jeanne, the music teacher, or three successive husbands, like Sylvia. No, Helen had always been a homemaker. Now her family needed sustenance, so she doubled every recipe and froze half. After all, there would be a memorial service, and shiva afterward. Helen could already picture Jeanne's students descending with their parents. Sylvia hadn't baked in years because Lew was diabetic. As for Melanie and Andrea—what would they throw together? A box of doughnut holes? No. Helen was the baker of the family. What she felt could not be purchased. She grieved from scratch.

And yet, Jeanne kept on living. Her sisters held vigil; her sons came up on weekends. In the kitchen, her family nibbled Helen's lemon squares. Melanie urged brownies on the nurses. "Take these," she told Lorraine. "We can't eat them all, but Helen won't stop baking."

"Sweetheart," Lorraine said, "everybody mourns in their own way."

Helen mourned her sister deeply. She arrived each day with shopping bags. Her cake was tender with sliced apples, but her almond cookies crumbled at the touch. Her pecan bars were awful, sticky-sweet, and hard enough to break your teeth. They remained untouched in the dining room.

Sometimes Jeanne asked in a confused voice why everyone had come. And then there were moments when she remembered and took charge. She ordered Melanie to drive all the plants and flowers to Newton-Wellesley Hospital. She told Wendy to put her guitar away. After this she asked to speak to her sons alone. She lay in bed and watched Dan and Steve approach. This is it, the two of them were thinking. "We'll see," Jeanne said.

Guilty, nervous, Steve asked, "What did you say?"

"These are my wishes," Jeanne said.

Dan pulled up a chair, but Steve paced up and down.

"Stop that," Jeanne said.

"What are your wishes?" Dan asked.

"First of all," Jeanne looked at Steve, "don't pace."

"Second of all . . ."

They waited.

"No funeral."

"A private burial?" Dan ventured.

"No burial."

Astonished, Steve said, "You have the plot." He might as well have added, and it's paid for.

"I don't want it."

Steve protested, "But it's next to Dad."

"Yes, I am aware of that."

Dan's glasses were fogging up. He took them off and wiped them with the edge of his sweater. "You shared your life with Dad for twenty-five years."

Jeanne looked at him sharply. "I certainly did."

If Jeanne had another plan, she did not reveal it to her sons. If she had a good word to say about their father, she did not say it. Fiercely, she insisted there would be no burial. No memorial. Privately, she decided not to die.

Jeanne's voice grew stronger as she kept living. Outside, the leaves were turning. AAA Sparkling Windows and Gutter Cleaning arrived with ladders. Still, she endured.

Uneasily, the family dispersed. Jeanne's grandsons returned to school. Jeanne's sons and their wives went back to work. Even Melanie stopped crying. Her mother-in-law was a medical miracle. She was going to outlast them all. Only the nurses kept the faith. Lorraine said that sometimes older people held on for an occasion. They willed themselves to stay alive for one final milestone. A wedding. A grandchild's graduation.

No one could think of a milestone, apart from Richard's divorce. Nobody was marrying or graduating. Everyone had shared a moment. Nieces and nephews and grandchildren and . . . Wait! They had forgotten Phoebe, writing poetry in Michigan, refusing to fly.

Melanie and Dan spoke to Phoebe on the phone. They called her from Jeanne's house, and then Melanie called again from the car as Dan drove home. She talked to Phoebe about respect and compassion—thinking about others, not just the earth.

Meanwhile, Helen and Sylvia kept coming every day, baleful, fearful, sorry for their lot. Helen wanted to bring her rabbi to the house.

"No rabbis," Jeanne said. "No members of the clergy."

"Well, what would you suggest?" Helen demanded.

Sylvia cried, "How dare you scream at her?"

"Only one of us is screaming," Helen said.

Sylvia left the room, and then she left the house. Maybe she raised her voice at times. Maybe she felt overwhelmed. The situation was overwhelming. Jeanne's death unimaginable, and now—even worse—postponed. There was nothing to be done, and yet Helen managed to do it. As usual, she took over everything. Sylvia was up all night; she was so upset. "It's all about Helen," Sylvia told her husband, Lew. "Her plan, her rabbi, her stale old pecan bars."

That weekend the family reconvened. They sat with Jeanne and paced the hall while she was sleeping. The house was desolate, the air stale until Sylvia and Lew arrived with fresh-baked apple cake, warm from the oven, fragrant in its pan.

Heads up, suddenly alert, Jeanne's huge grandsons sniffed the air. Can I have a piece? Can I have some?

Sylvia turned the cake out on a plate in the kitchen and sliced big wedges for the boys. Then Dan and Melanie had pieces, as did Steve and Andrea. In the dining room, Helen's defrosted brownies, pecan bars, and almond cookies remained untouched. Helen's husband, Charles, took a brownie out of loyalty, but he slipped into the kitchen for Sylvia's cake.

"I smell baked apples," Jeanne whispered in the studio. The bed seemed to swallow her up, and yet she spoke. She scented Sylvia's cake.

"It's my recipe," said Helen. "I gave that recipe to Sylvia twenty years ago."

"Yes, I remember," said Jeanne. "She bakes a very good apple cake."

"I bake the same one! I brought you apple cake last week!"

"I know, but I like hers better." Jeanne said.

Helen marched into the kitchen and gazed at the last crumbs of Sylvia's cake. Zach and Nate were eating standing up. Melanie and Dan, Steve and Andrea, Sylvia and Lew were eating at the table. Then Helen caught her own husband throwing away a paper plate.

"Et tu, Charles," Lew said.

"You used my recipe," Helen told Sylvia.

"Yes, I did," Sylvia replied with such an air that even Zach and Nate knew she meant What's it to you?

The next day, Sylvia brought homemade jelly rolls, soft sponges rolled with tangy apricot, dusted on top with coconut flakes. She had not baked jelly rolls in fifteen years, and the whole family fell upon them. Even Lew, who had to be careful, took a tiny piece. Only Helen and Jeanne abstained. Helen would not, and Jeanne could not partake.

She was sick of visitors, but she made an effort to say a few words to each. She advised her younger son, Dan, to look into hair replacement therapy. She told Melanie to try antidepressants. Maybe they would help her lose some weight. As for Steve and Andrea, they were neglecting music. Neither of their boys played an instrument. Jeanne advised Andrea to look into marching band, since the boys loved sports so much. Or if they refused to practice, there were youth choirs. With some ear training, they might learn to sing.

Andrea was speechless for a moment. Then she said slowly, "I realize that music is important to you."

"My life," Jeanne whispered.

"Would you like to see your students?" Steve asked.

Jeanne thought of her young violinists—George with his sweet tone and tendency to rush. Maisie, who forgot to count. Caleb had a good ear but didn't work at all. Emily could not relax her tight goat-trill vibrato.

Andrea said, "Would you like some of them to come and play for you?"

"God no," Jeanne said.

Sisters, sons, daughters-in-law were always begging to know what they could do. Jeanne gazed out the window at her sugar maple, and she told them what she wanted, since they asked.

They carried her into the garden, where she could see the trees. Tethered to her wheelchair and oxygen, she turned her face up to the fiery maples, the gold oaks, the breezy sky. How good the world smelled, the fresh damp grass.

She leaned back smiling, and her family thought she was at peace—but she was not. Quite the opposite; she was full of plans.

She told Helen she would see the rabbi. She would have a conversation with him. "Thank you," Helen said.

When the rabbi arrived the next day, Jeanne forgot that she had asked to see him. "Who is that?" she asked Helen.

"Rabbi Lieber," Helen said.

"It's good to meet you, Mrs. Rubinstein." The rabbi looked about thirteen. In his suit he seemed like a Bar Mitzvah boy.

"Jeanne wanted to have a conversation with you," Helen said, and then, officiously, "Should I go?"

Jeanne ignored the question and told the rabbi, "You should know that I'm an atheist."

The rabbi nodded. "Yes, I understand."

Jeanne added, "I don't have time for organized religion."

"You're in good company," the rabbi said.

Jeanne frowned to find him so accommodating. Didn't rabbis believe anything anymore? "But you believe in God," she said.

"I do."

Jeanne looked at Helen. "That's a relief."

"You see?" Helen told Jeanne, and she meant You see, it's a relief—a comfort—to think of the creator.

"Belief is very personal," the rabbi said.

"I agree," said Jeanne. "That's why we should keep it to ourselves."

Thc rabbi smiled.

"My family would like to bury me."

Helen broke in. "You know that's not true."

"They want to bury me next to my late husband," Jeanne said. "I would like to go somewhere else."

The rabbi asked, "Where would you like to go?"

"I'd like to be scattered," Jeanne said.

"Cremated?" Lieber asked delicately.

"That's not Jewish," Helen declared.

Jeanne looked at the rabbi, who seemed reluctant to speak.

"It's not our tradition," he said at last.

"Good."

"How would we visit you?" Helen demanded.

Jeanne said, "Why do you assume that I want visitors?"

Helen's tears startled Jeanne. Not you, she thought. Melanie's sniffling angered her, but Helen never cried. "I would visit," Helen said.

"Oh fine," Jeanne told the rabbi. "Go ahead and bury me. I won't mind."

"Thank you," Helen whispered.

After all, Jeanne reasoned, she would never feel it. She wouldn't even know. "Do what you want," she told Helen and Rabbi Lieber. "Cover me with rocks."

They wore her down. They came in shifts. Jeanne closed her eyes and pretended she was sleeping. Half-conscious, she listened to the house. Doors closing. Water running. The crackle of crumbs flying up the vacuum cleaner. Raised voices. Furious words. Helen brought mandelbrot from their mother Lillian's recipe. Sylvia countered with Lillian's honey cake.

Jeanne tasted none of it, but she remained the cause, the crux of the matter, the still fixed point of the entire family. How long had she been sleeping? When would she wake? She was as surprised as anyone to find herself alive again each morning. She opened her eyes, and everyone turned to her as to an oracle. She did her best to keep them busy. "Take a day off," she told Helen. "Serve on a committee. See a friend." She turned to Sylvia. "Bake another apple cake."

"You're angry at me," Helen told Jeanne later when they were alone.

Jeanne shook her head.

"You're angry because I have beliefs."

"No, I don't hold any of your beliefs against you." Jeanne said this, but she added silently, I do think less of you. As Jeanne weakened, Helen became more prayerful, a bid, Jeanne thought, to avoid her younger sister's fate.

"Sylvia covers her apples with brown sugar," Helen said. "She sugars everything."

"Of course she does," Jeanne said. After all, people liked sweet things. Anything sweet and easy, simple, fast. Whether in music, or in food, or life, the bitter, dark, and complicated could not compete. This had always pained her before, but she enjoyed the injustice of it now. She looked out the window and saw scarlet trees. How dazzling the world was. How strange.

She heard voices at her door and saw a beautiful girl, dressed all in rags. At last, her granddaughter Phoebe had arrived with her gold hair trailing down her back. She'd come on the bus from Michigan, and she'd brought a young man, a huntsman in a rough flannel shirt.

Jeanne clasped her granddaughter's hand, but Phoebe started back, shocked by Jeanne's ghastly face.

Oh, you're afraid of me, thought Jeanne. Grandmother, what big eyes you have, what withered cheeks.

"Sharp nails," Phoebe murmured, glancing at Jeanne's claws.

The wolf inside Jeanne whispered, The better to eat you with my dear. But Jeanne said, "Introduce me."

Phoebe didn't understand.

Jeanne turned to Phoebe's deerslayer. "What's your name?"

"I'm Chris."

"Short for Christopher?"

"No, Christian."

Jeanne's laugh rattled. She had no breath, but laughter racked her body anyway. She held on to Phoebe, and she began to shake.

Dan and Melanie did not find Phoebe's boyfriend funny, nor did they laugh about his name. He was twenty-eight years old without a full-time job. He talked about organic farming. He said he was interested in blueberries—and they said nothing. They did not appreciate meeting him like this. They did not appreciate meeting him at all. Chris sat on the couch with his arms wrapped around Phoebe and withstood every hint, and every disapproving look. He nuzzled their only child, and he ate. Unblinking, he finished off Helen's rock-hard pecan bars. He devoured Sylvia's apple cake.

Now that Phoebe had arrived, Jeanne was supposed to let go, but she stayed alive to gaze at Phoebe's lovely face. "Where's your violin?" she asked.

Phoebe looked down at her hiking boots.

"You sold it, didn't you?"

Phoebe began to cry.

"It doesn't matter. In the grand scheme of things . . ."

Phoebe waited. Then she said, "In the grand scheme of things . . . what?"

Oh, who can remember, Jeanne thought. Maybe she was sleeping. It was hard to tell. She could have been dreaming or talking in her sleep. She herself didn't know. "You played well—but other people play much better."

"Thanks, Grandma," Phoebe said, and suddenly Jeanne saw her as a little child, golden-haired, sitting in the sand. She could see Phoebe sand-dusted in her bathing suit. The rippling tide around her, wet sand, white foam.

"Write this down," Jeanne told her.

When Phoebe found her notebook she had to turn nearly all the pages, because they were full of poetry. "What should I write?"

"Write down the ocean."

Jeanne lost consciousness the next day. Dan and Steve kissed their mother's forehead. Once more, everybody said goodbye, but another day passed, and then a third. Finally, at night when she was all alone except for Shawn, Jeanne cried out.

"Mrs. Rubinstein!" Shawn tried to make her comfortable, but she fought him. She didn't want help. She wanted to open her eyes, to rise from her bed. She wanted music and she wanted apples. She wanted to touch the sandy beach, to feel summer's heat. She wanted all this, but she couldn't have it. She died because she couldn't breathe.

In the morning, Jeanne's sons tried to make arrangements. They sat in the dining room and Helen said that her rabbi should lead prayers.

Sylvia turned on her. "She said no memorial service. You know she hated organized religion!"

"Stop shrieking at me," Helen snapped.

"We are honoring Jeanne's life, not yours."

Dan intervened. "A simple burial."

"No service," added Steve.

"But she didn't want a burial," Sylvia reminded them.

Helen drew herself up. "She said fine."

"Because you pressured her!"

"I would never pressure anyone," Helen said.

"Oh really!"

"She told me fine."

"Nobody heard her say that."

"I heard. The rabbi heard."

"Because the two of you were pressuring her into it." Sylvia had beliefs as well. She belonged to a temple. She went for holidays, but she wouldn't foist her rabbi on anybody!

"For the last time, she wasn't pressured," Helen exploded. "She said yes. Bury me."

"Because she was dying! That's why she agreed."

Even as they argued in the dining room, the rental company came to collect Jeanne's canisters of oxygen. Someone was on the phone about the hospital bed, now stripped bare.

"She wanted to be scattered," Sylvia declared. "You know that," she told Dan and Steve, who sat together near the head of the dining table. She turned to Helen. "So do you."

"She said bury me. She told the rabbi."

"She didn't believe in rabbis!"

"Does that mean he never existed?" Helen shot back. "Does that mean the conversation never happened?"

"Stop," Dan begged, but they ignored him.

"As far as you're concerned," said Sylvia, "the only conversations that happen are the ones happening to you."

Now Helen lost her temper. "I asked her to make plans, and you accused me of having no feelings! I talked about instructions because I knew this was going to happen!"

"She stated her wishes a thousand times." Sylvia spoke with resolve. "She said she wanted to be scattered."

"That is what she said," Dan admitted.

"She never wavered," Sylvia told Helen.

"She changed her mind!" Helen cried out, but nobody believed her. Once Helen had been the sane one. Now they treated her as though she were delusional. Sylvia had begun the insurrection. She'd waged this war for weeks. Helen's voice broke, even as she appealed to them all, "Jeanne talked to the rabbi and she talked to me and she said bury me, and that's the truth!"

Sylvia fixed her eyes on Helen. "Don't get hysterical."

But, of course, it wasn't up to them. Dan and Steve were in charge, and they decided. There would be no burial, just a celebration of Jeanne's life.

Privately, their wives spoke to Sylvia and Helen. They said the reception after the service would be catered, and for the sake of the family, they requested no homemade desserts. They asked Jeanne's sisters to promise. No cookies, no pecan bars. Absolutely no cake.

"I will do whatever you decide," Helen declared.

"And so will I," said Sylvia.

Helen added, "I would never use an occasion like this to call attention to myself."

No rabbis spoke at the celebration of Jeanne's life. Jeanne's student Emily played Bach, and Dan spoke about how Jeanne's music filled the house. Steve talked about what he had learned from his mother. "Don't quit. Don't feel sorry for yourself. Don't just stand there." These were the lessons he remembered, although Jeanne's actual words had been don't pace.

In the front row of the funeral chapel, Sylvia wore tinted glasses. She didn't think that she could speak. However, when the time came, she walked up to the lectern and the words began to come. She had written them on college-ruled paper.

"All my friends were jealous when she was born," Sylvia said. "But I didn't even let them touch her. She was a perfect baby and an angel. From the time she was born, she was my special charge. I used to dress her and play with her. I was her teacher when we played school on the porch. And this is why . . . this is why it's so difficult . . . impossible to . . ."

Sylvia broke down, and her son rushed to the lectern to comfort her, which made her cry even more. How could he keep smoking after all this? How could Richard's wife, his first love, leave him?

Lew was standing. He helped Sylvia to her chair, and she sat between the two of them, her husband and her son. The tears kept coming—until Helen began to speak.

"It is perhaps appropriate that I speak last, because I knew Jeanne longest," Helen said. "And yet I have no monopoly on my sister. Like every human, she belonged to many people, not just one. She had parents." Helen stood at the lectern and stared straight at Sylvia. "She had *two* older sisters. She was a beloved member of our family. Daughter, sister, mother, aunt, grandmother, friend. She was a musician. She was a teacher who spent countless hours instructing children. She was not sentimental, but she was giving."

Now Sylvia took off her glasses. Now she wiped the last tears from her eyes.

"She did not love tradition," Helen said, "but in her final days she spoke of God."

"Not true!" Sylvia whispered to Lew, who took her hand.

"She talked about belief."

Louder, Sylvia whispered to her husband, "That's just not true!"

As Helen spoke, Sylvia rattled her notes, her own words left unsaid. She longed to stand and finish her eulogy. To deliver her bright version of Jeanne's life, the true picture, unvarnished with religiosity, but she'd missed her chance. Already Helen was speaking about eternity. Already she was reciting kaddish.

Sylvia wanted to jump up from her chair and drown out the prayer. She whispered loud enough for those around her to hear, "This was not Jeanne's wish!" She turned to the mourners behind her and said, "This is exactly what Jeanne wanted to avoid!" Apart from that, she suffered in silence. She would not ruin the memorial. She would never make a scene.

To close the service, Jeanne's twelve-year-old student George played the meditation on a theme from *Thaïs*. He didn't rush until the last cascading phrases at the end. Horse knows the way, Jeanne would have said.

After the celebration, the family convened at Jeanne's house to sit shiva for one day, because no one could take off another week. Silent, staring, Helen watched caterers set out quiche and crudités and sweet noodle kugel in a silver chafing dish. Fresh fruit platters stood in for dessert, along with factory-made cookies and weak coffee.

In the living room, Melanie and Andrea tried to comfort friends shaken by Jeanne's passing. Several confided that Jeanne's death had prompted them to enjoy life while they could. Jeanne's neighbors, the Auerbachs, were planning a cruise to the Galápagos Islands to see the tortoises.

In Jeanne's studio, Dan and Steve and their cousins Pam, Wendy, and Richard talked about how they used to play wiffle ball together in the backyard. Someone asked Helen to look for the photo albums, but she did not respond. As for Sylvia, she was nowhere to be seen.

Only as the guests began to leave did Sylvia slip into the house. Sober, Lew followed, carrying a Bundt pan.

"Lew?" Andrea said in a warning voice. "What is that?"

Lew kept moving. He knew this was the nuclear option, and he felt culpable, but he loved his wife.

In the dining room, Sylvia turned out and sliced her fresh-baked apple cake. The caterers were packing up. Their chafing dishes were hardly cold when the house filled with the cake's fragrance. Jeanne's grandsons ran straight to the table. Chris appeared with Phoebe right behind him.

The scent of apples woke Helen from her trance. She marched into the dining room and saw the family eating; she knew what Sylvia had done. Eyes bright, mouth set, she turned and walked out again.

That was the end.

Melanie tried. Everybody tried. Nobody could reconcile Jeanne's sisters. This was all a misunderstanding, their children said. Don't be stubborn, their children pleaded. Andrea said they only had each other now, but they refused to listen. Dan said life was short. They didn't care. In fact, they knew it wasn't true. Their lives were long.

Lorraine was right. Everybody mourned in their own way. Phoebe wrote a poem, and Melanie did, in fact, start taking antidepressants. Richard began dating a woman he'd met at a bar. Pam adopted an Irish setter. As for Jeanne's sisters, they would not forgive each other for her death. Helen and Sylvia would not reconcile, even when the whole family gathered at Singing Beach in the spring to scatter Jeanne's ashes in the ocean. Wendy stood on the sand and asked the sisters, in Jeanne's memory, to open their hearts and to embrace each other so that they might begin to heal, but no, not even then.

2

New Frames

He had been seeing Corinne for just a few months when he realized he needed new glasses. In fact, she was the one who told him. "You're squinting all the time."

"You think I'm old and blind."

"Yeah. Definitely."

Gradually, Richard's eyesight had been getting worse, but now he found himself misreading faces at short distances. Colleague or commuter? Summer intern or some random kid? Two blocks off, he couldn't tell. Even one block away, he wasn't sure.

The world had softened, just a little. Distinctions he had once assumed began to blur so that, as he walked downtown in twilight, the buildings wavered, floating gently in the dusk. He watched the evening stars appear and then realized he was looking at white lights threading through the trees.

He needed an eye exam, but he had deadlines—and then, when he was with Corinne, she filled his field of vision. On weekends with his kids, he had no time.

He was forty-five and scrambling to buy kitchen utensils. After demanding a divorce, his wife held on to the children and the house, the toaster, and all the spatulas and spoons, along with the new car and the dog. When Richard had asked for joint custody of his own pet, Debra explained that Max was *the girls'* dog, not his. She always said the girls with emphasis, a reminder that she thought only of Sophie and Lily; she kept nothing for herself. This was Debra's stance in every argument. She didn't take; she gave—as in, I gave up my career. (She had hated law, but never mind.) Richard was mercenary, feckless, terminally selfish, while Debra was pro bono, nonprofit, *real*. Her clothes were comfortable. Her hair was proudly gray.

An angry ex, two daughters, a giant mortgage, not to mention rent for his place—these were the facts, but the details no longer seemed so hard and fast. In the early days dating Corinne, Richard lost track of his keys and calendar. One Friday—an occasion Debra added to his list of misdemeanors—he forgot to take Sophie to her piano lesson. Carefree, he didn't see the mess in his apartment.

Saturday morning, Lily found a purple jogging bra on the floor in Richard's bedroom. "What's *that*?" She sounded like her mother, although she was just eleven.

"Hmm," said Richard as though he wasn't sure.

"Come on, Dad," said Sophie, who was fourteen. Disdainful. Embarrassed by his equivocation.

Two weeks later they glimpsed Corinne herself. It was Veterans Day, and the schedule had changed. Richard had forgotten to warn her, and she dashed in after a morning run. Opening the door with her own key, Corinne saw Richard and his daughters on the couch and realized it was his weekend.

"Oh hey!" Corinne stood there for a split second while the girls stared at her long legs and glowing body, the red mark on her arm where she had strapped her phone. Then she ran away again.

"Time for breakfast!" Richard headed to the kitchen and started buttering the skillet. He kept Sophie busy cracking eggs for French toast while Lily sliced the bread. He even got the kids to call his mother, but as they took turns on the phone—Hi, Grandma . . . Good . . . Dad told me to—he sensed his daughters' disapproval. Silently they processed his stealth girlfriend.

"What did Grandma say?" Richard asked when Sophie hung up.

"Last week was her birthday."

"Oh shit." He had forgotten.

"Don't *swear,*" Lily said.

At the office, Richard kept precise accounts, billing to the minute, but when he was with Corinne, his job seemed fuzzy, his professional objectives strange. He described his work as defending patents. He told Corinne, "We chase patent trolls," and suddenly he envisioned a troll figurine with pink hair. "Like those ceramic things in people's yards."

Corinne said, "No, those are garden gnomes."

She was clear-eyed, precise, and *twenty-five,* as Debra pointed out. Debra had never set eyes on Richard's girlfriend, but she had looked her up. She knew where Corinne had gone to school and, of course, Corinne's birthday was online, along with pictures. "She's eleven years older than Sophie," Debra said.

For years Richard had done nothing right. He knew this because Debra had told him. Apart from working constantly and making French toast, he had done nothing for his family. He had not picked up the girls from school. He had not picked up a goddamn sock. At one point, when Debra had been overwhelmed, Richard had suggested hiring some help, thus failing a major test of character. It had never occurred to Richard that *he* was the one who needed to pitch in, regardless of filing deadlines. Apparently, he had become so self-absorbed that the only one he saw when he came home was Max. In the months before their separation, Debra had used the dog as evidence against him. She had smelled cigarettes in Max's thick fur—proof that despite his promises, Richard had begun smoking again.

Now Richard could smoke in peace (although officially he'd quit). He could drink. He could stay out all night or go home with Corinne. Apart from the girls' visits, he could be himself. Other people found this hard to take. Richard had lost friends, particularly those in bad relationships. They had sympathized when Debra left. They had been right there with Richard in his misery, but now he was enjoying himself. This, his friends could not forgive, because he had abandoned them.

The family dentist, long married, melancholy, suffering from back pain, looked askance when Richard bounded in for cleaning.

"Sorry I'm late," Richard said.

Dr. Davis did not say no worries. He spoke in a monotone as he lowered Richard's chair. "How are you?"

"Wonderful."

"No medical changes?"

"I'm happy."

"Flossing?"

Richard sank deeper. Lying on his back, he gazed into his dentist's aggrieved gray eyes. "You have pockets," Dr. Davis observed. Then he added for the hygienist's benefit, "Over here, number fourteen could be a candidate for a crown."

Just a candidate, Richard thought. That's not so bad.

"There are several places we'll be watching," Dr. Davis said.

Everyone was watching, waiting to attack. Richard thought of his Grandma Lillian's saying, *smile and the whole world smiles with you*. Wrong! If you were too lucky, or too distracted, or too much in love, the world was out to get you.

One day he couldn't start his car. Every time he tried, the engine sputtered and cut out. He called AAA to his driveway, but when the truck arrived, he didn't need towing or a new battery. It turned out he had forgotten to buy gas.

"You're sure it's not mechanical?" asked Richard.

"Trust me, I've seen this before." The AAA guy smirked, and Richard thought, Really? What else have you seen? Then, suddenly self-conscious—What do you see in me?

His barber actually attacked. Maybe he had been having a bad day. Maybe his own marriage was ending. Or quite possibly, Antonio, who was bald himself, had tired of Richard's full head of hair and idiot grin. Antonio clipped so much that when Richard put on his glasses, he hardly recognized the guy with the buzz cut in the mirror.

"Are you fucking kidding me?"

"You don't like it?" Antonio asked coolly.

When Corinne saw Richard that night, she said, "Oh no!" and then she laughed.

They were waiting for a table at a crowded Japanese place, and Richard frowned.

"What? Are you mad?" Corinne asked.

He was studying a wide-hipped woman leaving the bar. "For a second I thought that was Debra."

"Really?" Corinne was all curiosity.

"She could be Debra's twin."

"You're so paranoid!"

"If you had this haircut, you'd be paranoid too."

"Aw, it will grow back. Eventually."

"Let's get out of here," Richard said.

"Appearances don't matter," Corinne declared, as they walked to the parking lot.

"Do you believe that?"

"Did the barber charge you?"

They walked to a pizza place and Richard said, "Can I ask you something?"

"What?"

"Would you love me if I was bald?"

"How bald?"

He couldn't help laughing. "That was a serious question!"

"That was a serious answer!"

You're funny, he thought, and then with some surprise—I'm old. Corinne teased him all the time, but now he felt it. He was ancient—not only old, but undeserving.

He was quiet as they drove home and serious as they began to kiss in bed.

"What's wrong?" Corinne asked.

"Nothing."

She was so young that she believed him. Or maybe she was just sleepy. She curled up next to him and closed her eyes, leaving Richard to wonder. Did she love him? Really? He stroked her back and thought, This is not serious for you.

She was lighthearted, happy with him now—but she could be happy later on with someone else. She took joy for granted.

Richard was the opposite. Bruised by marriage, he had given up on happiness, and now every moment seemed a revelation and reprieve. She'll hurt you, his heart whispered. She'll leave you, and it serves you right—but he decided not to listen. Not when his heart spoke like his ex-wife.

He avoided Debra when he came for the girls on Saturday. He would have waited in the car, except that this was his only chance to see Max. He knelt in the doorway and opened his arms as his fluffy dog came running.

Walking down the stairs, Debra took a good look at Richard's haircut, but offered no condolences. "You're half an hour late."

"Hey Maxy," Richard said. "What's new? How have you been?" He could hear the girls thumping around upstairs.

Debra said, "You could have called."

"Why? They aren't even ready."

Debra didn't answer. This was one of her new things. She did not engage—except sometimes she did.

When the girls ran downstairs with their backpacks, Debra

clipped a leash to Max's collar to prevent him from running after them. Max snuffed Richard's shoes, and Richard said, "I'm sorry, boy." It was hard to be apart. He could text his daughters, but he had no way to reach his dog.

"Could I just take him for the weekend?" Richard blurted out. "Couldn't he just come with the girls, since he's their dog?"

Debra stared at him as if to say, Really? Did we not put all this in writing? The girls' dog wasn't going anywhere.

She followed him outside with Max on the leash, and once the girls were in the car, she peered through the windows, as though she didn't trust the vehicle. Then with their daughters behind glass, she stepped back onto the curb and told Richard, "I should meet her."

"What are you talking about?"

"You know exactly what I'm talking about. Corinne."

Max pricked his ears, and Richard sensed danger too. "Oh no you don't."

All reason and responsibility, Debra faced him down. "If this is someone you're living with, then I should meet her. I'm not exposing the girls to strangers."

"First of all, I'm not living with her."

"But you could. You might. You probably will." Debra spoke as though his whole life were a foregone conclusion. "You could marry her."

"Don't be ridiculous!"

"I'm thinking about the girls."

"Nobody's getting married."

"So, this isn't serious. This is actually not a serious thing."

"It's none of your business. That's what it is."

"If she's in my daughters' lives, I need to meet her."

"They saw her once, for like two seconds."

"I should sit down and talk to her."

"What, you're going to interview her?"

"Dad?" Sophie opened her door and poked her head out.

Immediately Debra stopped talking and smiled at the girls and waved. She was brave and appropriate, while Richard hissed, "You are not sitting down with Corinne. Ever!"

Jesus, he thought as he drove off with his daughters clamoring to go out for dinner. What would Debra say to Corinne? What poisoned apple would she offer?

He tried to shake his bad mood, but the weekend did not go well. The girls fought, and Sophie talked back. Mom lets me have my phone in bed, she said. No, she doesn't, Richard told her. How would you know? she asked him.

Then Lily was up in the night because she was hot and, as she told her mother on the phone, afraid of Richard's house. Also, she missed Max.

See? Richard texted Debra, but she ignored him.

Sunday morning, he left Debra a long voicemail about Lily and the dog, the spirit versus the letter of the law. Then he rushed the girls to skating and forgot his coat.

Walking into Skate World, he felt an arctic wind. He knelt, struggling to help Sophie, whose lace was in a knot.

"Dad. Stop! Leave me alone." Not fit to tie your boots, he thought.

When lessons started, his daughters flew away like birds. Lithe and fearless they practiced spins and waltz jumps in their small groups on the ice. First, they unzipped their coats, and then they threw them on the barrier. Lily was working on her arabesque and laughed as though the night before had never happened. Meanwhile Richard shivered in the bleachers.

Other parents had dressed for freezing temperatures. They held up phones, filming their kids, but Richard didn't try. The whole scene made him queasy. His daughters wore white skates, black fleeces, and black leggings, each with a single stripe spiraling around calf and thigh so that, spinning, the girls looked like barber poles.

"Dad, did you see that?" Lily called out.

"Wow! Do it again!" Richard bit into a large, salted pretzel, dry as wood. Addict that he was, he drank the snack bar's coffee, and felt the way it tasted. Stale, acrid, lame.

He texted Corinne. *miss you.*

His heart jumped when his phone rang just a second later, but it wasn't Corinne calling.

"Hello?" an anxious voice inquired.

"Hi, Mom."

"Richard?" Sylvia spoke as though she had not heard his voice in years. "Are you busy?"

"I'm at skating."

"Skating! When did you learn to skate?"

"I'm just watching the girls."

"Take a picture!"

"Okay."

"Take a video on your phone."

"I'm talking to you on my phone."

"All right, sweetheart. We'll talk later."

"Wait. Mom?"

"You have your hands full."

"No, I don't. What's going on?"

"Nothing! I have a little vertigo."

Vertigo? Was that a thing? He felt guilty for not knowing, for not calling, for not thinking about his mother. She made him crazy—but that was no excuse.

"I don't think it's bad," Sylvia assured him. "I'm just going to the hospital for tests."

"The hospital!"

"They want to observe me."

"When?"

"You remember I felt dizzy at the celebration of Jeanne's life."

"I meant when are they observing you?"

"I thought it was my grief, but I'm off balance now."

"Can you walk?"

"Oh yes! But I have to hold on to something, or I fall."

"You fell? You never told me!"

"That's why they want me to come in. So they can observe me—and rule out other things."

"What things?" Even as he watched his daughters glide, Richard felt a sense of dread.

"They're admitting me tomorrow, but I don't want you to worry," Sylvia told him, and this meant Come here now.

"I could take an early train." He was thinking, Is this an actual crisis, or a bid for a quick visit?

"I know you're very busy," Sylvia said, and this meant You're my only child.

"Could I talk to Lew?" Richard's stepfather was known in the family for his calm demeanor, and firm grasp on reality.

"I'm worried," Lew said on the phone, and now Richard knew that this was serious. "She's having an MRI."

"Oh boy." Richard started pacing. He didn't even see his daughters anymore.

Sylvia chimed in, "I'm not really so concerned." This meant I'm probably dying. "I've had a good life. For the most part."

Richard canceled his whole Monday and took the early train to Boston. Opening his laptop in the Quiet Car, he tried to work but stared out the window where winter trees flashed past.

This was the other shoe. This was the universe clamping down. STOP. You're not allowed to be so happy. Back to Boston with you. Then of course he felt ashamed viewing the situation as a verdict on *his* life. As Debra said, he thought everything was about him.

Untrue. He was anxious for his mother. Was she really sick? He thought of nothing else, except Corinne.

He watched New Jersey flashing past. Leafless trees and snowy roofs. He wondered about the people who owned houses near the tracks. What was it like, hearing trains incessantly? Was that how people in those houses marked the hours? The years? He had been losing track of time.

He rushed to Beth Israel Deaconess, took the wrong elevator, backtracked, and tried another. He raced down long halls past patients deathly white, until he found Sylvia at last. She was sitting up in bed.

"Mom." He took her hands.

"Hello, dear," she said. "Are you all right?"

"I got here as soon as I could."

She nodded. "I know."

"What happened?"

"It was a surprise!" she told him. "I've passed all my tests. We're checking out at two. Lew went to pick up lunch. They've ruled out everything."

"You don't have vertigo?"

"I do! They've ruled out everything else."

Richard dropped her hands. "That's good news."

"You look terrible," Sylvia said.

"What do you mean?"

"Your eyes are puffy! What happened to your eyes?"

"I took a six A.M. train! I got no sleep—and Lily was up the night before." He sank into the chair next to his mother's bed. He was so relieved and so annoyed.

Of course, Sylvia looked great, well-rested, silver hair cut on the bias. She was wearing a silk dressing gown. No hospital johnnies for Richard's mother. "Sweetie," she said. "Who do you think just called? Debra!"

Richard started back. "What did she want?"

"Nothing! She wanted to see how I was. She was thinking of me. We had a long conversation about everything."

"Everything?" he said uneasily.

"I know you have your differences, but Debra is a wonderful

mother. You say that yourself—and I agree! She's worried about the girls. She doesn't know how your girlfriends will affect them."

"My girlfriends? Now it's girlfriends?"

"I don't remember whether she said girlfriend or girlfriends. She's worried about exposing Sophie and Lily."

"Oh, for God's sake," Richard exploded. "No one's exposing them to anything."

"She mentioned someone named Corinne."

"She called about Corinne? She doesn't know her. She has never met her."

"That's what she told me!"

"She's manipulating you."

"How can you say that?" Sylvia drew herself up against her pillows.

"How can you defend her?"

"Who is this girlfriend?"

"Someone I'm seeing, that's all."

"But why are you seeing her?"

"Mom," said Richard. "Listen. Debra called you behind my back."

"She is a good person," Sylvia said, although she knew very well what Debra and her lawyer had done to him.

"She is a controlling, angry, vengeful—"

Sylvia interrupted. "But she is still my daughter-in-law."

"No, Mom. She is not."

"To me, she is!" Sylvia spoke like this—although she had been divorced twice.

"Knock knock," said a nurse, standing in the open doorway.

"This is my son, Richard," Sylvia said, because good manners never failed her.

"Pardon my reach." The nurse maneuvered past him to check Sylvia's blood pressure.

"I'll just step out," Richard said.

Walking the corridors, he came upon his stepfather returning with take-out bags from Genki Ya. Lew's hair was white, but he was trim and fit; he looked fantastic for his age. He had been a judge on the First Circuit and still read law journals, kept in touch with former clerks, monitored his blood sugar, and walked two miles a day. "Richard! You made it! Have some lunch."

"Let me get some fresh air first."

"Don't tell your mother; it will kill her," Lew warned.

Richard hurried out through the glass hospital doors and lit a cigarette in the wind near Public Parking. He was the problem. Smoking when he said he'd quit. Dating someone much too young. He was Debra's eternal quarry, and she would hunt him down, even to his mother's sickbed—even when his mother wasn't sick.

He was the sick one. Sylvia was wonderful, as she told everyone. Lew did everything right, but Richard returned to Philly with a raw cough and sore throat. He leaned against the train window and when he closed his eyes he saw Debra sitting down to interrogate Corinne.

By the time he got home, he felt like crap. This is what he told Corinne on the phone. He couldn't see anyone, not even her. "Trust me, it's bad," he said. For three days, all he could do was drag himself to work, drink Scotch, and sleep.

"Don't kiss me," he warned when Corinne came over Friday night. "You'll catch my cold. It's a terrible cold."

She wasn't afraid of colds. She sat with him, sharing his armchair, and he wanted to confide in her. He wanted to tell her his worries and his fears—but in the end what could he say? Debra was after him, his taxes were overdue, his body ached, he missed Max, and he felt guilty about missing his dog so much. He had children, after all. "I feel behind," he told Corinne at last.

"What do you mean?"

"I'm behind on everything."

"Make a list!"

He stroked her arm. She was so practical, and, of course, she had no idea.

She said, "Seriously. Let me help you!"

"You can't."

Corinne straightened, resisting his resistance. She worked as a project manager. She planned entire kitchens! "Just tell me what you have to do."

"Okay, first of all, I have to make sure I don't screw up my kids."

"No, I'm talking about stuff you can actually get done—like this week."

He shook his head at her.

"Just do the little things first."

"There are no little things! I'm talking about my entire life."

"Okay," she said quietly.

"Not everything fits into a list."

"I know that."

"I'm sorry." He realized that he'd offended her.

She rested her head on his shoulder. "I'm just saying you have to start somewhere."

"You're right," he said. "I'll get new glasses."

"Yeah!" Corinne brightened immediately. "That's what I'm talking about." She took off his rimless glasses and her blue eyes blurred; her hair poured over her shoulders. He sensed rather than saw her loveliness.

"I need a new prescription," he told her.

"You need new frames," she said.

He asked her to go with him to 4EYES, and she practically skipped into the store. He spoke tentatively to the salesperson, but Corinne was already plucking frames off the displays.

Standing back, Corinne watched Richard try on each. No. No. No. *No*.

"Really?" he said, after eleven pairs.

"Trust me."

"I'll have to." Without his own glasses, Richard couldn't see himself.

"No way," she declared when he slipped on gold-rimmed aviator glasses.

Richard turned to the salesperson, Nora, a puffy woman his own age. "She's decisive."

"That's the way to do it," Nora said.

"I guess I'm trying on everything in the store," he said, even as Corinne handed him a pair of black rectangular frames.

"Yes," she said as soon as he put them on. "Those are amazing."

Nora said, "Wow. Just wow."

"These are the ones?" Richard squinted at the mirror.

"Don't you feel like a new person?" Corinne said.

Phototrophic, he turned toward her bright spirit, and he said yes. I'll take these. He said, These are good, but he meant Corinne's hope and confidence. He handed Nora his prescription and filled out paperwork and it felt right to choose new frames.

"You two take care now," Nora said, as he walked out with Corinne.

"You two!" Corinne whispered, laughing.

At the end of the week, Richard picked up his new glasses. Nora was there, and all the displays, just as he had left them, but he came alone. The errand was ordinary, gray—until he left the store with his new lenses. Then the world changed. The train, the streets, the smallest details were precise.

Revelation. Upgrade! At work he recognized his colleagues all the way down the hall. In restaurants he no longer mistook every pear-shaped woman for Debra. With his new prescription, he could read street signs. Walking through Old City he could discern individual red bricks. At Lily's orchestra concert, he could pick her out playing her half-size cello, way up on the risers.

There was a downside to such clarity. He noticed thick dust covering his shelves, a faint water stain on his kitchen ceiling. Outside he saw rotting leaves shellacked to sidewalks. Peeling paint. Wires wrapping tree branches, not just twinkling lights.

Of course, no one else noticed Richard's new lenses. Everyone remarked on his new frames.

"Dude," the guy at the gas station said approvingly.

"Hey, hey, hey," Richard's assistant at work exclaimed.

He heard that he was hot, that he looked like a novelist, that he seemed European. He went alone to a bar after work and a young man approached at closing time. A very young guy, even younger than Corinne.

"My name is Milo." The kid's eyes were liquid brown and earnest. He had faint stubble on his chin. "Pardon me for staring."

What is happening? Richard asked himself, although he knew exactly what was happening.

Milo said, "I think you're very interesting."

Richard stood and shook the kid's hand in a manner almost fatherly. "It's good to meet you, Milo."

The boy looked hurt, curious, and finally amused as Richard buttoned up his coat and walked out, stepping heavily, trying to embody age and experience, maybe even wisdom, although his black frames told a different story.

Could new frames make such a difference? Richard remembered a cartoon from his childhood. An ordinary insect donning square eyeglasses to become the mighty Fearless Fly.

His daughters approached warily. Sophie said, "Dad!" as though he had embarrassed her again.

Lily mourned the old frames. At night, she cried into her pillow. "Why did you change?"

"They're just glasses. I'll take them off. I'm taking them off." Richard bent over her.

Lily wailed, "Now you can't see me!"

He didn't need to see. He knew what Lily was thinking. He was not the same; he would never be the same.

He sat up worrying, but as usual, Lily felt better in the morning. The girls got used to his new look. His friends stopped commenting. Fashion victim. Narcissist. They judged him silently, but what did Richard care? He had confirmed their worst opinions long before. The scary part was the way Corinne began to treat him.

Was it his new frames? Or had he spooked her by admitting his sadness and fears? Somehow she lost her banter. She was sweet—even concerned—while she had joked before.

Standing outside the Miller Theater for *Chicago,* the national tour, she looked at him with tenderness, even concern. "Don't smoke."

He paused but lit his cigarette anyway.

She had never lectured him before. In fact, she had smoked with him on occasion. Now she said, "Seriously, don't."

"What's going on?" he asked.

"Nothing! I just don't want you to die."

He waited for some quip to follow, but that was all. "You sound like Lily."

She didn't take offense. She mused, "I should probably meet her."

"What?"

"I mean, sooner or later I have to meet them," Corinne explained. "Debra messaged me."

"Debra?"

"She was really casual like *Hey this doesn't have to be awkward I'd love to talk sometime p.s. I don't bite.*"

"P.S. Debra is not casual." Richard took a long drag. "Everything she does is preplanned. Do not go near that woman. She'll eat you alive." He was trying to find words dark enough, but he had been a father for too long. "This is not okay!"

"She sounded pretty—reasonable."

"She *hates* me."

"Maybe now she's in a different place."

He put out his cigarette to pick up their tickets at the Will Call window. "Richard Eisen," he said. "Thank you." Then, in a low voice to Corinne, "She is not in a different place. She's in the same place as before. Living in my house, driving my car. She would actually kill me if she could get away with it."

"She would not."

"You don't know her! This is a woman who won't let me visit my own dog."

"That *is* sad," Corinne admitted.

"Do not write back."

She hesitated.

"You answered her?"

"I didn't want to be rude."

He threw up his hands. "What did you tell her?"

"Nothing specific," Corinne said. "Just sure maybe sometime soon. I wasn't trying to upset you. Sorry!"

Enough. Richard confronted Debra about her proxy wars. He stood in the foyer of his old house and his voice was low but furious. "Stop. Just stop. Do not talk to my mother or Corinne behind my back. You want to tell me something, speak to me directly. Do not manipulate them."

"I'm not manipulating anybody," Debra whispered back.

"You crossed the line."

"*I* crossed the line?"

"The children are not pawns," he said.

"Don't start."

"What are you talking about? Don't start what?"

"Don't talk to me about pawns."

Their volume was escalating, but they cut off as the girls ran downstairs.

That week at parent-teacher conferences, Richard and Debra sat as far apart as possible. Lily's teacher had to turn her head to speak to each of them.

"Sometimes Lily looks tired. I think she's having trouble concentrating." Mrs. Grolnick placed a math quiz on the table.

Richard tried to make out Lily's answers slashed with red. "Is she sleeping in class?"

"No, but she's having trouble focusing. She seems down."

"What do you mean down?" Richard asked.

"There's a lot going on," said Debra, and Richard shot her a look because he knew those words were meant for him.

"What happened here?" Debra bent over the quiz.

Mrs. Grolnick said, "Well, this was the unit test. I think she's having trouble with the . . ."

Richard tried to understand the teacher's explanation, but like a man with tinnitus all he heard was Debra berating him and Lily crying. He heard Lily's voice, SEE ME, although those were the teacher's words in pen.

"Listen," Debra told him in the hall afterward. "We're going to have to work together on this."

"Yes," Richard said.

"We can't let Lily spiral into math anxiety."

"Agreed," Richard said.

"So, I'm going to look for a tutor, and we're going to work with her at night. And also, I think she needs to see someone about her anxiety. My sister knows someone who specializes in anxious kids."

"Okay, yes. Good," Richard said.

"Thank you."

Debra drove off in Richard's ex-car to his ex-house and he ducked into the boys' bathroom.

The urinals were short. The tiled room was empty. He stared at himself in the mirror washing his hands. What was he doing with those ridiculous black frames? He took his glasses off and his eyes were shadowed, slightly red.

He went to 4EYES and got Nora to find him rimless glasses like his old ones, self-effacing.

"I have to say, I like the square ones," Nora said shyly. "They're showstoppers."

"That's the problem," Richard said.

Two days later he picked up his new frames.

When he met Corinne that night for drinks her face fell. "Ohh, what happened?" she exclaimed, as though he'd hurt himself. "Why did you change back?"

"The new frames weren't good."

"The ones I found you?"

"Yeah, I didn't like them."

Puzzled, she said, "Yes you did!"

"They looked ridiculous."

"What do you mean? You looked amazing."

"Well," he said wearily, "what if I don't want to look amazing?"

"You liked them before," she insisted.

"*You* liked them."

She looked confused.

"I really have to concentrate," he told her.

"And those ugly glasses help?"

"Yes!"

"Okay," Corinne said, slowly.

"Lily's failing math."

Corinne didn't see the connection, but she tried to follow him. "Maybe she can get a tutor."

"We are. We are getting her a tutor, obviously."

"You don't have to be mean."

"It's not just Lily. It's Sophie too."

"What's wrong with her?"

"Nothing. She hates me."

"How are you so sure?"

"She's my kid," Richard said simply.

"Therefore, she hates you?"

"Therefore, I know."

Corinne sighed.

"You don't want to hear all this."

"Yes I do." She had been carefree, lighthearted before. Now she was involved with him.

He said, "I'm not dragging you into my kids' problems."

"That's okay!"

He could see her hurt and confusion as he said, "No. Not happening."

She flinched, and he hated himself, but what else could he do? Wryly, he admitted, "The thing is, I can't run away with you."

"I *know,*" she told him.

He said, "I have to think."

"About what?"

"You're wonderful," he said. "You deserve everything. But I have to help Lily. I've been distracted."

She didn't answer.

"You're so young," he said.

She stared at the table.

"I've got to pay attention."

"I thought you were paying attention before."

"Only to you," he said.

"Okay." She did not lift her eyes.

"Okay?" he echoed hopefully. He just wanted to avoid a scene and tears. He wanted Corinne to laugh with him as she had in the past. To end this lightly. But she did not laugh.

He kept talking and explaining. He said, Believe me, if it were different, but she did not say, I understand. He said, The children need me, but she did not say, Of course. Please, he said, but she would not engage. She wouldn't even look at him.

3

F.A.Q.s

Phoebe found the house almost unchanged. Same furniture, same couch cushions worn out in the same old places, practically the same stack of magazines. Phoebe's parents, Melanie and Dan, looked just as she had left them, and so their new coffee maker startled her.

"Where did that come from?"

"Your mother bought it."

"The old one broke," Melanie said, defending herself.

Of course, Phoebe saw that the new machine stood right where the scrap bucket had been. All composting had ceased the minute she had gone to college. Sweetie, it smelled so bad, had been Melanie's excuse.

And yet Phoebe's parents had planted vegetables with her when she was little. They had hired a handyman to build a chicken coop in the backyard. The coop stood empty now, just a few downy feathers blowing in the wind. Freshman year a fox had killed the hen named Scout. Weeks after that, Scout's sister, Carrie, had disappeared. During spring semester, the last chicken, Mrs. Dalloway, had passed.

Sometimes Phoebe questioned the level of care Mrs. Dalloway had received from Melanie and Dan. They had reverted so quickly to supermarket eggs.

"I'll carry those," Dan said.

"No that's okay." Phoebe shouldered her backpack and dragged her giant duffle upstairs. Nervously, her parents followed, weighted down with unasked questions. What had happened? Was the boyfriend really history?

"Let me help you get that through the door." Dan picked up the bottom of the duffle and squeezed the bag sausage-like through the doorframe. Phoebe was already inside, gazing at another acquisition, an elliptical trainer in the middle of her room. "We can move it." Dan had opposed the purchase, predicting correctly that it would gather dust. He had knee problems, so he never exercised.

"We'll take it down to the basement," Melanie said. She had only installed the trainer in Phoebe's room because she felt closer to her daughter there. Two birds. She'd missed Phoebe, and she was trying to lose weight. Missing trumped motivation, however, and after several minutes of exercise, Melanie usually ended up on Phoebe's bed.

When Phoebe stepped onto the machine, she heard a trilling sound like bells.

"WELCOME" she read on the small screen. "HOW OLD ARE YOU?"

Phoebe typed "100."

Without blinking, the elliptical asked "HOW MUCH DO YOU WEIGH?"

Once again, Phoebe typed "100."

"I got you rice milk," Melanie said. "And oat cakes," she added hopefully. Phoebe looked so thin. Her long blond hair had lost its spring; she'd tied it with a repurposed rubber band.

Melanie opened the closet door, revealing bins of clothes and toys, boxed board games and puzzles, including the Great Barrier Reef and the solar system. On the top shelf lay Grandma Jeanne's violin in its brown cloth-covered case. This was Phoebe's inheritance, but no one mentioned it.

Dan said, "We can consolidate these boxes."

Melanie said, "I'll get more hangers."

"Hey, it's almost midnight. Don't you have work tomorrow?" Phoebe ushered her parents out into the hall.

She was so tired she didn't even brush her teeth. She undressed completely and slipped between clean sheets.

Phoebe did not come down the next morning.

"Is she okay?" Melanie asked.

"What do you mean? She's exhausted, obviously." Dan spoke as though Melanie missed the point entirely, but he was just as anxious. He hovered in the kitchen while Melanie washed dishes. Then he followed her upstairs to wait in the hallway where each willed the other to knock first. Their daughter was home safe, but silent. What did it mean?

At last Melanie called, "Phoebe?"

No answer.

"Let her rest," Dan said.

Reluctantly, they left for work in separate cars. Dan drove to Progressive Insurance, and Melanie headed for New Jersey Medical. At ten o'clock she texted Phoebe, *I left you granola*. At noon, she texted her again. *Did you get some sleep?* Then at one: *Phoebe? Are you there?*

Still no answer. Was Phoebe really sleeping? Her bedroom had been preternaturally still. Not a rustle, not a breath escaped the cracks around the door. What if she had done something? Taken something? Drugged herself to disappear?

Melanie was planning to drive home when Phoebe texted. *Yes.*

Thank God. Melanie felt grateful and foolish. Now she could go about her day. Then she wondered, Did yes mean of course I'm here;

leave me alone? Or was it a broader affirmation? Yes, oh yes, granola with flaxseeds, rolled oats, dried cranberries. Yes, I have returned.

The first few days, Phoebe listened to music with her headphones on. She said she was unpacking, but she never did hang up her shirts, or fill her dresser drawers.

When she had the energy, she pulled clean clothes from her suitcase. At night, she left her dirty laundry on the floor. After she had worn all her shirts and underwear, she did the wash. Then she rigged up a clothesline in the backyard. From the kitchen window, Dan watched her tying one end of a nylon rope to the back porch and the other to the crab apple. She made a neat job of it; she had even found a tub of clothespins. Methodically she hung her clothes on the line. After that burst of activity, she drifted back inside and slept.

"I guess she needs it," Melanie ventured.

"I don't know," Dan said.

They remembered how much Phoebe had slept when she returned from summer camp, but this was different. After a week at home, she still couldn't stay awake.

Melanie worried about mono, ticks, and Lyme disease. She kept saying, "I think we should take you in." But Phoebe said no.

"What did he do to you?" Dan was always blaming Phoebe's ex.

"Oh, come on," Phoebe said, because did he really think she would tell him about her boyfriend?

"Could you be pregnant?" Melanie asked when she got Phoebe alone.

"Mom!"

Melanie was always looking for a diagnosis; Dan had to find someone to blame.

Each day, Phoebe waited in her room until they left for work. Then she shuffled down to sort pictures on her phone. Photos from college; photos from the berry farm. This took a long time because she studied each before she made it disappear. Once she ventured into the backyard. She checked the empty coop. She rolled her bike out of the garage and pumped up the tires. Then she rolled it back inside.

She felt disembodied, ghostly. She lived like Emily Dickinson. Yeah, right. She wished! No poems came to her, although she had the recluse part down. Phoebe watched children play across the street and imagined lowering a basket of gingerbread as Dickinson had done. Of course, she would get arrested. Food from strangers, nut allergies. She practiced flitting behind blinds instead.

At dusk, her parents returned like chattering birds. The house was small with thin walls and one narrow upstairs hallway, so Phoebe heard the arguments. How long would this go on? Was Phoebe home for the whole summer? And if she was, what would she be doing? Obviously, she should get a job, said Dan. But how and where? She wouldn't talk about her plans. She didn't talk at all. All they knew was Phoebe had spent a year living with Chris, and now they weren't together. What next? Their daughter said nothing, did nothing, wanted nothing. Melanie said Phoebe should see somebody. Dan said great, rush her into therapy.

Listening in bed, Phoebe remembered how her parents had fought when she was little. Once her father had told her mother, "If you're that unhappy *leave*." Melanie drove off but returned an hour later. She'd only gone as far as Edison.

From an early age, Phoebe had kept the family together. Melanie was tired; Dan was out of patience. Therefore, Phoebe had worked as hard as possible at math, poetry, physics, and violin—especially violin. In high school, she had practiced at least three hours a day. Now, as her parents snapped at each other, she thought of ways to reassure them. She would apply for internships. Teacher training? Arts administration? She would draft a five-year plan. The trouble was getting out of bed. She managed most days, but she didn't always make it down the stairs.

True to character, Dan lost it first. He turned to Phoebe at dinner and said, "All right, you've been here almost two weeks."

Melanie interrupted, "This is her home, Dan."

"You've been sleeping, what, twelve, fourteen hours a day?"

Melanie said, "You can see that she's run-down."

Dan kept after Phoebe. "What you're doing isn't healthy and it isn't fair."

"What do you mean, fair?" Melanie demanded.

"It's not fair to the rest of us! From now on we're having some house rules. First of all, no pajamas at the table."

Melanie protested, "She's not wearing—"

"She wore them yesterday. Second of all." Dan paused to think of his second point. "No sleeping more than ten hours. You have got to pull yourself together!"

Late that night, Phoebe heard a clattering of dishes in the kitchen as Melanie took Dan to task. "You don't just tell someone to pull herself together."

Dan said, "I'm not walking on eggshells while my twenty-one-year-old regresses."

"She's not regressing. She's recovering."

"From what?"

"I mean clearly—"

"She's growing *down*!"

Lying in bed, feet rooting underneath the covers, Phoebe imagined herself a misfit carrot, a fingerling potato.

"She doesn't drive; she doesn't even ride her bike," said Dan. "She was more capable at twelve. At ten! I'm calling her on it."

"You know that doesn't work."

"Oh, now you're speaking from experience?"

Melanie's voice wobbled. "I know it doesn't work."

"So, what would you suggest?"

———

The next night at dinner Phoebe told her parents she was sorry. She was really, really sorry.

"Don't apologize," said Dan. "Don't sit there apologizing to the world. Get up and do something."

Phoebe said that she would wash the dishes. When she was done, she sat with Melanie on the couch while Dan leaned back with his laptop in the reading chair.

Emboldened, Melanie hugged Phoebe. "You're great."

This was lame, so Phoebe didn't answer.

"Breaking up is hard, but you'll get through this," Melanie said.

Embarrassed for her mother, Phoebe patted Melanie on the shoulder.

Melanie hesitated. Then she said, "We've got Uncle Steve and Aunt Andrea coming over with the boys on Friday night, okay?"

Dan closed his computer. "Why are you asking? Are you asking her permission?"

"I'm not asking."

"That's what it sounded like."

"I wasn't asking a question. Even if I was!"

"Oh my God," Phoebe said. "Stop."

Immediately the bickering ended. Bright-eyed, expectant, her parents turned toward her. Their daughter had come alive again.

Were they expecting a speech? A manifesto? Phoebe had nothing.

"I just wanted to give you the heads-up," said Melanie.

"It's fine," said Phoebe. Uncle Steve and his family wouldn't make her feel better or worse. Phoebe barely knew what grades her cousins were in.

On Friday night, Phoebe watched through the living room window as her father's brother and his wife arrived. They lived only three miles away, but she could not remember the last time she had seen them. Last October when Grandma Jeanne passed away? Approaching the house, they looked familiar and awkward all at once, like animals who had learned to walk on their hind legs. Andrea brought a bottle of wine. Steve carried a wedge-shaped pillow for his back. In the entryway, their sons, Zach and Nate, crowded in behind them.

"Nate is looking at colleges," Andrea told Phoebe. "You can tell him about Michigan!"

Melanie and Dan exchanged looks, but Phoebe didn't take offense. She was watching her younger cousins—huge, laconic, grazing the light fixtures. Zach brushed against a side table and knocked off a glass paperweight, but he was quick and caught it with one hand.

"Good save," said Nate, who did not ask Phoebe about Michigan.

The three kids sat together at one end of the table, and it was peaceful there. Zach and Nate devoured Melanie's brisket, while Phoebe picked at her wild rice. The adults did all the talking, discussing dehumidifiers. They spoke about French drains and cars, but they kept their eyes fixed on the children. Not that anybody made comparisons. Just that the boys had grown so much, and Phoebe looked—crushed. What was she wearing? Nobody asked, but Melanie knew what her sister-in-law was thinking. Phoebe's post-consumer dress was faded blue, and nearly shapeless. Not a dress, but an apology for one. Oh why? Melanie wailed silently.

"Good to be home?" Andrea asked Phoebe. "Nice and quiet?"

Phoebe said, "I keep busy."

Dan could not conceal his surprise.

Melanie tensed, but Andrea saw an opening. "How do you like the violin?"

For a moment, Phoebe didn't know what her aunt was talking about. Then she remembered Jeanne's instrument, unopened in her closet. "I don't know," she said. "I quit."

"What?" Steve said slowly. Supposedly the whole point of Jeanne's bequest was that Phoebe would play it. (His sons had received nothing.)

"She'll get back to it," said Dan.

Poor Dad, thought Phoebe. Never say die!

"When did you quit?" Steve asked.

"Like a year ago."

Even her cousins stared, absorbing this news. They had grown up with Phoebe's recitals. Her music endless, wordless, intricate. All their lives they'd settled down to listen.

Slowly Andrea said, "Well, that's a shame."

Phoebe knew what that meant; the instrument was worth a lot of money. "Maybe someone else should have it."

"Oh no you don't," her father cut her off.

Melanie said, "Jeanne wanted you to have that violin."

"She wanted somebody to play it," Steve corrected.

"She didn't want just anybody. She gave it to Phoebe," Melanie said. "It was her wish."

The others settled in their chairs. Dan furious, Steve and Andrea not angry but surprised and disappointed. Okay, smoldering.

That night the violin kept Phoebe awake. She'd barely noticed it before, but now she sensed it suffering. Jeanne's gift seemed to her a wounded thing. Her closet, her room, her house could not contain the blood gushing from that violin. Blood soaked the carpet, stained the walls. Even so, she didn't scream; she didn't move. She couldn't wake her parents. Instead, she watched the window, waiting for the sky to brighten.

Daylight wouldn't come. The sun would not rise. She turned on her light and stole from bed. Softly she opened her closet door and took down the sealed casket. Then softly, softly she carried it downstairs, scanning cabinets and pantry shelves for a place to hide her inheritance. The kitchen was too cluttered for a violin. The mudroom was too cold. She sank into the couch and rocked slightly with

Jeanne's gift in her lap. Her parents found her in the morning sleeping there. In its case, the violin sat mildly on the coffee table.

"Oh, sweetie," Melanie said. Phoebe opened her eyes and sat up as her mother said, "They upset you."

"They had no right," Dan began.

But Phoebe cut him off. "They were fine. Everything's fine."

"Everything is not fine," Dan told her. "Look at you."

She tried to look at herself sitting on the couch in sweatpants and an Interlochen T-shirt. She was clutching her knees to her chest.

Melanie didn't want to leave Phoebe in the house all day.

"There's nothing to worry about," Phoebe told her mother.

"Prove it," Dan said.

"I'm going for a walk," Phoebe said.

"Where?" Melanie asked.

"Just to get some exercise."

As soon as her parents left, Phoebe pulled on a clean shirt, combed her hair, and stepped out, blinking in the sunlight. Then she felt awkward because she had nowhere to go. Nothing to do, no bags to carry. She retreated to the house and took Jeanne's violin, carrying it like a briefcase to the end of the street and then around the corner. A Rutgers shuttle bus stopped there, and she climbed aboard. The bus was free, half-full of summer students. Phoebe chose a window seat and rode from one campus to another. Busch, Livingston, Douglass. She watched trees rustling near the Raritan and saw one orange leaf in all the green. It was the first week of July.

The next morning, after her parents had left for work, Phoebe headed out again with the violin as briefcase, carry-on baggage. She got home just after three and sat in the kitchen gazing at the groceries Melanie had bought in her honor. Oats and nuts and grains and sprouted wheat berries and unsweetened coconut piled up in bags on the kitchen counter. Nobody really ate these things. Her mom poured herself sugary cereal. Her dad skipped breakfast. He was supposed to watch his cholesterol but he loved cookies and Icelandic chocolate.

Phoebe preheated the oven and mixed the grains and nuts along with coconut oil and diced pieces of crystallized ginger. Then she toasted everything on a pair of cookie sheets. The result was a lot of lumpy granola which she divided into snack-sized bags.

"This is for you." She handed her mother a little bag that night. "And this is for you," she said, handing one to her father.

"This is awful," her father told her.

"Dan," said Melanie.

"I don't like your tone of voice with her," Melanie told him later when they were alone.

"What tone?"

"Your hostility and sarcasm."

"That's the way I talk," he said. "That's my natural voice. The hostile one is you."

"I was just—"

"Listen to yourself!"

In the morning, Phoebe took the shuttle bus again. She got off at New Brunswick and sat outside the library. She didn't have a library card, but, carrying her instrument, she might have been an undergraduate. She liked the possibilities. She could have been a music student; she could have been a tourist. It was hot out, but she sat on a bench in the midsummer sun.

When she got home, she showed Melanie an article about cruciferous vegetables. "Phoebe?" Melanie said.

Phoebe said, "I think you should eat more of these."

Dan and Melanie were seeing someone in Edison, a psychologist recommended by a colleague of Melanie's. The doctor counseled them to wait patiently and allow Phoebe to lead the way. But where was Phoebe leading? She liked to turn off all the lights. Her parents would sit in the living room at night, and Phoebe would turn off the lamps around them. Could we not sit in the dark? Dan said. Meanwhile, Phoebe kept Jeanne's violin with her on the couch.

Melanie asked Phoebe to go with them to Edison. Phoebe said no thank you. Melanie asked if Phoebe would like to take lessons with her old teacher. Phoebe spoke cheerfully. "Not really."

She took the train to the city, boarding with her violin. The train rattled through Brunswick and Rahway and Elizabeth. Gazing out the window, Phoebe saw black benches and vistas of chain-link fence.

When Phoebe got to Penn Station, she thought about walking around, maybe visiting the Egyptian tombs at the Met. She bought a MetroCard and entered the subway, but she didn't go anywhere. She sat on a bench on the platform and watched tides of people rising and sinking away again.

A young woman and two small boys were struggling to carry a stroller with a sleeping baby up the stairs. Phoebe rushed to help. She picked up the crosspiece of the stroller and together with the mother and the children, got it to the top. Everybody thanked her, as the baby slept. "No problem," Phoebe said. She sauntered back to her bench at the bottom of the stairs. Wait. Her heart jumped. The violin was gone.

How could that be? It wasn't true. The whole thing was a dream—the station, the woman with her stroller and her children. Phoebe stood bewildered, looking up and down, but, of course, she wasn't dreaming. She was an idiot. That's how fast she lurched into self-loathing. Seriously? Seriously? Had she left Jeanne's gift in the subway? Had she fucked this up too? At which point she realized that she had returned to the wrong bench. Her violin was one bench over with a security guard hovering.

"Do not leave bags unattended," he intoned, even as she snatched the instrument. She clutched Jeanne's gift to her chest and ran away.

As soon as she was out of sight, she knelt, unzipped the case, unfolded a piece of green velvet, and took out the violin to check for injuries.

There were two bows in the case, and Phoebe tightened one, stood up, and started tuning. She closed her eyes and listened to the *whoosh* and roar of trains, the tide of people all around her. No one stopped and no one looked as she played scales. Mercifully, no one could hear her blunder through folk songs and scraps of Bach, Mozart, Lalo, the music she had known. Her fingers were thick, her bowing scratchy. After a few minutes, Phoebe stowed the instrument again.

The next day, she went back. Once again, she took the train into the city. This time she didn't even make it to the subway. In the station, there was a guy playing an amplified acoustic guitar, so she drifted farther down. Passing commuters drowned her out. Unamplified, her music could not carry, and that was a relief. Nobody heard and nobody cared how rough she sounded.

Scales, arpeggios. She practiced until her hands grew warm. One by one, she played pieces she had learned at five, "The Irish Washerwoman," a Hanukkah medley. Snatches of Vivaldi returned to her. Bits of Corelli.

Glancing down, she was embarrassed to find seven dollars and change in her violin case. She had not exactly earned the money. Her first thought was that someone had felt sorry for her.

Thinking she would give the cash away, she looked for the guitarist near the bench, but he had disappeared. The morning crowds had thinned, and it was lunchtime now. By the station clock she saw that she'd been playing for two hours.

She took her cash out to the concourse and went to a doughnut shop to buy some water. She should have brought her own. She was against disposable bottles, but she was so thirsty she bought one anyway.

"Anything else?" the cashier asked.

Phoebe gazed at the racks of muffins, crullers, doughnuts, cronuts. "Just one of those."

"The glazed?"

"Yeah, that one," Phoebe said.

She had read that nutritionally, doughnuts had no redeeming value; that they were literally nothing, empty calories—but as sugar melted on her tongue, the pillowy doughnut filled her. She had eaten real food for so long, she had forgotten how good nothing tasted.

She began spending any money thrown her way on cheap treats in the station. A cookie or a cup of super sweet hot chocolate. She earned only a few dollars, enough for a cruller or a candy bar. Even so, she enjoyed spending the cash.

She was rusty. She almost returned a ten-dollar bill because she thought it was too much. She was ridiculously overpaid. That was why she began working through a Bach partita—so that she would be worth people's time and money. This is practice, she decided, even though she played in public. This is practice and this is practice. She rehearsed her Bach for hours and days until she got some of it back, the double stops and the cascading phrases. Then, right after a train announcement, she decided, now I am performing. She stepped into her music and her heart pounded. She felt a strange stage fright. No mistakes! This was her recital, although she told nobody.

She performed at least once each day. She would set up and practice, playing at half speed, rehearsing one passage at a time. In slow motion, she would play each phrase. Safe in all the noise, she did her work until she decided she was ready. Then she would take a breath and start. Sometimes two, sometimes three people gathered.

She tried the cream doughnuts, the jelly-filled, the chocolate sprinkles. She purchased orange soda. She went to the greasy pizza place and bought calzone. At home her mother said, "A healthy young woman can't live on almonds!"

Her father said, "I don't understand what you do all day."

"I'm thinking," Phoebe said.

They looked at her. "What are you thinking about?" her mother asked nervously.

"Right now?" Phoebe deflected the question. "I'm thinking about you."

They were touched, but they weren't satisfied. "We want you to be safe," her mother said.

"I want you to take public transportation," said Phoebe. "You don't need two cars." She showed her parents the bus schedule. From where they lived, her father could get to the office on two buses. Her mother could just take one bus if she walked 1.9 miles—and that would be exercise!

Of course, her parents didn't listen. They argued late at night instead. Dan was tired of Phoebe's dogmatism. Melanie thought Phoebe seemed more herself. "I think she's doing better!" Melanie insisted on this point, until Phoebe began cleaning out the closets. All through the weekend, Phoebe gathered piles of old coats, forgotten shoes, discolored T-shirts. She left most of the stuffed animals, but she stacked up games and puzzles to carry downstairs. "I'm not sure about this," Melanie began, and then she said, "No, not the solar system!"

"Thank you," Dan said. *"Yes,"* he cheered softly when a YMCA van pulled up to cart the pile away.

Two days later, Melanie returned home to find Phoebe sitting on the couch with a young man! A high school friend? A new acquaintance? Melanie did not recognize him, but he and Phoebe were talking eagerly. It took Melanie a moment to see that they were working through some papers on a clipboard. Phoebe had contacted this guy for a free estimate on solar panels.

"They'd barely cost you anything," she told her parents at dinner.

This time, Melanie was the good one, studying the paperwork. Dan was recalcitrant and wouldn't look, even after Phoebe took a magnet and posted the estimate on the refrigerator. Dan said solar was ridiculous because their roof had the wrong angles. Even so, he didn't throw the estimate away.

It's a process, Phoebe thought, as she took the rattling, swishing morning train. Little by little, she told herself, arriving at the station. She had her parents composting again, although Dan told her straight out: No new chickens.

Melanie thought that Phoebe's eyes shone brighter. Dan was afraid she had a manic look. Both her parents sensed a shift. They studied Phoebe's face, her battered shoes, her hands. Melanie glimpsed calluses, the old grooves on Phoebe's fingertips. "Are you playing again?" she asked, and she was sure of it when Phoebe didn't answer.

It couldn't last, this secret life, this music in plain sight. One morning she heard a man calling her name.

"Phoebe?" It was Uncle Steve standing in disbelief with his coffee and bagel. He worked in the city, and, inevitably, even in the crowds, he'd found her. "What are you doing here?"

What does it look like? Phoebe thought, but she said, "Just practicing."

That was the end. She knew Steve would tell immediately.

Even before she arrived home, her parents pounced. On the train, her phone lit up with questions. Where was she? Was she really busking in Penn Station? Was it true? Was it safe? Was she okay?

That night they sat her down and asked what was happening, and how long this had been going on. Their words were anxious, but their voices eager. Initiative! Hadn't Dan predicted that Phoebe would return to music? Hadn't Melanie said don't rush her? Well, that's what she'd been thinking, anyway. Drifting off to sleep, Phoebe heard rueful laughter, a wistful conspiracy to follow her.

For two days, she evaded them. She played near the escalators—ready to run. She tried a spot outside, but the humidity wasn't good for Jeanne's violin. Phoebe retreated to her usual place.

On the third day, while playing Bach, Phoebe saw two phones held high—her parents filming. They'd found her. Run her down at last! She bent into the music, but they saw everything, loose coins in her open case, a bag of—were they gummy worms? Turning away,

Phoebe missed her parents' wide eyes. *Really?* And she had them eating pumpkin seeds?

Phoebe played on, as far as memory would take her. To be honest, she had been better at fourteen. As a young child, she had been quicker, sweeter. Where she was patchy now, she had been sure and true. Her tone had been deeper, although she'd felt the music less.

Even so, she had Bach in her hands. Her parents heard that, despite the trains. Phoebe finished her partita with a flourish, and her father punched the air. Her parents whooped and clapped so that people turned around, even in their hurry.

"Stop. You guys!"

"What?" Melanie asked, all saintly, unconditional.

"Good job, sweetie," Dan said.

Phoebe just shook her head.

One more piece, Dan and Melanie pleaded, as she packed up the violin. Just one more. But it was time, past time to go home.

"Come on."

"Where to?" her father asked.

"Let's get lunch," Melanie suggested.

They were all set for a day out in the city, but Phoebe told them no. She had to pack, and figure out her housing, not to mention classes. "Winter break," she promised. She loved her parents, but she couldn't take care of them forever.

4

Ambrose

Lily wants to live in the old days. Her mom Debra says no you don't, because in the old days all you did was cook and sew and die in childbirth, but Lily still wishes she could travel back in time. Her older sister Sophie says stop you just hate school, and that is true. Lily hates sixth grade. However, Lily hates other things too, like parties and kissing games, and boys keeping score. Guess what? Sophie says. There were parties in the old days too.

Sophie is more pragmatic than Lily. Debra says so on the phone late at night. Lily is more anxious, Debra says. Then Lily thinks, Am I? She sits up in bed and strains to hear her mom's voice downstairs.

"Yeah," her mom says. "Yeah, I know. Well, she's upset."

She's wrong, though. Lily is not upset. She just wants to live in a castle, or a secret cottage in the woods. She is writing a novel about a girl named Ambrose who becomes a swan at night. The novel is in a journal her teacher gave her. It's a black-and-white composition book for her feelings, or whatever she wants to say.

East of the sun and west of the moon lived Princess Ambrose with her mother the Queen, her father the King, and her eleven sisters. She was a regular princess except for one thing. Every night at dusk she turned into a swan.

"How?" says Sophie, but Lily's teacher comments in green pen, *Lily, what a wonderful story! Tell me more about the swan.*

"Why is her name Ambrose?" Lily's dad Richard asks when she's at his house that weekend.

"It's short for Amber Rose," Lily explains.

He says, "Of course. Why didn't I think of that?"

Ambrose kept her wings under her bed and at night she slipped them over her shoulders to fly across the sky and gather tiny stars. She poured the stars into the drawer of her nightstand where they sparkled secretly. She loved to look at them but in the morning she must sit at her loom with her eleven sisters and weave nonstop. Her mother is always telling her, hurry up, work faster.

"Oh wonderful," Debra says. "Is that supposed to be me?"

What are the sisters weaving? Lily's teacher asks in green.

Lily doesn't answer questions. Home with her mom, she cuts pictures of flowers and swans and diamonds from magazines. First, she glues roses and sunflowers and red poppies to the cardboard cover of her composition book. Then she adds the diamonds. Finally, she pastes a swan with outstretched wings. The swan is much smaller than the roses and poppies, but that's just perspective. When Lily is done gluing her pictures, Debra says it's beautiful, but you need to protect the edges, so they drive to Michael's and buy Mod Podge to brush over the collage.

"Just keep it on the newspaper," Lily's mom tells her.

Lily shoots her mom a look because everyone remembers how Lily opened nail polish on the couch and splattered the cushions, but she has not ruined anything in years.

She is named after her Great-Grandma Lillian who made all her own clothes, including her coats. Not only that, but she upholstered her own furniture and sewed all the curtains for her house. And they were *lined*. Lillian went to the Lower East Side and bought Schumacher fabric covered with roses. Her house in Brooklyn was filled with roses on the curtains and the sofa. When she and Great-Grandpa Morris moved to Brookline, Lillian cut roses from her garden. The Brookline house was always blossoming. In the dining room, Lillian polished her silver until it gleamed. In the kitchen, she baked rugelach, Linzer tortes, and mandelbrot. For dinner parties she served her own napoleons, and then she was so exhausted she had to lie down. Lily imagines Lillian lying on a bed of roses.

At night when she is supposed to be doing her homework Lily lies on the couch and writes.

> *She loved to feel the wind in her feathers, but she was always looking for something where were the other swans?*

Her teacher comments, *I hope she finds them! (Watch out for run-on sentences.)*

In her cement and glass school, Lily opens her book, now covered with roses and red poppies.

> *All day long, Ambrose waited to change into a swan and fly again. After waiting for her eleven sisters to brush their teeth, she locked herself in the bathroom and fastened her wings.*

During lunch, Lily hides in her empty classroom and writes.

> *The reason she flew all night was to look for the other swan girls who she knew were in the sky if only she could find them. She flew and flew until finally she saw a large bird coming toward her.*

"Lily?" says Mrs. Berman. "What are you doing?"

"Working," Lily says.

"But at lunch, you need to be in the lunchroom, honey."

When she's supposed to be at Assembly, Lily sits in the hall and writes.

Ambrose flapped her wings and quickly met the other bird in midair. Are you a swan? she asked. No I am not said the other bird. Sorry about that I am a pelican but don't lose heart. Go! Fly to the . . .

"What's wrong?" Mrs. Berman almost trips over her. "Lily? Why are you sitting out here?"

"So I can concentrate," says Lily.

"I hear what you are saying," Mrs. Berman says. "It's hard to concentrate sometimes."

"Yes," says Lily.

"Come on into the auditorium."

"No thank you," says Lily.

"That wasn't a question," Mrs. Berman tells her.

"Just a second." Lily is trying to finish her sentence.

"I'll tell you what. Why don't you take your notebook with you?" says Mrs. Berman.

Then Lily scrambles to her feet, because that is also not a question.

"Thank you," Mrs. Berman says. "I want you to know we are all on the same side." But later that week, she calls a team meeting. The team is Mrs. Berman, and Dr. C. from the Learning Center, and Lily, and both of Lily's parents. She can't stop staring at her mom and dad sitting on the same side of the table.

First of all, Mrs. Berman explains, this meeting is about safety. It is about respecting Lily's needs and at the same time making sure everybody knows where she is. There might be a way for Lily to alert a teacher that she needs a break from an activity like lunch, and if there is staff available, she might be able to step outside for a few minutes and come back when she is ready.

Lily's parents are nodding while Lily wonders what second of all is going to be. There should be a second, but Mrs. Berman never gets to it. She just keeps talking. If you were an animal, Lily asks Mrs. Berman silently, what kind would you be?

Debra and Richard turn toward Mrs. Berman at the same time, but Richard starts drumming his fingers on the table and ruins the symmetry.

"Dad!" Lily whispers. "Stop that!" He looks confused, and she says, "Stop fidgeting."

In the car, on the way to ballet, Lily's mom says, "Were you even paying attention?"

"Yes." Lily pulls on her tights and leotard in the back seat because she had no time to change at school.

"What did Mrs. Berman say?"

"I can alert a teacher."

"Why?" asks Sophie from the front seat. "What did you do?"

"Nothing!" Lily is pinning her bun as fast as she can. Sophie is fine because Level Seven starts later, but Lily needs split-second timing.

As soon as her mom pulls up at the studio, Lily jumps out. Inside the studio building, she races up carpeted stairs with her dance bag and backpack. She can't be late. She's already been late twice, and her teacher Gwen says if you are late again you can't come in. But it's not Lily's fault she had to go to a team meeting.

In the waiting room she pulls off her boots and stuffs her feet into ballet slippers. Through the glass studio wall, she can see everybody standing at the barre. Softly, she opens the inner door.

"Lily!" Gwen snaps. "No. Just no."

Lily retreats and sinks into the waiting room couch. If she could have explained—but no excuses is her teacher's motto. Gwen's hair is short, and she has a short temper. She chops off everything, even her own name, which should be Guinevere.

If Lily were in Level Seven, she would be early. She would be changing with Sophie in the dressing room. Lily watches the girls of Level Seven walk like ducks in their pointe shoes to the big studio. As they pass through the waiting room, Lily tucks her legs under her, so she'll be inconspicuous—but Sophie's teacher sees her. Sophie's teacher Nastia owns the studio, and she sees everything, even a speck of lint, because she trained at the Vaganova Academy in St. Petersburg where you had to *work* even when you were tiny children. Nastia wears black tracksuits. Only black. Her voice is harsh, even as she says, "What's wrong, sweetie?"

"I was late," Lily confesses. For a second, she hopes Nastia will take her to class and tell Gwen to let her in—but no.

Nastia declares, "Late students waste *ev*erybody's time."

And so, Lily spends ninety minutes on the couch with two mothers sewing spangles onto tutus. One tutu is lilac and silver for the Lilac Fairy. The other is crimson and jet black for Don Q.

"This was Hannah's," the lilac mother says, "but I had to get it altered for Olivia."

"You can't win," says the crimson mother. "I had to get this altered and it's new."

"They keep growing," the lilac mother says as Chopin seeps from the big studio.

When Level Six is done, Maddy and Scarlett rush out to tell Lily they feel so bad and Gwen is so mean, but then they zip up their coats and run downstairs because their moms are waiting. All the girls run down, but Lily has to wait for Sophie's class to finish before her mom comes.

She pulls out her book and violet gel pen.

In the sky, Ambrose spent all her time gathering new diamond stars but while she did that she was looking for the other swans. If she could find them the spell would be broken and she could fly all day.

She is still writing when class is done, and she keeps writing in the car. At night she sits up writing because she cannot sleep.

The next day she writes in the lunchroom, but it's so loud, she takes refuge under a table.

Her classmate Rachel bends down to look at her. "Are you okay?"

"Oh my God, Lily's sitting on the floor," says a girl named Kaya who posts pictures of herself with boys.

"Honey, you can't sit under there," says Mrs. Berman. "Come on out now. Do you need a break?"

Lily takes a break in the nurse's office with its jars of cotton balls and Popsicle sticks. Her temperature is fine and so is her blood pressure. She tells the nurse she is not sick, and the nurse says, I know. We just check everybody. Then a seventh-grade boy comes in with a staple in his hand and it's almost an emergency. While the nurse is taking care of him, Lily grabs her bag and escapes to the girls' bathroom. She waits and waits for a stall. Once inside, she pulls off her clothes, wriggles into tights and leotard, and pulls her jeans and shirt on top. Camouflaged, she stands at the sink and pins up her hair as though she were the Lilac Fairy preparing for a ball. By the time she is done, she has missed social studies.

On the phone that night, Debra says, "But I do worry about her."

Why is her mom always talking about her? Lily slips out of bed and creeps to the stairs. Sitting on the landing high above the entrance hall, she sees Debra pacing below. "Mom?"

"Lily Anne Eisen!" Debra says, as though Lily is the one doing something wrong. "Get back in bed."

Phone in hand, Debra runs upstairs and tucks Lily in and tells her she loves her, and Dad loves her, and Sophie loves her.

"And Max," says Lily because she can't forget the dog.

"Right," says Debra. And they will always be a family and that will never change.

Once her mom is gone, Lily sits up in bed with her novel and her little clip-on booklight.

> *The spell originated from a witch who turned swans into girls. The witch sends girls down from the swan kingdom to live on earth.*
>
> *The witch wears black from head to toe and sees everything with X-ray eyes. She calls you sweetie but she is not.*

In the morning, Lily has trouble waking up. When she is supposed to be eating breakfast she says, "I'm sick. Can I stay home?"

Her mom says, "What are your symptoms?"

"I'm tired."

"Tired isn't a symptom," Sophie points out.

Lily says, "Yes, it is."

Since being tired is Lily's only symptom, Debra makes her go to school and then to tutoring with Megan and then to therapy with Danielle. By that time, Lily can barely keep her eyes open. She sits on a blue couch near a window with a large plant on the sill. The plant is a philodendron with drooping leaves.

Danielle says, How are you feeling, and Lily says sleepy. Danielle says, You look sleepy. Then she asks, How is the novel going? Lily says good. Danielle says okay!

There are board games in Danielle's office, but Lily would rather rest. She closes her eyes for a few minutes—actually, for half an hour.

"Lily?"

She opens her eyes.

Danielle says, "I hear you are having trouble sleeping at night."

Lily says, "I think that plant needs more sun."

Danielle says, "You're probably right."

"You could get a plant light."

"It's not really my plant," says Danielle. "It's a shared office. I'm only here Tuesdays and Thursdays."

Lily feels bad—not for Danielle, but for the philodendron who never asked to be here. "It's sad," she says.

Danielle looks at her encouragingly. Lily looks at the plant.

Unfortunately, the less Lily talks, the more everybody wants to know what she is thinking. On the weekend, her dad says, "How's Ambrose?" But she does not show her book to him—or anyone.

In bed at her dad's house, Lily writes Chapter Four, which is about how Ambrose runs into trouble. Her mischievous ninth sister Ruby steals her wings and it's a disaster because only Ambrose can fly. If anyone else tries, they will end up plummeting to their deaths. So now, Ambrose has to steal back her wings and save her littlest sister whose name is Pearl. Meanwhile, it looks like the witch is about to reappear.

"Hey, Lily." Her dad walks into her room without knocking. "It's almost midnight."

"You should be asleep," she tells him.

"You're funny." Richard sits on her bed.

"Dad," she says, "I'm trying to work."

"Maybe you should work during the daytime, kiddo."

She closes her book. "I don't have time."

"Really?"

"Dad, I'm busy every minute."

"You've been taking some expensive naps."

She looks at him puzzled. Then she understands, and she's a little scared. "How much does Danielle cost?"

"That's not important."

"But you said she's expensive."

He's getting irritated. "She's not expensive if you're awake."

"I don't have to go."

"You said you like Danielle."

"I do! But I don't want to spend all your money."

"I'm not talking about money." He shifts his weight on the bed.

"Then why did you say expensive naps?"

"Okay, that's not the point. That's not the message I want to convey."

"What do you want to convey?"

"Your mom and I—" he begins.

"Why do you always say your mom and I?" Lily asks, because who else would he be talking about? Some other person's mom?

"Listen to me. We're worried about you."

"What are you worried about?"

"School," he tells her. "Sleep. How you are feeling."

"Can I be homeschooled?"

"No!"

"Why not?"

"Who's going to homeschool you?"

"Mom?"

"Don't you think Mom does enough?"

"If we homeschool, she won't have to drive me anymore."

"No. The point is, you need to go to actual school and see people."

"But I don't like people."

"Lily." He looks like he might laugh, but he does not.

"What?"

"Nothing."

"I don't like school."

"Nobody likes sixth grade."

"Sophie did."

"This is not about Sophie."

Lily hugs her novel to her chest. "She's more pragmatic."

"Where do you come up with this stuff?" her dad says.

Then Lily feels guilty, because her mom came up with that and now it's plagiarism. "Forget I said it."

Her dad leans over and hugs her hard. "Just tell me what's on your mind."

She swallows. "Dad, I just don't like—"

"You don't like—?" He seems to dread her answer.

"This time period."

"What?"

"I mean, I don't want to die in childbirth, but."

"Lily, what are you talking about?"

Her voice is pleading. "I don't like this century."

Her dad shakes his head, bewildered. He adjusts his glasses. "Well, what century would you prefer?"

Then she's stuck because all the centuries were terrible for girls, just like her mother told her, and she knows that they were bad for Jews. As a Jewish girl she would probably be dead. "It's just so sad," she says.

"What's making you sad?" Richard asks. "Is it me?"

"No, not you," she reassures him.

"You know you can tell me anything," Richard says. "You know I'd do anything for you."

Then come back, she thinks. Live with us all the time. In the nights and in the mornings. But since she can't have that, she asks, "Could I just try learning at home?"

"You can't run away from school."

"I'll do better at home! I learn better one-on-one."

"Yeah, that's why you have Megan."

"I know but—"

"Are you learning better with her?" He's got her now, because she is still failing math, even though she works with Megan twice a week. "Prove it to me," Richard tells her. "Prove that you learn better one-on-one."

Lily sits with Megan, and they fill in the missing numbers in equations. There is something about if there's a ten it's easy and if there's a five you can pretend it's ten and divide everything in half.

"Don't let decimals scare you," Megan says. She has golden hair and sapphire eyes. She could be a princess if she wanted, and she loves math. Megan used to be a ski instructor, but then she broke up with her boyfriend. She drove all the way from Aspen Colorado to Cherry Hill New Jersey to be a teacher, except she makes more money tutoring. Now she has a new boyfriend, and they are getting married in June. Lily has seen pictures of Megan's dress which is strapless. Megan says, "Just multiply and then deal with the decimals at the end. Don't be intimidated."

"Okay," says Lily.

"Don't guess," says Megan. "Use the method. Are you with me?"

Lily is staring and staring at the numbers 6 x _ = 4.2. "Seven?" she says.

"Good," Megan says. "You know six times seven is forty-two. But what we have here is four point two. Where do you put the decimal point?"

"Is it point seven?" Lily asks.

"Exactly!" Megan says. "Ding ding ding!"

Megan was a cheerleader in high school. She is a little bit dramatic, but a good teacher nonetheless. Lily loves that word, nonetheless. When you are with Megan you feel like you know what you are doing. Nonetheless, you take the test alone.

All alone, Lily sits with her math test in Mrs. Berman's office. It's because she got a 12% the first time. She sits with her chin in her hand, and she has a method, and she's practiced, but there are a lot of problems. Fractions and ratios and cross-multiplication. There are also word problems which Lily was not expecting.

If one bag of sugar weighs 14.5 kg, how much would 6 bags weigh?

Isn't that a lot of sugar? Why would you need that much sugar for anything? Maybe if you were a bakery? Multiply, she thinks. Worry about the decimal later. But multiplying is tricky because you end up with more place values than you had before. She hears Megan's voice. Don't be intimidated! She hears her dad's voice. Prove it! But she isn't sure where to put the decimal point. She isn't sure she multiplied right either.

"How was the test?" her mom asks as soon as Lily gets into the car after school.

"I don't know." She regrets sitting in front where her mom can see her easily.

"Better than last time?"

"I'm not sure." Lily pins up her hair as they drive to the high school to pick up Sophie.

"Megan says you are doing great work," Debra says.

"But it's different when she's not there."

Lily's mom scans the building. "Where is your sister?"

Sophie is five minutes late. Then seven minutes late.

Lily's arms are tired as she pins and then unpins her hair to try again. "If I'm late, I can't go to class."

"Stop it."

Lily pulls out her book and rereads the ending of Chapter Four.

You are not going to get your chance, said the evil witch. I have scattered all the other swan girls and you will never find them. Yes I will said Ambrose, even if I have to travel to the ends of the earth. The pelican will help me I will find her on the mountain. Good luck said the evil witch you'll need it.

"Hi." The car door slams.

"Could you not slam the door?" Debra says as she starts driving.

"You're making me late!" Lily accuses her sister.

"No, I'm not."

"Yes, you are, obviously! If your class was first, you'd come out to the car on time."

"Oh my God stop," says Sophie.

Lily turns around to glare. "You only care about yourself and your friends."

"At least I have some."

"I'm going to pull over," Debra says.

"No!" Lily sobs, because she doesn't have time for that.

"What is your problem?" Sophie demands.

Lily is clutching her novel as tears pour down her face. "Please, Mom, keep driving."

"Apologize to your sister," Debra tells Sophie.

"Because she's crying?"

"Because you made her cry."

"She makes herself cry!"

"Now."

"I'm sorry!" Sophie says as they pull up at the studio. She snatches her bag and leaves, not quite slamming the door, but closing it hard.

Lily should follow, but she doesn't. "It's too late."

"No, it's not. You have two minutes," her mom says.

"I can't go in there looking like this." Lily's hair is half up, half down, her face is hot and red in the passenger-side mirror.

"Sweetie." Her mom hugs her as best she can over the gearbox and the emergency brake.

"I wish I was little again," sobs Lily.

"Me too," says her mom.

"You wish I were little, or you wish you were little?"

"I don't know. Both!" her mom says. "All of the above."

"Why are you crying?" Lily asks.

"Because you are."

They look at each other and Lily says, "I think I failed my test."

"It doesn't matter," Debra says.

"Yes, it does!"

"We'll figure it out."

"But how?"

"We'll talk to Megan," Debra says. "We'll talk to your teacher. We'll make a plan."

"It's too late."

"Go!" her mom says like the pelican. "You can do it. Run."

Go, Lily tells herself. Go, nonetheless. She plunges *Ambrose* into her dance bag, wipes her face with her jacket sleeve. Dashes up the stairs. She runs as fast as she can, but she doesn't make it.

She hears the music. Through the glass wall she sees everybody at the barre. She almost runs downstairs again—but then she realizes that it's not Gwen teaching class. They have a substitute! It's Cassandra who isn't strict at all.

Lily pins up her hair and takes a breath. She slips into the studio to stand between Maddy and Scarlett.

"You got lucky," Maddy whispers, because Cassandra doesn't mind whispering.

"I know!" Lily says.

"Stand tall," says Cassandra. "Shoulders down. Elbows up."

Lily stands tall; she points her toes as she extends her leg. Her arms are tired, and in the mirror her face is flushed, but she doesn't think anyone can tell that she was crying. By the time barre is done, her cheeks don't even look that red anymore.

Cassandra says, "Come out to center." The class stands spaced apart. "That's it," Cassandra says. "Lily, lift your head."

Through the glass wall of the studio, Lily glimpses Nastia, all in black. Nastia who sees everything—but she didn't catch Lily sneaking in.

Lily's classmates know that she was late, but they have already forgotten. That's how it is when you are dancing. You only think what you are doing now. You breathe. You bend and you come up again. You stand with your chest open and your shoulders back. Line up in threes to practice leaps. Wait in your corner and lift your wings to fly.

5

Kumquat

Helen was not bitter. She did not covet other people's grandchildren—nor did she indulge in wishful thinking about her childless daughters. She never asked herself, What if Pam had married? What if Wendy had found a man? No, Helen did not indulge in alternate history. When her book club read *The Plot Against America,* her comment had been, But Roosevelt *didn't* lose the election in 1940. She did not dwell in possibility.

Admittedly, she practiced self-defense, avoiding her Radcliffe classmates' notes in *Harvard Magazine,* and skipping over ads for family learning tours in Tuscany. She was a punctual and generous great-aunt, quick with a birthday card and check, but she tended to miss the recitals, championship games, and graduations of her sisters' grandchildren. (Jeanne had three and Sylvia had two—not that anyone was counting!)

Who said comparison is the thief of joy? Or was it only on a pillow? Helen did not keep score. She took a longer, sadder view. After all, Jeanne had not lived to enjoy her descendants. It seemed to

Helen that every gain was offset by some loss. She mentioned this in her Great Jewish Ideas class, and her rabbi suggested, "Or could it also be the other way around? *B'erev yalin bechi, v'leboker rina.* Weeping endures for a night—but joy comes in the morning."

Helen smiled. She liked Rabbi Lieber, but she thought, You'll learn. You're only forty.

Her own life was rich and orderly but full of troubles, the worst of these her husband's health, because Charles had Parkinson's. There was the question of the house, which he refused to sell, thus jeopardizing a place on the waiting list at Hebrew SeniorLife. And then, of course, their daughter Pam, who suffered from depression that only worsened with words of encouragement and advice. With her therapist as witness, Pam had declared, in no uncertain terms, that her mother's visits exacerbated her condition—and so Helen was forced to worry from a distance. All of this kept Helen up at night, even as she puzzled about renewing season tickets to the symphony. On dark winter days, she found this problem every bit as difficult as all the rest.

"It's a shame," said Charles.

Helen threw up her hands. "What can I do?"

"You know what you could do." His voice had an edge.

They had prime real estate, front row left mezzanine. Soloists seemed almost close enough to touch—but their seats abutted those belonging to Sylvia and her husband. A benefit for twenty years, proximity had become intolerable, because the sisters were not speaking. This was not a little tiff. It was not simply, as some liked to suggest, a misunderstanding. Sylvia had done something unconscionable. Because of this, Helen went only to performances of new music, which she knew Sylvia would skip, along with programs of Mahler, who gave Sylvia headaches, and Shostakovich, who made her anxious to the point that she once said, in her dramatic way, "I can't listen to this. I feel short of breath!"

Charles still spoke on occasion to Sylvia's husband, Lew, and Helen bore no grudge against Sylvia's son, Richard—but the rift remained. In this, as in many things, Helen suffered most. After all, Sylvia had two granddaughters to distract her. Helen had none.

Sometimes she thought she'd had it coming. She had been too proud, too pleased with her own life. Grimly, she remembered her superiority, dressing up her daughters, while Jeanne and Sylvia had sons. Helen looked at her framed pictures—dark-eyed Pam, and Wendy with her auburn curls. Now Pam lived alone, and Wendy had married a woman in a ceremony with much singing. Why? Wendy said that she had always loved women but had been closeted—a word Helen found strangely offensive. She had great closets. She'd organized them long before closet organizing became a sport and a profession. The thought of her own daughter closeted seemed an insult not only to Helen's intelligence, but to her housekeeping.

Of course, her feelings were immaterial. These were the facts: Her daughters were no longer lovely girls, but stolid women in their fifties. Pam had cut off all her hair, and Wendy's curls were gray. Pam had a dog and Wendy had Jill, who had sworn off babies. "I'm the oldest of seven, so no kids," Jill had declared, practically the first time she came to dinner.

"The technology is very good," said Charles, who was a retired physician. "You don't need to carry or even conceive your own child these days."

"Yeah, but I don't want to raise one," Jill explained.

Wendy added, "And we're just too old."

I am old, I am old, thought Helen, who had studied English literature sixty years before. Bits of poetry rattled inside her.

She kept busy, hosting her book group and serving on the board of the Brookline Public Library. She drove Charles to the doctor and his poker game. And in the end, she renewed her subscription to the BSO. She did this because she wanted to support the orchestra, and because she could always donate unused tickets for resale, and because Charles wanted to go. He could no longer play tennis or golf, and she would not deny him another pleasure. But mostly she renewed because it was not in her nature to give in. Sylvia would never cancel her subscription; she never gave up anything she liked—so why should Helen? She loved music just as much. Of course, Jeanne had enjoyed the symphony the most. She had been a violinist, after all. Helen renewed in memory of Jeanne, and because she saw Mahler on the schedule.

It was an icy December night, so they took a cab which rattled and squealed alarmingly. Looking out at freezing rain, Charles said, "I wonder who will come in this."

Helen said, "We will, apparently."

She imagined a small audience, but the portico was swarming with umbrellas. Inside, the house was nearly full, and Helen worried briefly that Sylvia would show up, even if Mahler made her ill. She loved anything popular. However, her seat was empty, as was Lew's.

The orchestra was tuning up when a rustling began far down the row of chairs. An usher's penlight, and Helen's heart jumped as someone said, "Excuse me. Sorry!" Not Sylvia, but a slender girl, followed by a tall ambling boy. "Hi, Aunt Helen," the girl whispered, and Helen recognized her great-niece, Phoebe, who was supposed to be away at college.

"Aren't you in school?" Helen asked, somewhat inarticulately.

"Winter break! Aunt Sylvia gave me tickets. This is Wyatt."

Wyatt waved from one seat over. "Hey."

Applause again as the conductor took the stage. Phoebe said, "We went to string camp together."

Charles half rose to shake Wyatt's hand. Missing his patients as he did, he loved any sort of company. "What do you play?"

Before Wyatt could answer, a strange melee began—not Mahler—but a pair of new pieces. The first involved orchestral wailing and a sobbing disco beat. The second sounded like a Bach cantata floating lonely in the wind after threshing by a tractor-mower.

"Well!" Charles said when the piece ended after a half-dozen false alarms.

Phoebe leaned back in her seat. "I just want them to play it all again."

Wyatt nodded. "Same."

"Really!" said Charles. "I want a drink." And he insisted on taking the kids down to the bar. Stubbornly, he refused the elevator, which worried Helen, who hovered, while Phoebe and Wyatt trailed behind, unaware of danger.

Wyatt was long-limbed and graceful, although his clothes were terrible. Phoebe, golden-haired and fair, pre-Raphaelite as her mother Melanie had once been.

"I play cello," Wyatt told Charles.

"Good for you." Charles had a glass of Scotch, ignoring Helen's disapproving look. But it wasn't just disapproval, it was love for him! Her husband, who insisted that alcohol didn't make his symptoms worse—although Helen saw it did. Her husband, who had been an athlete and a dancer, now sporting a moustache because it was difficult to shave with trembling hands.

Meanwhile, Phoebe and Wyatt looked shy when Charles asked them what they wanted and ordered Cokes like children.

Helen told Phoebe, "You should have mentioned you were coming. You could have stayed with us!"

Phoebe looked confused and then apologetic. "I didn't even think of that."

You told Sylvia, Helen thought. She gave you tickets! But you never thought of visiting me. Why? Was she so frightening? She was harsh, supposedly, although the opposite was true! Did she not bleed when family came to town without a word? Downcast, Helen sipped her cold white wine.

Some people found Helen overwhelming. She couldn't help it, but her simplest statements sounded like commands. "Time to go back," Helen announced as soon as the lights dimmed. Immediately, Phoebe and Wyatt set down their glasses.

"How is Jeanne's violin?" she asked Phoebe as they took their seats.

"It's good." Phoebe hesitated. "There was a little wobble on the fingerboard, but I think I've fixed it."

"A wobble! What do you mean fixed it?" Helen exclaimed as the conductor made his entrance for the Mahler. "You tried fixing it yourself?" The audience was applauding as she said, "You don't fool around with an instrument like that."

A trumpet, sad, sardonic, filled the hall. A wave of sound below. All hands on deck—every instrument, and harp, and whip, and glockenspiel. Phoebe leaned forward, visibly relieved that Helen could not continue scolding. Saved by Mahler's Fifth, she clasped Wyatt's hand.

Meanwhile, Helen fretted. Possibly Jeanne's violin was fine. She shouldn't have assumed the worst—but she had no time to mend the conversation, no chance to soften the impression she had made.

Helen had heard this music many times in Boston and at Tanglewood, where birds called out to Mahler's flutes—but tonight the drums and horns filled her with dread. There were moments of joy, triumphant brass, and woodwinds scurrying. There was one reprieve, an adagietto like a remembered afternoon, a clearing in the trees, where strings played alone and everybody else put down their weapons. Trumpets silent. Percussion mute. Briefly Charles drifted off, but even here, horns lurked in shadow, armed and dangerous. As the symphony built to its finale, Helen felt a grim foreboding about icy streets. Charles would slip and break his leg.

"Let's go now so I can find a cab," she told him during the ovation, but he yelled "Bravo!" ignoring the logistics. "*Charles.*" She took him by the arm.

Then Phoebe called out above the applause. "Wait, we can give you guys a ride. We have Uncle Lew's car."

Before Helen could speak, Charles said, "That would be swell."

Phoebe drove and Wyatt rode shotgun, while Helen and Charles sat in back. The kids sang snatches of the score. "The horns!" said Phoebe.

Wyatt said, "I know!"

Charles added, "And the strings were beautiful."

Wyatt said, *"Adagietto!"*

"Perfect," Charles agreed.

"You slept through it," Helen pointed out.

He shot her a look.

Phoebe turned onto Longwood Ave. "We played that part in camp."

"Yeah, that was the best," said Wyatt, "because Mr. Landau always cried."

Phoebe said, "I used to wonder if he was crying for the music, or because his career was conducting us."

What was that? Helen thought. What did you say? Surprise, confusion, and a flash of pleasure to hear Phoebe sound so knowing and so shrewd.

"Is this where you live?" said Phoebe.

"Yes." Helen peered into the dark.

"I can pull into the driveway." Phoebe eased the car in as close as she could.

"Bye, Aunt Helen," Phoebe said.

"Hold on," said Helen. "About your violin."

"It's okay."

"I'll send you the address of Jeanne's luthier in Brookline."

"I'm not sure I have time to drop it off," said Phoebe.

"How long is winter break?"

"Four weeks—but we're going to my parents'."

Helen dismissed this. "If we take it in now, he'll have time for the repairs."

"Well, I'd have to get an estimate," Phoebe said.

Helen leaned forward from the back seat. "I'll pay for it."

"Oh my gosh," Phoebe said. Oh my gosh thank you, she kept repeating as Helen and Charles got out.

"You overwhelmed her," Charles said, after the kids drove off.

"I didn't mean to."

"I know," Charles answered, as if to say, You have a gift.

Three days later, a jittery Phoebe rode with Helen to Brookline Village. She was holding Jeanne's violin case in her lap, as though she were about to be apprehended.

I'm not judging you, Helen told Phoebe silently, although she had many thoughts. Certainly, Phoebe's clothes were criminal. The girl wore a raggedy shirt over leggings and salt-stained boots. Her long blond tresses spilled over her open bomber jacket. Helen's instinct was to take her shopping—but she restrained herself. She parked near Brookline Strings and led the way as Phoebe followed with the violin.

The shop smelled of varnish and emery boards and rosin. Violins lay neckless, bridgeless, naked, stacked on shelves.

"Leonid, this is Jeanne's granddaughter," Helen said.

"Hi," Phoebe said.

"Good good. Open up." Safety glasses magnified Leonid's blue eyes. As soon as Phoebe unclipped and opened her violin case, he plucked out the injured instrument and lifted it to see the fingerboard. "You glued!" he announced, immediately.

"Um." Phoebe hedged but could not hide.

Leonid could see and feel everything. His nails were long, his fingertips stained yellow. "Never glue yourself. You see this?" He tapped Jeanne's violin. "Bridge. String. Sound post. Top. One piece goes and the others fall. Disaster! What do you use for practicing?"

"Just a . . . I've been borrowing."

Already he was distracted by something else. "On the back, what happened? You dropped it!"

"No!"

Leonid stared Phoebe down. "You took it in the cold."

"I tried to keep it warm."

He examined the violin's torso. "This is a crack. You see how this gets a little crack?"

Phoebe was blinking. No crying, thought Helen. It was bad enough to hear about the damage. Now the poor girl looked so sorry and so sad.

"Who fixed this?" Leonid demanded. "What happened after grandmother is gone?"

"That doesn't matter." Helen cut him off. "We're here for restoration."

"You will need complete repair and cleaning."

"Good," said Helen. She told Leonid to do everything, fingerboard, bridge, sound post, crack.

"This looks like I will take the instrument apart," Leonid said.

"Do it," Helen told him.

"I will give you quotes," said Leonid.

"Call me later." Helen didn't want Phoebe to hear what a complete overhaul would cost.

As Helen swept out of the shop, Phoebe kept murmuring, "I feel so bad."

"Yes, well," Helen told her on the sidewalk. "No point in that. I'm taking care of this."

"Thank you so so much."

Helen gazed across the street at Orinoco, which was a decent Venezuelan restaurant. "We'll get some lunch."

"I didn't know it would be so serious," Phoebe told Helen at the table.

Oh, sit up straight, thought Helen. Eat your veggie empanadas. What she said was, "It's about as serious as I expected."

Phoebe looked surprised, and then just a little bit amused. "You expected all of that?"

Helen caught it again, a glint of wit. "At least some of it."

The glint didn't last. "It's just so sad," Phoebe said. "Because it's like I was playing the instrument too much. I was feeling like I'd rediscovered performing. I was finally returning to my original dream—and that's how I broke the violin."

"Lesson learned," said Helen.

"I was playing Bach when it happened," Phoebe confessed. "It was like an omen."

Helen said, "By the way, your grandmother did not believe in omens."

"No?"

"No, not at all."

"It was just the timing. I was playing in my room, and I thought I'm going to take next year just to practice."

"A whole year!"

"I decided to play Bach, busking cross-country."

"Busking?"

"Like Matt Haimovitz when he traveled with the cello suites! I had this vision and just then—at that exact moment the fingerboard popped off—and I was so sad. I started wondering, What is Jeanne trying to tell me?"

"Don't do it," Helen answered immediately.

"That's how you interpret it?"

"Absolutely."

"So, *you* believe in omens."

"I believe in common sense. It's not safe busking!"

"Well, I'd be with Wyatt," said Phoebe.

Helen tried to parse this. "Don't you want to finish your degree? I thought you were studying arts administration."

Phoebe shifted her weight nervously. "But I only like art."

Well, that's unfortunate, Helen thought, but she said, "You could graduate first and then go and—"

"But I feel like I have to go now," Phoebe said.

Now? thought Helen. Halfway through the year? "You need to study."

“I need music,” Phoebe said. “I’ve lost so much time. I need to play. I mean, I’m a musician.”

“Your grandmother was a musician,” Helen said slowly. “But she taught lessons. And, of course, she married an attorney.”

Phoebe frowned.

Helen knew it was bad form to admit Jeanne’s husband had supported her—but facts were facts. “The point is, Jeanne never earned a living from her music.”

“But if it’s what you love,” said Phoebe. “If music is the one thing you want to do, then maybe you have no choice.”

“You’re choosing to live in a car?” asked Helen.

“We’d have a van,” said Phoebe, as though this explained everything.

“A van?” The question slipped out, along with Helen’s skepticism. Not just disapproval. Disbelief.

Phoebe’s body straightened. Her eyes were guarded now. Mechanically, she said thank you as Helen paid the bill.

Outside, Phoebe thanked Helen once again for lunch and for the ride. When Helen dropped her off in Allston, Phoebe zipped up her little jacket, took out her keys, and strode toward Wyatt’s apartment building. Suddenly she looked much more grown-up, as though she knew better now. She would no longer tell her dreams to hostile relatives.

And Helen watched her go and she thought, Why? Why do I have this effect on people?

“I’ve offended Phoebe,” she told Charles in the stillness of their lamplit living room.

He looked up from his crossword puzzle. “You offered her money?”

“No, I told the truth.”

“Even worse.”

"Very funny."

"Four-letter humanoid?"

"Yeti."

"That's good! Thank you."

"I just want to help. I don't want to drive her away."

"I know, dear, but you're bracing."

"Bracing!"

"You say what you think—and not everyone is used to that. It's an acquired taste—like kumquats, or Seville marmalade."

"Kumquats?" Helen protested. Bitter marmalade was one thing. Delicious. But kumquats? Was she so sour? Was her skin so thin? "*I* don't like kumquats."

"Well, there you go," said Charles. "I do."

He was gallant and at the same time making fun of her. That was the trouble with her husband. A kumquat was a terrible little fruit. If Charles liked them, she had never seen him eat one. If he'd ever tasted kumquat, it must have been in that orange pickle that came with Indian food. "So I should say nothing," Helen said.

"Probably," Charles answered.

He had maintained a light touch, but unfortunately, Helen had become more forthright with age. Somehow, she was fated to say what people needed—not what they wanted to hear.

She considered this in the car and at the hairdresser, and when she sat with Charles at the symphony. She thought about those sour orange kumquats in Great Jewish Ideas where her class learned Maimonides's Eight Degrees of Charity. The lowest level was to give when asked; the higher levels involved giving to others when they did not ask or even know their benefactor. "So, the less said the better," she murmured.

"Yes," Rabbi Lieber said. "Exactly."

Weeks later, in February, Helen got the call from Brookline Strings. "I have the instrument," said Leonid, like a kidnapper.

"Were you able to repair it?"

"Yes, yes! I will show you."

"It's not mine," she reminded him.

"Yes, tell granddaughter."

At that moment, Helen decided to pay over the phone. She would settle the bill and let Phoebe pick up the instrument alone when she returned to visit Wyatt. Helen would take herself out of the equation. Phoebe wouldn't even see her. "I'll pay now," she said.

"No credit card," Leonid told her. "Come in for pickup. Cash or check only."

This ruined everything. Helen felt demoted to Maimonides's lower levels. At the same time, secretly, irrationally, she was glad. Like a spurned lover, she wanted to see Phoebe again, although she knew nothing would come of it. She called Phoebe and left a message. Then she called again, and her great-niece said she could meet Helen anytime.

So, you did leave school, Helen thought, but didn't say it.

"I'm actually in Boston now," said Phoebe.

You're living with Wyatt, Helen thought. You went ahead and moved in! What are you thinking? Your poor parents. Poor Melanie and Dan. But she didn't say any of it. She was silent.

Why then was Phoebe so nervous when they met at the store? Had she heard Helen's disapproval even without words?

As soon as she entered the shop, Helen saw that Phoebe had brought Wyatt for protection. The two of them were talking to Leonid and when they saw her they startled like a pair of woodland creatures, drawing back unconsciously. They flee from me, thought Helen, but that was overstatement. Of course, they didn't flee. They chattered nervously about strings and fingerboards and snowstorms, as Leonid unwrapped Jeanne's violin, restored and gleaming.

"Oh wow," Phoebe said.

"Holy shit," said Wyatt. "Sorry!"

"Try," Leonid told Phoebe, and she began tuning, hesitantly. She seemed almost afraid to touch the instrument, and when a peg slipped, she looked up. "Tune, tune," Leonid ordered, impatiently. She finished and played a few notes, then a snatch of scratchy Bach. "Play!" Leonid encouraged her.

Phoebe started a fragment of something else. "No wait." She began the Bach again slowly, softly, readjusting. Helen could hear her dipping under the surface where the current of the music drew her. And now Phoebe seemed to find herself in a familiar place. Her tone deepened. Her bowing flowed. She closed her eyes, and a partita filled the cluttered shop. A glow, a warmth, a sense of order, as though the world were fair.

Oh, you are lovely, Helen thought. You really are sweet. You can do anything you want. You're right. Music is your life and that's enough. Go ahead. Be like the lilies of the field, as happy as you can stand to be. Shack up with your cellist. Drive west. What's a salary?

"Very nice. Very good," said Leonid, after the last note died away.

Wyatt lifted his hand for Phoebe to high-five, but Helen was still standing in a dream.

Fortunately, she recovered quickly. She unsnapped her purse and extracted her black pen to write a check. This was her contribution, large but unpoetic, as Phoebe stowed Jeanne's ivory-tipped bow and wrapped Jeanne's violin in velvet.

Phoebe set her instrument in its case like a newborn in a cradle, and Helen thought, Kid gloves for the next few days. Then you'll start playing on the street and in motels and truck stops, greasy spoons. And when will you get tired of it? When will you be sick of traveling?

Did Phoebe and Wyatt know what she was thinking? When Helen offered them a ride they said they were good, although it had started sleeting.

"Thank you thank you," Phoebe repeated on the street.

"That's enough of that," said Helen, because it was too much and wasn't what she wanted, anyway. She longed for music. To share in Phoebe's life—not from a distance, but close enough to touch. She wanted to impart her wisdom. Keep your job, and practice hard, and marry well. Helen yearned to say all this, but what she knew pushed everyone away.

Phoebe and Wyatt were waving goodbye, walking off together, and Helen sat alone in her big car, driving slowly alongside them.

The kids bent their heads into the wet wind, and it was absurd. They'd catch their deaths. She opened her passenger-side window and called, "Take this."

Alarmed, they watched a bayonet emerge, the tip of Charles's golf umbrella. "No, that's okay," Phoebe said. They only had to walk a little bit. They had their hoods.

"Take it anyway." Surely Helen had hit rock bottom, not just giving, but forcing aid on those in need. "Please," she said. "Do me a favor. Take this from me."

6

Wendybird

After the 2016 election, but before the demonstrations—Wendy knit her sister Pam a pussy hat. Everybody wanted one to protest the new president who had boasted about grabbing women by the pussy, and Wendy, who had skills, felt a responsibility to those, like Pam, who could not knit their own.

She finished the project on Saturday and mailed it priority, which meant it would arrive in Providence by Tuesday. Well wrapped in tissue paper, the hat was 100 percent organic wool and Wendy enclosed a card inscribed SISTERHOOD! But Tuesday came and Wednesday followed with no email or text, although the post office confirmed delivery. Had the package ended up with neighbors?

"Just call and ask," said Wendy's wife, Jill.

But Wendy could not bring herself to do it. She woke up in the night, instead. Possibly Pam thought the hat was dumb, or, more likely, she was bitter, because Wendy had worked so hard for Bernie Sanders, and Bernie was her first choice, even now—especially now. Hillary Clinton had never moved Wendy, but, obviously, Pam felt differently. Wendy's sister took after their mother, Helen. Stoic, solvent, and somewhat grim. At the best of times, she looked askance.

A week went by, and Wendy pictured her offering consumed by squirrels. Fragments of pink yarn would appear in birds' nests in the spring.

"Message her," Jill said, square-shouldered, forthright.

"*Now?* After all this time has passed?"

"That's your own fault. You *let* the time pass."

"What would I say?"

"Just WTF? I'll do it for you."

"No!"

"Then you'll never know what happened."

This was rational, but untrue. Wendy knew exactly what was going on. Pam was an attorney and pro bono tax advisor, turning the wheels of justice, righting, or at least recalibrating, wrongs. She had opened her mail and oh God, there was Wendy, all crafts and fiber, a fuzzy artist and song leader—nothing but lint. "I sent my message."

"So, you're suffering in silence when you could just say, You piss me off."

"My family . . ." Wendy began.

"Uh-huh." Jill knew all about Wendy's strange and estranged family—their unspoken expectations, silent feuds, exhausting birthdays. And yet Wendy was always rushing to their deathbeds and sending hats and letters, even cardigans.

In all her life, apart from sleepaway camp, Jill had sent one letter to her family. She had opened her heart, coming out at the end of college, and when her parents answered that no, they were not happy, no, in fact, they were not proud, Jill had done what any self-respecting person would. She had shut her heart again to carry elsewhere. For whatever reason, even at fifty-three, Wendy could not manage this. Family was her addiction. She could not stop loving them.

Wendy told Jill, "It's just when you make something with your hands."

"Wendy." Jill knelt in front of the couch. "You are an *amazing* knitter. You did that hat in like two hours."

"Two nights."

"Whatever." Jill fingered the fringe of Wendy's wool throw. "For you, a pussy hat is not a stretch."

"This is symbolic of my relationship with her."

"So, tell her it's over. Bingo."

Then Wendy laughed a little because Jill was so tough; she was a police officer—yet she threw in bingo, which changed the whole tone, somehow. She had a funny way with words.

Jill tried to cheer her up, but Wendy was sad about her sister—and sad that she was sad, because her own job required uplift—peace at the bare minimum. Saturday morning, Wendy tried to meditate on the subway with her guitar in her lap. As the train swayed and rocked, she imagined her soul shooting through the darkness into light.

When Wendy emerged, the city was gray with garbage cans strewn everywhere. Even so, she made her way to Sunrise Jewish Senior Living, scanned her ID card, greeted people in the multipurpose room—part social hall, part sanctuary—brushed back her long curly hair, and lifted her voice to sing, supporting Rabbi Hannah with *Modeh Ani* in the Debbie Friedman melody.

Modeh ani lefanecha, melekh chai v'kayam, shehechazarta bi nishmati . . . I give thanks to You, eternal and living King, for You have restored my soul . . .

Wendy looked out at her congregants. There was Mr. Batkin, snoring lightly in his wheelchair, and Mrs. Kantrowitz fast asleep with family visiting, her daughter whispering furiously. Why was she medicated *before* services? And Wendy thought, By definition, a gift requires nothing in return. *B'chemlah . . . b'chemlah . . . rabah emunatekha.* With mercy . . . with mercy . . . Your great faithfulness . . .

At this moment, tiny Mrs. Guttman decided she was done.

"Mrs. Guttman?" Rabbi Hannah called out above Wendy's guitar. "We're just getting started!" But Mrs. Guttman was one hundred and one. She gave the signal, and her aide wheeled her away.

Such was art and prayer and senior life. Wendy didn't take offense, and she wouldn't take offense at her own sister either. She would forget the whole thing. Soon!

Of course, there was another possibility. What if Pam's silence signaled something terrible? A diagnosis. A break-in—or breakdown!

"It's like your superpower," Jill said that night, as Wendy picked up the phone to call her mother. "Imagining disasters."

"I have other powers," Wendy protested, fishing a little.

"It's your Jewish superpower," said Jill, who identified as small *c* catholic.

"Shh. Hi, Mom? It's Wendy."

"Yes, I know," Helen said. "How are you?"

"Okay. How are you?"

"Concerned."

"About what?" Wendy asked—not really defensive, just a little bit on edge.

"Take your pick."

Wendy felt a rush of gratitude that her mother meant the new president, the country, the environment, the status of women, the entire world—not her. "Yeah, I know. I can hardly sleep at night."

Helen said, "Well, that doesn't do anybody any good."

"Is Pam okay?"

"No."

"No?" Wendy's eyes locked with Jill's, and for a weird moment she wasn't sure whether she felt fear or vindication.

"Shadow passed away."

The cat! Wendy mouthed to Jill.

"She had kidney disease," said Helen.

"Oh, I'm sorry!"

"The dog walks around the house looking for her." Pam's Irish setter had a name, Rosie, but Helen called her the dog, because she didn't like her.

"When did this happen?"

"A week ago, Wednesday."

"I wish I'd known!"

"Well," said Helen, dry as toast.

"You were right. It wasn't me," Wendy told Jill after she put down the phone.

"But you were right too; something happened." Jill gave Wendy her due.

"I'll call her," Wendy decided, but when she did, all she got was her sister's voicemail. "I think Pam's avoiding me," Wendy said.

"Her loss!" Jill said.

In the morning, Wendy went to her Sunday gig, teaching nine middle schoolers to sing *"U'macha"* in something like harmony. *U'macha Hashem dima me'al kol panim.* And God will wipe the tears from all faces . . . and the whole time, she thought about her sister.

As soon as she got home, she took her deckle-edged blank cards and India ink pen and drew Shadow curled up in a basket. Then she wrote in beautiful block print.

Dear Pam,

I am so sorry for your loss. It is hard to lose the ones we love, but please know you are not alone! You have my whole heart.

Love,

Wendybird

P.S. Did you get the hat I sent you?

Jill photographed the picture, because Wendy didn't even keep a record when she gave away her art.

"Do you think it's good?" Wendy asked.

"The picture? It's amazing."

"I meant the note," Wendy said.

"It's what you feel, right?"

"Right!"

The second she mailed her condolence card, Wendy felt lighter, happier. How had she forgotten? It was so much better to do, to make, to give, than to sit in silence. Simmering resentment—that wasn't Wendy. That was her mother. Helen had a gift for grudges. Wendy's whole family did, but she would not live like that, even if Pam shunned her.

Three days after she decided this, she heard back from her sister.

> Wendy! Sorry I've been out of touch—it's been insane. Thank you for the beautiful card and hat. You are so thoughtful I really appreciate it.
>
> Sent from my iPhone

"What do you think?" Wendy said.

"I think it's . . ." Jill was about to say pretty cold but stopped herself. "She seems rushed."

"She seems overwhelmed. Maybe I should go up and see her."

"Sweetie, no," said Jill, because this would not end well—Wendy's warmth and love versus Pam's dark places.

But Wendy was feeling guilty in her good fortune. There she sat with Jill in their apartment with hooked rugs and crocheted pillows, a gallery of instruments hanging on the walls. Guitar, lute, melon-backed mandolin. "Pammy's all alone."

Jill said, "There's Rosie."

"Yes, but a dog can't really understand how bad it is right now."

"Dogs know a lot."

"I mean politically."

Jill sat back on the couch. How could she put this? Wendy's sister was a black hole at the best of times. "I don't think you should go up there right this second."

"Why not?"

"She just said that quote it's been insane. And you're gonna see her in January—unless you decide to skip it." Every year, Wendy took the train to Boston for her mom's birthday. Everybody went, except for Jill and people disinvited like Sylvia, Helen's only remaining sister, who had done something unforgivable, involving a cake. Of course, Helen was crazy. That went without saying.

"I can't skip," Wendy said.

"Okay, then I'll go with you," said Jill.

"Really? You hate visiting them." Jill had not come up to Boston in years.

"Yeah, but I'll go anyway." Jill had one thought only—to protect her wife.

For this purpose, Jill spent a week in Helen's overdecorated Tudor and slept in Wendy's childhood room with its ivy-patterned wallpaper, stuffed rabbit, and limp teddy bear. Wendy had the bed, and Jill the trundle, like a child sleeping over.

For Wendy's sake, Jill ate breakfast with Helen, while Wendy's tall, slightly stooped dad, Charles, watched the Inauguration in his paneled den. *America will start winning again,* the new president said. *Winning like never before.*

All week, Wendy's parents speculated about Pam's arrival, postponed to Sunday morning because of dog sitters and filing deadlines. Pam worked Very Hard. Helen said this in grim tones, as though no one else held down a job.

Jill had to get out. She had to escape. She wanted to go running, and at the same time, she couldn't leave Wendy to her mother. Fierce and watchful, Jill stayed close in that close house, but by Saturday afternoon, she was desperate for air.

"Go," said Wendy.

"Go like go? Or go like I'll just sit here in the dark?"

"Nobody's sitting in the dark."

"Okay." Jill changed into long shorts and a hoodie. She sat on the kitchen window seat and laced up her shoes, but she kept glancing at Wendy, who had settled next to her mother at the table.

"Steve and Andrea are coming tomorrow," Helen said, totting up the cousins at dinner. "And they're bringing Nate."

"They're driving all that way?" said Wendy.

"Don't worry. They're not driving just for us. They're on a college tour," Charles said.

Wendy ventured, "What about Aunt Sylvia? She lives right here."

Silence. Shadow. Winter in the kitchen.

Uh-oh, thought Jill, with her hand on the doorknob, but the next moment, Helen spoke mildly. "Could you get me more coffee, dear?"

Wendy poured another cup and Helen said thank you.

"Go ahead," Wendy encouraged Jill.

"I'll be right back," Jill promised as she headed out.

Only when she was gone did Wendy follow up, earnest and a tiny bit rebellious. "I wish Sylvia could come."

"Don't provoke your mother," Charles warned, because he was a pragmatist, but Wendy was a peacemaker.

"I miss Aunt Sylvia," she said.

Helen didn't answer.

"It's just so sad," said Wendy. "She's your only sister, and she lives thirty minutes away!"

"I had two sisters," Helen said.

"And what if you lose Sylvia too, and you never have a chance to forgive her?"

Iron-gray, Helen answered, "I don't tell you how to live your life."

When Jill returned, she found Wendy in the bedroom, sitting atop her little white child's desk with her feet on her little white chair. She was playing "Here Comes the Sun."

"What happened?" Jill asked.

Wendy shook her head and bent over her guitar, because how could she explain what she felt about her mother?

And Jill stood there flushed and healthy from her run, and she saw that the longer they stayed, the smaller Wendy became. She never laughed in her parents' house. She never felt like going anywhere. Jill said, "Let's just leave. Seriously. Pam had the right idea to stay home."

Wendy looked alarmed. "You don't think she's coming?"

"I mean, who knows?"

"I'm worried about her," Wendy said. "I think that cat broke her heart."

Jill swiped the stuffed rabbit from the dresser and started tossing it from hand to hand.

"You know she suffers from depression," Wendy said.

"Uh-huh."

"She tried to kill herself in college."

"Really?" Jill palmed the rabbit. "How?"

"Jill!"

"Sorry!" Jill was sheepish, because okay, yes, how was maybe not the first thing you should ask.

"She swallowed a whole bottle of muscle relaxant," Wendy said.

"Hmm."

"They had to pump her stomach. It was bad!"

"Okay."

Wendy shot Jill a look. "Don't be like that."

"Like what?"

"Like it was just a call for help."

"I would never say that!"

"You would think it."

"I think a lot of things."

"I'm just saying, Pam is going through something."

"Yeah, definitely—but you know what? If you're going through something, you probably don't go to Helen."

The next morning, Helen's guests began to gather, but Pam did not arrive. All was ready. The buffet was set, and still Pam didn't come.

Of course, Helen did not call to find out what was going on. She did not ask questions. She endured, serving fruit salad, bagels, lox, white fish, dry mandelbrot, heavy apple cake.

There were a dozen friends to feed, along with the New Jersey cousins. Steve and Andrea talked about their visits to BU, Tufts, Northeastern, and Brown, while their kid, Nate, said nothing. Wendy's cousin Dan and his wife Melanie arrived. They held up Dan's phone to show a video of their daughter, Phoebe, playing her violin in a subway station. Long gold hair and blue-gray eyes. Gorgeous strands of sound, until the train came roaring like a monster. Phoebe reminded Jill of Wendy, making music despite everything.

In the kitchen, Wendy was arranging miniature Danish on a tray. "How's that?" she asked her mother.

Helen frowned and said, "It's fine."

Then Jill watched Wendy hide her disappointment, because fine meant terrible. Opening her presents, Helen examined the handknit cowl Wendy gave her, studying each row for flaws. Suck it, Jill thought. You won't find anything.

Meanwhile, Wendy kept hoping for the best and, what do you know? Long after Helen had given up on Pam, Wendy saw her sister's car through the kitchen window.

"She's here!" Wendy called out, breathless.

Pam came the back way through the garden and screened porch. Everything about her was tiny, her thin little arms, her pixie cut, and she was loaded down with bags and leash and Rosie barking everywhere. "My backup sitter fell through," Pam apologized, and Helen actually said it didn't matter, and kissed her briskly on the cheek. The dog would sleep in her crate on the porch—that went without saying—but catastrophe had been averted. Helen would not disown her. No, on the contrary, joy suffused Helen's face, softening her disapproving lines. Amazing, thought Jill. Even with the late arrival, even with her hyper and unwelcome dog, Pam remained the favorite.

Wendy took Pam's coat. She cut her a slice of cake, but Pam turned to everybody else—Cousin Steve and Andrea and even Nate, who favored her with his deep, rumbling, almost inaudible replies. Good. I don't know. I'm not sure.

Whenever Wendy tried to talk to her sister, Pam looked away, distracted. She had to eat. She had to speak to someone else. In the real world, Wendy was next-level. Renaissance! She could rewire a lamp, explain Judaism, bake a three-tier wedding cake. Here in her mom's house, she was extraneous.

Jill stalked out to the porch where Rosie paced, worrying a tennis ball. Instantly, Rosie was up in her face.

"Down. Down! Wow, you are so lonely." Jill tried to pry the ball from Rosie's mouth. "I can't throw the ball if you don't let go." She opened the porch door. "Okay, girl. Get it!"

Rosie sprinted through Helen's muddy flower beds. Every time, she brought the ball back, slobbering, and every time, Jill had to talk her into giving the thing up. Sweet dog, but not super bright.

They stayed in the backyard until people began leaving, some waving to Jill through Helen's kitchen windows. "Take care," Jill called back, waving. "Talk soon!"

She entertained the dog until the cold pinched her toes, and her nose started running, and the last guests were gone. Then she called Rosie and tossed the ball into the crate.

A flash of pink.

"Whoa." Jill reached in. "What do you have here?" An old blanket, some rubber toy, and in the back, the shredded remnants of a pink yarn hat. "Where did you get this?" Jill asked Rosie. Then she said, "Don't answer that." The hat was all clawed up and ruined, as if Rosie had been teething on it. "Pam gave this to you!"

Rosie was jumpy, eager to run out again. She had more energy than one little screened-in porch or yard could hold. She kept nudging, pleading, but Jill ignored her. She balled up the rat's nest that had been Wendy's gift and hid it in her sweatshirt pocket.

In the living room, Charles was stacking wood in his deliberate way, tending the fireplace. Helen sat on the couch with Pam on one side and Wendy on the other. There was room for Jill, but she said, "That's okay."

"Thanks for playing with Rosie," Pam told Jill. "She was cooped up in the car so long."

Jill said, "Sure." You're welcome, bitch, she added silently.

Maybe Rosie had snatched the hat and slobbered on it and Pam just gave it to her. Maybe Rosie had chewed the padded envelope itself. She'd got into the mail and destroyed it. The dog was so bored. She needed to be out hunting, not cooped up in Pam's car or townhouse. Probably the mailman was the only living soul she saw all day. Pam didn't deserve a dog. Or a sister. When Jill went upstairs to change, she shoved her sweatshirt with the ruined hat into her open duffle bag.

At dinner Pam talked about her work, and Charles mentioned installing a new fence. Wendy ventured something about the kids she taught at After School, and how some of them were discovering they could sing. She believed, in her pure way, that anyone could learn.

Her mother countered, "I'm not so sure."

"With the right teacher, they can," Jill interjected, startling everyone. She spent the rest of the dinner mulling the things nobody mentioned—starting with Pam's cat.

After dinner, she and Wendy retreated upstairs. Wendy brushed her teeth and put on her nightgown and dove into bed, while Jill rummaged through the white bookcase full of children's books. *What the Moon Brought. All-of-a-Kind Family. All-of-a-Kind Family Uptown. Hurry Henrietta: A Biography of Henrietta Szold.*

"Who was . . . ?" Jill said and broke off when she saw that Wendy was asleep. Poor thing. She was tired out. Jill, on the other hand, was full of energy. She skimmed *The Man Who Loved Laughter,* a biography of Sholom Aleichem. Kneeling, she started reading *The Adventures of K'tonton: A Little Jewish Tom Thumb.* The kid was just a few inches tall, but nobody ignored him.

Footsteps. Someone on the stairs. Jill stole out to the landing, listened for a second, and then ducked back into Wendy's room to grab her sweatshirt.

The house was dark, but she heard a prowler in the kitchen. No, the den. Softly, trained in surveillance, Jill glided down the stairs and found Pam in front of Charles's liquor cabinet.

Jill came up right behind her. "Boo."

"Oh God," Pam gasped. "You scared me."

"Too bad," said Jill.

"What's that supposed to mean?" Pam asked shakily.

"Let me," Jill said more kindly, as she poured two shots of Scotch. "Sit."

Pam sank into her dad's big leather chair, and Jill handed her a drink.

"Cheers." Jill perched on the chair's matching ottoman. "Wow." This Scotch went down like liquid gold. Charles didn't fool around. Pam didn't either. She chugged her drink immediately.

Look at you, Jill thought, as she refilled Pam's glass.

"I can't sleep here. My bed is terrible," Pam said.

Jill made common cause. "I'm in a trundle."

"Wendy's little trundle?"

"Yup."

"That's ridiculous."

"In Wendy's shrine with the stuffed animals."

"Parsley, the rabbit."

"Parsley?" Jill was impressed and also annoyed by Pam's name-dropping. Parsley the rabbit. No one had told her that.

Know-it-all Pam said, "You can see the stitches where his ears ripped. Wendy sewed them on when she was five."

"She could sew at five?"

Pam leaned back in her father's chair like a specialist in Wendyana. "Absolutely. That was her thing."

"What else was?" Jill filled Pam's glass again.

Pam thought for a moment. "She built these little dollhouses from cardboard. She would sew blankets, and then she'd tuck her dolls in and sing to them."

"Aw. What else?"

Blankly, Pam looked at Jill.

"Tell me everything."

When Jill poured a new shot, Pam drank it like medicine, even as her words slowed down. "I remember when I was ten. She must have been seven. We were out in the yard, and she found a bird. He was alive but couldn't fly. I said, Don't touch that! Everybody told her don't touch it, but she got a shoebox and lined it with cotton to make a bed, so she could take the bird inside. Mom said, You can't touch that bird. They have parasites; they're filthy, but Wendy picked him up anyway. As soon as she had him in her hands, he opened his wings. I think he had flown into a window and was stunned. The second Wendy picked him up, he woke from his trance and flew away. She cried and cried."

"Why? Wasn't she glad?"

"No, she wanted to nurse that bird back to health! She always wanted something to take care of. She was very sweet," Pam added dreamily.

"Mmm," said Jill, allowing Pam her moment. Then time was up. "Can I ask you something?"

"What?"

"Why do you treat her like shit?"

Pam started, flushed and disbelieving. "I don't!"

"Your sister calls, and you don't answer. She sends you presents, and you don't acknowledge them."

"That's not true!"

"You're gonna sit there and deny it?" Jill leaned in close and threatening. "You and your parents. The three of you think Wendy is like Santa's little helper. She's not even human to you. She's some kind of elf."

Pam protested, "I don't think Wendy is an elf."

"Telling me she's sweet. What the hell is that? Sweet? You mean *less*—because she knits!"

"I don't think of her as less."

"You don't think of her at all, and when you see her, which is hardly ever, you look down on her."

"I do not."

"So tell me. What is she to you? The entertainment? The warm-up act before you walk in with your dumbass dog?"

"You don't know what she is to me."

"Oh really?" Jill threw the sodden hat into Pam's lap. "You took Wendy's work and used it for a rag."

"What is that?"

"The hat. Remember the hat?"

Gingerly, Pam lifted the wet yarn. Jill saw confusion in her face and finally recognition and defensiveness and shame. "Rosie got it!"

"Yeah, right. The dog ate it. And why was that? Because you let her!"

Pam shrank back, but Jill leaned over her, hand on the chair, her face in Pam's face. "Get away from me," Pam gasped.

"Listen up," Jill whispered in her ear. "If you ever *evèr* disrespect my wife again, you lose the dog. Wherever Shadow went, that's where Rosie's going too. If you in any way ignore, discard, or deface Wendy's work, the dog is gone. You understand?" Jill didn't wait for an answer. "This shit stops now. You get your high-functioning ass in gear and answer your phone when Wendy calls. And if a present comes, you send a fucking thank-you note. Within twenty-four hours. And a photo. With the gift fully visible."

Jill stood and left Pam sitting in the dark.

———

Of course, Wendy would have been horrified. Jill was horrified herself, by morning. Truthfully, she had no plan to murder Rosie. She would never hurt a dog. Wendy's sister was another story.

Jill scanned the living room as Wendy said her goodbyes. Maybe Pam had thrown the ruined hat in the garbage. Maybe she'd returned it to Rosie. It was nowhere to be seen. Pam stood meekly with Charles as Wendy said, "Goodbye, Daddy."

Meanwhile, Jill stared at Pam. Her eyes burned through Wendy's sister.

It was good to be home. Jill ran out for milk, and the next day she and Wendy returned to work, keeping the peace and bringing joy in their respective jobs. Weeks passed, and Jill never mentioned confronting Pam. She did not say a word about the Scotch, the ruined hat, the late-night conversation. Because of this, Wendy was startled to receive a thank-you text the very day of Pam's March birthday.

"Look at this," she told Jill.

"What is it?"

"A thank-you for the present I sent."

"Let me see that." Jill picked up Wendy's phone.

Dear Wendybird, the message began. *Thank you so much for your beautiful and thoughtful donation in my honor . . .*

"Uh-huh, uh-huh," Jill said, skimming.

"And look at the photo."

Jill studied the picture. Like a suspect in a lineup, Pam clutched a certificate of appreciation from Arts for Incarcerated Youth. "Okay," Jill said. "That's what I'm talking about."

7

Redemption Song

In every generation, you should feel as though you personally left Egypt.

—Haggadah

On Passover, Dan and Melanie hosted the first night, Dan's brother Steve and his wife Andrea the second. Divide and conquer, Dan said. You don't have to be so grim, Melanie told him. I'm not grim at all, he said. I just want to get it over with.

Passover was weighty for Dan, and for his brother too. It had been terrible for them, growing up. Their father, Irving, had been a survivor, and he'd ruined the holiday for everyone because it meant so much to him.

Irving had always been difficult, but on Pesach he spread misery, accusing Dan and Steve of misbehavior, fighting with their mother, finding fault with everything. More than once, Irving had left the table with a migraine—hinting darkly that they, the children, were the cause. Steve, the firstborn, had pushed back hardest, demanding, What did we do? Wide-eyed, Dan had watched. Of course, as adults, the brothers knew they had not been the cause of anything. Their dad was long gone, and they had long forgiven him, but they had a hard time celebrating. With seders looming, Dan became punctilious; Steve grew anxious and called often.

"Just double-checking," Steve said. "We're bringing salad?"

"Right," said Dan.

"And sponge cake?"

"No, unfortunately. No can do."

"They're vegan again?" Steve was talking about Dan's daughter, Phoebe, and her boyfriend, Wyatt.

"Yup."

"Shit. What will you feed them?"

"No idea."

"You can't use tofu. Or seitan. No tempeh!"

"I am aware of that." Dan didn't need his brother to spell it out—or rub it in. Dan and Melanie talked of nothing else. Soy, corn, wheat, rice, peanuts, legumes, were all prohibited on Pesach. What did that leave vegans? As for the seder plate—this holiday was not plant-based. What would they use for the roasted egg? A baked potato? And what about the shank bone? Some kind of radish?

"Please, please don't be so negative," Melanie told Dan as they took stock at the kitchen table.

"We have five days to get ready."

"So, we'll make it work! Nobody has allergies. Nobody's sick. Nobody's in pain." Melanie didn't say, Remember how fortunate we are, but Dan could hear it. He had grown up hectored about poor children starving, and now he was married to a gastroenterologist. "We'll figure it out!" Melanie said. "There are lots of vegan seders. Some people use sunflower seeds."

"For what?"

"I don't know. I think they . . ."

"Sprinkle them over the tablecloth?"

"Dan."

"And what about this mess?" Dan gestured at the bags of groceries covering the kitchen counters, the clock radio and toaster oven, the standing mixer no one used. Stacks of bills and tax forms swamped the kitchen island; the recycling bin was overflowing. Meanwhile, a newly purchased case of matzo sat on the floor.

"It's a process. It's going to happen. It is all going to happen," Melanie intoned.

Dan stood on a footstool to pull down the shoebox where he kept his Icelandic chocolate.

"I'm going to make moussaka," Melanie said.

"You think you can cook in here?" Dan demanded as he nibbled a grainy chocolate bar.

"I cook here all the time."

"We'd better clear the decks."

"Don't worry," Melanie assured him. "I'm on call tomorrow but we can start this weekend."

Something in her tone just maddened Dan, because every day she said, We'll start this weekend—and this weekend the kids would be here! Why couldn't she see? The house was sinking. They were going under, drowning in groceries and paperwork. "Not this weekend. *Now*." Dan jumped off his stool, threw down his chocolate, and started unplugging small appliances. He swept up bills and heaped them on the kitchen table.

"I had those in separate piles for a reason," Melanie said.

"Pile them elsewhere." Dan shook out a black garbage bag and started tossing cottage cheese, yogurts, hummus.

"Wait!"

"Yeah, we're done waiting. Waiting is the problem." Opening the produce drawers, he deep-sixed dimpled grapefruits and bendy celery and perfectly good potatoes along with sprouting onions.

"Stop!" Melanie had seen Dan manic about Pesach, but this was the worst he'd ever been. "Don't throw away good food."

Dan shouldered a load and hauled it outside to the trash. Then he heated a kettle of water and pulled out the grotty refrigerator shelves. He tilted each into the sink for cleansing with boiling water. "Dry these," he ordered. "Please."

Melanie began drying the glass shelves with paper towel so that they were not only clean but sparkling—but, as soon as she turned her back, Dan opened the lower cabinets. Pans clattered. Lids crashed.

Melanie spun around. "What are you doing?"

"Purging." Dan opened a new trash bag and tossed all of Melanie's empty cottage cheese containers.

"Dan, I need those!"

"Nope. No, you don't."

Melanie knew Pesach was hard for him. She had grown up in LA, with Hebrew School and Camp Ramah—singing Debbie Friedman in a circle. Dan was from Boston where everything was small and cold. Where, at their father's insistence, Dan and his brother had attended an Orthodox day school called Maimonides. At this school, which he described as excellent but dreary, Dan had studied Talmud every day, so when it came to food and Shabbat and holidays, he knew all the things you could do wrong. It wasn't his fault that his religion was all rules. But where did it say you couldn't keep your cottage cheese containers?

Melanie tried an I statement, as she had learned in counseling. "I feel threatened when you throw away my stuff."

"I feel great," said Dan.

By morning, the counters were bare. Dan had left Melanie the coffee maker. That was all. The fridge was antiseptic with nothing in it. Not even a carrot.

The freezer was empty. No frozen waffles, no frosty bags of bagels. No chicken pieces, pizza, or ice cream. Nothing. Melanie checked the cabinets. All crackers, cereal, and baking supplies were gone. Even the salt and the vanilla. Dan had purged everything, not just perishables. They had no pasta now or peanut butter or canned soup.

Oh, but I bet he kept one thing, she thought. She stood on the stool to open the cabinet above the fridge—but Dan's chocolate was nowhere to be found.

It was as if they had died and stagers had arrived to prep the house for sale. The sink was sparkling. The kitchen was as clean and beautiful as a 1970s kitchen in a 1920s Tudor 3 BR 2½ Bath could be.

Melanie felt erased. She donned her white coat embroidered **Melanie Rubinstein M.D.** and wondered, Who is she?

She carried her travel mug of coffee to the driveway and saw stacks and stacks of trash bags—but what was that? Visitors had come in the night to claw open plastic and feast on chicken nuggets. Frozen waffles and smashed yogurt containers littered the front yard.

Melanie ran through the minefield of debris, jumped into her Subaru, and slammed the door. What was wrong with Dan? It wasn't like he kept kosher the rest of the year. He was dormant and then, suddenly, Krakatoa! She wanted to scream. Yes, you had a difficult childhood, but do you have to traumatize everybody else too? Haven't you heard of food banks? Instead, she texted *Racoons. fix it.*

He apologized. That night when Melanie returned, the debris was gone, and two shiny metal garbage cans stood in front of the garage. Even as she stepped from the car, Dan opened the front door. "I'm sorry I went postal. I'm not trying to threaten you. I'm just doing what has to be done."

"But that's just it. You don't have to do any of this."

"You want to bury yourself in frozen food?"

She sighed and walked past him to the kitchen. Then she said, "I'm nervous too."

The truth was, they dreaded Phoebe's arrival. Their daughter, once so directed, then so fragile, was now busking full-time with her boyfriend. Once they had worried Phoebe had given up on music, never to play her violin again. Now music was all she did. Melanie and Dan had been proactive. They had been supportive. They had spoken gently and harshly to their daughter. We want you to be happy, Melanie said. We've already paid your tuition, Dan put in. Then Melanie made him stop. I'm gonna kill him, Dan said of Phoebe's boyfriend, and Melanie said, It's not just him. It's her.

"I have nothing against Wyatt," Dan said now.

"I know," said Melanie.

"I'd just like to understand what he is thinking."

"But remember," Melanie warned.

They had made a pact. There would be no confrontations. No recriminations. No harping on what they had told Phoebe already. As for Wyatt—Dan would not attack.

No, he was not even thinking of murdering the kid. He continued his great purge instead, emptying dresser drawers and storage bins, filling bags for Big Brother Big Sister.

Melanie sat downstairs and meditated. She popped in her earbuds to lose herself in surf and breaking waves. Then she gave up and listened to Dan stomping through the bedrooms.

She found him in Phoebe's room, bagging stuffed animals. Melanie said, "Those aren't even yours."

"She's fine with it." Dan flashed his phone.

Declutteringnow he had texted Phoebe.

Go dad! she'd texted back.

"Does she know you're taking *all* her animals?" Melanie whipped out her own phone and called her daughter. "Phoebe, he's bagging every single one."

"So now other kids can play with them," Phoebe said, amused.

"He's got Lyle, Lyle, Crocodile!"

"Mom, I'm twenty-two."

"All right," said Melanie, because at least she'd warned her. Then she said, "Dad's crazed."

"He's just doing what he should have done ten years ago!"

Meanwhile, Dan's phone was ringing. Steve again. "So, here's my question. Can we bring two desserts?"

Dan knew what Steve was thinking. Could they bring one vegan dessert and one good one? But he said, "I don't think it would be fair."

"You're going all in?"

"Yeah," said Dan. "And no complaining. Eat before you get here."

"Would they be mortally offended," Steve asked, "if we have non-vegan options at our seder?"

Dan took his phone out to the hall. "Look, at your house you can do whatever you want. We're eating vegan because you know—they're staying with us."

"You're vegan for the whole week?"

"Do you have a problem with that?" Dan demanded.

Steve hung up.

"You're antagonizing everybody," Melanie said later.

"Not true," Dan declared, but that weekend he lost it when he caught Melanie adding lentils to her vegan moussaka. "You can't do that! No lentils on Pesach."

"What?" Melanie stepped back from the kitchen counter. "What's wrong with lentils?"

"We went over this!"

"When?"

"When we wrote the master list. When I ordered all the groceries. How did you buy lentils?"

"I figured you forgot them, so I just picked some up."

"I didn't forget. I thought we had a plan."

"Maybe we should do two separate menus like Steve and Andrea."

"We're not cooking two separate dinners! We're doing one dinner right!"

"Except you keep vetoing everything."

"Obviously you can't use lentils!"

"You're making this impossible."

"*I* am? *I'm* making this impossible? You were the one who said we should have a vegan seder."

"I did not."

"You said people use sunflower seeds."

"Don't you use that tone of voice with me," said Melanie.

"What tone?"

"Listen to yourself!"

"I'm quoting your own words!"

"Against me!"

A van was pulling up. Dan and Melanie ran for the door.

Phoebe and Wyatt had arrived with their suitcases and backpacks, keyboard, cello, banjo, and violin. They were unpacking their Chevrolet Rocky Ridge Weekender—home, and command central for their alternative folk Bach—what would you call it? Revival? Silk Road Ensemble? Boondoggle?

"Hi, sweetie." Dan hugged his long-legged daughter. "How are ya?" he greeted Phoebe's boyfriend, although he never said how are ya.

"Oh my God, the house!" said Phoebe. "It's so clean! You are officially minimalists now."

"Not really," Dan said. "We've got boxes in the garage, and in the basement."

Melanie added, "We've still got our books."

"A lot of people keep their books," Phoebe reassured her parents.

"And your old music," Dan said.

"Oh wow," Phoebe cried out. "The kitchen looks incredible!"

"Well, there's nothing in it anymore," said Melanie.

"What are you making?" Phoebe glanced at the kitchen island heaped with tomatoes, yellow squash, russet potatoes.

"Work in progress," said Melanie.

"We can cook!" Wyatt volunteered.

Phoebe said, "Just let us get some sleep and we'll help in the morning."

In the morning, Melanie was broiling eggplant. She had pivoted from moussaka to an all-vegetable lasagna with layers of broiled eggplant, zucchini, and fresh herbs. Dan took a long look, checking the ingredients.

Melanie started humming. The tune was unrecognizable, but the tone and timbre of her humming was familiar, high-pitched, and breathy. "Mmmhmmhmmhmmmhhhh."

"Could you just?" said Dan.

"Mmmhmmmhmm."

"Do we have grapefruits?" Phoebe was standing in the doorway.

"No, Dad threw them away," said Melanie.

"Do we have spinach?"

"We can get some," Dan said.

"*You* can get some," said Melanie, because she was right in the middle, checking on the broiler while trying to slice potatoes thinly.

Dan asked Phoebe to come with him to the store, but she and Wyatt were busy researching flourless eggless dairy-free chocolate cakes, so he drove off alone, while Melanie kept cooking. She grilled portobello mushrooms and diced tomatoes and cucumbers and chopped parsley for an Israeli salad. She made vichyssoise and potato kugel and arranged the seder plate. Nobody ate lunch, and nobody washed dishes.

By evening, Melanie lay on the couch with her feet up.

"Mom, you should try acupuncture," said Phoebe.

Dan set out Maxwell House Haggadahs. "Done," he said. "Now we need the wine."

"I'm on it." Wyatt ran down to the basement for the bottles, which Dan appreciated. To be clear, he did not hate Wyatt.

"Okay, we're just about ready," Dan said.

"Why do you keep announcing things?" asked Melanie.

"He's getting ready to lead the seder," said Phoebe, who had changed into a long black cotton dress which she wore like an apron over a white T-shirt.

But Dan would never be ready. His head was aching by the time Steve and Andrea and Zach and Nate arrived. Andrea came bearing a basket of spring flowers. Zach carried a giant salad.

"Oh, thank you!" said Melanie, and she set both on the table, even though there was hardly any room.

"Hey, Phoebe, I love your dress," said Andrea. "Is that new?"

"New to me," said Phoebe.

"Hi, Wyatt!" Andrea said. "How's the music?"

Dan cut off the small talk. "All right, everybody."

Everybody took their places, and with a steely look, Dan began chanting. They took turns. They went around the table so that each person read one part of the Haggadah, but Dan set the pace (fast) and the tone (stentorian). He was the director, assigning all the parts. "Who's the youngest here? Nate. Go ahead."

Nate sang the Four Questions in Hebrew while everybody followed along in English, beginning *Why is this night different from other nights?*

Wyatt began humming a camp tune after the last question. "Okay!" Dan cut him off. "Moving on!" And Melanie thought, On this night my husband is a control freak. That's how he celebrates freedom from slavery.

If only she knew. Dan had ceded all control, relaxing standards entirely. When he explained the items on the seder plate, he lifted a gnarly piece of ginger root and said, "This piece of ginger represents the shank bone which represents the sacrifice of Passover to the Lord who passed over the house of the Children of Israel when He smote the Egyptians."

When it was Phoebe's turn, she read in English of the enslaved Israelites crying out for help—and referred to God as she. *And God heard their groaning, and God remembered the covenant She had made with them.* And the whole time, Phoebe was leaning against Wyatt, as if she couldn't sit up on her own. *And She saw our affliction,* Phoebe read. Dan looked at her and thought, No kidding.

Meanwhile, Dan's older nephew was texting at the table, and his younger nephew was tilting his chair back and back to the point that Dan yelled, "Stop that!"

"Dan," Melanie chided, as though he was supposed to encourage Nate's behavior.

None of it was right. None of it was the way it should be done, and Dan grieved. Not for a person, or a place, but for the unbroken recitation of the passage out of Egypt. "Our ancestors were *slaves,*" he said.

For a split second everybody looked at him. Dan remembered his own father who had stopped the seder once, demanding, "Doesn't this holiday mean anything to you?" And then the moment passed. Phoebe and Wyatt were cuddling again.

When, at last, Melanie and Phoebe carried out the vegan feast, the family was ravenous. Every last bite of lasagna, mushroom, and potato kugel vanished. Talk about locusts. Not a leaf was left of Andrea's huge salad. As for dessert, the flourless, eggless, dairy-free chocolate cake was gone in seconds. And after all the hours of cooking, chopping, and grocery shopping, Dan's nephews were still hungry. Nate finished off the matzo. Zach consumed all the parsley left on the table. He didn't bother dipping the greens into the salt water representing the Israelites' tears.

Melanie thought, Why oh why didn't I make pot roast for the rest of us? Why did I agree to vegan solidarity? And Dan poured a sixth bottle of wine and thought, We're animals. We don't remember anything.

"So, how's the big tour?" Andrea said, turning to Phoebe.

Big tour? Dan thought. Is that supposed to be funny?

"What's next?" Steve asked Phoebe. "Back to school?"

"Nope."

"What happened to arts administration?" said Steve.

"Hey." Dan was not going to listen to his brother interrogate Phoebe. Obviously, Dan had asked his daughter the same question, but that was different.

Phoebe said, "I realized administration is not for me."

"An income is nice," said Steve.

"Music is our lives," Phoebe explained.

Steve smiled. No, he wasn't smiling; he was smirking. "The only question is how to earn a living."

"Drop it," Dan told his brother.

Now the elders had the kids' attention. At their end of the table, Phoebe and Wyatt, Zach and Nate watched, fascinated.

"Excuse me?" Steve said.

"You should talk," said Dan, because his brother knew *nothing* about earning a living. He worked in academic publishing, for God's sake. How dare he take this sanctimonious tone? "What were you doing besides smoking pot at her age?"

"Nice, Dad," said Nate.

Zach was laughing.

For the first time, the boys were engaged, but Steve stood to go. "Okay, that's enough."

"Steve," said Andrea. "We're not done."

"I think we are."

"Go ahead. Goodbye," said Dan.

Andrea and Melanie looked at each other in dismay. They maintained a certain bond, and they were wondering the same thing. Was this just a brief skirmish, or the beginning of a thirty-year feud? In the Rubinstein family, it could go either way.

All watched. All waited.

Then, even as Steve stood in front of him, Dan opened his Haggadah and began chanting rapidly in Hebrew. Andrea shot Steve a look that meant You're being ridiculous, and, also, You're embarrassing me. At last, Steve took his seat and Dan raced through Hallel.

By the time everybody left, Melanie was so tired she was seeing dots.

"Time to clean up," Dan said.

"We can do it," Wyatt volunteered.

But Phoebe looked at the kitchen and said, "In the morning." And the two of them hightailed it upstairs.

"Did you have to pick a fight?" said Melanie.

"Don't start." Dan locked himself in the bathroom. As for Melanie, she sank onto the couch and closed her eyes. She could not imagine enduring another seder the next day.

Dan decided not to go. He felt lousy in the morning, and nobody had cleaned the kitchen. The kids were playing bluegrass in the living room instead.

He tried to eat matzo and jam in the dining room, but Melanie hovered over him.

"I figure we'll bring the vegan seder plate tonight," said Melanie. "No reason for them to reinvent the wheel."

"And I'll stay here," Dan said.

"No, Dan!"

"I'm sorry. I'm sick."

"You are not."

"I have a headache." Dan spoke over fiddling and thumping.

"Dan. You only have one brother."

"I know how many brothers I have."

"You were hangry."

Dan's matzo cracked down the middle. "Hangry?" He abhorred Melanie's reductionism. "Don't start diagnosing me."

"Don't start issuing ultimatums."

"I'm feeling sick. That's all."

"So now you're diagnosing yourself."

"You know what?" Dan shouted. The music stopped, and suddenly he had no cover. He lowered his voice and said, "Do not tell me what I should and shouldn't do or say."

He was not going. He was not doing anything. But that afternoon, Phoebe approached and said, "Can we take a walk?"

"Just us?" he asked.

"Yeah."

He knew that Phoebe was trying to manage him. She was going to tell him to calm down. To forgive. To lighten up. He knew it was a ruse—but a walk alone? Time with his only child? He had no pride.

He jumped at the chance. Of course, he had an ulterior motive too. No lecturing, he reminded himself. No harping. But he would influence his daughter if he could. Tell her, ever so subtly, to get her shit together.

He strolled with Phoebe past old Tudors and brick colonials and swing sets and daffodils to the old elementary school playground, where she sat on a swing. "Listen," he began, but she interrupted.

"Dad, can you come with us tonight?"

He shot her a look.

"It's so fun at their seder."

Dan was hurt by the implied contrast. "Nobody's stopping you from going."

"I mean, our seder is fun too!" This wasn't strictly true, so Phoebe added, "In a different way! It's hard to do the first one when everybody's so tired from getting ready."

He sat on the swing next to hers and admitted, "I was exhausted."

"You didn't have to yell at Uncle Steve."

"I was defending you!" he said.

"From what?" Phoebe asked, oblivious, supremely confident.

From being judged, Dan thought. From hearing you're a slacker. From my brother's double standard—pointing out that you can't earn a living when he spent years thinking he could be a poet—but Dan said simply, "I was tired. We all were. End of story."

"But now you're rested."

"I am not rested."

"Dad, your work is done." She pushed off with her feet and pumped her legs because she was still a little girl. "You don't have to do anything at their house."

"I'll see how I feel."

"Okay!"

"Just tell me you aren't going to elope with Wyatt to New Mexico."

"What's in New Mexico?"

"I don't know, just for example. You know what I mean."

"Nobody's eloping. We don't believe in marriage."

Great, he thought, you'll just sleep together with three kids on one mattress in your van. "Phoebe, I want you to have a good life—and by the way, there is nothing wrong with money."

"So, you and Uncle Steve agree," Phoebe said maddeningly.

"Leave him out of it! I'm talking about you."

"I'm fine."

"If you would finish senior year. You're so close!"

"Stop." She slowed the swing with her feet.

Don't come on too strong, he reminded himself. All he said was, "I don't want you to be poor."

"I won't be," she told him, and this was the problem. At the end of the day, she knew that he and Melanie would support her. She could deny it, and he could pretend otherwise, but this wasn't life or death; it was success or aimlessness.

"You're not thinking long term," he said.

She smiled at him. "You're such an actuary!"

What could he do? She was in love, she was happy, and she knew everything. "Well, you can finish your degree later," he murmured, mostly to himself.

"That's what I've been telling you."

"If you don't get totally sidetracked."

"I'm not sidetracked at all!"

Yeah, right, he thought. What he said was, "Look, I'm not going to argue with you. It's just that—"

"Could you come tonight?"

And this was the whole trouble. He could not say no to her.

"Please?" she asked.

"Maybe."

"Yay," Phoebe cheered softly.

Dan drove, and Melanie carried the seder plate. Phoebe and Wyatt sat in back with a bowl of fruit salad between them. When they arrived, Dan handed Steve a case of Bartenura Moscato which was kosher, sparkling, and sweet. Melanie and Phoebe and Wyatt were all taking off their shoes because Andrea had a no shoes rule, but they looked up to see Steve accept this inexpensive offering. "I love this stuff."

Dan said, "I know."

Steve's house was small, and the seder table extended from the dining room into the living room. The extension was a wobbly card table for the kids, but white tablecloths covered the whole thing. Once you sat down, it was hard to get up because the space was so tight. Only Andrea could maneuver at the head of the table where she served the soup and led the singing.

While Dan was non-practicing Orthodox, Steve was egalitarian, which meant Andrea did everything. She had compiled her own Haggadah with readings from Emma Lazarus to Emma Goldman. At Andrea's table, you never knew what would turn up. An orange for oppressed humans. A tomato for migrant farmers. A banana for refugees. It was like Melanie's childhood seders where everybody took a moment to write a postcard on behalf of Soviet Jews. Cousin Wendy was there with her wife, Jill, and Nate had invited his girlfriend, Mackenzie.

Instead of taking turns, everybody read together. Instead of moving everyone along, Andrea stopped to ask deep questions. "What is freedom? What is it, Nate?"

"Um," he said.

"Is it doing whatever you want?"

The seventeen-year-old knew better than to say yes.

"What is it? Other people? Dan?"

Dan shifted in his chair because he hated off-road Judaism. The unscripted seder. The personal connection. Although he felt oppressed by the old rituals, he preferred them, which was why he brought his own Haggadah.

"I'm not letting you off the hook," said Andrea.

Dan sighed and said, "Freedom means making choices that are sustainable."

"Great!"

"That's beautiful," said Cousin Wendy. Doubtless she thought Dan's sustainable choices involved the ecosystem. In fact, he had been thinking of his daughter.

"Anybody else?" Andrea said.

Jill said, "Freedom is being true to who you are."

Mackenzie was raising her hand as if she were at school. "Mom," said Nate. "Call on Mackenzie."

"Go for it," Andrea said.

"Freedom is telling the truth."

"Wonderful!" Andrea declared. "We have great definitions of freedom, but what is Redemption? Who wants to take a stab at that one? Zach?" She looked down the table at her older son.

"Being saved from sin, error, or evil," he said immediately.

"He's reading that off his phone," Nate reported.

"Okay, who's doing the saving?" Andrea pressed on.

"In what context?" Steve asked.

Andrea said, "You tell me."

"In the Haggadah it's God," said Steve.

"Okay, it can be God," Andrea said.

"No, Steve's right," Dan said. "It *is* God, literally." He read aloud. *"And the Eternal brought us forth from Egypt: not an angel, not a Seraph, not a messenger; but the most Holy, blessed be He, in His own glory."*

Look at you, thought Melanie. Rallying to support your brother.

"I, myself and not a messenger," Dan read.

"And who else saved the Israelites?" Andrea asked.

"Themselves," said Jill, who wore a kippah from Nate's Bar Mitzvah.

"Say more!"

"They were the ones they were waiting for—with Miriam and Moses."

"Perfect! Turn to page twenty-three."

When Israel was in Egypt's land. / Let my people go. / Oppressed so hard they could not stand. / Let my people go.

Everyone was singing except for Dan, who wasn't feeling it, as the kids would say. And Steve, who stood for a moment and then disappeared into the living room.

"Is he okay?" asked Melanie.

"It's his back," said Andrea, as everyone began the chorus. *Go down, Moses. Waaaay down in Egypt laaaand. Tell old Pharaoh . . .* "He can't sit so long."

Phoebe said, "I feel weird singing this, because it's like cultural appropriation."

Wendy looked hurt. "We always sing 'Go Down Moses.'"

"I know but."

Jill said, "Where's Moses from, anyway? The Torah. So who's appropriating who?"

"Whom!" Steve corrected from the next room.

Go down, Moses. Waaay down in Egypt laaand. Wyatt and Zach and Nate were bellowing and pounding merrily, and suddenly the card table collapsed.

"Nooo!"

"Get paper towels."

"Pull it up from underneath. Wait! Grab the plates!"

The vegan seder plate was drenched in wine and everybody was bumping into chairs and trying to clean up and laughing—but Dan used the opportunity to slip away. He stepped into the living room where Steve was lying on the floor.

Dan sat on the couch and watched Steve prone on his back, lifting his legs slowly so his muscles wouldn't seize.

"Dad wouldn't have lasted two minutes in there," Steve said as he looked up at the ceiling.

"No kidding."

"Remember the . . ." said Steve.

"Yeah."

Steve didn't need to say it. They had been just ten and eight when their father had heart pain at the seder. Their mother wanted to call an ambulance. Their dad said no. She said, You need to go to the hospital! Their dad said, Put down the phone. They fought until Irving had to lie on the couch. Then, finally, Jeanne convinced him to get into the car and she drove him to the hospital while Dan and Steve waited at home, wondering if their dad would come back. They sat on the couch and then they went to their rooms and then they waited on the stairs. They ate nothing, although the kitchen was full of food. They didn't even take a sip of water.

Their parents did come back, late that night, and Irving announced the pain was nothing. Only palpitations. He also said, It's lucky we didn't have guests.

"Remember how Mom said, Go to sleep now?" Steve said.

Dan nodded. It was the middle of the night, and the two of them were wondering if it had all been a dream, when their dad commanded, "Come here."

"Irving," Jeanne protested.

He ignored her. "Sit down," he ordered Dan and Steve. And so, they sat at the table while their dad bent over his Haggadah, finishing the seder. The food was cold, and they weren't hungry. Their dad was chanting furiously.

"Give me a hand," said Steve.

Dan pulled him gently into a sitting position.

People were calling from the next room. Dan? Steve? But Steve noticed the case of Moscato still sitting on the coffee table, and he told Dan, "Grab the corkscrew."

"Hey, where are you taking that?" Melanie asked, as Dan stole the corkscrew and two glasses from the table. "Where are you going?" But the kids were singing again. *Rocka my Soul in the Bosom of Abraham.*

In the living room, Steve uncorked a bottle. "Cheers."

The brothers sat on the couch to sip their wine as the seder continued in the next room. There were readings from Hannah Senesh and Primo Levi and Yehuda Amichai. They could hear Cousin Wendy playing her guitar.

"Musical instruments at the seder!" Dan said. Needless to say, he and Steve had not grown up with that. They had grown up reading from the Haggadah while their dad corrected them.

Tight-lipped, Jeanne would clear the dishes as the seder dragged on and Irving would say, Can you wait? Please? Then Jeanne had to put off the dishes until the very end, which meant she stayed up late cleaning. Irving would stay up too, because he had trouble sleeping, but of course he didn't help. He sat in his chair reading the paper because he followed the news religiously. Not sports, not arts, but politics, and Israel, and wars, and famines. Tragedies.

"What would Dad say if he were here?" Dan asked.

Irving would not have done well with rowdy kids and collapsing tables. He had not condoned loud singing. He had not condoned a lot of things. That was why he had those palpitations, although the heart attack that killed him came years later.

Holding his glass, Steve stood to contemplate the entryway littered with shoes. "You know what Dad would say. Look at that mess."

And why are you taking off your shoes to have a seder in your socks? Dan added silently. What kind of thing is that? And who is that young man? Who is that luftmensch with Phoebe? But then Irving would not have recognized Phoebe either. He had not lived to see his grandchildren, and they, in turn, had no idea what he had been about. Sometimes Dan thought that was a good thing. Other times he wished his father had lived to see and hear all this. The kids' joy, their ignorance, their sheer volume. They were bellowing Bob Marley's "Redemption Song."

"Come sing with us!" Andrea called from the dining room.

"Soon!" Steve answered.

Dan and Steve were sidelined—but they would make their comeback. They would return for dinner, and more singing. They who had not suffered compared to other people. They who had grown up free.

8

Sheba

She was cursed with the kind of roommates mothers love—a postdoc in astronomy and a med student at Tufts. The postdoc, Thad, went to Hawaii to observe sunspots for weeks on end. The medical student, Celia, was getting a master's in public health. Jamie, on the other hand, worked as a canine companion—okay, a dog walker.

She strolled with a Rhodesian ridgeback and went running with a fleet and feckless Irish setter. She bathed a phobic sheepdog named Puggles because nobody in his family would. Individual attention for each animal. No group outings. Every dog at his or her own pace. She did not jumble clients together, clutching all their leashes in one hand. Because of this, she walked some of the most privileged animals in Cambridge. The standard poodle of a Nobel laureate in economics, the golden retriever of a Miltonist, the beagle of an architect who designed transparent libraries.

First thing in the morning, Jamie and the golden ran once around Fresh Pond and sniffed the autumn air. Mud and damp and bright decaying leaves and other dogs approaching. Quick barks of recognition. Sidelong glances. Please, please, please. Jamie held on while Sunny strained the leash. Then, at Little Fresh Pond, she released him. Hurled his tennis ball into the water where he swam, rippling with joy, paddling quickly, nosing tattered lily pads.

If only they were all so easy. Frank, the beagle, nipped. The poodle, Sheba, had a melancholy air, a sadness behind the ears that nobody could scratch.

"You have a good home," Jamie told Sheba, as they walked on Avon Hill. "You have a great yard."

Sheba ignored this. Tall, gray, elegant, never one to settle for a hug and a tickle, Sheba snapped up treats but wouldn't beg for more. She gazed instead with searching eyes, as if to say, Is that all there is?

"What am I going to do with you?" Jamie said.

She dropped off Sheba and went home to her apartment, one-third of a blue Victorian on Russell Street. Celia was asleep. Thad, the postdoc, was pacing as he talked on the phone. He was a surfer, and he walked with a rolling gait, as though the earth was not challenging enough. Jamie was the conscientious one. Opening the door, she saw that nobody had cleaned the kitchen and it looked bad. It was so bad that after she scrubbed, vacuumed, and mopped, her roommates bought her lilies and roses at Whole Foods. The arrangement came in a glass vase with a ribbon. The lilies stank and shed pollen. The roses opened, but by morning hung their heads.

Jamie threw out the flowers. Washing the vase reminded her of the fish tank she had when she was twelve. She would take a toothbrush and scrub out the algae, because there was no one else to do it. Jamie's oldest sisters, Lissa and Heather, were in high school, and she barely saw them. Her third sister, Amanda, was in middle school, and Jamie saw her all the time. Amanda looked at the tank in the sink and said, "Eeew no."

"It's just algae," Jamie said.

"I don't like fish," Amanda told her.

"Why not?"

"Because they're always dying."

"We live, we die," said Jamie, who had been reading *Charlotte's Web*.

"Especially in aquariums," said Amanda.

She'd been right about the fish. One by one, they went belly-up, until only two angelfish remained. These two attacked each other, nicking fins and tails, until the larger killed the smaller one. For a time, the larger swam alone in splendor. Then death came to him as well.

"They didn't last long, did they?"

Jamie looked up startled and saw Celia dressed for class. "I guess not—but we can reuse the vase."

"You're so good." Celia came from Hong Kong, and she spoke with an English accent. She said that she aspired to neatness. "When are you applying to divinity school?"

"In the fall," said Jamie.

"You should get in, if there is a God," said Celia. "Sorry."

Jamie had been raised atheist. Technically, her parents were Jewish, but only technically. Paul and Judy taught labor relations at Cornell. They were atheist, socialist, and feminist, although Judy had been Paul's student. (Look, it was a different time, Paul said.) They had tried to instill humanist values in their four daughters, but each identified as Jewish.

Amanda, who was engaged to a Harvard law student, planned for a rabbi to officiate at her wedding. "Maybe *you* should be the rabbi," she told Jamie when they walked together that afternoon.

"Div school isn't training to be clergy." Jamie wrangled the beagle, Frank.

"So you want to study all religions?"

"Belief," said Jamie. "And why we believe and why we—"

Amanda interrupted. "You like Buddhism, right?"

"You don't *like* Buddhism," Jamie said. "You study. You practice."

"Stop! I'm thinking who to introduce you to."

Frank tugged the leash as Jamie said, "You don't have to introduce me to anyone."

"I know, but I want to."

"You have paint in your hair," Jamie told her sister.

"Really?"

"By your ear."

"I'm going to introduce you to a Buddhist at our party," Amanda said.

The party was at the Plough and Stars to celebrate Amanda's engagement to Jonathan, the law student. Amanda wore a lime-green minidress and platform shoes. Jamie wore jeans and a pin-striped shirt. The band was so loud you couldn't speak or hear. When Jamie said hi to Jonathan, he didn't see her.

"Come here!" Amanda called. She kept pulling Jamie over to talk to people, but Jamie could not hear what they were saying. There was a guy named Simon with bright brown eyes and thinning hair. Jamie wondered if he was the Buddhist one. He wore a T-shirt printed I WOULD PREFER NOT TO.

"Are you a student?" Simon called above the music.

"Well—I'm going back to school. Hopefully."

"Cool. What are you going to study?"

Jamie looked for Amanda, but she was gone. She could move fast in four-inch heels.

"I'm thinking about theodicy," Jamie told Simon.

"What was that?"

"The-od-i-cy," Jamie enunciated.

"Go, Homer!" he cheered.

Jamie did not correct him.

"I wish I was a student," Simon said. "I envy you."

"What are you doing instead?"

"Do you want to go outside?" Simon said.

Outside, the air was cool, and Jamie's ears were ringing.

"I'm in cybersecurity," Simon said. "I do recruiting."

"I don't know anything about cybersecurity," she said.

"That's okay."

"At the moment I'm a dog walker."

"You get to walk dogs?" he said. "Can I come?"

"He's sort of overfriendly," Jamie told Sheba the next morning.

Sheba sniffed Jamie's wrist which smelled of soap and detergent, a crisp hopefulness. A little smoke.

"Should we let him walk with us?" Jamie asked. "Bark once for yes."

Sheba did not bark. She looked at Jamie as if to say, You are too good for him.

But Jamie did not think she was too good. She told Simon she could walk with him any day but Sunday.

On Sunday mornings, she volunteered at the Porter Square T stop where the interfaith ministry held outdoor services. Father Anthony pushed a tea trolley stocked with grape juice, laminated hymns, and communion wafers. Jamie assisted.

While Father Anthony read the service, a woman named Dawna organized the contents of her shopping cart.

"The Lord is my Shepherd," Father Anthony read. "I shall not want."

"Yeah, right," a shaggy man said.

After the homily, Jamie played her flute.

"What was that you played?" Dawna asked.

"'Sheep May Safely Graze,'" said Jamie.

"What else you got?"

"Don't listen to her," the shaggy man told Jamie. "She's fucking ignorant."

But Jamie did listen. What was she doing playing the flute? Praying at the T stop? She should be giving out food and cash and lobbying Congress. The question haunted her. *What else you got?*

"Maybe I should be a social worker," Jamie told Amanda, the next time they walked Frank.

"But you'd be terrible," Amanda said.

"Why?"

"You'd just get upset."

"Maybe I should be upset," Jamie said.

The next day, Frank nipped Jamie's finger. His owner was away overseeing a center for reconciliation in the Middle East.

"I get it," Jamie told the dog. "You don't have to take it out on me."

Puggles bolted before Jamie could rinse the shampoo from his fur. He streaked down the stairs while Jamie raced behind.

As Jamie walked to Sheba's place, Celia called to say that the washing machine had flooded the basement. Their landlord was on a ten-day bicycle trip.

Jamie was glad to find Sheba waiting at the window of her chocolate-shingled house. Sheba barked once as the housekeeper let her out.

"Hey." Jamie offered Sheba an old rubber ball.

Sheba nudged it with her paw, but only to humor Jamie. She knew it didn't squeak.

"Listen," Jamie said. "We have a visitor. His name is Simon and he's good with animals."

Sheba looked at Jamie as if to say, What makes you think I am an animal?

"He's just here to say hi."

Sheba glanced at the gate where a young man was waiting.

"He's just going to hang out with us for a little while." Jamie fastened a leash to her collar, even though Sheba didn't need one. "Shall we?" Jamie said, and Sheba could not say no.

Regal, stately, Sheba led the way to the garden gate. As soon as Sheba stepped onto the sidewalk, Simon held out his sweaty hand, palm up.

"Hello, beautiful girl," he told Sheba. "Wow. You are gorgeous!"

Sheba stood unyielding while Simon petted her. He was indeed too friendly—but Jamie didn't mind. They walked along and Sheba trotted in front listening to them chatter about school and Cambridge and roommates and jobs and finding what you love. Sheba glanced back at Jamie. Love already?

They walked through leafy streets. They strolled through Harvard Square where people hunched at tables playing chess and a young man played the cello. He was sitting on a stool while a girl with long blond hair stood near, playing the violin.

Jamie was trying to explain. "I'm interested in suffering. I mean, don't take it the wrong way. It's not like I'm looking to suffer, or I have a morbid fascination, but—"

"You want to understand it?"

"Yeah. Exactly."

"Like, why do bad things happen to good people?"

"No, it's more like, why do bad things happen to anybody?"

A car was coming, and Jamie didn't even notice as she followed Simon into the street. Sheba barked in warning.

Then Jamie and Simon remembered where they were and stepped back onto the curb. "She's such a good dog," Jamie told Simon. "Aren't you?" she added for Sheba's benefit.

Sheba did not nuzzle Jamie's hand.

The next time, Jamie and Simon went without Sheba to Simon's Coffee Shop. At first it was a joke. Simon would say, let's meet at Simon's Coffee—no relation. Then they began meeting there regularly. Simon's was narrow as a railcar. Its tables were lined up one behind the other parallel to the long counter. The toasted bagels were not great. The chocolate chip cookies were big and soft and way too sweet, but the coffee was good—and there was something about how narrow the place was. You felt hidden there, as though you could say anything.

"I'd like to go back to school," Simon confided. "I don't love recruiting."

"What would you study?" Jamie asked.

"Photography."

"What kind?"

"It's unrealistic," he said, "but I would work for *National Geographic*. I'd take pictures of endangered species and the effects of global warming."

Jamie said, "I don't think it's unrealistic."

They went together to the MFA and stood in front of Guanyin's statue. The light was dim, and Guanyin sat casually on a pillar with one leg up and one leg down. Was she a woman or a man? Maybe a woman? Her skin was gold; her flowing robes were painted.

"Look at her face," Jamie said.

"Peaceful," said Simon.

"But she knows." Jamie gazed at Guanyin's downcast eyes and quiet mouth. The Bodhisattva knew all the problems in the world. All the troubles and the disappointments and the pain.

"She's like an angel," Simon said.

"She's like Sheba."

"Totally."

"He's not like other guys," Jamie told Sheba when she came to get her at the house.

Sheba thought, Who, Simon? He is exactly like other guys.

"He wants to be a photographer." Jamie scratched the back of Sheba's head.

He wants you, thought Sheba. She saw the way he circled Jamie.

"He's thoughtful," Jamie said.

Sheba turned toward the fence. Simon was pulling up, locking his bike to a RESIDENT PARKING ONLY sign. When he took off his helmet, he ran his hand through his thinning hair.

As soon as he approached, Jamie jumped up to meet him. He looked at her and forgot to close the gate.

Jamie said, "I have to show you this tree."

It was a massive beech with deep green leaves. Jamie and Simon looked up at branches that seemed to touch the sky. "It's even bigger than the ones at the library," Jamie said.

Simon said, "It's definitely taller."

"Who has a yard this big?" Simon asked.

"I know! In Cambridge? It's crazy." Jamie picked up Sheba's leash and they all walked to the side of the house. "Look at this."

It was the old barn. Sheba's master kept it as a garden shed. Through the open door, Sheba smelled squirrels, potting soil, old musty crocus bulbs, damp flowerpots, everything good, but she waited outside as Jamie and Simon stepped in.

"Up there you can see the hayloft."

"What's up there now?"

Sheba's leash trailed on the ground. She was forgotten.

In the shadows Simon was whispering, and Jamie whispered back. They were rustling softly beyond the potting soil, beyond the flowerpots. They were like wind in the trees. The softest wind. The smallest leaves.

Sheba was gone when they stepped out again.

They called and called for her. They ran through the garden out onto the street. "It's my fault," Simon said. "I didn't close the gate."

"No, it was me," Jamie said. "I dropped the leash."

Jamie whistled. Simon said she couldn't have gone far. They split up—Jamie running down Lancaster Street, Simon biking up Mass Ave.

Sheba was not walking around the block, nor was she strolling on Mass Ave.

Simon biked all the way to Arlington and then circled back. He found Jamie crumpled on the stairs outside Susanna's dress shop. She was trying to phone Sheba's master.

Simon knelt at Jamie's feet. "Don't call him yet. We've just started looking."

Jamie said, "I have to take responsibility."

All that afternoon they walked through Avon Hill. They searched every street and cul-de-sac. Simon was sure they would find Sheba. Jamie was sure that they would not.

She stapled LOST DOG notices to every telephone pole. She told Sheba's master she would return all her wages. She walked the streets. She pinned offers of rewards to bulletin boards as far as Christina's Homemade Ice Cream.

Her roommates tried to help. Thad posted online. Celia brought Jamie tea.

A week passed. Ten days. Jamie couldn't sleep.

She composed a resignation letter for her employers. She explained that she had been careless. She had experienced a lapse in judgment, and she took full responsibility. Regretfully, she could no longer continue walking dogs. Losing Sheba, she had betrayed a sacred trust.

Thad said, "I think this might be overkill."

Jamie said no.

Simon called. Her parents called. Everybody tried to comfort her.

"How is it negligence if the dog ran away from her own backyard?" Jamie's dad said.

Jamie said, "I left the gate open, and she ran away because of me."

Eventually, she stopped answering her phone.

Amanda came over and sat on Jamie's bed. She said, "So now you're not speaking to Simon? Are you blaming him, or something?"

"I blame myself," said Jamie.

On Sunday she assisted Father Anthony again. As they began the service at the Porter Square T stop, the shaggy man told Jamie, "You look like hell."

Father Anthony said, “If anyone here has seen a gray standard poodle, please let us know.”

Cars whizzed past as Father Anthony said, “Let us raise our voices in the Hebrew prayer for peace. He led everyone in singing *Shalom Aleichem* but Jamie hardly sang at all.

“I saw the dog,” an old, bearded guy told Jamie after the service. “She’s near Davis Square.”

“What?” Jamie’s hand flew to her heart. “Please,” she whispered.

“You want to see her?”

Jamie nodded, because she could not speak.

“Okay.”

The bearded guy led the way up Mass Ave and Jamie followed, almost afraid to breathe. “How much will you give me for her?” the guy asked.

“What do you mean?”

“I never did anything to your dog,” the old, bearded guy said.

“She’s not my dog. Her name is Sheba and she’s not mine to lose.”

“Not mine to lose?” the old guy echoed lightly.

“Where did you take her?” Jamie demanded.

The old guy’s skin was leathery, his eyes bright, narrow, dark. He wore jeans and a plaid shirt and a pair of black dress shoes. He hurried past the post office and a decrepit Tibetan rug store and Jamie followed. He walked even faster, and Jamie was practically running to keep up. Then suddenly he stopped in front of a Bank of America ATM.

“Why are you stopping?” Jamie asked.

“I’m cash only.”

“Bring Sheba here,” Jamie said.

“Maybe I will,” the old, bearded guy said as he walked off. “Maybe I won’t.”

Jamie withdrew $200 from her bank account and then she waited. She watched a pair of students carrying a blue armchair. She saw a mother encouraging a tiny girl on a pink scooter. The sun beat down. Jamie began to think the old guy was never coming back—but she could not give up watching for him.

She felt she had been watching the whole day. She felt as though the sun would set, even though it had only been an hour. Then, in the distance, she saw a man walking down Mass Ave with a tall dog. She ran toward them, and the dog was Sheba.

She had no collar and no leash. Her fur was dirty, and she looked gaunt.

Jamie knelt at Sheba's side, examining her, lifting her paws.

Sheba listened to Jamie scolding softly. "How could you? How could you leave like that? Were you punishing me? Is that what you were doing?"

"Where's the money?" the old guy interrupted.

Still kneeling, Jamie offered up the cash.

The man snatched the bills and barely glanced at them before he kicked Jamie in the ribs. He kicked the breath out of her with his black shoe.

Jamie doubled over, even as Sheba exploded, barking. She bit the man's arm and when he screamed and tried to fight her off, she charged at him again.

He ran.

She pursued him all the way to the edge of the traffic on Mass Ave.

He plunged in and sprinted across the street, but Sheba did not chase, because she knew not to run into the road.

She returned to Jamie who was scrambling to her feet. "Why did he kick me like that?" Jamie asked with a little cry in her voice.

Sheba knew why. The man kicked Jamie because he was bigger. He kicked Jamie because she was not on guard. Kneeling, she had given him an opening.

Jamie was trembling and Sheba stayed close. *Stick with me*, Sheba said silently, but Jamie wasn't listening. She was already calling Simon.

"I found her. I've got her," Jamie said. "Corner of Mass Ave and Meacham."

When Simon arrived, he was driving an old maroon car. He jumped out and rushed to Jamie and touched her where she hurt. He took her hand and helped her into the front seat. Sheba had to sit in back. From the rearview mirror hung a car freshener shaped like a little tree. The scent was fake pine needles.

They drove to Sheba's house and Simon helped Jamie out. Then Jamie freed Sheba. The three of them stood at the gate. "No, don't come in with me," Jamie told Simon. "I have to do this myself. It's my responsibility."

Sheba pricked up her ears, because responsibility meant her, not Simon. She walked in triumph through the garden gate.

As she followed Jamie up the path, Sheba smelled the old smells and saw the old toys. Her rubber ball lay hidden where she'd left it in the grass.

Jamie rang the doorbell and Sheba's master opened the door.

Jamie said, "I'm so, so sorry." The story of the bearded guy came pouring out. But Jamie did not say that she had paid for Sheba—and she did not say she had been kicked.

Sheba's master, Hal, knelt to embrace Sheba, who listened to him say how worried he had been. When at last he looked up, he told Jamie, "Come in."

"I should go," Jamie said.

"Not at all," said Hal.

Sheba followed Jamie into the house and drank a bowl of water and ate a bowl of food. Sheba's master told Jamie, "Sit."

Jamie sat on a hard chair. Sheba crouched at her master's feet, while he sat on the couch.

"Thank you for finding her," Hal said.

Jamie said, "Don't thank me."

"All's well that ends well."

Jamie said, "I can't forgive myself."

"Try," said Hal, "because I want you to keep walking her."

"You don't mean that," said Jamie.

"I do."

"Didn't you get my letter?" Jamie asked.

"I got your letter and I read it."

"Then how can you—"

"I don't accept your resignation," Hal said.

"What is the number one rule of dog walking?" Jamie asked. "Don't lose the dog."

Hal shook his head "Look, you can make this into a Greek tragedy if you want, but I don't do tragedies. I'm an economist."

"I can't keep working for you."

"At this point in time," Hal said, "there is no one on the planet more trustworthy than you. Listen. You know I'm right. You'll never let Sheba out of your sight again."

"You're too generous," said Jamie, choking up.

"It's not generosity," Hal insisted. "Now back to work, okay?"

"Okay."

Jamie stood and Sheba stood, looking at her. She longed to lick Jamie's face, but she was careful not to give herself away.

Don't you ever run away again, Jamie told Sheba silently.

Don't forget me, then, Sheba answered, silent in return. It's true that I belong to someone else, but you belong to me.

Sheba's master said, "How about a bath? And check for fleas."

"Come, Sheba," Jamie said.

Sheba did not obey.

"Come on," Jamie said.

Still, Sheba waited. She forgave Jamie, but she could not ignore her master on the couch or forget Simon lurking at the gate. She knew how quickly the world changed. The squirrel you thought you'd caught escaped. The love you thought you'd earned was cracked. She wanted Jamie to reach for her. She wanted Jamie to want her, so she held back. She had such height and elegance. Even in her filthy state, she acted like a queen.

9

Tanglewood

There had been a time the sisters picnicked on the lawn. Sylvia with her first husband, Helen with her family, Jeanne with hers. This was years and years ago when Sylvia wore cat-eye glasses. She had the pictures, now faded—her red dress changed to orange, the color of tomato soup. Grass bleached white, and all the children playing together. In the foreground, Pam and Wendy in peasant blouses, behind them Steve with his book, and frowning Dan, and Richard, Sylvia's son. Now the cousins had marriages and mortgages, children, and troubles of their own. If they did come back to Tanglewood, it wasn't all at once, or often. Did anyone remember those bright days, with Beethoven like distant thunder?

Sylvia still drove out each summer with her third husband, Lew, but they did not picnic. The sun was too much, so they bought tickets for the Music Shed.

"It's lonely," Sylvia told Richard, now a heavyset attorney. They were sitting on the porch in twilight, and the trees were lovely, and there were roses, but she said, "Everybody's gone."

"I'm here," Richard said. "The girls are here."

"For three and a half days!" Following their complicated custody arrangement, Debra brought the girls on Sunday and stayed with them till Wednesday. Richard took the rest of the week.

Slowly, Richard said, "I think it's fair."

"I think it's terrible."

"Thanks, Mom."

She was about to speak again when Lew came out with drinks and cut her off. "Let's enjoy everyone who's here."

Sylvia did not persist, but she looked mournfully at Richard all the same. She worried for her granddaughters. Maybe this split week was fair, but how could it be good? And who was her son texting? "Richard?"

When he looked up, a smile lingered on his face, and she was sure that he was seeing someone new. Then Sylvia felt for Debra, who was very much alone—and helpful! While visiting, Debra did what never occurred to Richard. She bought groceries and harvested tomatoes with Lew. She made sure the girls cleared the table and washed dishes, insisted they unpack and put their clothes away.

Sylvia asked her son, "Who were you talking to?"

Richard pocketed his phone. As a kid, he had wondered when his mother's scrutiny would stop. When he went to college? When he married? When he became a father? When he made partner? He turned to his stepfather. "I'll always be an only child."

"And I'll always be your only mother," Sylvia said.

Admittedly, Richard was an anxious parent too. He hovered, but his children really were children. Sophie was fifteen, Lily just twelve.

"Dad." He heard Lily calling when he walked inside.

He climbed the stairs to the girls' room under the eaves. "What is it?"

"I can't sleep."

"Because it's still light out?" He sat on the edge of her bed.

"Because I miss Mom."

He looked at Lily's small face, her fine blond hair spread over the pillow. "You'll see her Sunday."

"I know, but."

"Go to sleep," Sophie intoned from her bed opposite.

"We'll have pancakes tomorrow," Richard promised Lily.

"Mom made pancakes yesterday."

"Oh."

"Dad?" Lily said.

"Stop talking." Sophie flipped over and covered her head with her pillow.

"You stop talking," Lily snapped.

"Don't speak that way to your sister," Richard told both of them. Then he thumped downstairs and walked out to the garden where he chewed gum and paced under the trees because bickering upset him, and he was guilty and exhausted—all of the above.

"These should be fluffy," Sylvia observed the next morning when Richard's pancakes fell flat—or flatter than they should have been.

"There's no buttermilk." Richard frowned at the stove.

"It's all right," said Sylvia. "I don't eat pancakes anymore."

"What do you mean, you don't eat them?"

"Well, Lew can't."

"I can, although I shouldn't," Lew said. "And sometimes I do."

Sylvia laughed at that, and Lew seemed pleased, but Richard remained glum.

At the table, the girls slouched, absorbed by their phones. "Stop it," Richard told them. "You know the rule." And he thought of course Debra would take the first half of the week when the girls were still excited to be out of school.

He suggested hiking, but his daughters didn't want to go. He said, What about glassblowing, and Sophie said, We did that. Sylvia showed Richard the girls' lumpen paperweights. And so, everybody sat inside and stared at screens—except for Lew, who read *The Wall Street Journal* since he had canceled *The New York Times* to protest its coverage of Israel.

The house was stuffy, and the only conversation was what to have for lunch—until Lily piped up from the living room. "Who's that?"

"Who's what?" said Lew.

"That van."

"Delivery?" Lew asked.

"Were you expecting someone, Mom?" Richard stood at the window and saw a young woman with a lanky young man. Suddenly he realized the woman was his cousin. "Phoebe!"

Sylvia threw the door open. "What a lovely surprise."

"Welcome, welcome," Lew said, as the girls crowded behind.

"I'm sorry we didn't warn you. We just wanted to say hi," said Phoebe. "This is my boyfriend, Wyatt."

"Come in! Have a drink!" said Lew. "Come cool down."

"Have lunch with us." Sylvia ushered them in.

"Wow, you guys grew!" Phoebe told the girls, who gazed at her in awe. Phoebe's arms were bare and freckled. Blond hair cascaded down her back. As for Wyatt, he was so tall, he seemed to touch the ceiling.

"One thing," Wyatt said. "Could we bring in our instruments? It's too hot to leave them in the van."

"Of course, of course," said Lew.

In a moment Wyatt was carrying in Phoebe's violin and his cello, almost an extra person. Phoebe was explaining all the patches and stickers on the cases. Yosemite. San Francisco.

"Did you drive the whole way?" asked Lily.

"Yeah, we drove cross-country and back—but we stopped a lot."

"That's so cool," said Sophie. "Where did you stay?"

"I hope you'll stay with us tonight," said Sylvia.

Lily volunteered, "You can have the room next to ours."

Suddenly the family threw off its lethargy. The girls ushered Wyatt and Phoebe upstairs. Sylvia started making chicken salad and sent Lew to town for apples. "Cake?" he asked, hopefully.

"We'll see." They all felt it, like sudden rain, the surprise and the relief, the romance of youth.

"This is your room," Lily told the newcomers. "Don't bump your head. This is your closet. Look. It's Narnia." She pushed back old coats and garment bags so they could see the closet extended all the way under the eaves.

"This is the bathroom. These are for you." Lily opened the linen closet in the hall and showed off stacks of towels. Phoebe and Wyatt glanced at each other. Everything was so rich and perfect. There were skylights. "And look," said Lily. On top of the bureau stood three antique doll beds, one wood, one brass, one carved four-poster. No dolls slept in them, but each bed had a tiny quilt.

"They must be super old," said Wyatt.

Lily said, "There's a dollhouse in our room from 1880."

"I want to see that," Wyatt said.

Phoebe promised, "After we clean up and change."

And so, Sophie and Lily backed away and waited in their room next door. They lay on their beds and listened to the shower running.

Then, after a moment, Lily knelt in front of the dollhouse, which stood in the gable, and straightened the kitchen, setting out four tiny plates and cups of speckleware. "What are you doing?" Sophie asked, and Lily couldn't really say. She was too old; she hadn't played with the house in years, but she wanted to see the look on Wyatt's face; to watch him pick up the pennies which fit perfectly on each burner of the stove—since, after all, she'd put them there.

Downstairs, in the real kitchen, Sylvia opened her green notebook of recipes copied from her mother, Lillian, who served napoleons, Sacher and Linzer tortes, rugelach that put bakeries to shame.

Sylvia was nowhere near as good; she had a knack, but she was impatient. She threw things together. She knew all this because her mother had told her.

Lillian had been prophetic, almost biblically insightful. She had blessed and cursed in equal measure. You have talent, she told Sylvia, but you will not cultivate it. You will never make good mandelbrot. How had she known? Sylvia could not manage sticky dough—or sticky situations. When Sylvia was just a girl, Lillian had predicted, You will be a nervous mother. And so, it came to pass. Sylvia feared for Richard all his days and worried even more about her granddaughters.

But Phoebe and Wyatt were delightful. She could feed and entertain and show them the laundry room without considering their future.

"Whoa!" said Wyatt.

"A built-in drying rack!" said Phoebe.

The simplest things amazed them. Central air! Running water! The washing machine hummed with their clothes.

Sylvia sliced apples, mixed batter, sprinkled brown sugar and cinnamon, and slid her Bundt pan into the oven. She waited and then, it happened every time, the scent filled the house. All through lunch, the family was conscious of the cake baking.

Silence, as everyone ate apple cake with its crisp topping and its luscious crumb. Lew, Sylvia, and Richard refrained from taking seconds, but the girls indulged, and so did Phoebe, who closed her eyes, and Wyatt, who said oh my God wow. Sylvia loved their innocence and hunger.

When lunch was over, the girls did not drift away. Phoebe and Wyatt started clearing plates, and Sylvia said, "No. You're guests!"

Lew said, "Play for us, instead."

Sophie and Lily cleared while Phoebe unpacked her violin and Wyatt adjusted his cello pin. Then in the living room the two tuned together, Wyatt in a straight-backed chair, Phoebe on her feet, leaning like a sunflower. "This is a fiddle tune, but we adapted it," Wyatt said. "Boil Them Cabbage Down."

The family were all sitting except for Lily standing at the kitchen door. When Phoebe started playing, Lily forgot the sponge in her hand. Phoebe's fingers were flying, her bow weaving up and down. Her eyes were on Wyatt the whole time, and when she took the melody he answered with a smile. Phoebe doubled up her notes and Wyatt followed. He sped up and she dashed after him. Pretty soon, they were racing, faster and faster until they tied at the end, lifting their bows to applause and laughter.

"What would you be boiling the cabbage for?" asked Sylvia.

"Soup?" Phoebe suggested.

"Holishkes?" mused Sylvia, thinking of stuffed cabbage. You boiled the leaves to wrap ground beef mixed with rice and minced onion.

"I don't think so, Mom," said Richard. "Wrong recipe."

"How do you know?"

"Wrong culture."

"Let's have another," Lew told the musicians.

They played "Cotton-Eyed Joe" and then "Ole Dan Tucker." Wyatt sang the verses, his voice deep, his bow choppy under Phoebe's filigree. *"Ole Dan Tucker was a fine old man. Washed his face in a frying pan. Combed his hair with a wagon wheel. Run away with a toothache in his heel."* When he came to the chorus, Wyatt nodded for everyone to join. *"Get out of the way for ole Dan Tucker. He's too late to get his supper. Supper's over and dinner's cooking. Ole Dan Tucker just astandin' there lookin'."*

Are they really my own cousins? Lily thought, as she stood there looking. Are they in my family? They are so happy.

They were both generous, but Wyatt especially. He did not forget the dollhouse. He knelt on the floor and examined all the beds, the dressers and the tiny lamps, the potbelly stove and copper pans. The stamp-sized cookbook Lily and Sophie had crafted themselves two years before. One recipe for chocolate cake, one staple for a binding. He said, "How did you write so small?" His own hands were huge; the fingertips on his left were notched from practicing.

It was a perfect afternoon, except that Sylvia decided they had to go to Tanglewood that evening. "Noooo," Lily mourned, as she and Sophie trudged upstairs to change. In this family you couldn't lie outside on the grass; you had to sit in chairs, while the orchestra performed for hours. Just when you couldn't take it anymore, a woman and a man and then another woman would stand and sing, and everyone would read translations in the program, like the High Holidays, on and on forever.

Sadly, the girls pulled on thin white cardigans and slipped their phones into their dress pockets. They wore gold lockets from their grandmother because she liked to see them. The lockets opened on tiny hinges, so you could fall in love and put a picture inside, but of course, both hearts were empty. "Phoebe and Wyatt are coming." Sophie tried to look on the bright side.

"They aren't even in our section!" said Lily, who had been listening on the stairs. At such late notice, their grandmother couldn't get seven seats together.

"No complaining," Richard warned. He drove the girls, so he had a chance to lecture, while Lew drove everybody else. "And no phones."

"What about your phone?" Sophie shot back from the passenger seat.

"Watch it," he growled, by which he meant your tone, your attitude, your disapproving glances, the resentment you are learning from your mom, or from your friends. But when he glanced in the rearview mirror, Sophie seemed hurt. Lily looked shaken. Too much, he thought. Too angry. Too many rules. And then with a pang, What am I doing? I'm ruining their lives. Debra left *me,* he defended himself silently. But in their words and in their eyes, the girls said, We don't care who started it—which was what he always said to them.

Silently, the girls followed Richard to the gate where the others waved at them. Of course, they were early because Lew insisted on being early for everything. He always said, Why rush? Which meant you rushed at home and then you waited. As for Sylvia, she liked to watch twilight settle on the grounds.

"Isn't it lovely?" Sylvia looked out at the sweeping lawn.

"Yes," Lew agreed as always, surveying the scene.

The picnickers were out with lawn chairs and checked tablecloths and champagne flutes and wicker baskets. The air was perfect, warm, but dry. This was not a humid, buggy evening.

"Look. Tablecloths," Phoebe said to Wyatt. The whole scene was so elegant. Phoebe had changed into an Indian gauze dress, and Wyatt wore a clean black T-shirt. Like pilgrims they had washed the dust from their cracked sandals. They had been busking for so long in parking lots and diners and on concrete steps. Now they were walking on lush grass.

Phoebe saw the tree first. It stood alone on the broad lawn, a great oak with many trunks, a grove unto itself. When she ran up, she could not tell whether the tree was several grown together, or whether it had split into this labyrinth of trunks and roots. "How wide is it?" she asked.

"Let's reach around it in a human chain!" said Wyatt, who had worked three summers at Eden Village Camp. He took Phoebe's hand on one side, and Lily's on the other. "Look how big it is. What do you think?" he asked Lily. He meant, What do you think the circumference is? But she could not guess. The world changed in all dimensions when he took her hand in his. "We need everybody!" he called out.

Not everybody joined. Sylvia and Lew and Sophie held hands, but Richard hung back to take pictures on his phone. He caught Lily smiling and Sophie childlike again. Lew reached for Phoebe. Sophie stretched her hand out to her grandmother. Each to each in the cool evening light. The old wanting to be young, the young wanting to be older. The tree standing in the center with so many trunks you couldn't tell which was first and which was last.

Wyatt said, "Everybody reach around the tree. Okay, it's five people around!"

"Is that an objective scientific measure?" asked Lew.

"Objective but unscientific," Wyatt answered.

Richard was still taking pictures, even as the magic circle broke. If only there had been more time—but bells were chiming for the concert, and Sylvia started fussing that they would be late.

The concert began with a Mozart piano concerto that seemed to Lily like floral curtains rippling. She sat between her dad and her sister, and she couldn't move. She was trapped in her chair listening to an endless melody. Piano cascading. Orchestra chiming in. She would have been all right if she had known when the piece would end, but every time the musicians took a breath they started up again. If Wyatt and Phoebe had been sitting with her, Lily could have watched them listen—but they had seats so far away they were invisible. All Lily saw was the back of her grandparents' heads. Sophie's head was down. Was she listening hard or sleeping? Lily bent her own head to see if Sophie's eyes were closed. No. She was awake. Lily looked again, and that was when she realized her sister had her phone hidden in the folds of her dress. Sophie was peeking at her messages.

"You're so busted," Lily whispered, scandalized and envious.

Sophie pinched Lily's arm.

"Ow!"

Immediately, Richard turned on them. "She was . . ." Lily began her whispered defense.

"She is such a . . ." Sophie said.

"Shh." Richard cut them off.

Too late. Their grandmother whipped around. Someone else turned too—a stranger, pained and furious.

Sylvia glared at Richard and he heard her silent reproach. Do something. Make them stop. For shame. Because of course it was his fault his daughters did not know how to behave.

Even now, the girls were whispering, fighting quietly.

The stranger shushed them.

Lew turned, mouthing, Take them out.

In the pause between movements while the audience was coughing, Lily felt an iron hand on her thin shoulder. Sophie felt it too.

Their father frog-marched them into the night.

"You're hurting me," Lily pleaded.

Their dad propelled them across the lawn past picnickers and candles flickering. He marched them to the gate where you could still hear notes of the piano, cascading like beads onto a tile floor.

"Give me your phones." Richard faced his daughters in the parking lot beside their car.

"Dad!" Sophie protested.

"Now."

"I'm *sorry,*" she told him. Too late. He wrested the phone from Sophie's hand.

Then he turned to Lily. She protested, "I wasn't using mine!"

But he took it anyway. He did that thing he always did, punishing equally, even when it wasn't fair.

"I didn't do anything," Lily protested. "I didn't even touch my phone."

Richard ignored her. "What is wrong with the two of you? Why can't you sit and listen?"

They looked at him with pale faces, and Lily began to speak. "Because it's . . ."

"What?"

In a small voice she said, "Boring."

Then for a moment he did not know what to say. He found the music boring too—but he couldn't admit it. In the war between children and adults he had pledged allegiance to the parental side. "I don't care if it's boring," he said at last. "Sitting at that concert is the one thing your grandmother asked you to do. Didn't I tell you no phones?"

The girls said nothing.

"Didn't I?"

Their silence infuriated him.

"Get in the car."

They got in and closed the doors and he leaned against his SUV and missed his children. He missed the feeling they were really his. He missed fatherhood, which was now a time-share. He missed his whole life, and he thought, I was happy before all this. It wasn't true. He had not been happy, but he had been unhappy in a different way.

He took a deep breath and gazed at the drivers who stood outside their buses smoking. Then he opened his car door and took his seat.

He drove in silence, conscious of the girls, white and scared in the rearview mirror.

When they reached the house, he got out and the girls followed timidly.

He looked at his sad daughters and returned their phones.

Thanks, Dad, they said.

"I won't take it out at a concert again," said Sophie.

For a minute they stood with him, and he spoke softly. "I'm sorry I lost my temper—but you embarrassed me!" He knew from couples counseling that I'm sorry but is not the greatest apology. You should just say I'm sorry period. But simply saying I'm sorry did not convey what he felt for his daughters. His fury and sympathy with them.

The girls climbed the stairs and hid up in their rooms while he sat on the porch scrolling on his phone until he saw Lew drive up with Sylvia, Phoebe, and Wyatt.

Richard was sure Sylvia would mention Sophie and Lily. Then he would have to apologize and justify himself. He might have to say, Look, they're just kids. They know nothing about Mozart, okay? He imagined saying, Yes, they were out of line but that's not necessarily an indication of my parenting abilities. This was an extreme situation! Also, you were the ones insisting on bringing them. But he did not need these retorts.

Walking up the porch steps, Sylvia did not mention the girls. Lew didn't either. Everyone was talking about Schubert, in the second half. How the symphony began to build. How it kept you in suspense. "It's got this great edge," Wyatt was saying as they walked inside.

Phoebe said, "It's like a cliff."

"I wish you could have heard it," Sylvia told Richard, mildly, as though she had forgotten why he'd left.

Wyatt was singing something for Lew, demonstrating the progression of the chords. The house was lively, and Lew was opening champagne.

"What a performance," Lew said.

Only late at night, after a second and third bottle, did everybody go to bed. Lew and Sylvia went first, and then Richard retired to his room on the second floor.

Phoebe and Wyatt went up last of all. Phoebe stumbled on the stairs to the third floor, and Wyatt laughed softly, "You're tipsy."

"No, I'm not," she countered, cozy and lightheaded.

"Hey, who is this?" Wyatt said when they reached the upper landing.

"Lily?" Phoebe peered at the little girl wrapped in her blanket. "Are you okay?"

"Yes."

"How long have you been sitting here?"

Lily didn't answer. Then she said, "A while."

"You should sleep."

"I know."

"What's wrong?" said Phoebe, but Wyatt darted her a look because they both knew. They had heard at intermission. "Have you tried counting something?"

"It doesn't work," said Lily.

"Yeah, it really doesn't," Wyatt agreed, as though he had been her age once too.

Phoebe started to say something else, but she couldn't help yawning, and Wyatt kissed her shoulder. He said, "You should go to bed," and she turned to go, but he stayed with Lily a moment longer. He did not forget her. "Listen," he told Lily. "Go back to your room, and I'll play for you."

Phoebe paused on the landing to warn, "You'll wake everybody up."

"Just very quietly." Wyatt spoke to Lily. "Go lie down, okay?" She didn't answer, but she stood with her blanket draped around her shoulders. He said, "Lie in your bed and wait."

She glanced back at him, and her look was wistful, almost disbelieving, but she did as he said. She padded to her room, slipped under the covers, and lay on her back, staring at the slanted ceiling.

No sound. For a long time, all was still, and then she heard heavy footsteps on the stairs. Was Wyatt carrying his cello? Was he on the landing? She heard him open his bedroom door and close it. Then a murmur and soft tuning. And finally, his music—not like the bluegrass in the afternoon, or the cascading piano. Music of the trees. The sound of leaves unfurling.

Richard heard it in his bedroom below and wondered, Why is he practicing now?

Sylvia heard it in her bed and said, "Lew? What is that?"

"Bach," said Lew, mostly asleep. "Turn off the radio."

But Lily heard vines growing all around her. Over and around her bed, they twined like thorny fairytale roses. She lay still with her eyes closed, surrounded by the woody sound, and she needed nothing. She missed no one. She was safe and dreaming. Hidden for a hundred years.

10

Days of Awe

In September, my people remember.
—Florence Jeanne Goodman

They are driving to see Grandma Sylvia and Grandpa Lew for Yom Kippur when Lily says, "I think I'm feeling worse."

Her dad Richard says, "What do you mean worse?"

Lily doesn't answer that because worse means worse. She's carsick. She's *always* carsick, her older sister Sophie says, but it's not true. Only when they drive to Boston.

Actually, it's not Boston; they are driving to Weston, where there is nothing to do. It's a six-hour drive and Lily is sitting in front, as per usual. That's how Sophie puts it.

"Come on, Soph," says Richard. "You have the whole back seat to yourself."

Sophie leans her head on her pillow and closes her eyes. She thinks Lily is faking so she can sit in front. Lily knows that. Her sister is fifteen and hardly believes anything about her. Lily is twelve and should have outgrown carsickness by now, but hasn't.

"Try eating something," her dad says.

Lily unzips her backpack and pulls out the peanut butter granola bar her mom packed for her. Even the orange wrapper makes her queasy. "Could we just stop and walk around?"

"We're making good time," Richard tells her. "We're almost there."

Suddenly she feels it coming. She tries to stop it, but she can't, so they have to pull over. Lily's dad cleans her seat while she changes in the women's room at the rest area. She stands at the sinks, and her face is freckled in the mirror; her arms are thin as sticks. She is wearing a clean T-shirt from her suitcase. Her dirty shirt is too disgusting to bring back to the car, so she throws it in the trash.

"Better?" her dad asks when they start driving again.

"Sort of."

"I wish we were there already," says Sophie.

"I wish we were home," says Lily. When her parents divided up the holidays, her dad got Yom Kippur. That's why they are driving to his parents'. "Dad?" she says, after a while.

"Open the window and lean out."

"I just have a question."

"Okay."

"Why can't Grandma and Grandpa come to us?"

"Because they like their own services."

"No, they don't. They're always in a bad mood."

"That's just Yom Kippur."

"It's not fun."

"It's not supposed to be."

"I wish I was a different religion."

"Well. All religions have something."

"Is Grandma Sylvia religious?"

Richard looks over at Lily. "No."

"Is Grandpa Lew?"

"Not at all."

"Then why do they celebrate Yom Kippur?"

"*Because* they're not religious."

"What does that mean?"

Sophie suggests, "They're guilty."

"They aren't guilty," Richard says.

"What are they then?" Lily asks.

"What do you mean, what are they? They're Jewish people who go to temple on Yom Kippur."

"But why?" Lily says. Because why did they pick this holiday—the depressing one? Why would you choose to sit in temple fasting in cold air-conditioning? Grandma Sylvia always says the air-conditioning is so cold someone should do something, and then she has a headache.

The Weston house is glass, so you can see the trees outside. The furniture and rugs are white. There are no stairs, and all the doors and cabinets are white, so you can't find anything.

"Hello, sweetheart!" Grandma Sylvia is not in a bad mood yet. She hugs Lily and smears lipstick on her cheek. Sophie gets a lipstick kiss too.

There is honey cake in the oven, and it smells sticky-sweet. Lily lingers in the kitchen, but they have to keep an eye on the time, because it's later than it's supposed to be. Grandpa Lew says, "Girls, go ahead and unpack and we'll have a quick bite."

Lew has a thing about unpacking. He always says, Don't live out of a suitcase—but Sophie and Lily do anyway. As soon as they get to their room, they stuff their suitcases into the closet without unzipping them.

Their bedroom is white with white twin beds and a black nightstand between them. The beds are so white and the duvets so fluffy that Lily is afraid to make a dent. On each bed stands a black pillow with a white cursive letter. *S* for Sophie. *L* for Lily.

"Why is this house so bleak?" Lily asks Sophie.

"Bleak?" Sophie jumps face down onto her bed.

"The Lenox house is pretty."

"This one is more important," Sophie says.

"For what?"

Before Sophie can answer, their dad knocks and opens the door. "Timc to change."

"Can I bring a book?" asks Lily.

"To *Kol Nidre*? No! And no phones either."

Everyone is in a rush, dressing up and eating dinner. The honey cake is golden brown, and it's got toasted walnuts and it's still warm, but Lew upsets Sylvia by having seconds. His blood sugar will go through the roof.

"Don't do that!" Sylvia says.

Lew talks back. "Don't mind if I do."

Sylvia says, "I thought you were worried we'd be late."

Meanwhile, Sophie whispers to Lily, "Isn't this so fun?" Sometimes, when she is away from all her friends, Sophie is sarcastic with Lily, instead of against her.

Side by side, the girls sit in the back of Grandpa Lew's black SUV while their dad drives Sylvia. Together, they walk into the temple and take their places next to their dad and behind their grandparents. At least five hundred people fill the sanctuary, but the girls don't know anybody.

They are wearing white which is the tradition so you'll look pure and think about the shroud you'll wear when you are dead. Sophie's dress has puffed sleeves and a square neckline. Lily's dress is sleeveless, but she is wearing a white cardigan. The dresses are babyish, but at least no one they know will see them. That's what Sophie says.

The rabbi is up there in a white robe, and the cantor is wearing white as well. She is slowly chanting *kol nidre, v'esserei, ushvuei* which means all vows and oaths because all promises are canceled on Yom Kippur. After this holiday you can start the year with a clean slate—except first you have to ask forgiveness for all the things that you have done and for all the things everybody else has done intentionally or unintentionally, and for all the things anybody might even have been thinking about doing.

"We ask as a community," says the rabbi. "Have we lived up to our potential? Have we been the people we should be?"

Lily runs her fingers over the brass plaque on the pew in front of her. IN MEMORY OF JEANNE RUBINSTEIN.

"Have we been good to each other?" The rabbi's voice is piercing. "Have we *done* good? There is injustice in our world. Hunger. Pain. Abuse. Discrimination. There is systemic racism in our country. Sexism. Violence. Think back on this year. Did we step up?" He pauses. "Or did we stand by?"

"Look," Lily whispers to Sophie very very softly so their dad won't take them out into the parking lot and lecture them.

"What?"

She points to the brass plaque. "It's Great-Aunt Jeanne."

Sophie leans forward to read the name. "Are you sure?"

"Who else could it be?" Jeanne was Sylvia's younger sister, the one who died of cancer. Sylvia has an older sister too. Her name is Helen, and she won't speak to Sylvia because when Jeanne died, Sylvia baked an apple cake. Why was that wrong? Nobody knows, but it's a feud.

"Please rise," the rabbi says.

Lily is already hungry on the ride back. By the time they get to the house, she's starving, even though she had dinner earlier. She shouldn't be hungry so soon. She's not even fasting, but her dad is, and Grandma Sylvia and Grandpa Lew are, and Sophie sort of is, and Lily can't eat in front of them.

Her grandparents and her dad sit in the family room which is open to the kitchen, so Lily can't sneak a bite.

She waits and waits, until at last she and Sophie can escape to their room. Then while Sophie is brushing her teeth, Lily finds the granola bar in her backpack. She hides it under her pillow and dives under the covers, pretending to sleep.

For a long time, Sophie sits cross-legged on her bed texting friends. She is sitting there laughing, while Lily's stomach growls. Finally, Sophie turns off the light on the nightstand, and Lily rips open the wrapper and starts nibbling. She takes the smallest bites possible and chews with her mouth closed, but after just one second Sophie says, "What are you eating?"

"Nothing."

Sophie turns on the light. "You're eating a peanut butter granola bar in *bed*?"

"Where else can I eat it? Everybody's fasting!"

"You're getting crumbs everywhere."

"No I'm not."

"Yes you are." Sophie turns off the light.

Lily rolls onto her stomach and pulls the duvet over her head, but even then, Sophie says, "Could you stop chewing?"

When Lily opens her eyes, the sun is shining through the trees. The room is green and gold, lovely as a secret garden. Sophie is fast asleep. All is quiet. Lily grabs her book and tiptoes to the kitchen.

She touches white cabinets, and they spring open, revealing coffee and sugar and spices and dried mushrooms. She opens a drawer, and it's a refrigerator full of yogurt but it's plain. She checks the other cabinets, one after another. There it is. The remains of the honey cake encased in plastic wrap. She finds a huge knife and cuts the cake on the white stone counter. The cake is amber and just a tiny bit sticky on the outside. Her slice is golden, tender, crumbly. It's ambrosia. Ambrose! She cuts a second piece and stuffs it in her mouth. She eats a third. Then there's just a little piece left, so she eats that too. She can't help it that she's growing.

Hidden in the kitchen wall stands the refrigerator, but all the milk is Lactaid, so Lily drinks tap water. She leans over and sticks her head under the faucet so she doesn't have to use a glass. After that, she throws away the plastic wrap and brushes the cake crumbs into the sink and washes them down the drain. She rinses the knife and dries it with a paper towel and puts it away. She is afraid someone will walk in and scold her—but no one does. Only in the distance she can hear running water. Someone's shower.

She jumps onto the white couch and opens *Ballet Shoes,* which she has read a hundred times. She has read all the shoe books by Noel Streatfeild—*Tennis Shoes, Circus Shoes, Skating Shoes, Theatre Shoes,* but *Ballet Shoes* is her favorite. It's about orphans in England who make a pact to be famous. They are sisters and they make a vow.

"Good morning, sweetheart." Grandpa Lew is already dressed and standing over her.

"Hi." Startled, she looks up at him.

"I said good morning." Grandpa Lew has a thing about greeting people properly. He has a lot of things.

"Good morning," Lily answers.

"Ready for the onslaught?"

She closes her book. "I wish we could stay here."

"You and me both," Lew tells her.

It's weird, because he is an adult so if he doesn't want to do something he doesn't have to. Why would a grown-up drive somewhere he doesn't want to go?

Once again Sylvia and Lew and Richard and the girls take two cars to the temple. Lily's father and grandfather are wearing dark suits and Sylvia is wearing a white suit with rough edges, like the fabric is going to unravel. Her skirt is narrow, and her pocketbook has its own gold feet.

Lily is wearing her white cardigan again, but this time her dress is black. She stares at her sandals as the service rolls over her. There is nothing to do and nothing to read but the prayer book with Hebrew on one side and English on the other. While the cantor sings about being poor, trembling, and unworthy, Lily leans forward and rests her head on the pew with the plaque for Jeanne.

"Lily?" her dad whispers. "Are you okay?"

"I think I'm getting carsick again," she whispers back.

"Oh, please," Sophie says.

But everyone else thinks she might actually throw up and that can't happen. Not in the sanctuary.

"She needs to eat," Richard tells Grandma Sylvia.

"Dad, she is not sick," Sophie protests.

"Shh."

"She's just trying to get out of here," Sophie whispers furiously.

"She's white as a sheet," says Grandpa Lew.

Richard says, "I think she's got to have some lunch."

"I'll take her." Sylvia is already picking up her pocketbook.

"It's okay, Mom. I can take her out," says Richard.

"No, I'll go." Sylvia leads Lily between the pews, into the social hall. Grandma Sylvia's heels tap the terrazzo floor out of the temple, past the police and into the parking lot.

"Where are we . . ." Lily begins.

"Not now."

"But can I ask you something?"

"Lily. I have a splitting headache. Get in the car."

Usually, Grandma Sylvia calls you darling. She says you and your sister are the apple of my eye, and Lily thinks wouldn't that be apples? Sylvia says she always wanted a daughter of her own, but it wasn't in the cards. That's why she is so happy to have two granddaughters. When they were little she bought them dolls and now she takes them clothes shopping—not for school clothes but for party dresses. She helped Lily pick out her Bat Mitzvah dress and silver sandals. Even with a headache, she is the fanciest person Lily knows. That's why it's strange to drive up to McDonald's.

"We're going to eat *here*?" Lily cannot picture her grandma sitting at one of those tables. What if she gets ketchup on her unraveled sleeves? Where will she put the pocketbook? But Grandma Sylvia knows what she is doing. She eases her Lexus into the drive-thru and orders, "One hamburger, one small fries. One large coffee, black."

"Wait," Lily says, because she is not allowed to drink coffee, but Sylvia ignores her.

"Anything else?" the lady inside asks.

Lily ventures, "One medium strawberry milkshake."

"Do you want whipped cream on that?" the lady asks.

Sylvia answers for Lily. "No thank you."

"Will that be all?"

"Yes." With a jingle of bracelets, Grandma Sylvia is pulling out her wallet.

They place the drinks in the cupholders between them, and Lily gobbles down her burger and fries. She eats and eats, and the whole time, she is staring at Grandma Sylvia, who is sipping the black coffee. "I thought you were fasting."

"I *am* fasting," Sylvia informs her.

It's raining lightly, and they are not returning to the temple. "Where are we going?"

"To visit my parents." Sylvia's voice is so strange that for a moment Lily is afraid of her. Her eyes are hard; her face is old. Lily feels almost kidnapped.

"How can we visit your parents?" Lily says, because they are dead. Then she sees the signs. They are driving to a cemetery.

"I thought they lived in Brooklyn."

Grandma Sylvia parks the car. "First they lived in Brooklyn, and then they moved to Brookline. Coolidge Corner! They died at Hebrew SeniorLife, and this is where they're buried. Come on out. No. Leave the milkshake."

Lily steps out of the car. Slowly, she follows her grandma into the cemetery with its rows of gravestones. "Stay on the path," Sylvia warns, and Lily realizes with a shock that when you walk on the grass you are stepping on bodies. She looks at the gentle mounds of earth and imagines all the dead people, lying on their backs. Face up. Toes up.

"Hurry," says Sylvia because it's drizzly and they have no umbrella. Lily buttons up her little sweater. "Here we are," her grandma tells her. They are facing two black granite gravestones. "You see," Sylvia says. "This is my father, Morris." She stands silently before the grave. She is quiet for so long that Lily turns to look at her. "He was a wonderful wonderful man," Sylvia says. "So patient. You know, he was a cardiologist. For many many years he practiced medicine at Beth Israel. All his life he healed people's hearts. That's his Hebrew name, Mordechai Yaacov. Can you read it?"

Lily sounds out the Hebrew letters. "Mor-de-chai Ya-a-cov."

"And here you are," her grandma tells her.

"Me?"

"Great-Grandma Lillian. And here's your Hebrew name. Leah Channah."

Lily stares at her namesake's gravestone. "Take a rock," her grandma tells her.

Lily finds a pebble. "Not that one. That's too small!" Sylvia sounds insulted.

Lily pries a bigger rock from the mud. It's round on the bottom but rough on top. "Go ahead," Sylvia says. "Put it right there."

Cautiously, Lily places the rock on top of Lillian's granite stone.

"And now one for Great-Grandpa Morris," Sylvia says.

Lily finds another rock and places that one too. Then she looks up hopefully, but her grandma isn't done. She just stands there.

At last, Sylvia sighs. "Well, here we are."

Lily says, "Yes."

"It's a cold, cold day."

"*Really* cold," Lily agrees.

"And I miss you," Sylvia says.

Then Lily realizes that her grandma isn't talking to her. She is talking to her parents in their graves. "I miss confiding in you," Sylvia says. "I miss your advice. I'm not like Jeanne and Helen. I don't always know better than everybody else. And now Jeanne is gone, and

Helen might as well be." Her voice trembles. "I would forgive her, but she won't let me."

For several minutes, Sylvia stands there. When she speaks again, her voice is wobbly. "We're scattered. Some of us in Boston, some in New Jersey. Brooklyn. I hardly see Richard and the girls."

"Grandma?" Lily says, because she is right here.

Sylvia amends, "Except for the occasional holiday." She opens her pocketbook and extracts her phone. Is she texting Lily's dad? Is she going to tell him we're on our way back and not to worry? No. She holds up her phone to show photos to Morris and Lillian lying underground. "This is the dinner we had for Lew's old law clerks. That was a wonderful occasion. This is Lew making a speech. And here's a picture of us at CJP—the fundraiser. We went to Paris in April. These are all photos from that trip. Here is Notre-Dame. And the Tuileries. See the fountain? We met a wonderful couple who know the Goldbergs. These were our peonies this year. The best we've ever had." Sylvia lingers over the next picture, and then she pans her phone from left to right so that both graves can get a look. "This is the girls and Cousin Phoebe and her boyfriend Wyatt at Tanglewood. We had a lovely time."

If Lily had her phone she would be texting her mom *help!* Because does her grandma really believe her parents can see these pictures and hear what she is telling them? Is she going crazy? "Mother, I made the Grossinger honey cake," Sylvia says. "It was perfect, but I used walnuts. You don't like them, but they add something. Right, Lily?"

Lily nearly jumps.

"I have Lily here," Sylvia tells her parents. "Lily, do you have anything to say?"

Lily shakes her head.

"You've got a Bat Mitzvah next month," Sylvia prompts. "Do you want to tell about that?" But all Lily wants to do is run away. "She's shy," Sylvia says. "She doesn't like to talk. We're hoping she grows out of that." She frowns at Lily. "All right, that's it," Sylvia tells her parents. "Just remember, I think about you all the time."

Hard raindrops pierce Lily's clothes as Sylvia turns to go. Head down, Lily follows, taking the path between the rows. "You need to speak up," Sylvia tells her in the parking lot.

To dead people? Lily thinks.

"You were never so quiet when you were younger." Sylvia unlocks the car.

"I'm sorry." Lily doesn't know why she says that.

"Well, I hope you'll visit me when I'm—" Sylvia says—and then she stops. Keys in her hand, she watches another car pull up. A black umbrella emerges, and Lily sees why her grandma can't move. It's Helen. It's the unforgiving Helen under there. Helen who is dressed for the weather in black rain boots.

Lily's first thought is to duck inside the Lexus, but Great-Aunt Helen sees her. She is coming closer. "Lily, is that you?" Helen says.

"Yes," Lily says faintly.

"How are you, sweetheart?" Helen talks as though she can't see Sylvia standing there.

"I'm good." Lily feels rain soaking through her sweater and her dress.

"And how is your father? And your sister?"

Lily senses Sylvia bristling. She can feel her grandma's indignation and her hurt, a whole private thunderstorm—but Sylvia says nothing. "They're fine," Lily says. At the same time, she thinks, I should speak up! "It's a coincidence," she says.

Helen says, "What is?"

Lily's heart is pounding. "That you both come here."

Even then, Helen does not acknowledge Sylvia. Helen says, "It's not a coincidence. I come here every year." And she adds, "Don't you have a raincoat? Or an umbrella? You'll catch cold."

"We're leaving," Sylvia declares, as though Helen is insulting her grandmother skills. Is she? Is that what's happening? "Get in," Sylvia tells Lily.

In an instant, Lily ducks inside, and her grandma follows, slamming the door.

For a second, Sylvia sits staring. Then she starts the car.

"Where are we going now?" Lily asks after a few minutes.

Her grandma answers, "You know where."

There are fewer people at temple in the afternoon. Apart from Lily's family, their row is empty.

"Where were you?" Sophie asks Lily, who is still dripping. "Did you get lunch?"

"Yes."

"Lucky!"

"But it was terrible!"

"Where did you go?"

Richard shushes them.

So they sit quietly, and Lily feels Sophie's curiosity. It's a strange tickling sensation. It's just so rare. Usually Lily doesn't have anything her sister wants.

"But did you—" Sophie whispers.

"Stop it," their dad whispers because the rabbi is speaking. He is in the middle of the afternoon sermon, and he is walking up and down. He wears a little headset with a microphone so everyone can hear him.

"Let me conclude with a story from our tradition. And this one is not about doing wrong. It's about doing right. Long ago, there were two brothers, and they were farmers on adjoining plots of land. One brother was successful. His farm was profitable. He had plenty of money, but he had no children. The other brother was less prosperous. He had much less money, but he had several children.

"When it was time, the two brothers harvested their wheat and gathered the grain. The prosperous one thought to himself, I have plenty—more than I need. I will give some of my grain to my brother who has less money. But he did not want to embarrass his brother, so he waited until night—and then he transferred the grain to his brother's pile.

"Meanwhile, the less prosperous one thought to himself, I have a large family, and my brother does not. I will give some grain to my brother who has no children. He did not want to call attention to his gift, and so he waited until night—and then he added grain to his brother's pile.

"In the morning the brothers were confused. Each had given away some grain, but his pile was the same size as it had been before. The prosperous brother said to himself, I will try again. Once again he waited until dark and added grain to the poorer brother's pile. Meanwhile, the poorer brother was thinking the same thing, and after dark, he added grain to the childless brother's pile. In the morning the brothers were confused again. Why were their piles undiminished? That night each brother went one last time to add grain to the other's harvest—but this time, the two stumbled upon each other in the dark. You! they exclaimed. You did this! And the brothers embraced!

"And it's said that their love illuminated the darkness!"

The rabbi pauses. Everybody in the sanctuary waits, but Lily hears a strange snuffling. She peeks over her dad and sees her grandma crying. She is bending over her pocketbook, taking out tissues, as tears pour down her face. Grandpa Lew is holding Sylvia's hand, but it's not helping, and Lily knows why.

"What if our secrets were good deeds instead of bad?" the rabbi says. "What if our missed signals stem from generosity and modesty, instead of stubbornness and pride? What if we plot to bring honor instead of shame? What if we sneak out to give instead of take? What would our lives be like? What would this world become? It's said that where the brothers came upon each other—that's where the temple was built in Jerusalem. What happened to that temple?"

The rabbi pauses. Then he says, "It was destroyed. But we remember love. We remember generosity. We hold out hope that we may rebuild that temple speedily in our days."

Sylvia and Lew and all the people left in temple say amen.

The cantor announces, "Please rise and read responsively," but Sylvia buries her head on Lew's shoulder.

"Grandma," Lily whispers.

Her dad says, "It's okay, Lily. She always cries." But he wasn't there. He doesn't know.

"Dad, I have to go out," Lily says. "I have to take a break."

"You just had a break," he tells her.

"I didn't!" Sophie says.

"We'll come back," Lily tells her dad. Then, before he can argue, she and Sophie slip away.

"Where did you go?" Sophie demands as soon as they step into the social hall.

"McDonald's."

"*What?* I've been sitting here starving and you went to McDonald's?"

"And Grandma had coffee."

"Are you joking?"

Lily shakes her head. "And we went to the cemetery!"

"Girls." It's an usher standing by the door.

"Come on." Lily leads the way, even though she doesn't know where she is going. She races into a hallway, and Sophie rushes after her. Lily stops and tries a door, but it's locked. She tries another. The second door opens and it's a medium-sized room with pews and two stained-glass windows. Sophie turns on the lights and Lily sees that it's an empty chapel. She stands with Sophie in the aisle. "Okay, you aren't going to believe this," Lily says.

"What?"

Lily speaks slowly, drawing out the suspense. "We went to the cemetery, and we talked to Great-Grandma and Great-Grandpa."

"What do you mean talked to them?"

"As if they were alive."

"That's so weird."

"I know!"

"That's so superstitious."

"And then we saw Great-Aunt Helen."

"In real life?"

"Yes! But she and Grandma would not say one word. It was like they were two ghosts. That's why she's crying."

"What do you mean?"

"That's why Grandma is crying. Because of the sermon. Because it's *symbolic*."

Sophie looks skeptical.

"You don't understand."

Sophie stretches out full length on a pew. "You mean I had to be there?"

"Yeah. It was terrible."

"What do you mean, terrible?" Sophie lifts her head. "You had lunch!"

"It's not my fault, I'm younger."

"Yes it is! I've been sitting here all day."

"You have not."

"Symbolically."

Lily frowns. "You're always mean."

"I'm always stuck in the sanctuary!"

"And you're never sorry," Lily says.

"Sorry not sorry."

"What?"

"Nothing."

"What if we get estranged?" Lily stands over Sophie.

"What are you talking about?"

"What if we grow up and stop speaking?"

"What if you just talked less?"

"You aren't nice to me." Lily's voice wobbles.

"You don't give me reason."

"I don't want to have a feud!"

"Are you going to start crying?" Sophie asks.

"No."

"Okay. Then we won't have a feud."

"You aren't even listening," Lily says.

"You aren't talking like a normal person."

"I'm serious."

Sophie closes her eyes. "Okay."

"Could you promise you won't pretend that I'm invisible?"

"Sure."

"You have to sit up! And say it like a vow."

"Like *Ballet Shoes*?"

"Swear."

Half laughing, Sophie sits up. "I, Sophie Rose Eisen, solemnly swear that I will not pretend you are invisible."

"And that we will never be estranged," Lily says.

"And that we will never be estranged. As long as we both shall live."

"Now me," says Lily. "I, Lily Anne Eisen, solemnly swear that I will never pretend you are invisible and we will never be estranged as long as we both shall live."

"Okay."

"We should take a needle and prick our fingers," Lily says.

"Um, *no*." Sophie starts walking around the room. The walls are covered with memorial plaques. You can read hundreds and hundreds of names in Hebrew and in English. SAMUEL FISCHELL. DOLLY FISCHELL. IDA RINGEL. HAL RINGEL. BELLE COHEN, HYMAN COHEN, ISIDORE BIRNBAUM, ANITA BIRNBAUM, GERTRUDE BIRNBAUM, HERBERT SCHWARZ, MILTON ENGEL, MILLIE NADLER, ANNIE LINZER, NATHANIEL BARZILAI, LESLIE LINZER, BEATRICE GOLDFARB, MYRA GLUSSMAN, ARTHUR GLUSSMAN, DOROTHY MARKOWITZ, RITA LEVINE, ABRAHAM LEVINE, FAY DERSHOWITZ . . .

"Look." Next to each name is a tiny lightbulb and when Sophie turns the bulb the light comes on.

"I don't think you're allowed to do that," Lily warns.

Sophie spins around. "I don't think you're allowed to finish a whole honey cake."

Lily gasps—because how did her sister see? "I was really really hungry."

"You don't know what hunger is!" Sophie keeps turning bulbs. She turns on every single memorial light, until they hear footsteps in the hall.

For a second, they freeze. All the tiny lights blaze down on them. Then they scoot out of the chapel.

"I told you not to!" Lily whispers to Sophie.

For once, Sophie looks nervous, because everyone who walks in will see the lights. "It's too late to change them back."

They hurry away from the chapel, hoping no one will see. Rushing through the Social Hall, they see caterers carrying tables, but the girls don't stay to watch. They race back to the sanctuary. At the big doors, they stop to catch their breaths. Then they walk down the aisle to their seats.

Prayer is an ocean. The girls stand, holding the pew in front of them, trying to endure the waves of song. It feels like a week, a year of standing. It feels like dissolving in a trance, but at last the cantor holds up the shofar and begins to blow. She blows and blows the horn and there is nothing anyone can do but listen.

Then, suddenly, the day is over, and the congregation pours into the Social Hall. The girls load up plates with bagels and cream cheese and lox and noodle kugel and apple kugel and pasta salad and brownies and chocolate-dipped cookies. Their dad is on his phone checking messages. Their grandpa is drinking schnapps. Their grandma is standing with the other ladies in their suits, and she is smiling. Her pocketbook is on her shoulder and a coffee cup is in her hand, and it's as if she never even went to the cemetery and she never saw her sister and she never cried.

When they get home, nobody even thinks of honey cake. The day was too long, and there were too many desserts at the Break Fast. It's only the next morning that Grandma Sylvia says, "What happened to the rest of the cake? I'm sure I put it in here. Lew?"

"I never touched it."

"Then where did it go?"

Grandma Sylvia looks at Lily, and so does her dad. Everyone is looking at her, and Lily thinks she should tell the truth. Admit she got so hungry that she couldn't help herself. But she is too embarrassed—and she is watching Sophie's face. It's a test! Was it real, what she promised? If the vow is binding, Sophie won't tell on Lily.

Scared, excited, eager, Lily waits.

Sophie doesn't say a word.

11

This Is Not About Us

You don't have to be with someone every minute of the day. Richard was eating dinner at his desk when it came to him. Obvious, but true. Everyone had left, even the janitors, and he was peaceful, borderline happy with his computer and red curry. In the aftermath of his divorce, he had been frantic for companionship, affection, even conversation, and now suddenly he remembered that he enjoyed his own company. He didn't feel desperate at all. It was also true that he was dating his daughter's Bat Mitzvah tutor—but that wasn't what it seemed.

Lily's tutor was thirty-four, not a college kid like you might think. Heather had dual degrees in Jewish education and art therapy. She was a certified adult. The temple youth director! And Richard's ex approved of her. Debra had hired her, after all, and she said, quote unquote, "Heather is amazing for Lily." Debra did not know that Heather was amazing for Richard too—but in due course he would tell her, and she would be . . . okay. Probably. Meanwhile, they were not going public because they were focusing on the Bat Mitzvah, which Heather said is not about us. Richard had never been with anyone so sane. It was strange, after so many years of crazy.

He and Debra had met when they were practically children, junior counselors at Ramah Palmer. Debra had been slender then, with beautiful dark eyes, and she had known exactly what she wanted. She had been particular from the beginning, always a planner, not just day to day, but for the future. She had a vision, and even though they went to different colleges, he to Penn, and she to Brandeis, she never doubted that they would adhere to their established course. True, Richard veered a little, but she brought him back. She told him to stop smoking and he stopped. She said why do you drink so much? and he admitted that he had no reason, except that it was fun. On weekends when she came to Philly, they went to the gym. It had been her idea to go to law school together, and they had married as 1Ls at Boston University. They would run along the river; she would tie back her black hair, and he had loved her, not just for herself, but for the way she loved him. Only life and time could change that.

How had it begun? Their family and their house and their two cars and even their dog required more attention than anybody had anticipated. Their older daughter, Sophie, had dyslexia, and Lily suffered from anxiety. Debra gave up her career to manage everyone at home, and the girls started ice-skating, piano, cello, ballet, and gymnastics. He got exhausted, and Debra got angry. It was the old story, only worse, because it was happening to them.

Richard worked more; they fought more. He started smoking again, which Debra took as a betrayal. She chopped off her hair, and he gained weight. She said he was not around. He said how could he be if he had to pay for everything? Short version—their lawyers fought it out, her lawyers won, and Richard could hardly remember those starry nights at Palmer. Well, that was thirty years ago, as Heather pointed out. She was so wise.

And she was calm. This was the first thing Richard had noticed—apart from her sea-green eyes and her long legs and lovely neck.

Sane and calm, she tutored Lily who had balked early on, and now learned eagerly.

He loved to watch when Lily had her lesson at his house. Lily sat with Heather to practice her Torah portion, the story of Noah, and even after Heather left, Lily would walk around murmuring and humming her parsha in Hebrew.

"She's into it," Richard told Heather when Lily was at her mother's house.

Heather said, "Yes. It's beautiful."

The Bat Mitzvah's less spiritual aspects were a source of stress. The caterer, the décor, the temple and its rules, one of which was that if your child wanted to chant that week's excerpt from the Prophets as well as the Torah portion, she had to speed through in under ten minutes. Rabbi Zlotnick explained, "Remember, we're doing two Bat Mitzvahs that day, so we have to keep the haftarah moving."

But what if your daughter felt a deep connection to Isaiah? What if she read slowly, but the haftarah was her favorite part, and her voice was so sweet she brought tears to your eyes? Still, ten minutes.

"She should just get up there and do it," Richard told Debra on the phone. "Who's going to stop her? It's not like the rabbi will have a stopwatch on the bima."

"They'll cut her off," Debra insisted. "If the rabbi doesn't, then the cantor will. She'll be crushed!"

"Have you seen anybody cut off on their Bar Mitzvah?"

"I've heard of it."

"Rabbi Z. would never let that happen." Questioningly, Richard looked at Heather, who was sitting with him on the couch, exactly where Lily sat for lessons when she came over.

Meanwhile, he heard Debra on the phone. "Do you want your daughter to be the first?"

"I'll take out anyone who stops Lily's haftarah," he said in all seriousness.

"Wonderful."

"Why don't you ask Heather what to do?" Richard suggested.

Heather gestured no, no, even as Debra said, "I can't call her now. It's past ten."

"Tomorrow then."

"Okay, but what about the party favors? Could you please look at the links I sent?"

After he got off the phone, Richard and Heather studied the links to Lily-branded favors for her school friends and ballet friends.

"Wow," said Heather.

"Expensive," said Richard—not objecting, just observing. After all, this wasn't his first rodeo. He had paid for Sophie's three years before, and he knew how much coming-of-age cost. A friend at work likened his son's Bar Mitzvah to purchasing a Mercedes and driving off a cliff. "Rabbi Z. wouldn't cut Lily off, right?"

"He'll time her at the rehearsal," Heather said, because of course she knew Rabbi Z. well. She worked for him. "She'll get it up to speed."

"Really?"

"Yeah."

Richard hugged Heather around the shoulders as he gazed at travel mugs in dusty rose with A Lil' Simcha printed in silver script. "Are these kids drinking coffee on their way to middle school?" He squinted at keychains with a frog on a lily pad. "Why does anybody need a Lily keychain?"

"Maybe these kids don't need anything," Heather ventured.

Yet another reason Richard loved her, but he had to say, "Debra's never gonna go for that. She's by the book."

"Get them blank books," said Heather, suddenly inspired. "That's so Lily."

"You're great," said Richard, which is how he ended up buying two dozen silver journals for Lily's friends, plus matching silver gel pens—but he didn't mind. He was at peace with Debra and the world. Living in the moment, driving to work, coming home and cooking dinner when Heather was free.

They walked together on the weekends. They watched movies on the couch, and they did not overplan. Heather still had her own apartment—at least until the lease was up. She was a Jewish educator who didn't preach, a vegetarian who didn't judge. With her encouragement, Lily was writing a poem about Noah and the animals for her Bat Mitzvah speech.

"Debra can't say enough about you," Richard told Heather, as they strolled to the duck pond where he and Debra used to take the girls.

"No, stop!" Heather covered her ears.

"You're funny," he said.

"I'm serious! Whenever you talk about Debra I feel unethical."

"What are you talking about?" Richard protested. "Unethical is dating your student—not your student's father."

"I don't know." Heather stared into the murky water. "I feel like it's a breach of trust."

"We're not a breach of anything."

"I'm not sure Debra would agree."

"What do you mean?"

"When she finds out."

"Then we'll tell her everything!"

"She'll be—"

"Okay yes, but—"

"Maybe we shouldn't see each other for the next three weeks."

"Don't be silly," Richard said.

"But it would help."

With what? he thought. They were adults, and they were free, for all intents and purposes. Legally, he and Debra were still married, but that was because their paperwork was still in process. And whose fault was that? Debra's lawyer who had spent two years demanding, contesting, and refusing everything. Richard and Heather had done nothing premeditated. They'd found each other by surprise. One Sunday morning Heather had come by for a lesson and it turned out Lily was at her mom's that weekend.

"I'm sorry," Heather kept apologizing. "I messed up the schedule."

"Come in, come in," he said, as Heather stood on the threshold calling Debra.

"Let's just pick it up next week," Richard heard Debra say, because it would take twenty minutes for Heather to drive over, and Lily had ballet. Heather apologized again, but Debra cut her off: "It's really no big deal." Clearly Debra adored her! "Not a problem," Debra insisted. Words she hardly said to anybody.

As soon as Heather ended the call, Richard had asked, "Would you like coffee?"

Heather hesitated. She'd kept him in suspense, and he was nervous, and she was shy—but then she stepped inside.

Even now, months later, he and Heather put Lily and Sophie and everybody else first. Heather was the most ethical person he had ever known, and never skittish—except for the Bat Mitzvah. "I'm just afraid we'll ruin Lily's day," she told Richard.

"What are you talking about?" he said.

Two weeks out, the menu, band, flowers, and balloons were set. They were going ahead with the haftarah, which Lily read confidently in ten minutes twenty seconds. (The rabbi wouldn't cut her off if she was that close. Right?) Lily had her expensive little dress, and Sophie had one too. Still, Heather worried.

At first, Richard thought she was anxious about Lily's big performance. Lily did have a history of stage fright—but Heather said, "No, that's not it."

"What then?" Richard asked. They were lying in his bed, and all was quiet. The girls were with their mom.

Heather said, "I just think . . ."

His phone rang and he leaned over the bed to find it on the floor. "Debra."

He was going to let it go to voicemail, but Heather said, "Answer it."

"Hi," Debra said.

"Hi."

Debra said, "We have a situation."

Overhearing, Heather scrambled out of bed. She didn't know that for Debra anything could qualify. An errant florist, a lost invitation. Just last week they'd learned that all balloons had to be inflated before sundown on Friday, because the synagogue did not allow inflating on Shabbat. And the balloons were helium, so they might start drooping if they went up too soon! These were Debra's situations. Why then was Heather getting dressed? He reached for her, but she shook her head.

"Okay, what is it?" he asked Debra.

"Your mother."

"Aha!" Just as he thought, this was no big deal.

Debra said, "What do you mean, aha? You need to talk to her."

"Okay. No problem."

"She found out Helen isn't coming."

"Why would Helen come when they aren't speaking?"

"I know, but she's distraught."

"Helen was never coming. Why did Mom think that?"

"You have to call her."

"And how is that going to help?" He was watching Heather put on her shoes.

"You know what, Richard?"

"Fine."

"There's a reason Sylvia called me first. There's a reason I know about all this."

"I said fine," Richard told Debra.

"Why am I *still* picking up the slack here?"

"I said I'd talk to her! Anything else?"

"Don't you speak that way to me."

Years ago, he might have said what way? And she would have said can you even hear yourself? And he would have said, what about you? How would you describe the way you're speaking now? But he didn't escalate. He said "Will do" and ended the call.

"I should go," Heather said.

"Please don't," he said.

"I told you. We should stay apart until after Lily's day."

"You're being superstitious."

"I'm not. I don't want to cause trouble."

"You could never do that. My mother will make trouble all by herself. My mother, and my aunt." His family was a weather system rolling in. Rain, wind, sleet.

Sylvia mourned on the phone that night. "It's because Helen doesn't have grandchildren of her own. She's jealous, and that's why she won't accept the invitation—to ruin it for me."

"Mom, why would Helen come? You haven't spoken since the cake!"

"What cake?"

"You know exactly what cake. Your apple cake."

"This has nothing to do with cake."

"Oh really?"

"Richard, you know what she did."

"No, actually," he began—but stopped himself. He wasn't going to argue about who did what. "The point is you're not speaking to her."

"I *am* speaking to her. She isn't speaking to me!"

"Okay, let's assume for a moment that all this could be true . . ."

"Don't lawyer me."

"Just let me ask you this. Why would Helen come to your granddaughter's Bat Mitzvah if she isn't speaking to you? Don't you think she would ruin it if she came?"

"No. She's ruining it now."

"Only if you let her," said Richard, with all the wisdom of his newfound happiness.

He was serene. He was listening to Heather, and they were staying apart. All they did was talk on the phone, and he was fine with that. Heather was the opposite of suffocating, and breathing felt so good—at least for the first few days. After a week, he called and said, "This might be overkill."

"It's not," said Heather. "We have to think of Debra."

"Believe me," Richard said, "I do."

"But it's different now."

"Don't be guilty."

"It's going to be weird."

"It will be okay," Richard insisted. "Eventually."

Don't look at me, Heather texted on Friday before pictures. The temple did not allow photography on Shabbat, so the family did formal photos on Friday afternoon. The photographer was setting up in the sanctuary as Richard texted back, *Won't look at you at all.* And he was good as his word, even when he and Debra and Heather had to huddle, double-checking who would have honors in the morning. He kept his eyes on Debra with her gray hair.

His mother and stepfather had arrived. His cousins were gathering for the family photos. Wendy and her wife, Jill. Dan and Melanie, with their waif Phoebe. Steve and Andrea with their huge sons. Everybody was embracing, although Debra's parents and her sister Becca stood apart. Becca had hated Richard from the beginning. She tucked her hair behind her ears (she was a large woman, but her ears were tiny) and whenever Richard glanced her way, he could hear her thinking, Overbearing selfish male asshole.

Silently, he defended himself, because he was not a monster. Male, yes, but he couldn't help that. Overbearing, no! Selfish, no!

He took the girls to nail appointments for God's sake. Endured every concert, school open house, and play.

"Which one of you is Sylvia?" The photographer consulted his cheat sheet. "Grandma, amiright? Which one of you is Lew?"

Once again, Richard didn't look at Heather as she set the Torah on the lectern and rolled the scrolls to the right place. He focused on Lily, posing with her blown-glass pointer, pretending to read.

His daughters stood before blush roses and cream lilies on the bima. "Beautiful girls," Sylvia said.

"It's true," he agreed.

"How lovely to be here together," Sylvia told Richard as his side of the family posed with the girls. "It's a blessing."

"It really is," he said, even as he sensed Heather standing just out of frame.

Sylvia sighed. "I just wish Helen could be here."

"Mom," Richard warned.

"I only have one sister left."

"Yup," said Richard, because that's what everybody had been saying since the feud began.

"But she's so stubborn; she'll die before she speaks to me. Or I'll die first."

"Good job, everyone," the photographer said.

There was a rehearsal dinner, but Heather didn't stay. The family sat at two long tables in the Social Hall and they ate a choice of prime rib or mushroom risotto. Richard texted Heather, *you good?*

And she texted back. *home now.*

All was well except for Sylvia, who grew maudlin as the evening ended, and began telling Lily about her namesake Lillian's last days. "There was nothing anyone could do, because the cancer spread to her spine," Sylvia told Lily. "Her bones broke like teacups, but she did not complain."

"Mom, do you think we could save that for another time?" said Richard.

In the parking lot as Debra prepared to take the girls home, Richard kissed Lily and said, "See you tomorrow, sweetie."

"Dad," Lily said, "why is Grandma always talking about dying?"

"She's just old," said Richard. "She's really very happy." Lily looked at him with her big eyes, and for a second she seemed almost tearful, but the moment passed and she ran off to Debra's car.

Richard woke alone to a perfect October day. He donned a new suit with a sky-blue tie and drove to temple, thinking how blessed he was, and how sweet his daughters were and how fortunate he was to have only two. This was the last event he would plan with Debra for years and years. They would never discuss caterers again—not until the weddings—and with any luck, Sophie would elope.

He arrived early, but the parking lot was almost full.

"I didn't realize we'd have such a crowd," Richard told the rabbi as he walked in.

"Well, it's a doubleheader," Rabbi Zlotnick said. "Not to mention we've got three baby namings. Shabbat shalom. It's a great day!" The rabbi greeted guests and congregants with his famous hugs. Meanwhile, Debra was consulting with Heather, who had her game face on.

"Where's your sister?" Richard asked Sophie.

"Car."

"What do you mean?"

"She's sitting in the car."

"In the parking lot?" Richard whipped out his phone.

"Don't," Debra warned. "I texted her already."

"Did you tell her the service is about to start?"

"She's coming," said Heather in her capacity as tutor. "She's just taking a moment."

"Well, I hope so," Richard said in his capacity as dad, the one who used to drive Lily home from sleepovers in the middle of the night.

Congregants were filing in. People from work. Richard's face was hot.

"We have to start," the associate rabbi Julie told him, even as Heather slipped out to see what she could do.

The cantor was singing from the bima, *"Ashrei yoshvei veitecha . . ."* Happy are those who dwell in your house, and Richard had no choice but to sit—but he kept glancing at the doors. There was time before the Torah reading, and it was true that Arielle, the other Bat Mitzvah girl, was first. They had split the chanting down the middle. Arielle was reading four aliyot and Lily was to read three plus the haftarah—if this wasn't a full-blown panic attack. She hadn't had one since she was nine, but here they all were, gathered at the temple. What better time?

Richard glanced at Debra sitting next to him, and she looked back as if to say, Don't move. Don't even breathe. The extended family rustled in the pews behind them, and they were curious—but he and Debra were in agony, because really? After all this? Was Lily going to punt now? Yes. He could see that Debra thought she would. No recrimination. No blame. They were united, because it was just as it had been when she was little. Lily was fine until the very end, until the moment all the other girls settled into sleeping bags, or the second that she had to step onstage. What fools they had been, pretending weekly therapy was enough to manage her anxiety. Obviously, Lily would never manage anything, and this would be their life with her forever. They were doomed . . . until Richard heard his mother whisper, "Oh, there she is."

A small pale Lily slipped into place next to Debra as Heather wrapped her striped tallis around her like a sheltering wing. Richard leaned forward just slightly, looking past Debra at Heather in her long blue cotton dress and woven tallis. He looked at her and she glanced back, half smiling.

And Debra saw and understood. She stared Richard straight in the face, and even after all their fights and all the litigation, his heart dropped, because she knew what he'd been keeping from her. Could you ever divorce, really? He had disappointed her again.

He tried to pretend nothing had happened. He knew that now of all times, he should maintain neutrality, but he wasn't neutral, and he was not an actor. Sitting with his family around him, in the midst of that congregation, he had stolen a look, and Heather had smiled. Of course, she was Lily's tutor and her coach and guide. She was the one who led Lily up the stairs to the bima and handed her the blown-glass yad, with its long pointer finger. He had reason to look, but Debra knew.

Concentrate on Lily. Think of her, he told himself as the rabbi called him up with Debra to bless Lily in Hebrew and English.

"May you be like Sarah, Rebecca, Rachel, and Leah." Richard and Debra recited together, his voice gentle, hers hurt and furious. He knew what she was thinking. He could hear her say it. Really? Our daughter's Bat Mitzvah teacher? And he was a terrible person. Wrong as always.

It was Lily who saved him. She who broke the spell. Her voice shook as she began her chanting, but she grew stronger as she went on. Keep it up, keep going, Richard cheered silently. He and Debra hovered on one side of the scroll while Heather and Rabbi Zlotnick presided on the other. Black letters swam before Richard's eyes. While Lily chanted, his guilt and indignation slipped away. If only she could chant forever! But the reading ended.

Now Richard descended from the bima while the Torah scrolls were furled and dressed in velvet, decked with silver crowns and paraded through the sanctuary. He had to sit with Debra while Lily stood with Heather to chant the haftarah. In pink satin, Lily read Isaiah, and she swayed unconsciously. She chanted fluidly and no one stopped her. No one made a move because she sang so fast.

Sing, O barren one. Richard followed along in the English translation, as Debra sat stone-faced at his side. *The holy one of Israel will redeem you . . .* Words of consolation, words of healing—until the next verse. *Can you cast off the wife of your youth?* he read with a little shock.

I didn't cast off anyone, he protested silently.

For a little while I forsook you. But with vast love I will bring you back.

The wife of Richard's youth was staring straight ahead at Lily. Nothing was bringing Debra back. That was for the best—but she shamed him with her averted eyes, the aggrieved angle of her chin.

Flustered, he glanced up at Lily reading while Heather followed along, ready to correct but beaming because there were no corrections necessary. Lily. Lily, he reminded himself. Just focus on her—and then he remembered, this is not about us. Those words comforted him. He was not important. He and Heather were not the topic here. This moment belonged to Lily and Isaiah—and the prophet was not talking about Richard and his first wife. These verses referred to God and Israel. It said so in the commentary at the bottom of the page.

In anger, for a moment, I hid my face, Richard read. *But with kindness everlasting, I will take you back in love.* He felt peaceful then and calm, until Lily finished, and the world rushed in again.

The luncheon in the Social Hall was co-sponsored by the Bat Mitzvah families in honor of the girls. There were sushi platters, mini knishes, mini quiches, stuffed mushrooms, couscous, grilled vegetables, peanut noodles, kugels sweet and savory. And, of course, a dessert table arrayed with cake pops, brownies, blondies, tiny cheesecakes, and pink and white cookies, some iced LILY, and some iced ARIELLE. Relatives and congregants were milling. People were handing Richard envelopes for Lily and telling him how great she was.

"Terrific," said Lew.

"She was so poised," said Sylvia.

As for Debra, she was talking to her sister, and introducing her parents to the rabbi. When Richard walked past, she turned away. She actually turned her back on him.

When Heather said goodbye, Debra granted a tight smile. "Good luck," she said.

Lily begged Heather to come to her party that night, and Heather said, "I'm so sorry. I wish I could, but I have a conflict."

"Debra's upset," Heather mourned that afternoon at Richard's place.

"It's my fault," Richard said. "She could see the way I looked at you."

"I told you don't look at me."

"I was trying! It's hard not to."

"Oh God." They were sitting on Richard's couch, and Heather buried her face in her hands.

"Debra loves to take offense," Richard said.

"She hates me now."

"She does not. She hates me—and you know what? It doesn't matter. Lily was great. And you! You saved her."

"She saved herself."

Heather would say that. She was such an educator.

"Everything will be fine," Richard said. "It's better this way. Rip off the Band-Aid."

"But what's going to happen when—"

"We'll cross that bridge too."

"I'm just so nervous."

"Wait for me here," Richard said as he dressed for the party.

"No, I'm going back to my place."

"Okay. But don't let Debra get to you!"

"I'm sad for her," Heather said in a small voice.

He held Heather in his arms. He loved her heart, but she did not understand. Debra knew what she was doing at all times—and he gave her credit, all the credit in the world. Her judgment was harsh, but also good. It had been her idea to join the temple so that the girls would have a Jewish identity. It had been her idea to hire Heather. "Debra calls the shots," Richard said.

"But she's alone."

"She wanted the divorce," said Richard, and he was not exaggerating. Debra had insisted. Demanded. Declared that they were done. And of course, that had been the right call too.

The Social Hall was glowing. Gold tablecloths shimmered. Orange and russet roses floated in glass vases. Glowing paper lanterns hung over the dance floor. All Lily's relatives and friends rejoiced, although the music was so loud you could not hear what anyone was saying.

The Bat Mitzvah girl was dancing with her classmates while photographers perched on ladders to shoot from above. Lily's blond hair flowed over one shoulder and her skirt twirled, just as you would expect, after so much ballet and skating.

"Richard," Sylvia shouted in the dark. "Could you say something to them please?" She was talking about the band.

Richard knocked back a Scotch and shouted back, "It's okay, Mom. They'll quiet down when we're eating."

At dinner he sat between Sylvia and Lew, who said, "A reprieve at last."

"I remember when you refused to have a Bar Mitzvah," Sylvia told Richard.

"Yeah, I remember too."

"I said, But Richard! I pleaded, but no. You weren't having anything to do with it."

"It's true."

Sylvia looked at Lew, who had not been her husband at the time, and said, "I've always regretted that."

"It was thirty-four years ago," Richard said—and then he thought, The year Heather was born.

"And now we're celebrating together," said Lew in what Sylvia called his judicial voice.

"Exactly. It's all good." Richard started his endive salad.

"Well . . ." Sylvia said.

"Mom," said Richard, "it's as good as it's ever gonna be."

This was his mantra the whole evening. When the waiters clashed with the photographers, Richard intervened. When his mother said she was tired and asked Lew to take her back to the hotel, he talked them into staying. When it was time for speeches, Richard took his place with Debra in front of the band. He stood with Lily and his ex-wife and he chose peace, and happiness.

Debra paraphrased Martha Graham. "There is a life force inside of you," she told Lily, "and since there is only one of you that energy is yours to use or lose."

No pressure, Richard thought.

"Lily," Debra told their daughter, "I hope you remember this wisdom. There is only one of you in all of time. Never lose your creativity."

But when Richard spoke, he said, "Lily, you read from the Torah about new beginnings. After a flood destroyed the entire world, Noah and his family and their animals rebuilt their lives. What is the takeaway? That you can improve and change. The Torah teaches that you can start again."

"I didn't know you were so religious," his cousin Steve teased later.

Richard was not religious, not at all, but he felt it at that moment, a sense of mystery and providence—a little fear, but mostly awe at what was happening—because on this night Debra knew about him and Heather. She knew they were together, and that was a relief. Actually, that was exactly what he wanted. There would be trouble. It would be awkward; it might be awful for a little while, but so much joy was waiting on the other side.

Lily adjusted the microphone as he and Debra stood behind her.

"Good evening," Lily said softly.

"Good evening!" her cousins and classmates and ballet friends answered.

"For my speech I have written a poem." For a moment, Lily paused. She stared at her typed words for so long that Richard began to worry. Then suddenly she started.

Oh, world flawed beyond repair,
There is no hope.
We have no prayer.
Oceans cover every place.
Flood waters rise
And not a trace
Of land remains.

"Louder!" Lew called helpfully.

But what of us?
Animals demand.
Should we die
For sins of man?
Take refuge,
God said,
In an ark
Abide with Noah
While it's dark.

How have we created someone so eloquent? Richard wondered as he stood with Debra. We, with all our squabbling? They basked in their child's poetry, but Debra could not resist coaching Lily from behind. "Slow down."

"Shh!" Richard shot her a look. It was ridiculous, her micromanagement. How could Lily's life force flow when Debra was always hovering?

Lily paused for just a moment, and then continued.

Animals arrived in pairs
To dwell together
Lambs, sheep, bears.
Ravens, cattle, swans, and slugs,
Mighty lions, miniscule bugs.

Was there a writing program Lily could try this summer? A poetry contest? Richard was sure that she would win.

Crammed together,
They survived,
Until a rainbow
Lit the sky.
Noah released them
With a sigh.
And they dispersed
To swim, run, and fly.
Will we learn from this to save the earth?
Will animals be free to range?
Or will we flood our shores with climate change?

Lily looked up.

The Bat Mitzvah guests gazed back at her in stunned silence. Was she done? Should they applaud?

"Lily! Lily!" Richard started the chant as he began clapping. "Lil-y. Lil-y." Debra was embracing his child. She'd moved in for the first hug, but Richard kept on in the background. LIL-Y. LIL-Y. All Lily's friends were joining in.

"Beautiful," Sylvia told Richard when he returned to the table. "But where was the ending?"

"What do you mean?" Richard asked.

"Nothing! I thought she ended a little bit abruptly."

Oh, he thought. You were waiting for her to thank everyone for coming. You wanted to hear her say thank you to my grandparents who came from Massachusetts. As if that was the point! As if Lily's relatives were the subject when they were not. Definitely not.

"I didn't know she wrote poetry," said Lew.

"She writes all the time," Richard said. "Heather had the idea for the speech."

"I'm not sure the earth is in such dire straits," Lew caviled.

Richard raised his hand to stop him. The earth *was* in dire straits, and all he felt was joy.

Meanwhile, Sylvia said, "Who's Heather?"

Richard didn't answer. Everyone would find out soon enough.

12

A Challenge You Have Overcome

They were a family of long marriages. You might sleep in separate bedrooms and wash dishes in a fury. You might find a moldy peach in the refrigerator and leave it on the counter for three days as evidence in some private trial—but you would never leave. Dan and Melanie had been married thirty years. Steve and Andrea were coming up on twenty-five. Andrea felt a certain vindication about this anniversary because she had married in, and her own parents had split when she was young.

Andrea's mother-in-law, Jeanne, used to ask in a melancholy way, "How is your mother?" and then, after a long pause, "How is your father?" Clearly divorce was hereditary, and Andrea a carrier. Real Rubinsteins had the marriage gene—except for Aunt Sylvia. And Cousin Richard, who was her son, so there you go.

And yet, despite Andrea's unfortunate heritage, she and Steve remained together. Were they happy? Yes, of course. They were at least as happy as everybody else. And why was happiness the criterion, anyway? They had endured health scares, teenagers, money problems. They were struggling even now because they had spent their professional lives in educational publishing. Steve hated what was left of his job, and Andrea had lost hers altogether. Nevertheless, Steve kept schlepping to the city, where he worked in an open-plan office and was allowed no shelves, no files, just one drawer. Andrea toiled at home as a private college counselor. Together they kept paying their mortgage, their taxes, their older son's tuition. Jeanne would have approved if she had lived. This was a woman who praised a shirt: It wears like iron. Who lay on her deathbed, refusing to accept that she was dying. As a couple, Steve and Andrea had staying power—a virtue Jeanne had prized more than youth, beauty, or joy. And why not? Youth ended, beauty faded, and where was joy when you needed it?

Joy was not the word that came to mind when Andrea remembered her late mother-in-law. Toward the end of her life, Jeanne lost patience with everyone, but particularly her grandsons, Zach and Nate. Their teams meant nothing to her. Their classes, friends, activities, did not register. In her delirious last days, Jeanne kept asking Andrea why her sons did not read. Why they did not talk. They *do* talk, Andrea protested, and Jeanne said, But why can't they carry on a conversation? The last time Jeanne saw the boys, she spoke obsessively of music and kept asking Nate, "What do you play?" She could not comprehend his answer—soccer.

No, Jeanne had not been sympathetic, and yet Andrea appreciated her now that she was gone. Was it pity? Was it distance? Was it knowing Jeanne could no longer hurt her? Or was it that Andrea's work required such extraordinary tact? Counseling students and consoling parents, Andrea remembered Jeanne's breathtaking honesty.

"I don't think there's enough of *you* in this essay," Andrea told a girl named Lizzie—but she knew what Jeanne would say. *Oh, I disagree. Less said, the better.*

"I think she'll have good options," Andrea reassured Lizzie's mother on the phone, but she could hear Jeanne. *With that transcript?*

At night, when Andrea heard Steve's heavy footsteps, she ascended the stairs. "Hello," she said, by which she meant How was your day?

"Hi," Steve answered, which meant Don't ask.

"Did you find the other clicker?" The garage door opener was broken.

Steve stared at Andrea as though he had never heard of a clicker, or a garage. "Are we having dinner? Or is everyone just fending for themselves?"

Andrea said, "You know what? I'm not even going to answer that."

Steve opened the fridge and gazed inside. Eventually, he took out the remains of Nate's birthday cake and cut himself an enormous slice.

You don't need that. It was strange, hearing your dead mother-in-law in the house. Weird, tragic, gothic, which didn't match the sixties split-level, but there she was.

There had been a time when Jeanne brought Andrea to tears. Then Steve would say, The truth is, my mom is a good person, but she has no filter. And Andrea would say, She hates me. And Steve would say, No! How could anybody hate you? These were their actual conversations. Now Andrea stood in the kitchen doorway and Jeanne hovered at her shoulder. Bad habit, guilty pleasure, good without a filter.

Meanwhile, Steve ate the cake with its thick slab of buttercream. "Where's Nate?"

Andrea glanced down at the tiled entryway. Nate's cleats were lying by the door, but his sneakers were missing, which meant he was with Mackenzie, his girlfriend. And what were they doing? Not college applications. Yes, while Andrea built spreadsheets and schedules with some of Nate's own classmates, he rejected such prosaic methods. He had joy to spare, and no sense of time. His parents worried, disapproved, and envied him.

"Wasn't he supposed to be here after practice?" Steve asked.

"I don't know," Andrea said. "I've been working."

"Well, so have I." Steve carried his plate to the kitchen counter. (No one but Andrea ever opened the dishwasher.) "You should talk to him."

"I tried!"

Steve could have answered this. He could have said, Why are you shouting? But he was beyond bickering. He sank down on the couch in the living room and closed his eyes, because if exhaustion were a competition, he would win. Andrea got to set her own hours, while he sifted ashes nine to six at Hillier-Nelson, where scarcely anyone remained, and Steve awaited termination. He was the working dead, his projects canceled, his assistant fired. He had nothing left—not even survivor's guilt. At one time he had acquired books. *Composition Across the Curriculum. Writing for Everyone.* As senior editor, he had shepherded each manuscript to publication. Now, he thought only of his severance package. No, that wasn't true. He mourned his house, once proud, once famous, merging, swelling, and collapsing like a dying star, retrenching to the backlist, selling dead authors, then giving up entirely on print editions.

Eyes closing, he drifted off, dreaming lightly of new titles. *Research Across the Universe. Writing Without Readers.* He saw paper and black print and poetry, his first love, the yellow wood he had forsaken.

The room chilled; the windy night rushed in. Steve woke with a start. "Nate."

"What?" His son was bounding up the stairs. He was always bounding, jumping, hair flopping in his face.

"What day is it?"

"Thursday," Nate said.

"No, tell me the date."

"October."

"It's October eleventh," Steve informed his son.

"Okay." Nate smiled, gracious and a little condescending, as if to say, I'm not gonna argue.

"So, when are you going to work with Mom on applications?"

Nate didn't answer, because, of course, he had no intention of working with his mom on anything. Other people paid good money for her services. Parents and students testified to Andrea's insight, her compassionate approach. No way did Nate want any part of that. He didn't know he needed an edge. He had good grades and great scores; he was a pretty decent athlete, but he had won no prizes; nobody was scouting him. Obviously, he needed all the help that he could get.

"Just use your common sense," Steve said. Unfortunately, Nate did not have any. He was applying November first to Brown, and he had not started his essays—or so he said. Secretly, Steve hoped his son was going it alone, crafting a brilliant piece of writing. Nate cultivated a careless look, but he was more motivated than he appeared. This was what Steve had always told his mother.

Jeanne never disputed the point. All she said was, "He should play an instrument." As a violinist, Jeanne saw music as a sign of character as well as competence—but Steve wasn't getting started with all that. He had labored at the piano all his childhood, practicing alone, then learning sonatas with his brother, who had it even worse, sawing his small gloomy cello. Beethoven should have been their birthright, except that they had no talent or interest in music. It was a great day when their father announced that they could stop, indeed they should stop playing for the good of everyone around them. Jeanne had never entirely forgiven him for that, just as her sons had never entirely forgiven her for forcing lessons on them all those years. Steve refused to repeat the experiment, and his sons grew up happy to a fault. Zach was now at Rutgers, mostly playing rugby. Nate, who really was quite bright, was gliding through the end of high school, last-minuting every assignment.

"You have to start," Andrea told Nate the next morning. "You have to put some time in. You can't just close your eyes and say I'm gonna get into Brown."

"You've got an in-house college counselor," Steve added, but Nate was rushing, gathering his stuff for school. Notebook, laptop, graphing calculator.

When Andrea said, "You're just leaving your bowl on the table?" he clattered cereal bowl and spoon into the sink. "Don't break them!" she snapped as he ran down the stairs and out the door.

Then Steve told Andrea, "You don't have to yell."

She said, "That wasn't me. It was your mother."

Andrea had to make a conscious effort to block Jeanne's voice, because she didn't want to speak that way. She was not so old, or angry, or so bitter. Even so, Jeanne tempted her.

A student named Jonah came to her that afternoon and at one point he said, "I'm not gonna get in anywhere."

Andrea whipped off her reading glasses. "Yes you will!" she declared. Because of course there was a school for everybody, even the worst student. There was absolutely a college out there. *A lid for every pot,* Jeanne whispered.

Too cynical. Too true. This is not who I am, Andrea told her mother-in-law. I never even liked you. *Yes, I know,* she heard Jeanne answer. Sometimes Andrea hummed to drown Jeanne out, but it was difficult. She felt haunted, although she did not believe in ghosts. Jeanne said, *I don't either*.

November first, Andrea made a supreme effort. When she saw Steve digging into the leftover Halloween candy, she did not say a thing.

When Nate skipped school to write his application, she did not say *Oh, now you're trying to do it all on the last day?* Her clients had already submitted. They had completed the process days ago. Meanwhile, her son holed up in his room.

Andrea stood outside his door and begged to help—but he would not relent. Hours passed, and she could hear Nate typing. Half a day, and she worked down in her office. Leave him alone, she told herself. No more pleading or berating. All she did was slip her Essay Guidelines under Nate's door. This was a two-page handout which included **TOPICS TO AVOID.**

1. Death of pet
2. Divorce of parents
3. Sports injury
4. Drugs, alcohol, mental health, cancer
5. Challenge you have overcome if it's one of the above . . .

Actually, Andrea steered her students away from writing about challenges of any kind. Asian, Jewish, and just plain white, her kids had real troubles, but they were not homeless, stateless, or first-gen anything. They had not walked across Sudan to freedom, or escaped the killing fields, or lived as refugees. Some had parents or grandparents who had done these things. Nate's own grandfather had been a Holocaust survivor who had rebuilt his life, working his way through college and then law school—but, to state the obvious, Zeyde was not the one applying. (Andrea's sixth topic to avoid was **Impressive relatives.**) Demographically, a kid like Nate just couldn't win. All he could do was write with wit, humility, and self-knowledge, in hopes that someone would take a second look at him.

At dinnertime, Nate emerged to refuel in the kitchen. He toasted two bagels and smothered them with cream cheese which melted through the holes.

"How are you doing?" Andrea asked, as he licked his fingers. "Do you want me to look?"

"No."

The garage door was rumbling open now that they had found the other clicker. Steve thumped up the stairs and said, "Hey, Nate. How's it going?"

"Okay."

"Taking a break?"

"Yeah."

"We should at least proofread," Andrea interjected.

"Shh," said Steve.

What? Andrea demanded silently, because hadn't she kept quiet almost the whole day? And wasn't her kid sending in his application that very night with no help, no oversight? (**Every essay will benefit from a second pair of eyes.**) She told Nate, "Just let me look for typos," but he was already running to his room with a one-pound bag of pretzels.

Steve turned on Andrea. "Can't you see you're triggering him?"

"I'm not triggering anyone!"

"You chased him right out of here."

"I did not."

"Now you'll never see that application."

"That's not my fault!"

"Because you are always ordering him around."

"I was making a suggestion."

"You are incapable of suggesting anything. Every statement is an injunction." Not for nothing had Steve edited *The Hillier Handbook for College Writing,* ninth edition.

"STOP!" That wasn't Jeanne talking; it was Andrea, trapped there in the kitchen with her husband. She, a college counselor, he, an editor, both banished by their son—and now what? They were supposed to take it calmly? Applaud his budding independence? Let go and watch him fail? The hell with that. Andrea did this for a living!

Her kid didn't have to be the one to learn the hard way. "I know how to help him."

"But you have no idea how to talk to him."

"I talk to people all day."

"That makes you even worse."

"*You* stay home and coach five kids an afternoon."

"I wish," said Steve. "I wish I had your job."

"You do not," Andrea shot back, and this was true. He didn't wish it. He wouldn't last five minutes; he would lose his mind. At the same time, she had no idea what he was going through. Andrea had been laid off two years before with lots of other people. There had been esprit de corps, and goodbye coffees, common cause. She'd left when business was merely bad. She had not seen worse. She had never known the loneliness, the dread, the poison in the air. He was about to say all this when Nate flew down the stairs.

"Nate!" Steve called, but his son was opening the front door.

"Hey," Nate said softly, and Steve thought, Oh great.

"Hi, Mackenzie," Andrea called down to Nate's first love, a junior with her whole life ahead of her, no applications for an entire year.

"Hi, Andrea," Mackenzie answered, as Nate rushed her to his room.

Jeanne said, *That's what she calls you?*

"Now Nate has his second pair of eyes," Andrea told Steve.

"Wonderful." Steve stalked to the living room couch and Andrea sat in the matching armchair. He opened a book. She wondered if Mackenzie could differentiate there and their. "What time is it?" Steve asked.

"Just eight."

Steve opened *The Hillier Anthology of Short Fiction* because this is what he did now. He salvaged old books from the office. These were the stories he had studied back in college. High school. This was his youth. "Araby" and "A&P." "Lady with a Lapdog." "The Horse Dealer's Daughter." He said, "I really thought they'd fire me today."

"Yeah, I know," said Andrea. November first was a good crisp date for termination. Slowly, she said, "It's been so long. They're never gonna let you go."

"Oh, they will." Steve's fate had been decided when his editorial director left, and her deputy left too, and the house restructured to bring in a new VP named Erin. This Erin, who was thirty-one years old, had an even younger assistant named Cody, who had a PhD in composition from Wayne State, and answered the phone "'Lo?" sounding remarkably like Nate. Who was upstairs in his room with his girlfriend and his application on his computer. "What was that song we used to sing to the kids?" Steve asked Andrea. "About the branch on the tree and the twig on the branch?"

"And the nest on the twig," she said immediately. "And the egg in the nest, and the bird in the egg, and the feather on the bird, and the flea on the feather."

"That's what it's like," he said, because the older you got, the faster everything went. Childhood, school, college, marriage, kids—egg, bird, feather—each nesting inside the other. You tried to hold on. You tried to get your kid to listen. You wanted to change the outcome somehow, but that wasn't happening.

Strange how much better Steve felt in the morning. Andrea was sipping coffee in the kitchen, and she looked better too. One minute before midnight, Nate had sent his application in. Relief! Of course, he would have many more to write. Andrea's students had a plan B and a plan C, their apps queued up like airplanes on a runway. Nate had nothing. He would spend all of winter break writing new supplemental essays after he was rejected from Brown—but you couldn't think about that now.

You just couldn't get this crazy every time. You could not let the darkness and the aggravation win. And what if, by some chance, Nate had done it right? Steve's secret hope returned. What if his son's essays sparkled with originality? And what if Mackenzie had actually done some proofreading, and Nate got into Brown without adults? What a triumph that would be—like navigating by the stars. For weeks, Steve thought of this. All that autumn, through Thanksgiving, even to the first days of December.

Every day, on the train to work, Steve hoped for Nate. The kid was funny. He was original. Brilliant, once you got to know him. Wouldn't Brown need a soccer-playing news junkie who was also good at math? In the office, Steve prayed for miracles while Erin presented new initiatives to what she called the team and what Steve knew as the remnants of the company.

"We're very excited about this project!" Erin declared. "We're taking our content off *The Hillier Handbook* and what we're doing is creating a series of interactive trainings." As she played video clips, Steve imagined telling people, I never read my kid's college essay. No! they would cry, disbelieving. How could you let him send them in without even proofreading? Modestly, Steve would say, He didn't need my help. He decided to go it alone, and I respected his decision.

"That's what's cool about this platform," Erin was telling everybody, and Steve remembered that he had not respected his son's decision. He still doubted Nate had done the right thing.

Nate hated personal essays. Although he was a whiz at math, and a political savant, he didn't read a lot offscreen. He was the student Erin hoped to reach—although Steve could not imagine Nate undergoing video trainings—not for writing.

He told Andrea that night, "This interactive thing is the end."

Andrea thought he was talking about the company. "Not necessarily."

"No, I mean the end of me. I'm writing my resignation letter."

Jeanne slipped out. "Oh please." Steve should have been writing cover letters. He should have been meeting with his headhunter. Instead, he offered up a yellow legal pad with a handwritten screed. *Dear Erin, As much as I enjoy your presentations—very—I find myself incapable of stepping onto your cool platform together with the team. I am a book editor, and content provider, aka writer. I am not an anima-*

tor, coder, or video editor. My texts do not need performers. They interact right here on the page.

Andrea said, "You're not serious, are you?" Because here she was, building her home business hour after compassionate hour, and all he wanted was to burn his ships. "You're not sending that anywhere."

"Why not?" He was proud of his manifesto, his jeremiad.

"You should be working on next steps."

"I am!"

"This is not one of them," Andrea said, because what was Steve thinking?

Actually, he was thinking about how he'd given up on poetry so he could earn a living. Ha, he thought, the joke's on me. He was thinking about technology and whether he could find another job without boot camp which Steve's brother, Dan, insisted was the answer. Dan knew a musicologist who had changed careers that way. You came to camp a baroque music specialist, coded nonstop, and emerged a programmer.

"Is that your phone?" said Andrea.

Steve picked up and said, "Speak of the devil," although he'd only been thinking about his brother.

"How's it going?" Dan said.

"I'm contemplating coding camp."

"Great. I'm telling you! It's the way to go," Dan said immediately.

"I'm not so sure."

"People do it all the time," said Dan.

"I'm not people," Steve replied.

"I'm just saying, think out of the box."

You're an insurance agent, thought Steve. Meanwhile, Dan's wife Melanie got on the phone. "Hey, happy anniversary!"

Steve exchanged looks with Andrea, who sat close enough to overhear. "Thanks," he said, as Melanie asked, "How are you guys celebrating?"

It felt like a trick question. Not what are you doing for your anniversary, but how are you guys doing?

When he got off the phone, Andrea said, "Only Melanie would remember that."

"So you forgot too," Steve ventured hopefully.

"Oh, I didn't forget."

"Well, you didn't mention it."

"You know what?" Andrea said. "I'm tired of reminding everyone of everything." She had been emailing students, and now she closed her laptop, because all she did was say, Don't forget to send me your next draft, and time to register for the next SAT. She was the scheduler and list-maker and timekeeper. *What else is new?* said Jeanne.

"You always take offense," said Steve. "You are personally offended at everything I do."

"No," said Andrea. "It's what you don't do. It's what you constantly ignore."

"I'm not ignoring anything."

"Nate heard from Brown today."

Instantly Steve's tone changed. "Was he rejected?"

"Yeah, I think so."

"What? He didn't tell you?"

"No, he didn't say anything."

Steve hoped against hope. "So maybe . . ."

"That's how I know."

Steve glanced down at the entryway to check for shoes. Nate must have taken refuge at Mackenzie's house. He didn't like his own house at the best of times—and Steve couldn't blame him. Unhappiness filled every room. Why should he come home? Why would he tell his parents anything? He would leave just like his brother; he would disappear into the ether, leaving them to bicker over dying houseplants.

Not yet. Steve and Andrea heard the garage door rumbling below and there was Nate in his bike helmet. No Mackenzie, just their own kid, huge and strong, nose red, cheeks glowing.

Nobody spoke—not even Jeanne. In fact, Andrea could not hear Jeanne's voice at all. She just walked up to Nate and wrapped her arms around his chest, which was the highest she could reach, and said, "I never went to Brown."

"I didn't either," Steve put in from the kitchen table. "And look at us. Look how well the two of us turned out."

Nate pulled away and Andrea studied his face. She saw stubbornness there, and frustration, a little sadness, but mostly surprise. It was the first time he had been rejected from anything. "You're gonna be great. Nate the Great!" she told him, and Steve remembered Nate at four in his homemade superhero cape. "This is just the beginning," said Andrea, and Steve loved her for that—for her hope, her battered optimism. If only she'd stopped there. As Nate headed to his room she could not help calling after him. "Why don't we sit down this weekend and plan your next applications?"

Nate's voice floated back. "No thanks."

Steve threw up his hands. "Did you have to mention that?"

Surely Jeanne would have had a comeback, but at that moment Andrea had no idea what she would say. It was a strange feeling, like shaking water from your ear. "Oh well," she told Steve, "I had to ask."

The next morning, Steve got the call. Cody ushered him into Erin's office, and she told him how much his work had been appreciated, and how much the company had changed and how unfortunately Hillier was restructuring, which meant new roles for everyone.

Steve said, "And no roles for some." This interruption startled Erin. She seemed to forget her lines, so Steve encouraged her, "Do go on."

He would have preferred to quit. Much preferred to type and send his letter, but he didn't have a chance. He simply walked out in the middle of the day. Briefcase in hand, he joined the throngs in midtown, the guys in ski hats, and the other guys in suits, and the tourists with their kids shopping for Christmas in the glass department stores.

So, this was freedom. Perfect emptiness. This was what he had been waiting for. What did it say about him that his first impulse was to buy something? He wanted to go out and spend his nonexistent money on a treat, a lavish gift—but of course he didn't. He kept walking. He walked all the way down to the West Village where you could purchase antique tricycles and letterpress stationery. Then he walked back to Penn Station.

What he really wanted was dark chocolate. Andrea liked good chocolate, especially with hazelnuts or almonds—but he didn't buy any, because she worried he was eating so much candy. He found a florist instead, and stood in front of the glass refrigerator case, a morgue for roses. You could get a dozen in a long box like a coffin.

"Special occasion?" the tiny saleslady asked.

"Anniversary. One day late." He wasn't sure why he confessed to that.

"Long stem red," the florist told him with authority, but the roses looked vampiric, almost black. The orange roses were much better, flaming colors, perfect for a firing—except the flowers weren't for him.

He looked at potted orchids, azaleas, cacti—maybe a little hostile for the occasion—and then he saw it, an overpriced ficus standing in a ceramic pot, an entire tree with a slender gray trunk, and abundant fluttering leaves. "I'll take that."

Now the saleslady frowned, as though she was concerned for him. She tied a red ribbon around the trunk and handed him a blank card. "Careful, careful," she warned, as he left the shop and struggled with the door.

The whole thing was a struggle. The heavy pot and tickling leaves right in his face. He almost fell stepping onto the escalator at the station. He wrenched his back, but he fought on, wrestling the tree onto the train. There he sat with the pot on the floor in front of him. Who bought a ficus in the city and took it to New Jersey? Apparently, he did. He should have asked Andrea what she wanted—probably nothing. His back was seizing, and he wished he'd bought the flaming roses—but a tree had roots. It was alive. Meanwhile, the florist's card was the size of a postage stamp—much too small to say what he was thinking. That he was starting over. That he was glad and disillusioned all at once. That he was lucky to come home to Andrea and Nate—and Zach, who had just arrived for winter break. That this tree reminded him of the song, although it didn't come with a bird or a feather or an egg.

13

The Last Grown-Up

She heard their footsteps on the stairs. Water running in their bathroom. She sensed her daughters everywhere—but it was just her imagination. They were gone. Of course, they would come back. They were safe, and it was just till Sunday. It wasn't death—it only felt like that. Her friends said, "Now you can rest! You can think. You can work out!" Theoretically, she could have done these things. She could have been thinking and going to the gym and resting, but when the girls left with their father, Debra sat on the couch and cried. Which was fine. Crying was good. Divorce was hard! All she had to do was call and her sister Becca would drive over, but Debra didn't want sympathy, so no one saw her tears, except the dog.

Max was a Samoyed, and pure of heart. If anyone was injured, he came running. When Lily fell headfirst from her bike, Max had rushed to lick her better. But where was Debra hurt? She could not explain, so she buried her face in his white fur.

Eventually Debra got up and preheated the oven to four-twenty-five. She poured a bag of frozen shoestring fries onto a cookie sheet.

A sprinkle of salt, a dollop of ketchup, and that was dinner, which she ate right on the couch. It wasn't good for her, but she was listening to her body, and her body said, Who cares?

She called her parents down in Florida and her mom said, "Hi, honey. How are you doing?"

"I'm okay," Debra said, balancing her plate on the arm of the couch.

"Ed?" her mom said. "Debra's on the phone."

Debra's dad picked up and said, "What's new?"

"Our paperwork is finished."

"It's finalized?" Her mom was disbelieving. It had been so long.

"Done."

She could hear her parents mulling what to say. The paperwork was done, and it was weird and painful, like picking off a scab, because the marriage itself had ended two years before.

"Well, that's a relief," her mom said.

But Debra's dad spoke in the voice he reserved for his deepest disappointments. "All right. That's that."

"I'm wondering," Debra's mom ventured. "Should I take down your wedding picture?"

"Cindy," her dad chided.

"You've still got that picture up?" said Debra.

Her mom sounded embarrassed. "I was just—"

Debra said, "It's fine. Either way."

"You don't mind?"

"Why should I mind a picture?" Debra asked, although in retrospect she thought her beaded gown unfortunate. "I have the whole album."

Her mother gasped. "You look at your album?"

"No, but I'm not going to get rid of it. The girls might want it! I'm not erasing history."

Silence, and she knew her mom was gazing at the photo in its gilt frame. "You look so happy."

"I *was* happy," Debra said.

"And Richard was so young!"

"Yes, Mom. He was young." Debra almost laughed—and then she felt guilty for mocking, even inwardly, because how could her parents know what to say? How could anybody? What clueless things would Debra tell her own daughters? They were in tenth and seventh grade, obviously a million years from marrying, let alone divorcing—but if they did. Would you admit the truth? Debra asked herself. Would you say this was not what I imagined? This was never what I hoped for you?

Debra took out the trash and picked up a package by the door. New earbuds for Sophie, who had lost hers. Then she took Max out to romp and sniff and chase his rubber ball in the backyard. The girls never set foot here anymore. At sixteen and thirteen, their days of romping and foraging were done, but Max never outgrew anything.

"*You* need a yard, Maxy. Yes, you do!" She threw the ball, and he streaked off, untiring through the autumn leaves. Did he wonder where the girls had gone? Debra was sure he missed them—and she was glad he didn't know it would get worse. In just two and a half years Sophie would leave for college, Lily would follow, and then what? Debra didn't want to sell the house, but could she and Max afford to stay? Would he even live that long? Oh no!

Admittedly, Debra tended toward the worst-case scenario. It made Richard crazy because she was always, as he said, fast-forwarding. But she had foresight. She prepared. She planned meals and vacations, scheduled lessons, preregistered for summer camp. Slow down, Richard would beg her. Cut back, get help! (Of course, he never considered helping. When they fought he said, But you insist on doing everything.)

This was true. No one had told Debra to stay home and do everything; that came from her. Nothing compelled her but her conscience and her common sense. When the girls were babies, she had given up free time and exercise. When they were older, she gave up her job, because she could not work the kind of hours Richard did and see her children while they were awake. And because she wanted to eat real food. And because she did not want to outsource every single aspect of her life. And because those were years you could not get back, and because she hoped someday she would return, if not to law, to something new. Education? Social justice? Counseling?

Together, Debra and Max examined icy puddles under the girls' old climbing structure and green slide. It was exhilarating to think of all the possibilities—how she might teach or advocate for immigrants—but when she thought of Richard, she saw his future as domestic. He would remarry. It was obvious to her—to everyone. He was already living with his girlfriend, Heather, who was smart and beautiful and sane. He had kept his relationship secret, which was childish, to say the least, but the relationship itself was great. The girls loved Heather, and Debra approved. As for Richard, he was better than he had ever been. Eating healthy, losing weight. The girls said he'd stopped sneaking cigarettes.

"Good for you," Debra had told him a few days earlier.

"Yeah, I'm doing it," Richard said.

She looked at him with sudden insight. He was taking the plunge. The paperwork was done. "You're going to propose!"

He looked startled. "I meant quitting."

"Oh! I'm sorry."

"I wouldn't propose without talking to the girls." He was reddening around the ears.

She nodded. "That's good."

"We want them to be—"

"Yeah," she said.

"Comfortable. We want it to be natural."

"They'll be ecstatic," she encouraged him.

"Thanks," he said.

A sweet moment, a really good exchange. "I was proud of us," Debra told her therapist, Suzanne, the next day. Truly she was happy for Richard, and relieved he was done dating women half his age. Heather was someone Debra could work with. Someone she could respect.

It was a good thing. It was the right thing—and at the same time, Debra knew Richard's remarriage would sting. The greater good would be another loss. "Does that even make sense?" she'd asked Suzanne.

"Totally."

"But what can I do about it?"

"Do you always have to do something?" Suzanne answered.

Debra sighed, because she knew that there was nothing to be done with feelings but to feel them. There was nothing to do about her ex-husband and his new relationship except to watch events unfold. Debra understood that. (She was good at therapy.) If only Richard and Heather would hurry up and get it over with.

That evening Lily called from Richard's place. "Guess what?" Lily said, and Debra's heart jumped. This was it.

"What?"

"We're making pizza from scratch."

"Oh."

"We should do this sometime," Lily told her.

"Okay. Sure!" Debra heard laughter in the background.

"Mom, we have to get a pizza stone."

"We have one."

"But it broke," Lily reminded her. "We should get another one."

"Okay."

"Then after dinner we're getting gelato."

That was when Richard and Heather would tell the girls—except they wouldn't tell them; they would ask. They would sit together, the four of them, and Richard would say, Girls, we have a question for you. Or Heather would speak humbly: I will never replace your mom, but I want to ask if I can be on your team and support you forever. Or they would say together, Girls, we have a present for you. You don't have to wear them all the time—or ever—but we want to give you these necklaces.

Debra could imagine it every which way, the squeals of delight. The delicate gold chains, everything sensitive and meaningful. Richard would be kneeling, or Heather—or both! And there would be hugs and happy tears. "Have a wonderful time," Debra told Lily now. "Let me know how it goes."

"Bye, Mom, love you."

Lily always said goodbye like that, and Sophie too. Love you, they chirped on every occasion—even when they called to say carpool was late. Love you, love you, until the words meant nothing. They might as well have said, Talk soon. Where did the kids get it from? Summer camp? It irked her, although it didn't bother anybody else. Plenty of parents spoke to their kids that way as well. Becca declared, "I always say 'Love you' because who knows what could happen? What if you were hit by a bus? Wouldn't you want your last words to be 'Love you'?"

Debra said, "Not if it's just habit." Love you. Killed by a bus. The whole thing made her sad. She walked through her empty house. Then she vacuumed the first floor and cleaned the girls' rooms.

The kids won't learn to clean up after themselves if you do it for them, Richard used to tell her. He had been scrupulous about ordering the girls to do whatever task Debra required. Do as I say, not as I do.

She shook her head and picked up laundry from the floor. School clothes, leotards, balled-up tights. Lily's rug was sea green, Sophie's fluffy white. She'd asked for white like Maxy's fur, and that was what she got. Her rug was furry, and it shed. Legos used to disappear. What was that, caught in the white shag? An earbud right at the foot of Sophie's bed. And there was the other. Debra almost called to say, I found them! Right after the new ones were delivered! But she resisted.

They'd be at the gelato place by now. Finishing up. Driving back to Richard's condo. Debra watched her phone, but nobody called.

How was the gelato? she texted at last.

Good, Lily texted back.

When the girls returned, nothing had changed. Richard and Heather were not engaged. Debra had been fast-forwarding again.

"Have you ever had Cherry Amaretto?" Sophie asked.

"Is that what you got?"

"We tried Heather's."

Debra tried to picture Heather with a fruit flavor. Heather seemed more Cookies and Cream.

"It was weird," Lily said.

But nothing else seemed strange to them. In fact, they were lighter, happier than when they had left. Trust Heather—a trail runner and a hiker—to leave kids better than she found them. The girls hugged Max, went up to their rooms, and did their homework. Even Lily, who worried at night, did not seem sad, and curled up in bed with a book about girls learning to be witches or possibly princesses at boarding school.

Life was good, and it was ordinary. It was school and ballet and groceries and dinner and pre-algebra and world history, and the next weekend Debra had the girls, and she made waffles. All was calm until the following Thursday.

Richard came in and played with Max while the girls were dragging their bags downstairs and he said in a low voice, "Debra, I have to tell you something."

That was a bad sign. "Go out to the car," Debra called to the girls as Richard started pacing. He forgot Max completely. "What is it?" Debra asked.

"Well—" he began.

"Is it Heather?"

"Yes."

She froze. Were he and Heather breaking up? Now? Now that the girls were used to her? Had he screwed up this relationship already? "You didn't."

"Didn't what?" he shot back.

"Richard. What's going on?"

He hesitated for just a second and then said, "We're expecting."

"Wait, what?" The words didn't even register at first.

"We're expecting a baby in January."

"But I thought you were— You aren't even— Aren't you getting engaged?"

"We're planning to."

"And when are you going to tell the girls? And when will you get married?"

"I wanted to ask you about telling them. I mean, it's good news."

She was calculating quickly. How long had they been expecting? Were they really . . . ? Yes. They'd been pregnant at Lily's Bat Mitzvah and they hadn't told her. "You could have said something."

"I know but you were already—"

"But you—"

"It would have been too much."

She nodded. It was too much now. Inside she heard the words Selfish! Unfair! But no. That wasn't true. They weren't selfish to live their lives. She swallowed. "It's a lot of good news at once."

"Exactly."

"Congratulations."

"Thank you."

"I'm just—"

"We didn't want to wait too long."

"But you did wait," she burst out, because he'd waited all this time to tell her.

"I meant wait to get pregnant."

"Oh."

"Lissa . . ."

"Who?"

"Heather's sister is having a terrible time. IVF and everything."

Debra stood there bewildered, because why were they talking about Heather's sister's infertility? "When are you getting married?"

"After the baby."

"Okay," she said slowly. She had foreseen engagement, then marriage, not an instant family.

He said, "Are you worried it will be weird for the girls?"

"Well, yeah."

"Because you think it's wrong to have a baby first?"

"No!" She wasn't going to be the bad guy, the moralistic one, the evil fairy at the christening! She realized something now. The king's first wife—that's who the evil fairy would have been. But that wasn't Debra. Not at all. She just needed a minute. She had never imagined Heather in a rush, or Richard so nervous and so glad, and she felt a pang, hearing his good fortune. Once upon a time Debra had wanted a third child, but Richard had objected, and she had listened. "It's just a lot to . . ."

"That's why we want to talk to them."

The front door opened. "Dad," Sophie said.

Lily called from the open car, "You're taking forever."

He called back, "One second."

"Let's figure out a plan," Debra told Richard.

"Great!" He took the cheerful tone they both used when the kids were near.

Debra said, "Team meeting."

The three of them met at the Abandoned Luncheonette. Richard sipped kombucha and Debra had black coffee. Heather had nothing.

"Why don't you try the water?" Debra suggested.

Heather smiled. She appreciated Debra's sense of humor. Of course she did, because she was perfect—even if she looked a little pale.

"How are you feeling?" Debra asked.

"Eh," Heather said, and Richard took her hand.

"She's a trouper." Richard could have been talking about Lily, but Heather didn't seem offended.

Debra asked, "Are you going to find out whether it's a boy or a girl?"

They spoke at the same time. "I think so," Richard said.

"I'm not sure," said Heather.

"Well, either way," said Richard.

Debra interjected, "But you're going to tell the girls that you're expecting."

"Of course!" said Heather.

Richard said, "We have to."

"Here's the thing," Debra told them, and now she saw Richard getting tense. He hated hearing a thing. "I think you should get engaged first and then let a little time pass before telling them about the . . . I think it's important for them to know—"

"That we're all in this together," Heather said.

"Exactly."

"That this is forever," Heather said.

Debra said, "Right."

As for Richard, he said nothing. He would do what Heather wanted. He, who had insisted he could not handle a third child. This was different. Debra understood that. This wouldn't be a third child born into their old family with their old wars. He and Heather were a new beginning. This was the way of things, that women had their babies and they stopped, while men lived like starfish, constantly regenerating.

"I love the girls so much," Heather was saying. "I want to include them when we get engaged."

I got that part right, Debra thought.

Heather said, "I want to dedicate myself to them."

You're great, Debra thought. You really are. And at the same time—you have no idea. Parenting times three. The sleepless nights ahead, the tantrums and book reports and standardized tests and the million ways kids in middle school are mean.

Heather said, "We'll write a family proposal."

"Thank you," Debra said, and meant it. "I think that will be wonderful," she told Heather, because why scare her? And the new baby would be beautiful. She envied Heather that, although she was grateful for the daughters that she had.

"I'm glad we did this!" Heather said when they were walking to the cars. Richard hugged his future fiancée's shoulders. He kissed her ear.

And Debra didn't feel alone at all. She did not mind watching the two of them. She just felt like the last grown-up on earth as she called after them, "I'm glad we're all on the same page."

The next weekend, she was forewarned and forearmed. She had in her possession a folder with the proposal. Heather had sent it, so Debra was like the press corps with the full text of the speech the president was about to give. And better than the press, she had printed two copies on archival paper. Even as her daughters were off listening to Richard and Heather pledge their troth, Debra was sitting at the kitchen table framing the documents, so that each girl would have a copy in her room.

Family Proposal

We propose to be there for each other every day.
To respect differences and appreciate each person for who they are.
To make sure everyone in our family is seen and heard.
To honor each other's feelings.
To be on one team.

Debra's phone was ringing. It was Lily and she was on speaker. Debra could hear Sophie and Heather and Richard in the background as Lily shouted, "We're engaged!"

"Mazel tov!"

"And we're expecting!" Sophie added.

"Oh wow," Debra said automatically. So much for letting a little time pass. "That's so great."

"Mom!" Sophie said. "You already knew, didn't you?"

"I can neither confirm nor deny," Debra said, and she heard Heather saying, Ha! "This is so great," Debra repeated. "This is really, really wonderful." She said it, but her body ached. Her arms, her legs, her heart.

"It's going to be a girl," Lily said.

Debra said, "They told you?"

"Lily just *wants* it to be a girl." That was Sophie's older sister voice.

The phone was ringing over there at Richard's place. Debra could hear it in the background. "Sorry, it's my parents," Heather said. "Mom? Hi!"

"We should talk to them," Richard said.

"And we need to make dinner," Heather reminded him.

Crashing sounds and laughter. Heather's voice, "Yes! We're here with the girls. We all proposed to each other!"

"Okay I have to go," Lily told Debra after a minute. "Love you!"

Everyone was happy. Everyone was young. As for Debra, she was relieved. She was actually glad that Richard and Heather had shared all their news at once. She almost wished that they'd revealed the gender too, and named the baby, and that their perfect child was in school, and Richard was showing just how involved he could be the second time around. I have so much more patience now, he would say, as older parents always did. I am so much calmer. Debra wished it had all happened already, so she didn't have to watch.

In twilight, she got the leash and took Max for a walk. The earth was damp and the grass tender. The neighbor kids were biking up and down the street, looping in parabolas. She stood watching, as she called her sister.

"Hey," she said.

Immediately Becca said, "The deed is done?"

"Yup."

"And how was it?"

"It was great. It was beautiful."

"Were you there? You sound like you were there."

"No! I wasn't there. I heard from the girls. And they also know about the baby."

"I thought Richard was waiting to tell them."

"Apparently not."

"I thought you had that big meeting."

"We did, and Richard sat there agreeing to everything."

There was a pause and then Becca said, "He's just bad."

"He isn't bad," Debra said numbly.

"Yes, he is!"

"He's inconsiderate," said Debra. "That doesn't make him bad."

"Whatever," Becca said. "You can call it what you want. He blind-sided you!"

"No, Max!" Debra called. He was barking, straining at his leash, excited by a beagle. "He's getting violent," Debra told Becca. "I have to go."

"Max isn't violent."

"He has a thing about little dogs." Debra was maligning her own sweet Max just to get off the phone.

"Hey, Debra. It's okay to be angry," said Becca, who taught creative movement. "You can scream! You can dance it out."

Debra pulled Max across the street. "Yeah, I don't think I'm in that kind of shape right now."

"No, anyone can do this! Listen. It takes two seconds. Plant your feet."

Debra planted her feet on the sidewalk as Max looked quizzically at her.

"Breathe in and tighten your whole body. Make fists."

"Uh-huh."

"Then open your hands. Release your breath. Let go."

Debra opened her left hand because she was still holding the leash in her right. She exhaled. Then she said, "Let what go?"

"The whole thing."

"Oh."

"I can show you some other ones," Becca said. "That's just a mini ritual. Anyone can practice that at whatever level. Just try it whenever you feel the need."

"Thanks," Debra said. "Will do."

She took Max home and let him run around the yard while she sat on the girls' old swing. He was looking for his ball. Several times he ran up as if to ask, Where did it go?

Max sniffed her knees. He wanted her to hunt, but she said, "I can't, Max. Sometimes you have to rest. You know?" His ears pricked up; he could detect even a hint of sadness. "It's okay. It will be okay. I promise," she told him. "You keep looking, and if you still can't find your ball, I'll buy a new one. And then as soon as I buy a new one, the old one will turn up." Max buried his head in her lap as she said, "I don't know why it happens. It's funny, right? But that's just how it goes."

14

$

In this family, you didn't talk about money—not even with euphemisms the way you spoke of cancer (she is very sick) or a disastrous get-together (it was very nice) or unforgivable behavior (it's not my business). Dan and Steve were silent when they inherited equal shares of their mother Jeanne's estate. It was just the way they had been raised. Talking about money was rude, and somehow dangerous.

Because of this, the brothers were surprised after Jeanne's death to learn of her many bank accounts and detailed bequests. She left generous sums to the Boston Symphony Orchestra, Jewish Family and Children's Services, and Mount Holyoke, her alma mater. Smaller gifts went to the YMCA in Brighton where she used to swim, and to the Longy School of Music where she had once taught. All good causes she had never mentioned. In her will, Jeanne left her piano to the All Newton Music School, and with some difficulty, her sons arranged to donate it. *I want my instruments to be played,* Jeanne stated, which was why she left her Vuillaume violin to Dan's daughter, Phoebe. To Steve's sons, she left nothing. "Well," Steve told his wife, Andrea, "she never liked boys."

After these donations, there wasn't much cash left—but Dan and Steve got the money from Jeanne's house. The big old Tudor in West Newton had sold for a fair amount, and after taxes and broker's fees, Dan and Steve each got a lump sum. A decent lump, but the brothers didn't let it show. In fact, they were just as stressed as they had been before, and the reasons were not hard to guess. Dan was supporting his mother-in-law in memory care, and Steve was unemployed. With a salary, Steve would have felt differently—but Andrea did not make nearly enough to support the family, so they were burning through his inheritance.

Of course, Steve was trying to find work, but after twenty-five years editing composition textbooks, he was highly specialized. He had applied for jobs in publishing, libraries, research institutes, and nonprofits—but his skills were old-school, and his habitat had dwindled. His interviews were informational at best.

He was working intermittently with a cheerful tattooed headhunter named Charlotte who specialized in creatives, as people like Steve were now called. The first time they'd met, Steve said, "I'm not sure I like being an adjective turned into a noun."

"Ha!" said Charlotte. "Good one."

She was a creative too, a photographer with an unflinching eye. Her portfolio was mostly insects—extreme close-ups of ants and iridescent flies and horrific praying mantises.

At their first meeting, they had talked about Steve's goals, and he had told her he would do anything he was qualified for except teach high school.

"Any specific reason?" Charlotte asked.

Where do I begin? he thought, but he said, "I hate kids."

Steve tried to come up with alternatives to education. He even considered bookselling. "Those jobs are hard to come by," Charlotte said. "Would you consider tutoring, or, like, college counseling?"

"My wife does that," Steve said. "Conflict of interest."

Charlotte looked puzzled, but Steve explained. "It would cause conflict, because I'm not interested."

After several months of this, Charlotte told Steve, "Honestly, you're overqualified for most of this shit."

"I wonder if it's something else," said Steve. He had been brooding about certain former colleagues who might blackball him. Sworn enemies now alighting on whatever slender opportunities remained in publishing.

"Nah," said Charlotte. "You're a bad demographic."

"Too white," said Steve, but he thought too male.

"Too old," said Charlotte.

Old as he was, Steve tried networking the old-fashioned way.

"Are you still in touch with Jeff?" he asked his brother on the phone.

"Jeff who?"

"Rosencrantz."

"Like once or twice a year. I think he's in Teaneck."

"And he's still married to Shira, right?"

"Yeah. Why do you ask?"

"Because he's in publishing."

"Really?"

"He's an indie publisher." Steve was standing at the picture window in his living room.

Dan sounded puzzled. "I thought he was in advertising."

"No, he's got his own publishing house now."

"Wow. What's it called?"

Steve hesitated. Then he said, "Cloverleaf."

"What's that?" said Dan.

"Never mind." Steve gazed at his snowy walk. Andrea was working downstairs, and Nate was off with his girlfriend so it was up to him to shovel and die of a heart attack. Not to be dramatic, but lately this had been his thinking. He had been out of work so long and he had spent so much time in New Jersey. He would perish in the most suburban way.

"I'll send you his email," Dan told him. "Is that what you want?"

"Maybe," Steve said.

Playwright, actor, beer pong champion, Jeff had been Steve's freshman roommate, and they had been close. It was only after the implosion of Steve's entire industry that reaching out began to feel humiliating. Steve had not contacted Jeff in years and now he thought, I cannot do this—but he forced himself to write anyway.

He sat down with a yellow legal pad and drafted a preamble in which he asked after Jeff and Shira and the whole family. Then fondly he recalled days at Emerson, and nights at the radio station, WERS. After which he meditated on the passage of time, and the growing up of children.

Once he got all that out of the way, Steve spilled his guts, explaining the cataclysm he had witnessed at his company.

Andrea padded up the stairs with her travel mug of coffee because she still behaved like a commuter, even though she had been working in the basement for the past five years. "I think we should probably shovel."

"I'll get to it," said Steve.

"What's wrong?"

"Nothing." He handed Andrea the yellow pad.

"You're writing to *Jeff*?"

"He's actually doing well."

"Huh," said Andrea, as she leafed through Steve's letter.

"Are you reading?"

"At the time I left Hillier-Nelson," Andrea read aloud, *"I felt we were chasing new platforms instead of developing ideas, sacrificing the good for the expedient. We were selling our birthright—giving up on books and readers. It was terrible to watch. In fact, it was a tragedy.*

Even so, despite everything, I still believe that—" Andrea looked up. "You sound like Anne Frank."

"Keep going."

"Books are not units. Content is not product. Good prose is vital, albeit increasingly rare, and we must resist the constant debasement and cheapening of words and the thoughts they represent. This is a sacred trust." She flipped the page. "When are you going to say you're looking for a job?"

"I don't know if there is a job," said Steve. "I'm reaching out."

"Oh, okay."

"You think it's too much."

She didn't answer.

"You think it's grandiloquent."

"I didn't say that!"

"You don't have to!"

She turned pages scribed heavily in ballpoint. "This must be three thousand words!"

"That's your response?"

"I thought you wanted me to look this over."

"I didn't ask for a word count."

"I wasn't counting!"

"Then tell me what you think."

She kept leafing. "It's heartfelt."

"Heartfelt?" He snatched back his legal pad.

"I didn't mean it pejoratively."

"Oh, you meant it in a *heartfelt* way?"

"Steve!"

"I'm just asking what you think."

"It's too long."

"Fine! I'll cut it."

He said this, but cut nothing. He typed just what he had written—not because it was good, but because it was true. *I still believe in art. I still believe in poetry. Cogent prose is the one resource we lack, and yet, clear writing is as important as fresh water and clean energy.* He reread these words and sent the email. Then he went out to brave the drifts.

After shoveling the walk and driveway (he did not die) Steve checked his inbox. Nothing. No reply for several hours. He did not hear back from Jeff all day.

The next morning it snowed again, but just a little. Steve dug out the car for Andrea and touched up the driveway. He didn't have to shovel perfectly, but it felt good once he started. He scraped off every bit of ice.

Then he stamped inside, kicked off his boots, and reread his credo. It was indeed grandiloquent, and he saw a typo—outage where he meant to say outrage. His message did seem bloated, and he had not, in fact, asked Jeff directly about employment; he'd only suggested meeting sometime for coffee. It was all too long, too weird, and at the same time way too subtle. Jeff wasn't gonna answer this.

But no! That evening, Jeff Rosencrantz wrote back. *Hi Steve! Great to hear from you. Your email came at such a great time. Our little outfit is expanding!*

And lo, Steve woke early Monday morning, and drove to Panera Bread, where Jeff was waiting with his laptop and a stack of books and coffee.

"Hey!" Jeff stood and shook Steve's hand, and clapped him on the shoulder, and he was just as friendly as if no time had passed, although he had no hair left, and he was fifty pounds heavier than he had been in college. "How are you, man?"

"I can't complain," said Steve, although this wasn't true.

"Still writing poetry?"

"A little," Steve said, although this wasn't true either.

"I loved your stuff," Jeff told him.

"Really?"

"I still remember the one about the orange. The one that got all those awards."

Steve nodded, although the poem had been about an apricot. "Just one award."

"Oh, only one!" Jeff said good-naturedly.

Steve went up to the counter, where he resisted a vanilla cinnamon roll. "Are you still writing plays?" he asked when he returned with coffee.

"No!" Jeff told him. "Work has been insane. Your message could not have come at a better time. I need good people. Desperately. We have so many books scheduled we cannot keep up."

Steve said, "Well, that's good to hear."

"Yeah, I know you think people aren't reading anymore," said Jeff, "and you're right. They're not. But everyone's writing like crazy. So, for self-publishing—we're riding a wave."

"What happens when it breaks?"

Jeff smiled. "I hear you. But that's just it! There's always another story coming. There is so much creativity out there it's scary. You've seen our website."

"Yes."

"So you know what we're about."

"Quality."

"Yup. Our books are *beautiful*—and we do them all in-house, soup to nuts—from editing, to cover design, to marketing." Jeff pulled a glossy sample off the stack on the table. "This is a collection of feminist oral histories. We're very proud of it. And this is a really smart vampire novel. Look at that cover design." Steve gazed at the blood-red cover marked with vampire teeth. "And here's a memoir. This guy is an obstetrician, and he's fascinating. He's a brilliant, brilliant guy. We vet all our authors, by the way."

Steve nodded, because he had indeed studied the Cloverleaf site. "They send you a writing sample."

"Right. We only take the most promising."

"But do you find that they're *all* mostly—promising?"

"No! Our potentials send us an excerpt and we do a sample edit on a thousand words and we talk about whether we're a fit. Then we match up author with editor—or writer."

"What's the writer for?"

"We're soup to nuts," Jeff reminded him.

"So, you not only edit, design, and market books but you . . ."

"Write them. Yeah!" Jeff said.

"Oh wow."

"Look, everybody has a story," Jeff said. "But not everybody has the words." He held up the obstetrician's memoir, which was titled *Baby Doc*. "Production is only a small part of what we do. The writing is the most rewarding, and the most time-consuming."

"So that's why you're hiring."

"We need wordsmiths," Jeff said. "Frankly, we need poets, and novelists. Storytellers. People who can take the rough ideas and—"

"Spin straw into gold?" Steve ventured.

Jeff did not take offense. "Exactly!"

At home, Steve sat on the couch, opened his laptop, and gazed at his first assignment. "It's a trial balloon," he told Andrea.

"What did they send you?"

Steve read the first paragraphs on his screen. "It looks like a family history of life in the Old Country."

"Oy. How bad is it?"

Steve read the opening silently. *Our family came from Bukovina in what is now Ukraine. We were descended from rabbis on both sides and naturally we were orthodox Jews (everybody in the village was very religious) and we spoke Yiddish. That was a given. It was a family where everybody loved each other but it was difficult because we were so poor. We had nothing except we had love which is everything. Along with Papa and Mama, there were seven brothers, Mendel, Yussel, Nachum, Dovid, Moisheh, Yitzchok, and Binyomin, and one sister (my grand-*

mother Feygie) but at any moment the Tsar's men might come knocking on the door to conscript her brothers for his army after which they might never return. They lived in fear!

"Well?" Andrea waited for the verdict.

"It's heartfelt."

"Steve!"

But he was reading Jeff's instructions. *"So, this needs oomph. Author says it's nonfiction, i.e. don't change characters or incidents."*

Oomph. Steve began walking up and down. He poured himself a drink—but he could not unsee that first paragraph. He looked at Andrea and shook his head.

"Okay," Andrea said.

Steve heard Andrea's resignation, and he knew how hard she worked all day rewriting college essays—or, rather, helping high schoolers find their voices. How was this any worse than what she did? He wanted to share the load. But seven brothers? Mendel and Yussel and . . . Christ.

He stepped outside without his coat and stood in the freezing air. All was still. Only one neighbor was out walking her dog.

Do it. Do it, he thought. "Come on!" he shouted aloud, as he did when he played tennis. Dog and neighbor turned around.

Steve waved. Then he retreated into his house, set himself up at the kitchen table, and started typing. *We live in fear. At any moment, the Tsar's men might ride up on their black horses. If they come and ask you for your sons, you cannot refuse. They must ride away to fight . . .*

He typed like this for half an hour and then he put the kettle on. *We eat only black bread,* he wrote, remembering something he had read. *Black bread with schmaltz if we are lucky. White bread is a delicacy—and in our village hard to find.* Steve thought for a moment and then he added, *We are always hungry.*

He worked and brewed some tea and worked some more. He looked up and thought about Sir Walter Scott, toiling by hand to pay his debts.

It was midnight when he sent his trial balloon back to Jeff. The house was quiet. Andrea was asleep. Back aching, Steve lay on the living room floor. He'd done this thing. He had spun a thousand words.

In the morning, Andrea took her travel mug down to the basement, and Steve took the car in for service, since it was squeaking whenever he turned corners. He set up his laptop in the waiting room and donned earbuds to block the sound on the wall-mounted TV. No response from Jeff, and it had been nine hours.

He opened his laptop even as news of bitcoin played on the television above his head. What *was* bitcoin? Imaginary money? Money that cost money? He gazed at the Cloverleaf website. There was an old-fashioned typewriter on the home page. *Yes, we publish first-time writers! Yes, we publish poetry.*

"Steve? Steve Rubinstein?"

It was the Subaru serviceperson, Gary, coming to find him. "Yes." Steve assumed his car was ready, but Gary knelt by his chair instead.

"So, we've got some issues," he said in a low voice, as though he was protecting the car's privacy.

"What kind of issues?"

Gary looked at him with regret and sympathy. "Steering column."

"What do you mean?"

"It's very unusual, but your steering column is cracked."

"How did that happen?"

"It's hard to say."

"How much would it be?"

Gary showed him the estimate on his diagnostic worksheet. "This includes parts and labor."

"Is it something we would have to do now?" Steve asked.

"Well," said Gary, "at this point you might want to consider buying another vehicle."

Uh-huh, thought Steve. With what? With your savings. With whatever you have left. Keep eating at it. Keep spending. And he sensed his mother's disapproval, her quick appraisal. She had always been quick. He said, "I don't want to buy another car."

"Understood." Gary was waiting for a decision, and Steve was staring at the enormous price of the repair. Wait, he thought. Wait, let me think.

Just then his phone lit up. It was Jeff! A text! *U NAILED it. sending Contract asap*

Steve felt a rush of affirmation, celebration. Pure adrenaline. "Let's do it!" he told Gary. "Let's fix this thing!"

"All *right*!" Gary sprang to his feet.

Seven hours later, Steve drove home with his new steering column, and he felt efficient, productive. Solvent. No longer spending his inheritance, counting down to bankruptcy. He thought of texting Charlotte the headhunter. Hey, I did find employment despite my advanced age, in case you were wondering.

"I got it," he told Andrea, who had finished work and was now lying on the couch.

"What?" She sat up. "Amazing!"

"They're sending me a contract."

"For how much?"

"I mean, I don't know the details."

"I was just wondering what kind of job it is. Like do you get paid by the project, or do you get a salary?"

"I said I don't *know* yet!"

"You didn't even ask, did you?"

"They are very successful." Steve thumped into the kitchen and opened the refrigerator. With one kid at college and the other never home, the shelves were almost bare. He saw condiments and leftovers and a dozen Greek yogurts, and he wanted to go out. He wanted a proper restaurant-cooked meal, because he had done this. He'd landed a job. Maybe it wouldn't be a lot of money. It wouldn't be a salary, but it was work. It was living by his wits.

Even so, he didn't want to jinx himself, going out to eat. He drove to the store for salmon and broccoli and cooked dinner. It was one of those sheet pan recipes where you gave the broccoli a head start, and then you glazed the fish with soy mustard brown sugar, and you broiled everything together and it came out great. Steve's father, Irving, had never cooked a meal in his life. He had left it all to Jeanne. But preparing food was not so bad. Neither was ghostwriting. It just took some patience—and ingenuity.

"I actually think I did a pretty good job," Steve told Andrea as they ate at the kitchen table.

"It's delicious," she said.

"I mean the memoir," he told her. "I think I captured the family's fear."

"What's that?" said Andrea.

His phone was buzzing. A text from Jeff. *Call me?*

"Uh-oh." Steve's mood changed instantly.

"What happened?"

"Not good."

"You don't know that."

"Yes, I do. Something's wrong." Calling back, he paced the kitchen while Jeff's phone was ringing.

"Steve!" Jeff said, as though everything was fine.

"Hi!" Steve answered, trying to match Jeff's tone.

"So, this is just a bump in the road."

You charlatan! Steve thought. You con artist. You aren't going to pay me! But he said, "What is it?"

"Our client." Jeff lowered his voice and suddenly he sounded like the Subaru serviceperson, Gary. "She has a few issues."

Steve tensed. "What do you mean?"

"Okay, listen. First of all, I want to reassure you this is very normal. It's just some questions. And they are all totally doable! The author wants to know why you are writing in the present tense when this book happened in the past."

"It's the historical present!" said Steve.

"*I* know that, and *you* know that," Jeff said. "Next, she wants to know, why is it so harsh?"

"Because they were living in the shtetl in poverty."

"Yeah, but she says she wants the tone to be more cozy."

"Cozy?" Steve glanced at Andrea in the kitchen. "This is supposed to be nonfiction."

"I'm just talking about tone. She wants it sweet and cozy."

"Like sepia-toned, rose-colored glasses?"

"Exactly."

"Nonfiction, but not real either?"

"Bingo."

"Who is this person?"

"She's the author," Jeff said, "and this is what she wants."

How incredibly simple, Steve thought. How straightforward. No need for criticism. No need for theory. The author has knowable intentions in case you're wondering. But then he thought, What about me? "I gave it my best shot," he told Jeff.

"Hey, this isn't the end!" Jeff said. "This is just the beginning!"

"You want me to rework this?"

"It's just tone," said Jeff. "It's rounding a few edges."

"What I did was good," Steve declared.

"No question," Jeff said. "But I don't have to tell you—there are a million ways to write a story."

Steve lay on the living room rug for his gentle back exercises. He lifted one leg just a few inches. Then the other.

"What did you decide?" Andrea was gazing down at him.

"You heard what I told him."

"You'll think about it?" Her eyes looked bigger from this perspective.

"I'll find something else. I'll contact Charlotte and ask how to make it in photography."

"Don't be that way," said Andrea.

"Don't look down on me."

"Fine!" She backed off, hurt.

Immediately, he sat up. "It was a joke!"

"You know what?" she said.

"Yes," he told her. "I know. I know. I know." Because he was not funny. He was not positive. His jokes sucked, as the kids would say. And in fact, he missed the kids, his sons so big and loud with muddy cleats. Unlike his mother, Steve liked boys—okay, he liked his own. Without them his house was deathly quiet. He could hear his line of credit dwindling.

"There are lots of things you can do," said Andrea.

"I know." Steve stood up gingerly.

He drove to Joe's, which was an excellent bar, and he found a nice table and set up his laptop and ordered a Rob Roy. "L'chaim." He toasted Sir Walter, drank up, and ordered another as he started typing.

"Mama, mama," cried little Feygeleh, "I see horses."

"What horses? Let me see!" Mama held Feygeleh tight and together they looked out the small window of their little house.

The horses were black. The men were tall and grim. The Tsar's Cossacks! They were riding through the village!

"Oy veyismere, what will we do?" Mama whispered. "Here we are all alone while Papa and your brothers are at shul."

The horses passed the house and swept through the village like the wind. Suddenly they were gone. "Thank God," Mama said, but Feygeleh was still frightened. "Don't cry, little one," Mama said. "We will clean the house and make our Shabbos meal and tonight we will have white bread!"

Now Mama took out her big broom and Feygeleh took out her little broom and together they swept the floor. Then Mama took out her big bowl and Feygeleh took out her little bowl and together they kneaded challah. They braided a big loaf for

Mama and a little loaf for Feygeleh. Soon the house was filled with the scent of baking bread.

"Can I get you something else?" asked Steve's server, Jayden.

"Absolutely," Steve said.

"You're workin' it," Jayden observed.

"I'm in a state of flow."

Steve wrote until the bar closed, and then he drove carefully to his own cozy house. The lights were off. Andrea had gone to sleep, but she had cleaned the kitchen. He sat at the table and reread his work and wrote even more. He wrote about a big pot of cabbage soup. He wrote about the Shabbos candles shining. *They were shining on all the faces of the family. Papa and Mama and all the brothers and little Feygeleh. They shone in the window, and they shone on falling snow.*

Toward dawn, the kitchen light flicked on, and he saw Andrea standing in the doorway. "Steve?" She was wearing her pajamas and her thick robe covered with stars.

"I'm a genius," he told her. "I am Laura Ingalls Wilder and *Fiddler on the Roof* and *Dubliners* and Joan Nathan rolled into one." He held up a cookbook Andrea's mom had given them years ago. It was called *The Children's Jewish Holiday Kitchen.*

"Listen." Andrea sat next to him. "This isn't worth it. This is not the job for you."

"I was born for this job." Steve pushed his laptop toward her.

She sat huddled in her robe, and she began to read. "Oh gosh," she said.

"What? Doesn't it scream rose-colored sepia glasses?"

She just shook her head at him. "I mean you can't send it, but . . ."

"I already did."

And the strange thing was he did not regret it, not even in the cold light of morning. He felt creative. He felt free. He loved his shtetl family. Their rosy cheeks, their flickering candles. Their warmth and their dirt floors. He loved protecting them from the Tsar's army. He was the writer, after all. He could do that, even if history did not. Was it art? Not at all. Was it satisfying? Totally. It was like assembling an entire breakfront with an Allen wrench.

However, he did not hear from Jeff all day, or the next day either. Two more days passed, and Steve began to understand something. The author might not find his work so charming. She might detect the tiniest bit of fakery and mania and drunkenness. Mockery! Clearly, this was the one thing you could not do. This was the unspoken rule. You had to take your author seriously.

He wrote to Jeff—just checking in! No answer. He wrote again. *You know, Jeff, I don't have time to write entire books on spec. If this is how you treat your so-called writers*—but he did not send that one.

Five full days passed. Andrea said, "Look, it's a blessing in disguise."

Steve called Charlotte to explore new options. "I'm ready to think out of the box," he said.

"Teaching?" she asked delicately.

"Bring it on."

"Even though you hate kids?"

"I don't hate them."

A moment of surprised silence. "Really?"

"It's adults I hate. It's just humanity."

"Okay cool!" said Charlotte. "I'll set you up with Emily."

"Another Brontë?"

"What?"

"Nothing."

"She does the private high schools," Charlotte said.

"Only private?"

"I mean you'd have to get certified to apply to public. It's not too late to look into that!"

"Nah," said Steve. "I want to start." He would teach American literature. He would take the veil, retreating to the classroom, which was practically the only place you could talk about poetry. Did he really like kids apart from his own? No. But maybe he would change a life or two. Maybe he would be the one his students looked back upon. Strict but fair. Tough but kind. Super smart (a little tragic). Weren't the best a little bit forbidding? He remembered his own English teacher, Mr. Spector, who had written his master's thesis on the works of Thomas Hardy. Maybe Steve would wear a tie.

"I'm doing it," he told Andrea that night.

"You'd have to coach something," she said doubtfully. "They always make you do an extracurricular at these prep schools."

"Literary magazine."

"And you'd have to be . . ."

"Sensitive? Politically correct? What are you talking about?" said Steve, who had edited the Hillier-Nelson anthology of essays by women of color. "Diversity's my middle name."

He slept well and woke refreshed. Even as his coffee brewed, he sat at the table to rework his resume—and that was when he saw Jeff's message with two attachments. One was a contract. The other was a 352-page document titled GRANDMA FEYGELEH A MEMOIR. *Steve! Sorry about the delay! Author had cataract surgery, but we are good to go!*

"Jeff?" Steve said when he reached his old friend on the phone.

"Hey!"

"I assumed when I didn't hear from you—"

"No, no, no. I'm sorry this took so long! I'm totally behind."

"She liked it?"

"*Loved*. She is ecstatic. It's exactly what she was dreaming of."

"I'm not sure I can keep this shit up for three hundred pages."

"You're too modest," Jeff said.

"Listen, I'm starting a full-time job soon," Steve said.

"Not a problem! We are totally flexible. That's the beauty of this line of work."

Steve gazed at his computer with both memoir and contract on his screen. The book contract was for almost as much as his car repair. "I don't think I can commit just now."

"Take your time," said Jeff. "Just take a day or two! Meanwhile, I'll put you in touch with Ruth."

"Who's Ruth?"

"Your author. She's delightful. She's eighty-six and smart as hell."

"I just don't know if I can spread myself so thin," said Steve. What he meant by that was, Oy vey, how are you suggesting such a paltry sum of money for this kind of aggravation?

But Jeff did not take the hint. "It doesn't have to be either or."

"Well," Steve countered.

"It can be both *and*."

"Never say die," Steve said.

"Exactly. And here's the thing to remember. There's a lot more where this came from."

The waves, Steve thought. The stories rolling endlessly.

He should be fixing Subarus. He should have gone into insurance like his brother—but no, he had become a poet, contemplating other kinds of loss. Was that a problem? No! he told himself. Come on! He could be a poet still. Nobody was stopping him. Nothing was getting in his way.

15

Nutcracker

The season was upon them. The scented boughs and glowing ornaments. Illuminated trees. The neighbors across the way were fully lit, their garden an enchanted forest, their porch, roof, and windows outlined in white lights.

"Why can't we have lights?" Sophie had asked when she was little.

Debra told her, "You know why—because we don't celebrate!"

Her husband, Richard, corrected, "You mean we don't celebrate *Christmas*."

"Isn't that what I said?"

"You make it sound like we don't celebrate anything."

Wide-eyed, Sophie had listened to this exchange. She must have thought her house would remain forever dark with her parents at cross purposes, but that was not her family's fate. Years later, each girl had two menorahs—one at Debra's house and one at the condo Richard shared with his fiancée. Of course this family celebrated.

They lit double sets of candles. There were presents to bestow. Gift cards for teachers, cute earrings, books, plush animals for friends at school—and this year Secret Santa for Level Seven at the studio. Sophie should have picked the gift, but she had no time, because of Nutcracker.

Oh, Nutcracker. That tinkling celesta. That supply list for performances. **Lipstick poppy red or scarlet NOT pink, coral, etc. False eyelashes required Level Seven.** This was Christmas for Lily and Sophie, who had risen through the ranks to become a Spanish dancer and a waltzing snowflake. They couldn't have Christmas lights at home, but every winter, they rehearsed the holiday.

When had Debra signed on for all of this? Just a few years before, her girls had been seedlings and bees. They had been tap-dancing vaudevillians tossing and sometimes catching hats and canes at Nicole's World of Dance. Then one fateful summer, Sophie's best friend, Eden, switched out and Sophie had followed her to Mishkin Ballet Academy, also known as MBA.

"She is be*hind*," Nastia Mishkin had informed Debra, after Sophie's audition at age ten, "but maybe possible." Then abruptly Nastia turned to seven-year-old Lily, who was just tagging along, and ordered, "Take off your shoes."

Standing at the barre in socks, Lily's eyes filled with light as Nastia declared, "Pretty feet."

And now? Class four times a week for thirteen-year-old Lily and five times a week including all of Saturday for sixteen-year-old Sophie. Dinner in the car, and homework late—this was their life. Eden was long gone. She played lacrosse and had a boyfriend with a car. However, Debra's daughters never wavered. They loved the turning, and the pirouetting, the pointe work blistering their toes. One by one, their other pastimes fell away. They quit piano, cello, tennis, even skating.

"You have to be on board," a mom named Joy had warned when

Debra began riding the couch in Nastia's waiting room. "You've gotta be all in."

"It's true," said another mom named Chelsea. "The kids get stepped on." Debra had been concerned to hear this—and then shocked, realizing that Chelsea meant it literally. "Nastia walks into the studio when the girls are stretching on the floor, and when they do their straddles, she'll step on their butts to push them down."

"You *saw* her?"

"I think she wanted us to," said Joy. "It was like a test for all the parents."

Debra had resolved that very day to speak to Nastia. A test for parents? She wasn't putting up with that. But when Sophie and Lily emerged from classes, they were beaming—and in the car when Debra demanded, "Did anybody step on you?" they said no.

She was an old hand now, sometimes amazed and sometimes horrified. She knew the tap and squeak of pointe shoes on the floor, and Nastia's fury when girls couldn't get it right. "Everybody work on speed and coordination. Especially *you*. And *you*!"

Debra understood the upside as well. Nastia was an inspired teacher, rigorous and pure. There was a reason her studio won New Jersey dance awards. The lows were lower at MBA—but the highs much higher. A perfect leap, as Sophie landed radiant. A compliment. Betterbetterbetter! An afternoon with Joshua the jazz teacher, who once upon a time had danced in *Dreamgirls* on Broadway. He whip-turned across the floor, and then spun around to watch his students following in threes. Whitney Houston belting, Joshua cheering. "Go Emily! Yaaas, Lydia! Come on, Rosie. *Live* your life!" In the next trio Sophie took off, powerful, broad-backed. She could jump!

Debra had hoped to catch a glimpse as she arrived with the Secret Santa gift for Sophie's friend Emma, but class was over, and everyone was packing up.

"Find your boots!" the dance moms called to their twelve-year-olds, small and light as hummingbirds.

"Come on let's go." They hurried their thirteen-year-olds, all legs. "Hurry, we have to get your brother."

The fifteen- and sixteen-year-olds were just emerging, girls with curves and blooming cheeks, and gauzy Degas practice tutus. They stepped into the dressing room to change, and then they flew downstairs while their mothers shouldered heavy bags and followed, earthbound.

"Where's Emma?" Debra asked the moms of Level Seven.

No one answered.

Oh great, Debra thought, because she had braved traffic to buy the perfect gift—a silver snowflake pendant—and now Emma was absent?

No. Emma's mother, Chelsea, was waiting outside the restroom. And now Emma appeared, her eyes red, her face puffy.

"Nastia said her turns weren't good," Joy whispered to Debra.

"That's ridiculous!" Debra replied, more loudly than she had intended, because Emma was Dewdrop! Nobody turned more beautifully. But here she was, crying faster than she could wipe her tears.

And here was Nastia striding through, her hair dyed black, her tracksuit black, her dance shoes black, her mood black too. Posters of Nastia dancing adorned the waiting room. Nastia performing Sugar Plum, and Dewdrop, and Juliet, her legs long, her face soft and dewy. This had been Nastia in Russia. Now she marched through the waiting room, and everyone stopped talking. "Hello. Hello." She nodded to parents, but she did not stop to chat. She stepped into her office and shut the door, leaving silent mothers and the weeping Emma in her wake.

It seemed the wrong time to approach, so Debra gave the Secret Santa gift to Chelsea. "This is from Sophie," she said, but she was thinking, Why aren't you comforting your daughter? And protesting!

It was not okay to make a young girl cry like that. Debra would have followed Nastia right into that office! But Chelsea did not. She was stoic, and a mom of six. She had enormous gravitas and a thundering gait. Only her mouth was small, drawn tight. "Thank you." She accepted Debra's little gift bag.

"Thank you so much!" Emma chimed in, even while crying and untying the ribbons on her shoes. Her hair was dark, done in a bun, revealing her slender neck. She did look like a Degas dancer bending down, her cheeks flushed, her arms taut.

"I hope you like it," Debra said.

"I will!" said Emma, tragically polite.

"What happened?" asked Debra, driving home as the girls ate dinner in the back seat.

"Nastia hates her," Sophie said.

"I thought she said Emma is best in class." Yes, Nastia actually said these things in front of everyone.

"Not anymore." Lily was gobbling up Debra's homemade stir-fry from a glass container.

Sophie explained, "She started doing her chaînés and Nastia kept stopping her!"

Lily put in, "She says Emma isn't working."

"How do *you* know?" Sophie said.

"Because I saw!"

"Weren't you in the other class?" Debra said.

"No. We got to watch Level Seven, and we were just sitting by the wall and Nastia said point your toes!" Safe in Level Six with her strict-but-fair intermediate teacher, Lily found Nastia thrilling—scary but awesome. An evil queen.

"If she ever makes you cry like that—" Debra didn't finish, but she was thinking, You'll be out of there so fast.

"She only makes you cry when you're really really good," Lily observed.

"That's not true," said Sophie.

"What do you mean?" Debra caught the sadness in Sophie's voice. "Did Nasty say something to *you*? Sophie?"

Silence as she pulled into the driveway of their house without lights or evergreen boughs. Silence as the girls carried backpacks and dance bags inside.

"Hey, Max! Hey, Maxy!" Sophie embraced the dog who had been waiting all day to see her. "No, you can't have that. It's not good for you." She set her stir-fry on the table.

"Don't you want any of it?" Debra asked.

"I had some."

"What did Nastia say?"

Lily ran upstairs and Sophie tried to follow—but Debra called, "Soph!"

"I have homework," Sophie said.

"Hold on."

"Mom!"

"What happened?"

Debra saw her older daughter hesitate, torn, wanting to escape and to confess. She saw the grief in Sophie's round face. "She said no bread for you," Sophie admitted at last.

"She said *what*?"

Now the tears came. "She said, salad salad salad."

"Are you joking?" Debra had to steady herself, hand on the banister. "I'm calling her."

"Nooo!"

"I'm talking to her now."

"Mom, please don't call!" Sophie begged. "Please, please!"

"This is abuse," said Debra, searching her phone for Nastia's number.

"If you call, she'll kick me out!" Sophie said.

"I'll kick *her* out!" Debra hardly knew what she was saying—but she was certainly no stoic.

"Mom!"

Nastia's phone was ringing. It rang and rang in Debra's ears, even as Sophie collapsed on the stairs, sobbing. What will I say? thought Debra. What will I tell that psycho? How dare you! How dare you make my daughter think that she can't eat? Do you want my lovely girl to look skeletal like you? She's sixteen years old, you horror show! Words crowded her mind—but Nastia did not pick up.

Debra sat with Sophie on the bottom stair. "She's inappropriate. You know that, right?"

"But she's a good teacher," Sophie said.

"Not if she talks that way to you. And makes Emma cry."

"I want to learn!" Max was snuffling Sophie's knees, and unconsciously she knit her fingers into his fluffy white fur. "I want to be a dancer."

Oh, Christ, thought Debra. Nutcracker was one thing. Dressing up and jumping, holding your head high. That was wonderful. But wanting to be a dancer, really to be one—to accept that pain? To compete and to be judged by your tummy and your breasts? "You can be a lot of things."

"I want to dance," said Sophie.

"You can always dance," said Debra. "You don't have to dance at MBA."

"But I love it there."

"Why?"

"Because I'm learning!"

"What are you learning? To hate your body?"

"Technique."

"Listen to me. You're growing! You can't look the way you did at twelve."

"I *know,*" said Sophie. But Debra thought, Do you really? "Just please don't call her," Sophie said. "I promise I'll eat!"

And Debra embraced her, and Max licked both of them, and they made up, as though they had been fighting—but what was the fight about? Just Debra trying to save her daughter from her teacher. From ballet itself. From the notion that puberty, like gravity, was a force you could transcend.

Sophie swore she would not think less of herself. She promised Debra she would remember she was beautiful just as she was. She said she had to study for her math test, and she wasn't sad. She was okay.

But what would happen at the next rehearsal—and the next? And what of Lily, still so slender at thirteen? Would she hate herself when she had hips?

Upstairs, all was calm. Sophie finished her practice problems. Lily sat on the floor of her room writing rapidly in her composition book.

"It's getting late," Debra said from the doorway.

"Okay." Lily did not look up.

"What are you working on?" Debra asked shyly.

Lily didn't answer. In the past, princesses had filled her pages. Twelve sisters in a castle, but she'd lowered the portcullis. She never talked about her writing now.

At ten, Debra corralled the girls to bed. They didn't fight her; their eyes were closing, even as Debra kissed each of them good night. Soon she heard them breathing deeply—but Debra couldn't stop thinking about the studio. She paced the hall outside their rooms and her heart warned, Don't take them back.

"It's my fault," Debra told her parents on the phone. "I let them stay too long. And now Sophie is in Level Seven, so she has Nastia all the time. They're doing competitions in the spring."

"Pull her out," said Debra's dad, Ed, the voice of reason from West Palm.

But how? Debra thought. If she pulled out Sophie, she would have to pull out Lily too. And then what? "They'll be crushed if I make them quit."

"They don't have to quit," said Debra's mom, Cindy.

"Find another studio," said Ed.

"Your sister switched a couple of times," Cindy pointed out. "And she was a wonderful dancer."

"They think they're in the best place! They won't let me switch them. It's not like kindergarten!"

"Little children, little problems," said Cindy. "Big children—"

"Thanks, Mom." Debra thought of Sophie's jumps, her innocent face. Lily's composition book decoupaged with magazine pictures of roses and diamonds.

"Sweetie?" Cindy asked. "Are you still there?"

"Yes."

For a long time, no one spoke. Then Ed said, "If parenting were easy—it would be easy."

Cindy added in her make-the-best-of-things voice, "We don't have to see the show. We're flying up to see you—not Nutcracker. We'll do something else!"

But even as she spoke, Debra knew her hands were tied. There was no way she could pull her daughters from rehearsals—not when they knew their grandparents were coming.

It was always going to be like this. Another performance and another. *Sleeping Beauty* in the spring. Scenes from *Giselle* in summer. Nastia had bewitched the children so that they craved class more and more. They lived for pointe shoes, tutus, sparkling sugar plums. All the sweets you could not eat.

In the morning, Debra's head ached as she drove the girls to school.

"Mom?" said Lily. "Can we have Christmas music?"

"I really think—" Debra began.

"No!" said Sophie.

"It's my turn," said Lily.

"But the songs are so bad," said Sophie.

Debra agreed—but Lily loved the Christmas station with its retro tunes, and it was her turn to choose, so Debra let her listen. "Santa Baby" filled the car, despite Sophie's protests.

Should I worry that she likes "White Christmas"? Debra had asked her dad. She's an old soul, he said. I know, said Debra, but should I worry about the content? What content? her dad answered. And by the way, those songs are all by Jews.

Even so, she worried. How could she not? She worried about the music. She worried about the dancing. She had done a terrible thing—buying into Nastia's studio. She had obeyed her children's wishes, against her better judgment. What if they got injured? They could ruin their feet. Blow out their knees. It hadn't happened yet—but if it did? And what if Sophie really did stop eating and starved herself and gave up on schoolwork? In Level Seven girls talked about auditions and conservatories, not college.

"Bye, Mom. Love you."

Debra realized she had arrived at Lily's middle school.

"Can you turn it off now?" Sophie said a few minutes later, as Debra pulled up at the high school.

Debra turned off the radio as her oldest opened the door and dashed out. "Have a wonderful day," Debra called after her, but she forgot to wish Sophie luck on her math test, and she felt wistful as she drove away.

Was everything worse now, or was Debra worse? Was it difficult for her because Nastia was dangerous? Or was it hard because she had dedicated so much of her life to mothering that she thought of nothing else?

When she talked to her parents, she said am I obsessing? And her mom said yes.

When she talked to her therapist that afternoon, she felt even worse. Suzanne asked, Do you think you're not enough? No, Debra said. I *know* I'm not enough.

She called her sister from her parked car immediately after the session.

"Ballet is evil. I told you that before," said Becca, who had studied dance for years, and now taught creative movement to people with developmental disabilities.

"Why did Mom and Dad let you do it then?" asked Debra.

Becca said, "What did they know?"

Debra thought back to her childhood. Her younger sister had not been thin. "*You* never had an eating disorder."

"Sure I did."

"Oh God."

"Just breathe," said Becca, as she always did.

"I can't just sit here breathing."

"That's your whole problem," Becca said.

"Okay, this is not helpful."

"Do you want me to tell you the kids are all right?"

"No. Because they're not—and I did not protect them."

"Do you want me to tell you how even though I danced as a kid I turned out fine? Eventually?"

"I want concrete suggestions!"

"Make Richard tell the girls they have to quit."

Debra burst out laughing.

Encouraged, Becca said, "Seriously, why are you still doing this shit on your own, even after you're divorced? Doesn't Richard have joint custody? Tell him what's happening and make *him* be the bad guy!"

Which Debra would never do. Of course she would never do that. But just hearing this was liberating. After all, the girls did have a father—and a future stepmother! Had they not all promised to be one team? Debra texted her co-parents. *emergency team meeting*.

Of course, once he figured out no one was dying, Richard said he was tied up, but he would try to juggle. His fiancée was the one who met Debra at Jersey Java. Heather came in huffing, out of breath, set down her giant bag, and heaved her pregnant self into a chair.

And Debra, who was there to talk about the sick diet culture of ballet, took one look at Heather and thought, Oh my God, you're huge. Heather's breasts had swollen. Even her face had widened. Wowwowwow, thought Debra, who had not seen Heather since October. Debra was not proud of her reaction. The irony did not escape her. *Nothing* escapes you, Richard used to say. But that wasn't true.

"Oof," Heather said.

"Almost there," Debra told her.

"Almost," said Heather. "I don't fit anything. I can't even wear my ring."

Sure enough, Heather's hand was bare. Debra still had the little diamond ring Richard had given her in law school. Sell it! her friends told her. Trade it in! "How are you feeling?" she asked Heather.

Shyly Heather said, "Were you kind of desperate at the end?"

"Totally."

"I'm already on leave," Heather said, "so I have way too much time."

Debra said, "I know what that's like."

"Really?"

"Oh yeah."

"Was it hard to go back?"

"It was bad," Debra said. "That's why I quit my job." And then she thought, Don't worry her. Don't scare her! "Let me bring you something. No, don't get up." Debra was almost afraid to see Heather walking around. How was Richard still at work? Seriously, what was he thinking? Was Debra going to be the one taking Heather to the hospital? Would she have to do that too?

She brought Heather juice because she wasn't drinking coffee. And she got her an orange ginger scone, which Heather hadn't asked for. Debra ended up drinking coffee and eating the scone.

"I was thinking of going back part-time," said Heather.

Debra thought, Aren't you working part-time now? Somehow Youth Director at the temple did not seem like a full-time job—but that was her own prejudice again. "You'll see how you feel," she said.

"I'll know more once I have the baby."

Debra nodded slowly, but she tried to sound encouraging. "The girls are excited!"

"Yes!"

"Do they eat at your house?" Debra picked apart the giant scone.

"Yes."

"Sophie too?"

"I think so."

"Her dance teacher is pressuring her," Debra said.

"What do you mean?"

Debra told Heather about no bread and salad salad salad.

"That's terrible," said Heather.

"What do you think I should do?"

"I don't know," Heather said nervously, as though Debra were asking a trick question.

"I mean what should *we* do?" Debra invoked the team.

Heather shifted her weight. She sipped her juice. "I think," she said at last, "maybe that question is for Sophie."

"She's sixteen," said Debra.

"That's what I'm thinking," Heather said. "Now that she's sixteen, maybe our job is just to give her tools to make decisions for herself?"

Debra stared at Heather. You have perspective, she thought. That's why you talk like this. You have distance. You see Sophie as a young adult with agency. Good for you. At the same time, she thought, Wait till you have your own kid. Wait till it's your baby.

Richard understood. Righteous indignation he could get behind. He called that night after Heather had briefed him about Nastia and said, "How dare that woman even *look* at Sophie?"

"Right?" said Debra.

"Yes, get the kids out of there. Obviously."

This was a relief. It was a huge relief to hear her ex-husband's certainty, until she mentioned the slight complication that the girls loved MBA.

"What do you mean love it?"

"They don't want to leave."

"Well, they might *need* to leave."

"And Nutcracker is in a week!"

"Okay," Richard said. "They'll do Nutcracker and then they won't come back after winter break."

"You aren't listening. They won't leave the studio ever."

"Have you asked them?"

"I don't have to ask."

"So you know exactly what they're thinking?"

"I do! And it's impossible to change their minds!"

Richard's voice tensed. "Oh, okay. Then can I ask why we're having this conversation?"

"Because I'm trying to parent with you!"

"How is this parenting with me? You tell me they have to leave the studio. I agree. You say they can't leave a week before Nutcracker. I say okay. You say actually they're never leaving. So, is there a reason you're asking my opinion?"

"I'm trying to have a discussion!" Debra burst out.

"But you've already made a decision."

"That's not true."

Silence. Then he said, "Maybe we should talk over winter break after the performance is over, and we have time to think."

"We need to make a plan."

"Okay, Debra."

This was maddening to hear. The voice of appeasement, as though she were hysterical (not true) for no reason (not true either). "I just don't understand," she said, "why even now I can't have an actual conversation with you."

"Maybe it's because you do all the talking," he said. "And the editing. And the revisions afterward."

"Maybe it's because you aren't interested in what I have to say, and you speak to me as though every problem is imaginary."

"I never said this problem is imaginary."

"You implied it."

"This is what I mean by editing."

"Listen," said Debra. "I'm trying to explain!" Because she was talking about the whole world, and the weightless ideal of femininity. The dewdrop sugar plum fairy of it all. The pointed toes and arabesques and silver filigree. And the auditions in the spring, and the vanishingly small chance that any of the girls at MBA would end up dancing for a living. She was talking about youth sports. The little soccer players and the tennis academies and, yes, the studios and skating rinks and gyms. What were they but puppy mills? "I'm worried about the girls. They're pawns! They're victims in this culture where women starve themselves to look like waifs—all for a dream that—"

"I get it." Richard cut her off. And that right there was why they were no longer married.

It's not worth it, she told herself at the dress rehearsal. It's twisted, this kind of training. She was waiting with the other moms backstage at the high school theater, rented for the occasion, and she could hear the silvery music and the sound of Nastia screaming, "Upupup! NO!"

"What is it now?" Debra asked Joy.

"Who knows?" Joy answered.

"It sounds bad," said Debra.

"I've heard worse."

"Gogogo! Arms!"

"What does she want from them?" Debra muttered. "These girls are not professionals. And they aren't going to be."

Now the other moms looked up from their phones. Joy and Chelsea and Brodie's mom, Lauren. They stared at Debra from the shadowy benches outside the dressing rooms.

No one spoke, but Debra felt a chill. She, who had given up her career for motherhood, felt her own commitment questioned. Because what was she saying? That she wouldn't take her daughters to New York and live with them if necessary? That she wouldn't spend weeks in a hotel while her girls competed in YAGP (Youth America Grand Prix, in case you were wondering)? That she wouldn't fly to Spain so that Sophie could try out for European companies? Did she really think her daughters—*their* daughters—were not worth it? And that Nastia's studio was built on lies—when several of her students had won competitions and were indeed dancing professionally in Latvia, Atlanta, Philly?

"Seriously. It's just wrong," said Debra.

But this was heresy. The other mothers turned away.

Strange to feel shunned. Even stranger that it had taken Debra so long to speak. How had she become one of these mothers waiting at rehearsal? That was not her. Not her at all. She was a feminist. Outspoken. How then had ballet lured her? Six years of Nutcrackers and summer classes, and pointe shoe fittings, and tutus. This was not what she had set out to do! But that was the nature of the beast. Mothering. Caregiving. It sucked resistance out of you. You woke up with a start and realized your daughters wanted to be princesses onstage—and you were financing gauze skirts and rhinestone crowns, even though you used to read them *Good Night Stories for Rebel Girls*. Debra covered her ears as Tchaikovsky played on. No! She knew she was opposed. Not to excellence, not to technique, not to dance itself—but to pursuing it this way.

If only her daughters felt the same. They bounded backstage and linked arms with their dance friends and laughed and pranced and posed for photos in their lovely costumes. They did not know their mother was recanting.

The day of Nutcracker, Debra arrived early with her parents and six tickets, and she made sure she was standing near the front of the line when the doors opened so that everyone could sit together.

"Not the front row," she told her mom. "That's too close. And those are reserved." Sure enough, Nastia had taped RESERVED signs to a block of seats where she would sit with the teachers. Nastia's husband, who owned a video business, was setting up to film the show.

"How about here?" Debra's dad said, standing midway among empty seats.

"No, too far back," she told Ed. "This is good." She chose the sixth row and then she and her parents spread out their coats and bags to save the seats. "Leave this one on the aisle for Heather."

"When is she due?" Cindy asked in the hushed voice she always used when talking about Richard's future wife.

"Next month I think? You guys sit down there," Debra said. "I'll sit next to them." It was still half an hour before curtain, but the audience was streaming in. Chelsea and her husband, along with Emma's brothers. Joy with her in-laws. Brodie's mom and Maddy's mom and Sabrina's mom.

There were siblings doing homework and grandparents visiting from Utah. There were several families speaking Russian. Debra had always thought the American moms were jealous of those who could speak to Nastia in her native tongue—as though they had an in.

"Should you leave the other tickets at the box office?" Cindy asked. "Where's Becca?"

"I'll go out and watch for everybody. Save these seats." Debra strode up to the lobby and as she went, she smiled at Chelsea—just to see what she would do. Chelsea didn't smile back. She was busy settling her kids, and obviously she hated Debra forever. Yes, this was high school.

"Hello. How are you?" Debra tested Joy in the lobby.

Joy smiled, but that was all. She did not answer.

What a relief to see Becca hurtling through the door. Wide-bodied, bright-eyed, Debra's sister blew past Joy. "Hey! How are you holding up? How are they treating you?"

"Okay, I guess." Becca was asking about their parents, but Debra was gazing at Nastia as she swept by in full regalia, a long gown with an oversized ruffle across the top—although it was two-thirty in the afternoon.

"Is that her?" Becca whispered.

Debra clutched Becca's arm, and they both burst out laughing. Oh, it was good to have a sister. What did other people do?

Becca sat on Debra's left as the lights dimmed in the theater. She held Debra's hand and passed out peppermints to Cindy and Ed while Nastia stood in front of the curtain. "Welcome, everyone."

Becca whispered, "How come Richard and Heather aren't here?"

"Parking?" Debra whispered back.

"Thank you for coming to our Nutcracker." Nastia looked small and nervous, nothing like her fire-breathing self. "We are so proud of our dancers and what they have done. We hope you will appreciate them. I would like to thank our preparatory teachers. Miss Megan Tanaka, Miss Gwen Sorenson, Mister Joshua Jackson . . ."

"There they are," Debra told Becca. Richard and Heather were standing in the back. She waved until at last they saw her. Then slowly they made their way down the aisle.

"Holy shit," Becca whispered to Debra. "How many months is she?"

"Shh." Debra shook her head as Richard approached.

He sat next to Debra with two bouquets of roses, and Heather eased herself into her seat on the aisle.

"Nice flowers," Debra told Richard.

"And lastly," said Nastia, "photography and filming is strictly forbidden. I want to thank my husband for help and support including filming today's performance. Order forms are in your programs. Thank you very much."

The theater went dark, heavenly music played, and infinitesimally small angels paraded across the stage. The four-year-olds wore white with silver haloes. Aww, breathed parents, straining to see. *The Nutcracker* did not usually begin with angels, but Nastia liked to get the littlest dancers out of the way.

As soon as the angels filed off, a dozen slightly bigger girls pranced out to dance with painted Nutcrackers, and they were followed by three boys marching and jumping with precision as toy soldiers.

Candy canes bounded on with hoops, and marzipans in little hats, and three girls dressed as Chinese dolls—or were they jumping jacks? Or little red silk cats? "Is that a tiny bit racist?" Becca asked during the applause.

There was no story in this Nutcracker. Nastia staged the ballet in scenes. Instead of a Christmas tree growing taller, the dancers grew before the audience's eyes as the youngest children yielded to tweens and teens. Here was the French Dance with girls in lilac and one careful boy, standing in the middle. Here were fairies—and suddenly, the Spanish Dance!

"There she is!" Disillusioned though she was, disgusted with ballet and all it stood for, Debra gripped Richard's arm—and he was smiling. They both were, because that was Lily in a red tutu and black lace, a red flower pinned to her blond hair.

Lily's eyes were huge and dark; her head tilted. Her body was a flame. She turned and spun and flew about the stage and she was theirs. She was their own child—but she was also something else. Something magic, self-aware and brave. It wasn't just her steps or her precision; it was her style. Anxious at school, afraid of the dark and fireworks and death, she opened like a flower under the lights.

"She kills it every time," said Richard, during the applause.

"I know," said Debra, as the Spanish dancers curtsied.

Lily ran off into the wings and she was still a Spanish lady holding out her arms and flicking up her skirts. *"Wow,"* said Becca. "She's the one you have to worry about."

Anxious, and delighted, Debra wanted to hear more, but the flowers were waltzing now.

Was it just Debra's imagination? Emma's Dewdrop was not compelling. Admittedly, the part was hard, but Emma's chaînés were not quite as fast as Debra had seen them in rehearsal. Had Nastia ruined her confidence, or was something really lacking? In her pale pink tutu, Emma danced with just a touch of fear. Joy's daughter, Fiona, cleaned up as Sugar Plum, along with a Cavalier Nastia had imported from the city. The Cavalier partnered decorously but Fiona attacked and sparkled as she turned.

"She's good," said Becca.

But now the snowflakes ran in from the wings, their waltz filled the stage, and Debra's mom said, "Is that one Sophie?" Because at first it was hard to tell. There were so many girls in white.

"That's her," said Debra. And her heart was pounding. Sophie was dancing with such care. She was lovely, but she was soft, and her body really was round, her face dimpled, her waist thick. She danced modestly, and while her steps were clean, they were not crystalline.

"I loved that!" Cindy told Debra as the curtain tumbled down and "Sleigh Ride" started playing.

"Lily was something," Becca said.

"Sophie was too," said Ed, who praised equally, no matter what.

"Where's Heather?" Debra asked Richard.

"She stepped out because her back was hurting."

Oh God, Debra thought, and she told Richard, "Go check on her."

But nothing was wrong. They found Heather in the lobby taking pictures of the costumed girls. There was Lily's teacher, Gwen, and there was the tall patient woman who taught the little kids. Only Joshua was missing. The girls' jazz teacher never came to Nutcracker.

"You were both so beautiful!" Cindy told the girls.

Richard presented the bouquets. "I know it wasn't easy."

"But it was so fun," said Lily.

Meanwhile, Debra asked Heather, "Hanging in there?"

She nodded. "I'm okay!"

"Let me take one of you and the girls." Debra took a photo of Heather with Sophie on one side and Lily on the other and they were both pointing to her belly as Nastia swept by.

"Better in rehearsal," she told Sophie. "Timing."

Sophie nodded humbly.

"But you!" Nastia told Lily. "A star!"

That's it, Debra thought, watching Sophie's face, resigned, anguished, jealous. We're out of here. Just you wait, she told Nastia silently. Just wait till I pull these girls. I'll save them from you. Break your spell. If looks could kill. But Nastia did not notice Debra glaring. "Next time you will listen to the music, yes?" Nastia told Sophie.

"Yes!" said Sophie, eager as a little soldier.

"You see what I mean about their teacher," Debra told Becca as they waited for the girls to change.

"Yeah, she's a bitch."

Debra fumed. "One kid isn't better than the other!"

"Well," Becca hedged.

"What?" Debra demanded.

"Lily is really good."

"Becca!" Debra chided, because how could she say that? How could her body-positive, movement-therapist sister talk that way?

"Sorry!" Becca threw up her hands. "She's got it. She's a natural."

"That isn't fair," said Debra.

"Yeah, I know."

"I'm not doing this anymore," Debra declared.

"Good luck."

The girls were reemerging in their clothes and coats. They were carrying their roses, and their faces were glowing with lipstick and mascara and rouge. Sophie's eyes were framed with long false lashes. You can be anything you want to be! Debra told her silently. Go on! Become an astronaut. A research scientist. A doctor. And yet she looked so lovely with her flowers. Hopeful, innocent, determined. How could Debra pull her from the studio?

Richard ran out to bring the car around for Heather. He said he had to get her home and Debra said no kidding.

The crowds dispersed. Debra and the girls and all the other dancers and their parents and siblings adjourned to the parking lot.

A snowflake named Olivia called out for Sophie and gave her a Secret Santa gift which was a little plush ballerina bear. Lily danced ahead with Audrey, Maddy, and Scarlett. It was bitter cold, but the girls didn't seem to notice.

They had another performance that night. There would always be another—until when? Until they woke up? Until they outgrew the music and these lights? Even then, how difficult it was to break away. You loved the floating skirts and jeweled bodices, arched feet, quick turns. You couldn't help it. That was the scary part. The spells still worked when you became a mother.

16

Deal Breaker

Pam is seeing someone, but she's not talking about it. Of course, her friends know, but she has not told her parents or her sister, Wendy. She would tell her father, Charles, because he doesn't pry—but then he would tell her mother, Helen. As for Wendy, she can't keep a secret from anyone—Helen least of all. If Helen knew, she would pry and pester and pass judgment—so Pam is keeping John from her. She's done being judged. Well, almost done. She's working on it.

John is not Jewish. For Helen that's a deal breaker—but this isn't Helen's deal to break! He is not young, but, at fifty-six, Pam is not young either. He is mostly bald. His knees are bad. He's heavy and he has a little twitch when he is nervous, a slight blink of his left eye. He's shy, soft-spoken, and *divorced,* which is, in Helen's mind, a moral failing. Helen would never say it, but Pam knows what she thinks. Helen, who has the most solicitous husband in the world, believes that divorced people give up easily.

For these reasons, Pam does not even mention John on the phone and her mother assumes that she is single. You know your mother worries, Charles tells Pam, and she feels a little guilty, but not enough to change the status quo, which is that she and John spend nearly every weekend together, either at her place in Providence or his in Jamaica Plain. He doesn't twitch at all when they're together. In fact, his eyes are wonderfully green. Like Pam, he is a lawyer, but he is a sole practitioner specializing in wills and trusts. Like Pam, he enjoys black coffee and good jazz. But those are surface details. More importantly, he is openhearted. He loves animals. His ginger, Taffy, passed recently, and he keeps her picture on his dresser. He does not think it strange that Pam still mourns her own cat, Shadow.

John is big, and his bulk comforts Pam, because she is so small. He is effusive, while Pam is more reserved. When he embraces her, he lifts her off the ground. He has a warmth about him, like an oven radiating heat. Pam warms her feet on him in bed. The first time, she said, "I'm sorry my feet are cold." And he said, "I don't mind. I like it."

They have been seeing each other for six months when he says he wants her to meet his daughter. Isabella is his only child, and he is careful with her. He does not rush to introduce her to people he is dating.

"Who else have you dated?" Pam asks, because he has only been divorced a year.

"Well, just you," says John. They are walking in the Arnold Arboretum on a clear October day. They take a path over gentle hills, and John says, "I want to introduce you because I think you'll really like each other."

"Oh!" Pam's heart jumps. She knows all about Isabella, although she has not met her yet. John's daughter is fourteen and she attends The Winsor School and sings. Pam has watched videos of Bella in choir—although it's hard to see which one she is. Isabella is a wonderful student. John keeps all her essays in a folder. And her math tests! She is good at math as well. She is gifted, John tells Pam, and she recognizes his partiality. She has other friends with children, and they are all loving, but those with just one child are lovesick, their attention undivided. An only child must be everything at once. Student, athlete, artist. Pam used to laugh about this, but when John praises his daughter, she looks at him with tenderness. Isabella is a writer and a mathematician and an artist and why not? At John's house, Pam gazes at Bella's acrylic paintings and says, "She's so talented!" Her portrait of her father looks just like him. The green eyes, the smooth dome of his head.

As they walk through the trees, John's cheeks are ruddy in the fresh crisp air. "I thought the three of us could go somewhere together."

He says it near a hemlock. All the trees in the arboretum are labeled with metal tags, and Pam takes note because she is going to remember this moment. "We could meet for lunch," she says.

"Maybe it would be better to do something," John suggests.

Pam tries to think. What's a good thing to do with a fourteen-year-old girl? Movies? Canoeing on the Charles? She hates canoeing. Trampolines? Not with John's knees. "How about a museum?" She is thinking of Isabella's art. "The MFA. Or what about the Gardner?"

"I haven't been there in years," John says.

"Me either," Pam says, but the memories rush in on her. The Italian palace right in Boston. The museum's courtyard like a fairy tale as you step inside. Walls pale pink like the inside of a shell, a glass roof far above, and at the courtyard's center an enchanted garden with a mosaic floor and fountain, delicate flowering vines.

"The Gardner is a great idea," John says.

"And you know what? She can get in for free," Pam tells him.

"What do you mean?"

"If your name is Isabella you can always get in free."

"Really?"

"In college I had a friend named Isabel, and it didn't count. You can't be Isabel or Izzy. You have to be Isabella like Isabella Stuart Gardner."

"Is that still true?"

"Look it up."

While he checks his phone, she hovers at his shoulder, and they laugh with pleasure because it's still true, just as Pam says. They are standing near the hemlock with its green and golden leaves, and everything seems meant to be.

However, they can't get to the museum right away. They need to wait for one of John's weekends, and even then, Isabella is busy. She's not just a singer and a painter. She plays soccer every Saturday. Pam knows the schedule, because John can't see her when Bella has a game. He's got to drive and watch and cheer. During the season there's hardly any time, and then it's Thanksgiving, which he and his ex-wife, Alison, choreograph to maximize relatives on both sides of the family. John takes Bella to his parents' in Winchester for dinner and then Bella and her mother and her aunts run in the Turkey Trot on Friday morning, and they all go to J.P. Licks for ice cream afterward.

"That's right near my parents' house," Pam says while they are eating breakfast at her place.

"Not the one in Brookline. The original J.P. Licks," John says, meaning the one in Jamaica Plain on Centre Street.

"But that's close too," says Pam.

John looks puzzled, as if to say, What are you suggesting? And for the first time she feels uncertain—trapped in a kind of Catch-22. She might be close. She *is* close, but she can't join him and his family, because she hasn't even met his daughter.

"I just wish," she says.

"Wish what?" he asks.

"That we could be together more."

"We will be." He kisses her, and uncertainty evaporates. There is something about the way he holds her face in his hands. When she was young the guys she'd loved had been charming, confident, a little mean. John is none of those things. When he takes her in his arms she wants to be with him forever. She wants everyone to know that they're together, everyone except her mother.

Thanksgiving is desolate with freezing rain. Pam drives to her parents' but her sister can't come because Jill is working on the holiday.

"What about Aunt Sylvia and Uncle Lew?" Pam asks when she arrives.

Her father shakes his head.

"They're just twenty minutes away." Pam shakes out her umbrella in the entryway.

"Leave it on the porch," her mother calls out from the kitchen. She can sense a wet umbrella without seeing it.

"Do you even know what Sylvia did?" Pam whispers to her dad.

"Your mother was very hurt," Charles tells her, as he always does.

"Hurt, or took offense?"

Charles shrugs as if to say, Is there a difference? Does it really matter?

Pam knows about taking offense. Like Sylvia, Pam's dog is not invited to Thanksgiving. The last time Pam brought her to the house, Rosie rampaged through the garden, trampling the flowers, and now she remains home with a sitter in Providence. So, it's just Pam and her parents and the secret Pam is keeping. Such a big secret that she nearly sets a fourth place at the table.

"This is a lot of food," Pam says when they sit down.

"I can always freeze the leftovers," says Helen.

Pam glances at her father, who will be eating turkey sandwiches and cornbread stuffing and roasted Brussels sprouts forever. "What about the Metzgers?"

"All the usual suspects are in Boca," says Charles.

"The Metzgers are in West Palm," Helen corrects him.

"Do you ever think about going down there?" Pam asks.

"Occasionally, in moments of weakness," Charles says. "But—"

Helen finishes his sentence. "We hate it there."

Pam says, "I hate to see you isolated."

"We aren't isolated." Charles refills Pam's glass.

"You seem that way." Pam's face is hot. She was a diver as a girl, and she recognizes the feeling. Flushed excitement, climbing the ladder. "You seem bored and lonely."

"I am never bored," Helen declares, as though Pam has accused her of a mortal sin. Laziness. Superficiality.

"I worry about you guys," says Pam.

"You don't have to worry about us," her father says.

"I worry that *you're* lonely," Helen tells Pam.

"Why?" She realizes how absurd this is—fighting about who's lonelier at a three-person Thanksgiving dinner.

"You've been single for a long time," Charles says in his gentle doctor's voice, courteous and at the same time chiding.

"How do you know I'm single?" Pam shoots back.

Helen turns on her. "You're seeing somebody!"

"I am." Suddenly, she's done it. The secret's out.

"Really!" Charles sets down his fork.

"Who is it?" Helen says.

Pam tilts her chair way back on its hind legs, just to get some distance from the table.

"Don't do that," her mother says.

"His name is John." Pam thumps to earth, all four chair legs on the floor.

"How did you meet?" Charles asks.

"John who?" says Helen, because, as she's told Pam many times, it's irritating when people are introduced by first name only.

"John O'Neill," says Pam.

"Okay," her dad says.

"What does he do?" asks Pam's mother.

"And no, he isn't Jewish." Pam's cheeks are burning now.

"I gathered that," Charles says. "I figured that out."

Helen says, "It doesn't matter."

"What?" Pam splutters, half laughing, half indignant. "You always said that was a deal breaker!"

"At your age?" says Helen.

Charles looks miffed. "Who do you take us for? Your sister married a woman."

"Okay, Dad."

"A Catholic woman," Helen adds.

"Right. Give us a little credit," Charles says.

"He's divorced." Pam tests her mother.

Helen doesn't even blink. "The main question is what he's like."

"He's a good person," Pam answers, and she resolves to say no more. Not another word. But her mother doesn't honor this.

"A good person? What does *good* mean?"

"Good. Just good," Pam tells her.

"So, you know him well?" says Charles.

"How long have you been dating?" Helen asks.

"Seven months."

Charles says. "All right. We're not going to put you on the spot." But then he can't resist. "What does he do?"

He kisses me, thinks Pam. He holds me in his arms at night. She says, "He's a lawyer."

"How long has he been divorced?" asks Helen.

Here we go, thinks Pam. "A year."

"That's not very long."

"How long should it be?" Pam laughs a little. She can't help it. Even speaking about John makes dinner bearable. Even speaking about him to her mother. Strangely she doesn't mind talking, now that she's begun. Somehow, nothing Helen says can hurt her. In fact, at this moment, her mother seems gentle.

What is happening? Helen's eyes are kind. She seems open, pleasantly surprised. Charles does too.

"Does he have children?" Helen asks.

"Yes," says Pam. "He has a daughter at Winsor."

"A good school," says Charles.

"What's her name?" says Helen.

For a moment, Pam doesn't want to answer. She wants to declare, I'm not at liberty to say, but she has come this far. She tells them. "Isabella."

"That's pretty," Charles says.

"Is she in high school?" Helen asks.

"She's in ninth grade."

"John must be much younger than you," Helen says.

"No, he's my age."

"Then he's quite an old father!"

Charles turns to Helen. "Lots of people have children late."

"I am aware," Helen tells him. Then she asks, "What's the daughter like?"

That question needles Pam. "I haven't met her yet. We're planning to do something together."

"Dinner?" Charles says.

"The Gardner Museum."

"Oh! Wonderful," says Helen. "Does she like art?"

"She's an artist." Pam feels the conversation spinning out of control, but she can't stop talking. "She's an amazing painter."

"You've seen her work?" her dad says, as though Bella is professional.

"I mean, only in John's kitchen." Why does she say that? Why does she say anything? Pam learned long ago not to confide in her parents, but now she's blushing, and it's not the wine. It's happiness. Here she is whipping out her phone to show them a photo of Isabella's painting. The portrait of John, radiant with his green eyes and the glowing dome of his pink forehead.

Helen says, "Hold on, I have to get my glasses."

Meanwhile, Charles squints at the phone. "That's very good. Is it her father?"

"Let me see." Helen takes a long look. "The flat face and green eyes remind me of Modigliani."

"Really?" says Pam.

"If he were painting a middle-aged man," Helen says without irony.

"With a short neck," says Charles.

"He doesn't have such a short neck," Pam defends John.

"You're right," Charles says. "It's not that his neck is short. It's that the necks in Modigliani's paintings are so long."

"She's talented," Helen declares.

"She is," says Pam.

Charles says, "When are you taking her to the museum?"

"We're trying to—we have to figure out the schedule."

"Oh." Helen sounds more like herself. Just a little colder. Firmer. "Because she's living with her mother."

"John has joint custody."

"And who is the mother?" Helen asks.

Pam thinks fast. Mostly, she knows what John told her, which is that his ex-wife broke his heart and smashed it into little pieces. "Her name is Alison. She's an oncologist at the Brigham." She says this for her dad's benefit, because he is a retired otolaryngologist. He is always modest about his career. He says he could never fix a broken heart like Grandpa Morris. Still, he was an Attending for many years at Mass Eye and Ear.

"Alison who?" Charles asks in case he knows her.

"Alison Friedlander."

"Jewish!" Helen says.

"You don't know that," Pam says.

"Of course I do."

"It's a Jewish name," says Charles.

"Isn't it German or something?"

"No," says Helen. "It's a Jewish name. She's Jewish."

Charles chimes in, "And you know what that means!"

They have that twinnish look they get when they solve the acrostic in the Sunday paper. Almost in unison, they say, "John's daughter is Jewish too."

"You guys are terrible!" Pam says, because what are they doing seizing this innocent child? Five minutes ago, Pam admitted she was dating, and now they've claimed a girl they haven't met. A girl *she* hasn't met. They're ready to adopt John's daughter. "You don't know anything about her."

"Her mother's name is Friedlander," Helen says.

"Believe me, no one's raising Isabella Jewish," says Pam.

"That doesn't matter," Helen tells her.

"She celebrates Christmas with John's parents."

"Doesn't matter," Charles intones.

"John and Isabella decorate a tree each year."

Helen dismisses this. "Her mother is Jewish, so she is a Jew."

"What else can she be?" says Charles.

They are so pleased. They have forgotten John entirely. They've nearly forgotten Pam across the table. It's as if they have an instant granddaughter. Already, they are plotting. Pam can see it in their eyes. "Don't get excited," she warns. "Don't jump to conclusions."

"Who's jumping?" Charles says.

"Just don't get your hopes up."

"About what?" says Charles.

"About anything!" Pam feels superstitious. Relieved and yet regretful that she told them. "Don't assume."

"I don't assume anything," Helen says, and yet she's smiling. "Charles, would you get dessert plates?"

Usually, Pam escapes as fast as possible. She'll drive home early, the morning after Thanksgiving. This weekend, she lingers most of Friday. Partly to stack firewood, because her dad can't do it anymore. Partly because her mother is so pleasant. Helen does not question Pam's short hair or tell her wistfully, But you could get the gray out. There are no dark comments about living alone. No mournful speeches starting with the words I worry . . . Most surprising, Helen does not interrogate Pam about John. Clearly Helen has decided—

maybe she and Charles have decided together—that they will not intrude.

It's like a staring contest, these two keeping their mouths shut. Helen does not say a word about Pam's relationship. Charles does almost as well. True to form, Helen maintains discipline, but Charles cracks.

They are standing in the driveway, and Pam is about to head home to Providence where Rosie waits for her. Helen says, "Good-bye, dear. I'm so glad you could come."

"Thanks, Mom," Pam says.

"Drive safely," Charles tells her. "Keep us posted."

Helen shoots him a warning look—but she's amused by his little hint as well. She's won! "Just let us know when you get home," she tells Pam.

"Okay, bye. I'll call you." Pam's words are swallowed up in her father's embrace.

And he cannot resist. "Tell us all about the Gardner."

"Only if you want to," says Helen, radiating curiosity and hope.

Pam's parents are funny, almost charming as they stand in front of their brick house. I love you, Pam thinks suddenly. "I will," she promises. "I'll tell you how it goes."

If only she had something to report. The visit to the Gardner keeps getting postponed. First it's Isabella's choir concert and then she has exams and then the holidays are coming and there will be no weekends left. Pam and John can hardly see each other, let alone take Isabella to the museum. All that's left is the Friday Isabella gets out of school for winter break, but after Pam reserves tickets, there's yet another problem.

She drives to John's office in Jamaica Plain so they can pick up Bella together. His building is a small Victorian that used to be a house. An orthodontist leases the first floor, and John shares the second floor with an insurance agent. John's space is in front. He's got a big bay window which would be perfect for plants, but he has none. The only pictures are those of Bella on his desk.

"Hold on." He is typing something on his phone. "One second."

Pam takes a seat in a blue-and-chrome chair and looks at Bella as a tiny girl on the beach and Bella in her choir robe and Bella smiling with braces on her teeth. Does she go to the orthodontist downstairs? Her eyes are brown. Her hair is long and shining, perfectly brushed. Burnished. That's the word that comes to mind. Some combination of brushed and polished. She is not just pretty. She is cherished.

"Hi," John says.

"Hi!"

"There's a problem."

Again? Pam thinks. Really?

"Alison broke her foot."

"What?" Pam blurts out. Then she says, "Oh no."

"She just had an X-ray."

"Why didn't you tell me?" Pam asks, because she's been driving for an hour.

"It just happened this morning, and now it looks like she'll need surgery to put a pin in—so I need to be there with Bella."

"Okay," Pam says, trying not to let her disappointment show. "We can reschedule. I just wish you'd called me."

"We were still figuring out what to do."

"But if I'd known I wouldn't have taken off work—"

"Well, it's an emergency."

"Yes but."

He stares at her. "What do you mean but?"

She tries not to let her disappointment show, but she can't help it. "I feel like we're cursed or something."

"What are you talking about?" His eye is twitching, just a little. He is looking at her as though she is an alien, thinking about museums at a time like this. "Alison's in the hospital."

Isn't she always in the hospital? Pam thinks. Doesn't she work there? "Okay. I guess I'll just go over to your house and wait."

"No, I'm taking Bella for the weekend," he tells her.

Pam nods, because of course she can't be at the house with them. Bella hasn't even met her. "I guess I should just turn around and drive home."

"No, don't do that," John says as he sits at his desk.

She feels distant as a client. "You didn't call me."

"The situation was unfolding!" he bursts out.

The situation? she thinks. What is the situation here? All she wanted was to meet his daughter. He'd suggested it himself, but there's no room for her. His heart is with Alison and Bella because he is a good person and they are family. "You have your hands full," she says.

"I'm not trying to ruin your plans."

"They're my plans now? I thought we were planning to take Bella to the Gardner together."

He is astonished. "Pam, Alison's foot is very badly broken!"

"It's always something."

"This is not just something."

Tears start in her eyes. "It's never going to happen. You're not going to let it happen."

"What are you talking about?"

"We'll never get to the museum."

"Why are you still talking about the museum? This has nothing to do with the museum."

"I know," says Pam. "It's about not seeing me."

He looks at her across his desk and says, "Do you think I'm trying to avoid you? Or exclude you?"

She takes a breath. "I don't feel excluded."

"Thank you."

She stands up. "I feel extraneous."

"I don't know what that means," he says.

"It's just that I'm alone," she tells him. "And my feelings are extraneous."

"Pam!" He walks around his desk and reaches for her. He is always reaching, but when he embraces her, she feels as though he's somewhere else. All the action in his life is happening without her. It's all offstage where she can't see. No. It's just the opposite. She's the one offstage in shadows.

"I'm sorry about Alison's foot," she says, collecting herself.

"I know."

They are standing there together, doing the right thing. Her voice is muffled because her face is pressed against his chest. "I just have a feeling that we'll never get to the Gardner."

"We will," he says. "We'll go together."

Just us? she thinks. Just us, without your daughter? She had envisioned stepping from winter into the pink courtyard and seeing it through Bella's eyes. She had imagined that surprise. The mosaic and the ferns and the climbing vines. The sudden burst of Italy. "I wanted to be there when she walks in for the first time."

"She's been there," John says with some surprise. "She went on a field trip with her class last year."

Pam pulls away. "You never told me that."

He points out the obvious. "Her school is right there."

"Oh." She should have thought of that. Winsor is practically across the street. Of course the girls would visit the Gardner. "I had a whole story in my mind!"

"What story?"

She is half laughing at herself. "I made up a whole story and none of it was true!"

"We'll figure it out," he promises.

She doesn't answer.

"Don't you believe me?"

She just shrugs. She can't give him what he wants. She doesn't have it in her to say yes.

"I'd better pick her up," he says.

"Okay."

"Don't look at me like that."

"How do I look?"

"Crestfallen," he says.

And it's true. She is so anxious and dramatic. This is the gulf between them. She has never been married. She has never been a parent. "You think I'm selfish."

"No," he says. "You're just not used to—"

"Putting other people first?"

"Changing the schedule sometimes."

"But I *am* used to it!" she says, because how many times have they postponed the museum trip? How many times have they rescheduled? She's been flexible. She's been hoping.

"And we will get to the museum."

"No, that's okay." Her voice sounds small and cold, but she can't help it. That's how she begins to feel. Chilly, as though she were outside again. She's zipping up her coat and John looks so sorry! He looks sorry for her. Righteous anger rushes in—or is it self-respect awakening? "Don't do me any favors," she says, because she has no desire to walk through the Gardner's doors. To see the Madonnas or the bits of lace, the altarpieces, the Rembrandt self-portrait. The one where he's so young and self-assured.

Quietly, John says, "I'm going to be late." He is disappointed in her. She can see it in his face. He is shocked by her behavior (as if she's in the wrong!), but even now, he's kind. "I'll call you later."

"Okay." With a sinking feeling she remembers that she called her parents from the road. She told them she was going to the Gardner with John and Bella that afternoon.

He drives off to collect his daughter. She sits in her car trying to figure out where to go. Not to the museum. Not to her parents'. They're just a few minutes away, but she can't face them. No way can she tell them about all of this.

She drives to Providence and picks up Rosie. Her dog panting, unquestioning, always thrilled when she returns. Jamie, the dog sitter, is surprised to see Pam back so soon.

"We were just going for a run," Jamie says.

"That's okay. I'll take her." Pam pays for three full days and takes Rosie home.

Her parents refrain from calling. Pam can tell, because they don't call for three days. They don't even text, but she can hear them wondering about her. They are in suspense. Then they are speculating. Didn't she say she'd tell them how it went?

She hears them wishing she would call, or at least send them a few words. Tap the hull of her drowned submarine. On the fourth day she texts to say she's fine.

Her mother texts back immediately *That's good to hear.* And Pam hears everything in those few words. Reproach, concern, regret.

That night Pam fortifies herself with a few drinks and answers when her parents call.

"Hello?" she says.

"Pam?" her mother says.

Who else would it be? Pam thinks. She says, "Hi. Yes."

"How are you?"

"Good," says Pam.

"Hold on. Let me put you on speaker."

"You're doing all right?" her dad asks.

"I'm fine."

"I figured as much," Helen says, because of course she has figured out everything.

"Yeah, we didn't get to the museum," Pam says.

"What happened?" Charles asks.

"I don't know. Scheduling. Medical emergency."

"Really!" Charles says.

"I mean, it wasn't life-threatening."

"I'm sorry," Helen says. For a split second it sounds like she's sorry the emergency was minor—but Pam knows what she means.

"It's okay," says Pam. "In the end I didn't really want to go."

"You broke up with him!" Helen is direct as always.

"Well," says Pam. "We're still speaking. He is very—"

"Very what?" says Helen.

"Committed."

"That's a good thing," Charles ventures.

"To his ex-wife and daughter."

Her mother says, "Oh."

Alone in her kitchen where no one can see, Pam tilts back her chair. "What do you call those trees that hold on to all their leaves even in the winter?"

"Persistent?" says Charles.

"Marcescent," says Helen, because she knows the word for everything. She is such a puzzler.

"That's how he is," Pam tells them.

"Good for him," says Helen, and Pam knows she means good riddance.

Charles's voice is gentler. "So, you haven't met Isabella."

Pam can hear his wistfulness and longing. She senses it in both her parents, although it's hidden in her mother.

"I told you not to get your hopes up," she says, but this is harsh, and she regrets it. "We're still friends," she amends. "We're on good terms."

They say nothing.

Their silence lasts so long that Pam asks, "Are you still there?"

"We're here," says Charles.

"Mom?"

"I'm here," she says. "I was just thinking."

"What are you thinking?" Pam asks, although she can imagine. Helen is thinking that John was a mirage and there won't be an instant granddaughter. Not even a granddaughter once removed, a step-granddaughter, a granddaughter by adoption. Helen says none of this, however. She asks, "Why don't you come here for the weekend?"

"I mean—" Pam starts.

"So you won't be alone."

"I'm not alone. I'm sitting here with Rosie."

"Wonderful."

"We're taking obedience classes."

"That's a good idea," Helen says.

"That way when she graduates, we can visit you together."

"No," Helen says immediately. "You are always welcome here. Without the dog."

Pam laughs at that. Strange to say, her mother's retort comforts her. Any wistfulness on Helen's part is over. She will not suffer fools or dogs or trees. She will not sigh about what might have been. Pam's dog will not return, and John won't set foot in Helen's house either. Has he failed a test? Absolutely. Pam can't help but admire her mother's clarity. Helen is difficult. She's daunting, but she is crisp. She never clings. She does not remain on good terms to avoid a scene, nor does she stay friends when she doesn't feel friendly. Helen has never met John, but that's no impediment. She is disowning him. She has never spoken to him, but it doesn't matter. If she had spoken to him, she would never speak to him again.

17

Poppy

Two years. Two years and two months—but who was counting? In all that time, the sisters had not exchanged a word. It was a heartbreak, but what could Sylvia do? Helen would not apologize. Meanwhile, Sylvia was eighty, and Helen two years older! Sylvia dreaded lying on her deathbed without seeing Helen—or, even worse, discovering her sister had passed away.

In all this time, Sylvia had nurtured one faint hope—that some higher cause would override their long estrangement. Some greater need. A flood or hurricane at home. A crisis, God forbid, in Israel. In the past, Helen and Sylvia had joined forces, or rather, Helen had enlisted Sylvia as donor and foot soldier. However, even this dream had ended months before.

That fateful day, Sylvia and Lew had been watching *The Marriage of Figaro* on *Great Performances* when Sylvia's phone rang.

"Richard!" she said. "Hello, sweetheart."

"Mom?" Richard sounded jubilant and nervous.

"Is something wrong?"

"No! Why do you always think something's wrong?"

"Your voice," said Sylvia.

"I have a question for you."

"Yes?"

"How would you like to be a grandma again?"

"Oh!" Sylvia turned startled to Lew.

"We're expecting in January!"

"You and Heather?"

"Who else?"

"Goodness!" Sylvia didn't mean to sound so surprised—but really. Richard was nearly fifty, and only just divorced. He and Heather were unmarried, and he had two daughters already. To think of starting a second family! "Do the girls know?"

"They're excited!"

"And Debra?" Sylvia was still fond of her ex-daughter-in-law.

"She's very happy!"

Very? thought Sylvia.

"We told her first!"

Onscreen, Count Almaviva tried to seduce Susanna. On the couch, Sylvia tried to imagine a new baby. Now? At this late date? She would have three grandchildren! And then she thought of Helen, who had none.

"Lew, did you hear?" Sylvia asked, although he was sitting right next to her.

"I heard," Lew said.

"But you just got engaged," Sylvia told Richard.

"Yes, Mom."

"Do you have a date?"

"New Year's Day."

"A New Year's wedding!"

"No, that's the due date," Richard said. "We'll plan the wedding for next summer."

Overhearing this, Lew chuckled.

"Shh," said Sylvia.

"I realize it's a surprise," Richard said.

"A wonderful surprise," Sylvia declared—but she could not stop thinking, Three for me, and none for Helen.

That was the end. There would be no reconciliation. Not even for Combined Jewish Philanthropies.

When she got off the phone, Sylvia told Lew, "She'll blame me for this."

"Who's blaming you?"

"Helen!"

"How can your sister blame you for another grandchild? You've got nothing to do with it," Lew protested. But he did not understand.

Week after week, Helen's silence grew.

Lew said, "Silence doesn't grow. Silence is silence." He did this sometimes, insisting on semantics. It was his legal background. He said, "You can't be more silent than you were before."

Sylvia said, "My sister can."

"Think of the baby," Lew advised.

"But that makes it harder."

"Why?"

"Because it will be so complicated!" Sylvia wasn't thinking of herself. On the contrary! She feared for Richard, who was taking on so much. After all, he had joint custody. He worked all hours, and he had the girls every other weekend. Lily had tutors, and Sophie had strained a calf muscle dancing. That meant physical therapy and more driving.

Lew showed Sylvia an article about how to manage worries. You were supposed to set aside a time each day to write them down.

"I'll think about it," Sylvia said.

She thought a lot. At night she crept out of bed and studied framed photos on the piano. How would Richard care for a baby at his age? And what if Heather had another? Would Richard live to see these children grow up? Would anyone? They were all too old for this. And then, inevitably, she thought of Helen and her husband, Charles. Two grown daughters with no children of their own. Sylvia felt no superiority—none at all. Only melancholy, as she contemplated that branch of the family ending.

An hour a night. At most two hours. That was all the sleep Sylvia was getting—but she did not tell anyone apart from Lew. She would not burden Richard, and certainly she could not confide in Heather, who needed to stay calm.

All Sylvia ever said to Richard was, "You should get married before the birth. If not for your sake, then for the baby." And all she said to Heather was, "How are you, sweetheart? How are you feeling?" There was nothing else that she could do. Richard and Heather had decided to keep the baby's gender secret, so Sylvia could not even go shopping.

"First of all," Richard told her, "you don't need to buy stereotypical baby clothes."

Sylvia protested, "How can I buy everything in mint green?"

"And second of all, you don't need to buy anything."

"Why?" Sylvia sensed something in his voice. Just a touch of resignation. "Is it another girl? Do you already have baby clothes?"

"Mom!"

No, of course he wouldn't have hand-me-downs from Sophie and Lily. Nobody kept baby clothes after so much time had passed. Even if she was a girl, this little one would be a different generation. Meanwhile, Sylvia had no guidelines. She could not buy pink dresses. Nor could she choose nautical pajamas. She had no theme.

"There is such a thing as unisex clothing," Richard told her.

"Yellow?" she said. "I don't like outfits that are neither here nor there."

"Well, you're behind the times," Richard informed her.

"I just want to help," she pleaded.

However, Richard was too busy to consider how she might contribute. Sylvia asked, Will there be a brunch after the baby naming? He told her, We're taking care of it. She said, What about caterers?

He said, Mom. And so, she was left thinking, What will everybody eat? Also, her friend's grandson had a heart defect requiring two surgeries! So much could go wrong. Sylvia worried like it was her job. Nine at night until five in the morning.

Then whenever she called with an idea, like Why don't I take care of the flowers? or Should I book a hotel for Christmas in case Heather gives birth early? Richard would say, Mom. Please, I'm in a meeting. As though she were being difficult, when in fact this baby was arriving at the most difficult time of year. Hotels *did* book up for the holidays.

Everything is under control, said Richard.

"He sounds so strange," Sylvia told Lew. "Is he trying to keep me at a distance?"

Lew said, "Probably."

But why? Sylvia wondered in the night. And why was it that Heather never picked up the phone? She had always been forthcoming in the past. Warm. Sociable. What was going on with her?

Lew said, "If something were wrong, Richard would tell you."

Sylvia said, "Not at all! He wouldn't tell me until it's too late!"

"Too late for what?" Lew said. "You realize that you cannot do anything about anything."

"Exactly!"

Lew would never understand. Only one person would recognize this anguished feeling, all the advice pent-up inside, and that was Helen.

In December, Sylvia started at each buzz of the phone. Lew said she had to calm down—but Heather was planning a home birth. How was that reassuring? What if God forbid something happened and they had to rush to the hospital, but they were too late?

Sylvia suggested this to Richard, and like a faceless bureaucrat he kept intoning, Everything is under control.

"Stop!" Sylvia said, because nothing was. Not if you were having a midwife. Not if you had only just finalized divorce and custody. More than once, Sylvia had seen her son's life spin out. Exhibit A, the end of his first marriage. B, this unexpected pregnancy.

"How do you know it was unexpected?" said Lew.

"Before their wedding? How can that be?"

Lew said, "People aren't always so traditional."

Then Sylvia woke up in the night thinking, What kind of example was Richard setting for the girls? She longed to call Helen and tell her everything.

After tiptoeing to the living room, Sylvia turned on the lights. She picked up her phone, although it was three twenty-three in the morning. She would do it. She would call and leave a message.

But she saw her own phone light up. A text from Richard. *Alls well in labor now.*

The baby was coming early! December twenty-fourth.

Sylvia rushed back to the bedroom. "Lew. She's in labor."

Lew sighed and rolled onto his back.

"They're having the baby!"

He opened his eyes. "Boy or girl?"

"I don't know!"

Lew buried his head in the pillow.

"Lew?"

"Tell me when something happens."

Lew had many virtues, but only during waking hours. Sylvia was the one who had to sit up imagining the baby in distress. How could Heather turn her back on modern medicine? Debra had gone straight to the hospital for Sophie and Lily.

Sylvia texted Richard. *Any news?*

He didn't answer.

She sent a message to Helen. *Richard is having another child don't ask. In labor at home. She is 13 years younger.*

Helen didn't answer.

A message came from Richard instead. *Hanging in there.*

Hanging? Hanging by a thread? Hanging in there despite everything? Richard had been practical with Debra. He had benefited from his first wife's good sense. Now Sylvia's heart raced. Was it the baby suspended between life and death? Who was this midwife? Who was Heather, really? She was from Ithaca New York. Who came from there? Of course, Heather's parents lived there—but they were academics. Her mother had been her father's graduate student, so they had the age difference too. And they were leftists. Terrible about Israel. Heather was not so extreme, but how could you know? What could you know about a person in such a short time? And Heather's thank-you notes were very very brief. Sometimes she didn't write at all.

Sylvia was up all night. She only closed her eyes briefly in the morning. She rested her head on the white couch—and then a moment later, she heard Lew's voice. He was leaning over her.

"Sylvia?"

"What is it?" She sat up immediately. "What happened?"

"They had a baby boy."

"A boy! When?"

"While you were sleeping."

"I wasn't sleeping. Is he all right?"

"I think so."

Lew showed her a picture on his phone and there was Heather holding a tiny naked infant against her bare breast. "She's in a birthing tub." Lew showed Sylvia another photo in which Heather was indeed half-submerged in water.

"A tub?" Sylvia was already phoning Richard. "Hello?"

"Mom?"

"Mazel tov! Do you have any blankets?"

"He's nice and warm. He's perfect!"

"He looks so small."

"He's six pounds thirteen ounces."

"That's very small."

"Not really."

"You were eight pounds six ounces."

"He's beautiful," said Richard. "Heather is amazing."

"Resting?"

"She's on the phone with her parents."

"Did you tell the girls?"

"The girls are here!"

"Already?"

"Yes! Lily went upstairs about midnight, but Sophie was here the whole time."

"Didn't you—" Sylvia looked wide-eyed at Lew. "Weren't you—" Because where did you even start with that? "You let Sophie . . . watch?"

"She was helping!" Richard's voice was buoyant.

"Heather wanted Sophie to help?" Sylvia had a hard time believing that.

"Yes!"

"And Debra agreed to it?"

"The girls were here anyway," Richard said in his lawyer voice. "It was our weekend."

"They watched the birth!" Sylvia whispered to Lew, her witness. "Can you believe that?"

Suddenly, Richard's voice was curt. "Here, I'll put them on."

"Hello," came a sleepy voice.

"Who is this? Sophie?"

"Hi, Grandma."

"Hello, darling. Mazel tov." Sylvia paused for a moment, uncertain what to say. "You have a brother."

"I know! He's so cute. We named him Froggy."

"That has a nice ring," Lew interjected from the couch. "Sophie, Lily, and Froggy."

"But that can't be his name," Sylvia said.

"Not officially," said Sophie. "It's just because he looked like a frog in the water."

"Where is he now?"

"Just hanging out."

"What do you mean?"

"He's on Heather's breast."

"Were you really there the whole time?"

"Yeah! And Dad was here and Heather's sisters, and the midwife, but Lily was only here at the beginning because she was afraid to look."

Lily called into the phone, "Because it was gross."

Sophie said, "But it was so cool."

Sylvia thought of Heather squatting in the birthing tub. Naked and panting and screaming in pain. How could Richard let a sixteen-year-old witness such a thing? But she deferred to her future daughter-in-law, even now. Even when she gave birth in a three-ring circus. All Sylvia said was, "That's not what I would have done."

"Oh my God, he's so cute," said Sophie.

"Ohh! Let me see." Sylvia put on her reading glasses and squinted at new photos coming in from Lily. A grandson! She had hardly dared to hope, and of course it didn't matter at all, but at last, a baby boy!

"Isn't he darling?" Sylvia showed a picture to Lew after she got off the phone. The baby was tiny and pink, eyes closed, one little hand curled up against his cheek.

"He doesn't know what's about to happen to him," said Lew.

"Lew! That's terrible."

"I'm just stating the obvious," Lew said.

Sylvia calculated quickly and then gasped. "A bris on New Year's Day."

"What's wrong with that?"

"We have nowhere to stay!"

She called, but everywhere was booked, just as she had predicted. All she could find was a Residence Inn.

"It will be fine," said Lew.

"You say that now."

They were in bed, watching the Weather Channel. "We're tracking a powerful storm that's going to affect a lot of us, particularly in the mid-Atlantic region," the forecaster said gleefully.

"Our flight will be canceled." Sylvia gazed at the weather map with the expected accumulation for Philadelphia. "We'll have to come in early."

"How early?"

"At least two days."

"We may as well go down now," said Lew.

"Well, we can't come late!"

But nobody knew exactly when the storm would start. And nobody said exactly what time the bris would be. Morning? Afternoon? Would there be lunch, or any kind of food? Nobody could explain the plan. If there was one! Sylvia didn't even know where the baby was registered. When she called Richard, he didn't answer, and when she emailed him questions, he did not reply, except to say that Heather didn't believe in registries.

"What does that mean?" Sylvia asked Lew. "What is there to believe?"

Sylvia and Lew would have to come early with whatever presents they could find in Boston. And now the storm looked like it was coming on the day of their new flight—so should they change again? *No,* said Lew.

The blizzard was imminent; all the forecasters agreed on that. Lew looked into trains, but there were no tickets left—and in heavy snow they wouldn't run.

"I'm not sure what we should do," Sylvia told Richard on the phone.

"Stay where you are," he said, a little too fast. "Stay safe. It's fine!"

"But we have to be there for the naming."

"We'll film it."

"You can't film a circumcision!"

"Why not?"

"No one wants to see that!"

"You just said you have to be there."

"I don't want to *look*."

Sylvia texted with one finger, picking out her SOS to Helen. *Baby was born luckily healthy all things considered bris is on New Year's Day and we might not get there due to snow!*

She sent this message—and once again, there was no reply.

Not to have a sister. A confidante. Confederate. Comrade in arms. Sylvia had always told her granddaughters how fortunate they were to have each other, and how she regretted that their father was an only child. She had been in the middle once, with a sister on each side. Now she was alone. Sylvia's sisters had abandoned her. Of course, Jeanne had an excuse because she was dead. But Helen!

"How can she be so cruel?" Sylvia asked Lew as their plane landed in Philly.

"Sylvia," he said, "it's up to you. You can decide whether to let Helen ruin this day."

And so, they took a terrible shuttle bus to the Marriott and then a taxi to Richard's place which was a townhouse, looking white and temporary, littered with boxes and a baby swing and nursing cushions.

You could hardly take a step without tripping over some equipment, but there on the couch sat Heather, huge, enveloping, with the baby curled up in her arms. "Oh, look at you!" said Sylvia, speaking to her grandson. "Aren't you precious!"

When Heather offered her the baby, Sylvia wept. It was because he was so small and warm and like a seed, curled into himself. And Helen would never know this feeling—holding a newborn grandchild in the crook of your arm. Sylvia would share this baby. She would share him without asking, if only Helen let her.

"What a doll," she told Lew, who was still carrying presents upstairs from the garage-level entryway.

"He looks like your Aunt Jeanne," Sylvia told Richard.

"Really?"

"Oh yes," said Sylvia, who remembered Jeanne at this size, small enough to fit into her doll's cradle. How she and Helen used to squabble over their baby sister! Of course, Helen acted as though the baby were all hers. When other children peered inside the baby carriage, Helen announced, You can look at her, but if you want to touch her, you have to ask me first. "He has Jeanne's face," said Sylvia. "But he has my father's nose."

"You can already see that?" Heather asked.

The baby's eyes were closed. His ears were translucent; he was so new. His nose was broad and flat, remarkably large in such a little face. "It's a very strong nose," Sylvia said.

"Hopefully, he'll grow into it," said Heather.

"My father was a wonderful man," said Sylvia. "You remember him, Richard."

He looked offended. "Of course!"

"He was a wonderful physician," Sylvia told Heather. "He practiced at Beth Israel Hospital for forty years. He healed thousands of hearts."

Sylvia did not say there was nobody in the family named after her father, Morris. Of his five great-grandchildren, not a single one. No, when it came to names, she would never suggest anything. Helen would have spoken up—but Sylvia was not a dictator. All she said was, "Richard, do you remember how Poppy used to give you a bowl of fresh-picked blueberries topped with sugar?"

"We brought baby clothes and we've got toys, and we brought cake," said Lew, pulling out a Bundt pan covered with plastic wrap.

"Yes! Apple cake!" said Richard, and Heather tried to stand, as though to find some plates.

"Sit!" Sylvia told her. "Tell me," she asked with a touch of melancholy, "how are your parents?"

"They're coming tomorrow," said Heather, "if they can."

"It's going to be a terrible storm." Sylvia held the baby closer.

"How would they fly from Ithaca?" asked Lew.

"They're going to drive."

"Oh no!" said Sylvia, but Richard gave her a warning look. "I hope they can make it," she amended. She did not say, But they'll be killed driving down the mountain in the snow! She did not ask, Why aren't they here already?

Sylvia's grandson stirred in her arms. His little hand crept up to his ear. Richard was distributing flimsy paper plates with pieces of apple cake. He was talking about how there were no bagels to be had and caterers were booked. Hadn't Sylvia warned him?

"But you're an angel," Sylvia told the baby.

The next day, snow blanketed New Jersey. Sylvia and Lew could barely get a cab to the temple where the family was gathering, and when the cabbie did start driving, they had to make their way so slowly, Sylvia was sure that they would miss the whole thing. Eight in the morning! Would there even be coffee? Sylvia could have organized a brunch. She could have done it long-distance and had flowers delivered. She would have chosen ivory roses and dark leaves and moss and pinecones. She gazed out the window at the white road and thought, Now there will be nothing.

"It will be fine," Lew said, reading her mind, as he often did.

She sighed because her grandson wasn't fine. He was perfect. He deserved a celebration! Not a cold, barren chapel at the temple without a single bloom.

Lew helped her out of the taxi, and they picked their way through the snow into the building where they found a scattering of people who must have been Richard's and Heather's friends. And there was Rabbi Zlotnick.

"Let's get started," Rabbi Zlotnick said. "The gang's all here!"

He led the way into the temple's chapel, which was blond wood, and there, in the front pew, stood Heather in a tentlike purple dress. She looked tearful already.

"Her parents got snowed in," Richard whispered to Sylvia.

"Oh, I'm sorry!"

"And her older sister is in LA."

"Her older sister?" Sylvia sighed. She knew what it was like to be alone.

Richard said, "But her younger sisters are here."

Sylvia watched as these young women, Amanda and Jamie, supported Heather, one on each side. Amanda's hair was very very short, almost a buzz cut. Jamie had a nose ring. They looked like teenagers, but they stood with Heather in solidarity.

The mohel had arrived with his doctor's bag. Bearded and dressed all in black, this gentleman named Moshe was both a rabbi and a urologist at CHOP. With all these credentials, he scarcely even glanced at the baby. "Cute!" he said in an offhand way.

Cute? Is that what he said to everybody?

"Hi, Grandma!" Sophie and Lily bounded in wearing bright sweaters and strategically ripped jeans. "Hi, Grandma! Hi, Lew!" they called out.

"Is anyone else here?" Sylvia asked Sophie. By anyone, she meant any other family.

"My mom is!" said Sophie.

And sure enough, there was Debra. Sylvia embraced her immediately. She was so glad—and so impressed. What a hero, attending the bris of her ex-husband's baby. "You are wonderful." Sylvia's voice broke a little.

Debra said briskly, "Well, the girls couldn't drive themselves."

What do you think of all this? Sylvia wanted to ask.

How wonderful the birth seemed, and how strange. How much had happened since the girls were born. And how she wished she could go back to the way the family used to be. But Sylvia did not say a word. She could only listen as the mohel welcomed everyone. Music began. Who was that on the guitar? Wendy! Helen's younger daughter. Sylvia felt a rush of gratitude, knowing Wendy had braved the storm to come from Brooklyn.

Wendy, in her woven tallis, was playing softly. She hummed a wordless tune, but Sylvia couldn't make out what it was. She was distracted, because Heather had given her the baby, who was sleeping on a pillow. Oh, how darling he looked in his tiny jumper—the striped one she had bought him. She could hold this baby forever. His eyes were closed, and he had no eyelashes yet, or eyebrows either. His ears were soft as velvet.

Unfortunately, the bris was happening. The mohel said, "We are inviting Lewis to be the *sandek*."

Lewis? For a second Sylvia and Lew looked at each other and then they realized that Richard was giving him the grandfather's special seat. He would be the one to hold the baby on his pillow. How lovely! Many years before, Richard's father, Sylvia's second ex-husband, had passed away, but Lew got the seat of honor.

The mohel set a stool under his feet. "This way your lap will be level," he explained.

"Oh yes, I see." Usually he was so poised and self-assured. Now Lew looked terrified.

"You'll be great," the mohel reassured him. "Just don't move."

"On this day," said Rabbi Zlotnick, "the eighth day of life, we celebrate a covenant with God and with our people."

Heather took the baby from Sylvia and handed him to Lew. The baby rested on his pillow in Lew's lap, and Lew held still, afraid to blink.

Unconcerned, the rabbi kept talking while the mohel took out his instruments. He dabbed a piece of gauze in wine and touched it to the baby's lips. But Sylvia's grandson knew what was what. As soon as the mohel started unsnapping his jumper, he began to cry. Poor thing! Sylvia wanted to snatch him away.

"This will be quick," the mohel said. Was he talking to his little victim? The baby wanted none of it. "They just don't like to be cold," the mohel told the assembled friends.

Of course, Sylvia knew it would be quick. She remembered Richard's bris perfectly, and she had been to many others. The procedure took just a few seconds—usually.

She stood in the back with Debra, who had an arm around each of her daughters. Smart woman. Debra didn't think every life cycle event had to be a lesson in anatomy. Sylvia and Debra and the girls could not see a thing, but Heather was hovering as the mohel took off the baby's diaper. Richard was standing at the mohel's side, and this bris was not quick. It was not as Sylvia remembered, the work of an instant, a flash of the knife. For some reason, the mohel kept leaning over, while the poor child cried and cried.

Wendy played soft Hebrew melodies, but Richard's friends shifted their feet. Why was the baby still crying? Heather was crying too. Huge tears were rolling down her face, and her sisters were comforting her. "It's okay," Jamie was murmuring. "It's okay."

"Heather," Sylvia beckoned. "Come back here with us."

But Heather shook her head. She was determined to stand up front, no matter what.

For at least five minutes, the mohel bent over the baby. And now Sylvia saw Richard turning white. It was too much! Heather's tears and the crying baby. Lew sat straight, scarcely breathing. Only when the mohel stood up and nodded did Lew relax his shoulders.

Rabbi Zlotnick was naming the baby in Hebrew. Heather was wiping away tears as the rabbi said in English, "And the baby's name in Israel shall be called Mordechai Yaacov."

"Ahh," said Sylvia, and now she began to weep as well. She felt such gratitude, joy, and regret. Richard had done it. If only Helen had been there to see. Mordechai Yaacov was their father's name.

All the other prayers flew by. The rabbi's words and Wendy's mazel tov, as Heather retrieved the baby. A murmur went up and everyone relaxed. Wendy put her guitar away.

"Now Richard will say a few words," said Rabbi Zlotnick.

Richard took a breath. He was leaning against the table. His face was drained of color. Fortunately, the mohel offered him a chair.

Richard sank down and spoke softly. "Thank you all for coming to our son's naming. I want to say a few words about my Poppy. He was a good man who dedicated himself to healing."

"True," Sylvia murmured to Debra and the girls.

"He loved children, and he loved his family. He was generous and kind. He was a man of integrity."

"A wonderful man," Sylvia murmured.

"If anyone was in need, he helped them, no questions asked. We hope that our son will inherit some of these qualities."

Is that all you have to say? Sylvia thought, because Richard made her father sound so bland. What about his dahlias? What about the house in Kaaterskill? The house no longer in the family. The apple tree there. The black potbellied stove. Morris used to wake early to build a fire in that stove. Sylvia had helped him, handing him pieces of applewood and then *The New York Times* for kindling.

What about the snapdragons Morris grew? And his little radio? He sat listening every day, following the news, but he never traveled overseas. He never left America after he arrived. He had seen what was coming in Europe and he did not go back. There was no U.S. citizen more grateful. And no better doctor. He worked every day so patiently. He always wore a coat and tie.

But Richard said none of this. Of course, he had not known Morris as Sylvia had. Grandchildren could never know. With a pang, Sylvia thought, What will this little baby remember about me?

"My Poppy was an immigrant, like so many others," Richard said, as though his grandfather was a dot on a graph. "He used to say he came to America to be free. For this reason, we are giving our son an English name which means free man. We are calling him Charlie."

"What was that?" Sylvia whispered to Debra.

"Charlie," Debra whispered back.

Sophie said, "Oh my God I love that name!"

Sylvia said, "I don't understand."

"It's such a cute name!" said Lily.

"But my father's name was Morris," said Sylvia. Of course, she would never say a word, but how did you get from Mordechai to Charlie?

"Charlie. Charlie," Sophie murmured.

Sylvia shook her head. What was this about a free man? What kind of cockamamie story? She turned to Debra. "It's just not my father's name."

"What can you do?" said Debra.

Ah, you understand, Sylvia thought. You understand everything.

There were a few bare tables set up in the Social Hall. Doughnuts and boxes of coffee. Meanwhile, Heather disappeared to nurse the baby in the temple library.

Sylvia did not comment. She did not criticize at all—but she would not touch anything. She watched Richard gobble up three doughnuts, one after the other, while his friends joked about how he'd been on the verge of fainting. I wasn't on the verge. I was all right, he insisted. No, you weren't, they told him. You were shook! We were getting ready to scrape you off the floor.

"It was good of you to come," Sylvia told her niece Wendy. "It was good of you to represent the family."

Immediately, Sylvia's niece embraced her. Her curly hair was long and gray, her body soft. Wendy had always been a hugger. Even now, in middle age, she remained affectionate, unlike others.

"Of course!" Wendy said. "I'm so happy to be here!" And she did look happy—until Sylvia asked, How is your mother?

"Well—" Wendy said.

"Is Helen sick!" Unconsciously, Sylvia clasped her hands together.

"No," said Wendy. "She's fine. The same as ever."

"Thank God!" said Sylvia. "I sent her messages, but she never answered."

Wendy sighed.

Sylvia asked, "Is something else the matter?"

"No," said Wendy. "I'm just sad for you guys."

"I reached out!" said Sylvia.

"I know."

"She told you? What did she say?"

In that undecorated Social Hall, the friends were all departing. Debra and the girls were cleaning up, consolidating doughnuts into two large boxes. "She said she's happy for you," Wendy told Sylvia.

"Really?" Sylvia said. But she didn't know what that meant without the tone of voice. Had there been a hint of joy, or had Helen been long-suffering? She could imagine Helen looking balefully at Wendy. "What else?"

"She sent a present."

Of course, thought Sylvia. Helen always sent a gift. The most beautiful things. Plush elephants. Wooden trains. She remembered every child's birthday.

"Let me take you to lunch," Sylvia told Wendy.

"Good idea. Let's find some real food," said Lew.

"Come to our place!" Richard was stepping up at last, fortified with coffee.

"I'll take you," Debra said. Sylvia and Lew and Wendy and the girls piled into Debra's minivan, and she drove through the snow. Sylvia hoped that she would stay, but heroic as she was, Debra had her limits. She dropped off the girls and drove away.

Sophie unlocked the door because they had arrived before Richard and Heather and the baby. Was his name really Charlie? How could they? And it was the same name as his Great-Uncle Charles. Had they thought of that? It was bad luck to name a child for a living relative. Sylvia would have warned Richard if she'd had the chance. She would have stopped him—but now it was too late.

The girls bounded upstairs, and Wendy followed, brushing snow from her guitar case. Once inside, Sylvia saw a bouncy seat and several boxes blocking the entrance to the kitchen. She felt a little shiver as she read the return address on each. Three boxes. Four! All from Helen.

"I'm sorry that took so long," said Richard as he burst through the door, carrying the car seat. There was the tiny baby fast asleep—his soft cheek resting on the seatbelt. A crocheted blanket trailed onto the floor, and Sylvia tucked it in immediately.

"Oh, this is beautiful." She looked at the white stitches, fine as lace.

Heather said, "Wendy crocheted it."

"We're taking lunch orders," Lew announced. "We've got one eggplant, two meatball subs, two house spaghetti."

"Four boxes from my sister!" Sylvia told Richard.

"What do you want, Grandma?" Sophie asked.

"I don't know," Sylvia said.

"Get her the Cobb salad," Lew told Sophie, who was placing the order on her phone.

Sylvia asked Wendy, "What did she send?"

"Let's open them!" Richard was in an expansive mood. "Lily, get me the utility knife."

"Be careful," Sylvia said automatically.

"Last call," said Lew.

"I'll have the eggplant parm," said Wendy.

"Me too," said Heather.

"Okay, Grandpa, just give me your credit card," said Sophie.

Lew said, "And eight cannoli."

"They must be books," said Richard. "The boxes are so heavy."

"Then it's a lot of them," Heather said, a little nervously.

Richard was slicing through the packing tape. "Yup." He drew out *The Adventures of K'tonton: A Little Jewish Tom Thumb.*

"I love that book," said Heather.

Richard pulled out *Tales of King David* and then *Tales of King Solomon. Ten and a Kid.* Five hardbound volumes of *All-of-a-Kind Family.*

"Oh wow!" said Heather.

Richard handed her *What the Moon Brought.*

"That's not even in print!" said Heather.

There were Yiddish folktales, and *The Wise Men of Chelm*. There was an entire box of children's biographies. *Pattern for a Heroine: The Life Story of Rebecca Gratz. Embattled Justice: The Story of Louis Dembitz Brandeis.* Richard pulled them out one after another. *Henrietta Szold. Albert Einstein. Sholom Aleichem. Lillian Wald. Eliezer Ben-Yehuda. Moe Berg.*

"These are incredible," said Heather.

"We'll have to buy a new bookcase," said Richard.

Sophie was the one who caught on first, because she remembered seeing the books in Brookline. She turned to Wendy on the couch and said, "They're from your house, aren't they?"

Wendy nodded. "They were ours. They belonged to Pam and me."

And Sylvia thought, Of course Helen had done this. Sending her daughters' books to Richard's son. A gift and a reproach.

"But if they're yours!" Heather told Wendy. "We would never take them from you and Pam."

"We don't need them," Wendy said.

Heather said, "Seriously, Charlie shouldn't have all these."

Wendy looked at the baby and said, "He should have everything."

How is it, Sylvia thought, that all my sister's sweetness went to you? How are you the best part of Helen? Wendy was gentler, kinder, and a better knitter, to be honest. "You crochet as well as Grandma Lillian," Sylvia said.

"Really?" Wendy reddened with pleasure.

Sylvia smiled, and then suddenly she felt lightheaded. "Oh, my goodness."

"What's wrong?" Richard asked.

"Nothing. I feel a little dizzy," Sylvia said. "Don't worry. I'm just hungry. That's all."

"Didn't you eat anything at the temple?"

"There was nothing there," Sylvia said—not in a judgmental way, just as a matter of record.

"That's not true," Richard said.

"You know I don't eat doughnuts in the morning."

"Oh, so you admit there was food."

"Richard, we could have hired a caterer. I would have organized it," Sylvia said, although she was officially not saying anything.

Lew lifted his hand to stop her. "That doesn't matter now, does it?"

"We have some doughnuts left," Richard said.

"No thank you," Sylvia said, although she didn't feel well, and lunch was taking so long.

By the time the food arrived, everyone was so hungry they would have eaten their sandwiches like wolves straight from the wrappers, except that Sylvia insisted on plates, and place mats, and proper napkins. The cannoli were the best part. Lew had one, and Heather ate two. Her parents called, and in her effusive way, Heather exclaimed, "I miss you so much!"

Meanwhile, Lily asked Wendy if she could try playing her guitar. Wendy showed her how to pick out "Baby Mine" and Sylvia watched them croon to the baby nestled in his car seat. Morris? Charlie? He didn't know his name. He had no knowledge of injustice or snowstorms, rifts or gifts. Not yet. He did not know all the ways that you could hurt, and all the ways that you could love. Eyes shut, he was breathing softly.

Acknowledgments

I am grateful to Cressida Leyshon and Deborah Treisman at *The New Yorker,* John Freeman at *Freeman's Quarterly,* and David Leavitt at *Subtropics,* for their excellent questions and suggestions.

My agent, Julie Barer, is a brilliant and rigorous first reader. My editor, Whitney Frick, has a unique ability to see the arc of a book and the details within. She sees the forest and the trees. How lucky I am to work with you both. You inspire me.

Thank you to the remarkable Hadassah-Brandeis Institute for a fellowship supporting my revision of this manuscript.

Special thanks to the readers who enjoyed parts of this book in magazines and sent me messages asking for more.

About the Author

Allegra Goodman is the author of seven novels, including the national bestsellers *Isola,* which was a Reese's Book Club pick, and *Sam,* which was a Read with Jenna selection; two short story collections; and a novel for young readers. Her fiction has appeared in *The New Yorker* and elsewhere, and has been anthologized in *The O. Henry Awards* and *Best American Short Stories*. She lives with her family in Cambridge, Massachusetts.

allegragoodman.com
Instagram: @allegragoodmanwriter

About the Type

This book was set in Fairfield, the first typeface from the hand of the distinguished American artist and engraver Rudolph Ruzicka (1883–1978). Ruzicka was born in Bohemia (in the present-day Czech Republic) and came to America in 1894. He set up his own shop, devoted to wood engraving and printing, in New York in 1913 after a varied career working as a wood engraver, in photoengraving and banknote printing plants, and as an art director and freelance artist. He designed and illustrated many books, and was the creator of a considerable list of individual prints—wood engravings, line engravings on copper, and aquatints.